PRAISE FOR
JAY BRANDON AND
LOCAL RULES

"Jay Brandon knows how to put together a tight, believable courtroom melodrama."

—Gene Lyons, *Entertainment Weekly*

"A crisp new story.... Brandon's readers have come to expect ... thoughtful storytelling with appealing and credible characters. *Local Rules* continues in this tradition."

—Ronald Scott, *Houston Chronicle*

"*Local Rules* is a great story and a terrific mystery with a surprise ending that will knock you out."

—James Wensits, *South Bend Tribune*

"Thoroughly entertaining.... excellent on all counts...."

—Mary Kate Tripp, Sunday *News-Globe* (Amarillo, TX)

"In swiftly moving prose and with an affectionately rendered, credible cast, Brandon delivers a solid string of riveting, detailed courtroom dramas—and some moving bedroom scenes as well."

—*Publishers Weekly*

"Readers who place Grisham and Turow at the top of their courtroom suspense list will be forced to revise the rankings. Excellent...."

—Wes Lukowsky, *Booklist*

A LITERARY GUILD SELECTION

A READER'S DIGEST CONDENSED BOOK

PRAISE FOR
JAY BRANDON'S
PREVIOUS NOVELS

LOOSE AMONG THE LAMBS

"Compulsive reading ... as vividly real as Scott Turow at his best."

—David Delman, *Philadelphia Inquirer*

Loose Among the Lambs rises above the crowd.... Tensely drawn ... and convincing."

—Chris Petrakos, *Chicago Tribune*

"Brandon pulls it off.... He knows how to tell a story and writes about the law with interest and humor."

—Elizabeth M. Cosin, *The Washington Times*

"Dramatic.... A novel of strong motivation, deep emotions, and intense compassion."

—Laurie Trimble, *Dallas Morning News*

"*Loose Among the Lambs* works up a good sweat on a case of child molestation.... Brandon goes straight for the showy stuff: the pathetic testimony of the little boy, the taut dynamics of cross-examination, the high drama of a surprise witness, and the tense interplay of the legal teams."

—Marilyn Stasio, *The New York Times Book Review*

RULES OF EVIDENCE

"When it comes to mystery thrillers, Jay Brandon ranks with the best. . . ."

—Lenny Litman, *Pittsburgh Press*

"A wild novel that has its own surprises. . . . The courtroom dialogue and drama are some of the finest I have seen in recent years."

—Francis Moul, *Lincoln* (NE) *Journal-Star*

"Brandon involves the reader in rich descriptions of the courtroom, verisimilitude of dialogue, a compelling plot, and the workaday lives of bigger-than-life characters. . . . A singular tour de force."

—Charles P. Thobae, *Houston Chronicle*

"The tension-filled relationship between Boudro and Stennett . . . propels *Rules of Evidence* to its highest level. Because they see crime and punishment from far different perspectives, their story raises fundamental questions about racism and the law."

—Richard Martins, *Chicago Tribune*

"A compelling, explosive conclusion. . . . Jay Brandon is a talent to be reckoned with."

—Toby Bromberg, *Rave Reviews*

Also by Jay Brandon

Deadbolt
Tripwire
Predator's Waltz
Fade the Heat
Rules of Evidence
Loose Among the Lambs

Published by POCKET BOOKS

Jay Brandon

LOCAL RULES

POCKET BOOKS

New York   London   Toronto   Sydney   Tokyo   Singapore

This book is a work of fiction. Names, characters, places and
incidents are products of the author's imagination or are used
fictitiously. Any resemblance to actual events or locales or per-
sons, living or dead, is entirely coincidental.

POCKET BOOKS, a division of Simon & Schuster Inc.
1230 Avenue of the Americas, New York, NY 10020

Copyright © 1995 by Jay Brandon

ISBN: 0-671-88409-3

First Pocket Books printing May 1996

10 9 8 7 6 5 4 3 2 1

POCKET and colophon are registered trademarks of
Simon & Schuster Inc.

Front cover illustration by Ben Perini

Printed in the U.S.A.

for Sam and Elizabeth
with love

I listened to some great music while writing this book. I'd like to thank particularly Mary-Chapin Carpenter, Chris Isaak, James McMurtry, and Rosanne Cash.

1

It was a long, boring highway with home at one end and water at the other, and nothing to slow down for in between. Flat, scrubby land that didn't snag the eye. The only sight was the horizon, and a man's foot tended to get heavy on the accelerator. Jordan had the Bonneville on cruise control, set on seventy-two, but half the time he kept his foot on the gas pedal and helped it out a little when that horizon didn't seem to be approaching fast enough. He must have been daydreaming, too, because he didn't even notice passing the patrol car. The first time he saw it was in his rearview mirror. He muttered a curse, didn't hit his brakes—that would have been too obvious—but turned off the cruise control and let the car ease down to the speed limit and below. The only effect that had was that the patrol car caught up to him faster. Its overhead lights came on as it did.

"Oh, hell," Jordan said again.

As he coasted to a stop in the gravel of the highway's shoulder, he struggled with his conscience, which, since he was a lawyer, meant he tried to decide what he could get away with. In the good old days—up to a few months ago— he had kept his driver's license inside the little black flip-open case that held his district attorney's office ID, so that when he handed over the license the law officer would see that Jordan was a prosecutor. In eight years he hadn't gotten one ticket.

But he didn't have the ID any more. They hadn't let him keep it even as a souvenir.

Nah, I won't try to take advantage, he decided. Just be a

1

common good citizen. In the mirror he saw that the officer was out of his patrol car. Jordan quickly jumped out to meet him, which he thought was the polite thing to do, but this officer didn't seem to like having him spring out of the car. He stopped jerkily and one hand dropped to his hip. Jordan held his own hands out away from his body and tried to look harmless, which was easy, since he was wearing shorts and a knit shirt and tennis shoes without socks and couldn't have been concealing anything more threatening than a keyring. The officer scowled as if Jordan had said something caustic and hurried forward, ticket book in hand. He wasn't highway patrol, he was a sheriff's deputy, Jordan saw, wondering what county he was in. The deputy wore a brown uniform and his arms were just as brown, except for a pale band on each arm just where the short shirtsleeve ended. There wasn't much to be seen of his face beneath his straw cowboy hat and mirrored sunglasses except a black, rather severely trimmed moustache. The lips beneath the moustache were tightly sealed.

"Hello, Officer. I hope there's not a problem." Jordan politely removed his own dark glasses. When he took them off, the heat hit him all at once. It was south Texas, it was July, the sun was intent on reducing the asphalt of the highway back to melted tar.

"Would you step back here behind the car, sir, and let me see your operator's license, please?"

Jordan complied. "It wasn't one of my brake lights, was it? I just had the car inspected."

"No, sir. You were exceeding the posted speed limit."

"Really? This isn't a speed zone, is it? The speed limit *is* sixty-five, isn't it? I don't believe I was going faster than that."

The deputy didn't respond. He looked as if he were trying to memorize the driver's license, then he looked at Jordan's face, comparing it. Jordan felt as stupid as anyone who's been caught for speeding. A car zoomed past, making his clothes ripple, the car's occupants no doubt enjoying a good laugh.

Satisfied, the officer flipped up the cover on his ticket

book, tucked it under the clamp of his clipboard, and clicked his ballpoint pen. As soon as the deputy touched pen to paper, Jordan knew, hope of mercy was gone. After the ticket was begun, the deputy couldn't tear it up; he'd have to explain the missing ticket to his superiors.

"I've seen a lot of cases that started out like this," Jordan said suddenly.

The deputy stopped, pen poised, its writing tip appearing to flicker in the heat like a snake's tongue. "Sir?"

"I've prosecuted a lot of cases that started out as traffic stops," Jordan said, enunciating distinctly on the second word.

"You're a prosecutor?" the deputy said. He folded his arms, removing the pen from the ticket. "Where?"

"Bexar County," Jordan said. His voice had deepened, as if he and the deputy were already chatting about the bad guys they'd put away. Jordan felt a little bad about the deception. A little.

"San Antonio," the deputy said with almost human feeling. "You know Nora Brown?"

"Sure."

"I testified for her once. She's something, isn't she?"

"Oh, yes." Nora was no longer in the office, but then neither was Jordan, but why get technical?

"Hmp. Well." The deputy was thinking it over; Jordan could tell from the way the officer's lip lifted as he sucked on a tooth. "Need to slow down a little," the deputy said.

"I definitely will." Departing tension dropped Jordan's shoulders.

The deputy took Jordan's driver's license off his clipboard, looked at it again, and said, "Let me see your ID, just to be sure."

"Uh. Well, I don't carry it when I'm on vacation, like now."

"You don't?" the deputy said, as if someone had suggested to him that maybe he shouldn't strap the big iron onto his hip first thing in the morning, before he brushed his teeth. His hand closed around Jordan's license. "I'll just make a call," he said, turning back toward his car.

"Uh," Jordan said, the one syllable enough to halt the officer's retreat. "I just left the office recently, as a matter of fact." He could feel his face reddening, as if he'd been out in this damned blazing sun for an hour. He felt like a jerk for having let the deputy jump to the wrong conclusion. The deputy's mouth had compressed again. "This is my first trip since I quit, actually," Jordan said hastily. "I was in the DA's office so long sometimes it seems like I'm still there. You know how that is."

There was no longer a person behind the mirrored lenses, there was only a law officer. The deputy snapped open his ticket book and started writing.

So eight years in prosecution didn't leave any reservoir of good feeling with former fellow law enforcement agents, like money still sitting in the state retirement fund? No, of course not, because when he admitted to being a *former* prosecuting attorney, that made Jordan *now* one of the most prized targets of law officers everywhere: a stinking, slimy *lawyer*.

Well, hell. Jordan glanced at the ticket, reading upside down. "Madera County? Is that where we are? Are we inside your jurisdiction?"

"We have statewide jurisdiction, sir."

Jordan didn't think that was true of sheriffs' deputies, but he couldn't remember offhand.

"Besides, you crossed the county line about a mile back," the deputy said smugly. "We both did."

"So you weren't even in your own county to start with? You're staked out in the neighboring county?"

The deputy said nothing for a moment to emphasize that he owed Jordan nothing, but he couldn't help justifying himself. "I'm on my way home, sir. From San Antonio." With a glint of superior amusement. Hey, I'm a world traveler, too.

"You mean you're not even on duty?"

"We're always on duty, sir. When you put on the uniform in the morning—"

Oh, Jesus. Out of all the cars on the highway heading to the Gulf coast, Jordan had had the bad luck to have Barney Fife coming up on his bumper. "So you're just bagging a trophy on your way back to the office to show the boss how alert you always are, even after a big time in San Antonio."

Oh, that brown face behind the mirrored lenses was taut. "We don't think of them as trophies, sir," the deputy said.

"All right, all right." Jordan put his own sunglasses back on, hope of human contact lost. "How fast do you say I was going?" he asked idly.

"Seventy-three, sir."

Brother. The speed limit on this stretch of rural interstate was sixty-five, and the universal wisdom was that you wouldn't be stopped for going less than ten miles over the limit. That is, not by a normal law officer.

"Mind if I verify that for myself?" Jordan asked. He was close enough to the patrol car to glance in its windshield.

"Step away from the vehicle, sir."

Jordan didn't. In fact, he stepped closer, puzzled. "Where's your radar?"

"Step away from the vehicle!" The deputy's hand was on his gun again. Jordan obeyed but stood with his hands on his hips, waiting for an answer. "This vehicle isn't equipped with radar," the deputy finally said. "It's not a traffic control vehicle."

"Then how do you know how fast I was going?"

"I was pacing you, sir."

"Pacing me?"

"I stayed behind you, driving the same speed you were going—"

"I know what pacing means."

"—and saw from my own speedometer that the speed was excessive."

"You drove the exact same speed as me, not one mile an hour's difference. Bull," Jordan said distinctly, as if he had completed the word. "Then how did you catch up to me?"

"*After* I determined your speed, I caught up to you and pulled you over."

Jordan shook his head. "No. You weren't hanging back there behind me long enough to clock me without me noticing." The deputy ignored him, continuing to write. "You're writing that down, seventy-three? I'm not going to agree to that."

"You'll have your chance to contest the ticket in court," the deputy said, holding out the clipboard toward him. Then something else occurred to Jordan.

"Wait a minute. You weren't out patrolling for speeders. You're on your way home from San Antonio. And you caught up to me. Which means if you say I was going seventy-three, then you were *really* speeding."

Jordan could feel the deputy's glare through both their sunglasses. It was time to back off, a little voice was telling him, but the voice was overpowered by the anger he felt at being bullied by this smug bureaucrat.

"I'm in a patrol vehicle, sir, we're allowed—"

"But you weren't *on* patrol, you were just on your way home. So you can go blasting down the road at whatever speed you want, but any ordinary citizens that get in your way, you'll pull them over and harass them just for the fun of it. Right?"

The deputy pulled the clipboard back, stuck it under his left arm, and laid his right hand on his gun again.

"Come with me," the deputy said flatly.

"What? Where?"

"I think we'd better go see the judge right now."

"No. I'm on my way. We'll hash this out—"

"What you're doing," the deputy snapped, "is coming with me."

"Why?"

"Because of your refusal to sign the ticket, promising to appear in court."

"I didn't refuse. Give me the ticket, I'll sign it."

The deputy, confident of having the upper hand again, wore a tight little smile, tiny as the button on a doll's shirt. "Sorry, sir, you only get one opportunity."

Jordan lifted his hands. "When was my one opportunity?"

"This is ridiculous," Jordan said, going up the steps of the courthouse. Deputy Delmore (Jordan had made sure to read his nameplate) was close behind him, occasionally touching

Jordan's back to herd him, which made Jordan flinch—from anger, not fear. "You know, if somebody smashes into my car, or steals it, your liability will be personal."

"If the judge assesses you a jail sentence, I'll retrieve your vehicle personally," Deputy Delmore said.

"Jail? You're crazy."

Walking into the courthouse in his shorts and thin shirt was like one of those bad dreams. As in a dream, too, the courthouse didn't look right. Jordan had never before seen the Madera County Courthouse. It wasn't a fourth the size of the Bexar County Courthouse he was used to, nor of the same antiquity. The building was red brick, which gave it a dark, cool appearance on the summer day. It created its own shade. They went through a simple glass door into the linoleum-floored interior.

Jordan began to relax a little. They were in his territory now, even if it was Deputy Delmore's home county, because in some fundamental way all courthouses are the same. The judge would be a lawyer, he and Jordan would implicitly acknowledge their professional camaraderie. They might drop a couple of phrases that would pass over the deputy's head. Now that the threat of being shot to death on the side of the road had passed, Jordan felt equal to the situation.

He just wished he weren't dressed like a college student on spring break.

The ground floor hallways were laid out in a simple "plus" sign with short arms. At the end of one of the arms, the deputy stopped outside an open office door. "Sit there," he said, indicating a wooden bench like a church pew. After Jordan sat, Delmore removed his hat and his sunglasses, revealing raccoon eyes from wearing the mirrored lenses in the sun all the time, and stepped just inside the doorway of the office. The sign above the door proclaimed the office as that of the clerk of the municipal court.

The deputy had only stepped halfway inside the doorway, so Jordan was able to hear the tone of the conversation inside the office. Deputy Delmore announced himself to little response, made his request, and was met with some kind of problem. Jordan listened happily as the deputy was reduced to cajoling and whining. The clerk, if that's who it was, was giving Delmore indifferent hell. The deputy had a problem, but it wasn't the clerk's problem, and she had no intention of sharing it.

"Judge Waverly's the only one here, and he said he'd handle whatever came in," came the clerk's peremptory voice.

Deputy Dimbulb reached to tip the hat he was no longer wearing and stepped away quickly. "Come on, you," he snarled at Jordan.

"Judge Lucas is on vacation," he added, more to himself than to his prisoner as they emerged from the hallway's arm and stopped for a moment at the foot of the stairs.

"It seems like an omen, doesn't it?" Jordan suggested.

"I don't work for omens," Delmore snapped. The exchange restored the deputy's feistiness and his almost invisible smile. "Up," he said.

Because the command was so peremptory, Jordan took his time on the stairs, putting his sunglasses back on. They somehow made him feel better dressed.

The atmosphere of the second, the top, floor of the courthouse was different from the first. The ground floor had hardly been an antbed of bustle, but there'd been a few people about and the halls had been lined with offices. Upstairs there was a hush. During working hours in Jordan's home courthouse there were always people in the halls, families moaning together, trials starting up or at least threatened. Here all was silence. It wasn't the hush of justice being performed, though. At the top of the stairs the pebbled glass door of the courtroom—*the* courtroom, Jordan noted wryly—was open, revealing the courtroom was empty.

Delmore passed him without a word, infected by the silence, and Jordan followed him to the door of the office that would be situated behind the courtroom. The deputy knocked quietly before entering.

"Hello, Cindy. I hate to bother the judge, but I need to see him if he's available."

The girl—little more than that—behind the desk in the office that was small enough to seem very crowded once

Delmore and Jordan were inside gave the deputy a smile of encouragement, paid Jordan no notice at all—after all, he was obviously a criminal—and said, "He doesn't have anybody with him, T. J. Go ahead and knock."

The deputy knocked on the only imposing door Jordan had yet seen in this courthouse—it was of solid dark wood, with ten inches of molding around its frame—and a voice from inside said a single quiet syllable.

Deputy Delmore took Jordan's arm—more for comfort, Jordan suddenly felt, than as an exercise of authority—and they entered. The inner office was four times the size of the secretary's. The desk alone seemed the size of the entire outer office. The office was dim. There were four windows on two walls, but the shade was only up on one of the four, so that the heat of the day outside was confined to a rectangle of sunlight that hit the desk's surface. Behind the desk, seated in a high-backed swivel chair, was a man in his fifties who wore age like an accomplishment, not like a disease to be avoided. In fact, he might have been younger than he looked; his hair was white but had receded only enough to make his forehead imposing; his head looked as if it contained activity. His hands, resting in the sunlight, were long-fingered and strong. The judge's eyes looked very dark. His most arresting feature was a nose that was remarkably strong, saved from hawkishness by flaring nostrils and a thick moustache.

The eyes did not blink or change their waiting expression as the two men came toward him.

"I'm sorry to bother you, Judge," Delmore began, "but Judge Lucas's clerk said that you were the only judge in the building and that you'd offered to handle whatever—"

"What can I do for you, Deputy?"

"Just setting bail, Judge. This fellow here—"

Jordan quickly doffed his sunglasses and stepped around the desk to shake hands. "Jordan Marshall, Your Honor, I'm an attorney from Bexar County. I'm afraid you need to instruct your officer here that speeding is not an arrestable offense in this state."

And Jordan stayed where he was, allied with the judge,

as if the two of them were judging the deputy who remained in front of the desk.

"Mr. Marshall is right about that, Deputy Delmore," the judge said mildly. "Or did you arrest him on some other charge as well?"

Delmore's hands were circumnavigating the brim of his hat. "Yes, sir, Your Honor, there was the matter of him misrepresenting himself to me as being an assistant district attorney, too. He tried to say—"

Jordan started to jump in with a contradiction, but before he could, the judge interrupted in that same mild, flat tone of voice as if he were simultaneously conducting some more important business inside his head.

"While falsely claiming to be a prosecuting attorney is certainly reprehensible, it is not, unless the legislature has been busy behind my back this week, a criminal offense. Besides, what difference would such a claim make to you anyway, Deputy, in issuing a speeding ticket?"

"Well, none, Judge, but—he perjured himself, and I thought—"

The judge's alertness increased. "You mean you had administered an oath to him before questioning him, there on the roadside?"

"No, sir."

"Then perjury is not the correct word. He may have lied"—the judge glanced upward and Jordan looked solemn—"but lying to a law officer is almost to be expected. I don't believe we've ever charged anyone with that, have we?"

"Well, he wouldn't sign the ticket either, Judge."

"I *begged* to sign the ticket," Jordan interjected.

"Now *there,* finally, we have a legal controversy," the judge said, but as if he were suddenly tired of it all. His hand rested on papers before him; he had been thinking about something when interrupted. "But since you're both in agreement now, why don't you have him sign the ticket, Deputy, and we can all go about our business?"

Delmore, rigid with the embarrassment of acting under someone else's command, fumbled out his ticket book, offered it and the clipboard to Jordan, and after Jordan had signed, tore off the copy and handed it over to his erstwhile prisoner, saying automatically, "Have a nice day."

"Have you sworn out the complaint yet?" the judge asked.

The deputy was almost standing at attention. "No, sir. Judge Lucas is on vacation, sir."

"I don't believe the judge is necessary to begin the paperwork. Judge Lucas's clerk should have the forms. Why don't you begin that process, Deputy Delmore, and we'll see if we can speed—that is, send—Mr. Marshall on his way."

"Yes, sir." The deputy beat a hasty retreat, closing the office door gently. Jordan stayed where he was, thinking how beautifully it had gone, how the scene could hardly have been improved if he had written the script for it himself.

"Thank you, Your Honor. I'm sorry we had to take up your time with this nonsense. I think your deputy there could use some training in the fine points of his job. You must get a lot of complaints about him."

"None we pay much attention to. It's true people he arrests aren't usually very happy with him, but by the time they're convicted, they'll usually admit that the arrest was perfectly justified."

Jordan realized that the judge hadn't been siding with him during his mild dressing-down of the deputy, it was just that Delmore had been doing the talking, and Judge Waverly had the kind of mind that seized on whatever it heard and dissected the statement for flaws. Jordan spoke more carefully.

"Judge, I've been a prosecutor for eight years, I've only recently left the office. I'm not some hardcore defense lawyer, I don't go around whining all the time that people's rights are being violated. I know the vast majority of defendants are guilty, and law officers get used to treating us all that way. By the way, I want to correct that misimpression. I did *not* tell the deputy that I'm still a prosecutor. Though as I say, I was for a long time."

The judge didn't answer, but not from inattention. He was studying Jordan quite frankly. It must have been difficult for the judge to give any weight to anything Jordan said as the younger man stood bare-legged before him. Jordan felt again that nightmare-quality embarrassment of having gone to work without his pants.

Judge Waverly's hand moved across the document beneath it as if he were reading by Braille.

"Well, I'm sorry to have taken up your time, Your Honor. I know you have more important things to deal with than speeding tickets." For Judge Waverly, as Jordan had seen on his office door, was the area's district judge, meaning he presided over trials of felony crimes and higher-stakes civil suits. Traffic offenses were literally, in this courthouse, beneath him. "I'll just—be on my way and see if I can find a ride back to my car. Thank you again for explaining the law to Deputy Delmore."

Jordan now sympathized with the deputy's eagerness to withdraw. Judge Waverly's steady perusal made him feel that if he lingered longer he would be found guilty of something. Jordan didn't think those dark eyes had blinked once since he'd come into the office.

"Perhaps," the judge said slowly, weight dragging down the words, "I could prevail on you to stay with us a bit and do me a favor."

"Certainly, Your Honor," Jordan said automatically, because that is the way lawyers answer requests from judges.

The judge appeared to regret having spoken. He glanced again at the papers before him. His mouth tightened in thought, then in decision, and he stood up. The judge wore black suit pants, a long-sleeved white shirt, and a tie muted to the point of solemnity.

"We're having an arraignment this morning. The defendant is eligible for a court-appointed attorney. It sounds from your experience as if you would be perfectly qualified, and certainly no one can fault your availability. Would you consider accepting the appointment? I can promise the case would not be time-consuming." He studied Jordan again. "Or perhaps you would rather not waste any more of your valuable time in Green Hills?"

"No, sir, Your Honor, it would be a privilege." It was a

little bit sickening the way Jordan's mouth said things like that with no support at all from his brain.

"It would be a privilege to waste time here?" the judge asked with the closest-to-humorous tone Jordan had yet heard from him, which was not very.

"Not at all, sir. I mean I would not consider it a waste of time and I'd be happy to accept the appointment. I should have made myself clearer."

"Yes," Judge Waverly agreed. "What, after all, is a legal education for?"

Jordan grinned, waiting for the punch line, then realized the question had been rhetorical.

The judge laid a hand on his shoulder as he guided him to the door. "Do you have any other clothes with you?"

"Yes, sir, but not a suit. I was on my way to Port Aransas."

"Of course. Well, we won't be very formal. And we'll still make sure you reach the beach today. Cindy, this is Mr. Marshall. He's going to represent Wayne Orkney. Would you please show him where he can confer with his client before the arraignment."

Wayne Orkney? It was maybe the guiltiest-sounding name Jordan had ever heard. Some local thug heading back to prison for his fifth or sixth conviction, probably. He hoped this wouldn't take long. Contrary to what he'd unctuously declared to the judge, he did consider every minute spent in Green Hills (was that the improbable name of this backwater?) a waste.

"I guess the judge means for you to talk to Wayne before they bring him over," the secretary said. She looked Jordan up and down, once, as if now that he'd been revealed as a lawyer rather than a criminal her opinion of him had declined.

As she wrote out an authorization, Jordan reflected that Deputy Delmore's dire forecast had proven accurate. He was on his way to jail after all.

When he should have been, by rights, close enough to the beach by now to smell the salt. This was the weirdest speed trap he'd ever heard of.

2

Attempted murder," the district attorney said. "And we'll consider taking a plea today if you're inclined."

"Well, wait a minute," Jordan said. "I couldn't do that. I need to do some investigation first."

The DA shrugged. "If you want. There's your witness list."

He had just handed Jordan a police report. Attached to it was a list of eyewitnesses that made it appear Jordan's as-yet-unseen client had committed the crime in the middle of a football stadium at halftime of a big game. "All these people and nobody tried to stop it?"

"It happened pretty quick. By the time anybody could get between them, Kevin Wainwright was just a heap in the dirt."

Jordan was quickly skimming the police report. "Well, this was just a fistfight. Aggravated assault at most. What makes it attempted murder? Where's your intent?"

The DA leaned forward to flip the report to its second page. "That will be tricky," he drawled. "We'll just have to go with the fact that he shouted, 'I'm going to kill you, you son of a bitch,' right before he jumped the victim."

Jordan cleared his throat. "I guess, yes, to a lay witness, without the benefit of legal training, that might be taken for intent to murder."

"Or to twelve lay jurors."

Jordan laughed. "Oh, sure, to a jury." The district attorney chuckled along with him. So far the prosecutor and Jordan weren't opponents, they were just fellow lawyers reviewing a case. If things went well, they could maintain that amiable relationship.

When the judge's clerk had called the jail, she had learned that Wayne Orkney was already in transit, so Jordan had decided to meet the prosecutor while he waited. As it turned out, the district attorney was handling the case personally rather than turning it over to his staff—that is, to his one assistant. The DA's name was Mike Arriendez. He had jet black hair but skin only slightly browner than Jordan's, as if he avoided the sun. He and Jordan were on friendly terms at once, especially after Jordan had explained that almost all his own legal career had been spent as a prosecutor and that he still felt like one.

He was still in the habit of analyzing a case from the prosecution viewpoint—assuming, for example, that most of the witnesses would condemn the defendant—instead of searching for signs hopeful to the defense. But even when he looked for the holes in the case before him, it still looked like a lay-down. No wonder the DA had decided to prosecute it personally.

So Jordan wouldn't be here long. He might as well make a pleasant experience of it. "First offense?" he asked, less than hopefully. There was no rap sheet in the thin sheaf of papers he'd been handed.

The DA nodded. "As good as. Couple of misdemeanors, but nothing serious."

That made things easier. Jordan ran it through the prosecution computer that was still part of his brain. First offense, really just a fight that got out of hand. It was a probation case, nothing more. He might be done with this case by noon after all, assuming his client was willing to do the right thing.

"So you have an offer?" he asked lazily.

"Twenty," Mike Arriendez answered just as lazily. "And for that we won't ask for an affirmative finding that his fists were deadly weapons."

"Twenty?" Twenty years was the maximum sentence for what the defendant was charged with, attempted murder. Leaving off an affirmative finding would make Wayne Orkney eligible for parole earlier, but it was still far from an enticing offer. For a first offense, it was a ridiculous offer. "I thought we were going to work this out quick," Jordan said. "I'm on my way to the beach."

Arriendez shrugged. "If we haggled over it for hours and hours, I might come down to eighteen, but that's as good as it would get. We couldn't accept anything less than that."

"Come on. You like this on all your cases? Where's my incentive to plead?"

The district attorney gestured at the police report. "Where's my incentive to come lower?"

Jordan said, "Well, I couldn't take that. I'd rather go to the judge for punishment without a recommendation."

"We could do it that way," Arriendez said easily, so easily it gave Jordan pause. He'd better ask around first, find out what kind of sentencer the old judge was. He remembered the dark eyes and acerbic humor. Mercy might be a seldom-used component of Judge Waverly's sentencing repertoire.

"I'll just talk to my client and get back to you."

"Do that," Arriendez said. Only two little syllables, but there was in them that same quality of restrained anticipation that had been in everything the prosecutor said, as if Arriendez knew of unhappy surprises lying in wait for Jordan.

Jordan lingered. "What's this Wayne Orkney like?"

Arriendez frowned. "He's the kind of guy who could try to beat his best friend to death."

"His best friend?" Jordan had a glimmer of an idea. "Where's the victim now?"

"Still in the hospital."

Jordan studied the prosecutor a moment longer. Arriendez looked only slightly older than Jordan, closer to forty than to thirty: young to hold his position of authority, especially in a county where conservative Anglos probably still outnumbered Mexican-Americans at the polls. Arriendez would be skilled at appeasing the public interests. There was something powerful about him or something devious, and Jordan felt sure he held a wealth of information, but he wouldn't be sharing it. One didn't get to Mike Arriendez's position by giving away secrets.

The courtroom was staffed when he returned to it. A bailiff—Mexican-American, young, but overweight in the traditional way of bailiffs—sat at his desk near the front of the room, opposite the jury box. He looked up quickly when Jordan entered, and his stare hardened. He didn't ask if Jordan needed help, which was a way of asking his business, so he must already have been informed of Jordan's reason for being there. The clerk, Cindy, busy at her station beside and below the judge's bench, saw Jordan and turned away and left the room.

The court reporter was loading paper into the machine she would use to record any testimony. Her hands, which were her livelihood, moved efficiently, even as she watched Jordan walk to the center of the room. Her mouth was held in a tight line, making her lips almost disappear. Her cheeks and nose thinned with disapproval.

For all the traditional south Texas friendliness evident in the room, he might as well have been in Dallas. The court staff had never seen Jordan before, and he doubted they were clothing critics, so the hostility must have been aimed at his client. In his own amiable way, the DA also obviously held a grudge against the defendant, with his twenty-year offer. This Wayne Orkney must be the terror of the town. They'd finally caught him at something, and they were going to hammer him. Well, fine. Jordan's role would just be to step to the side a little, which he was perfectly willing to do if someone would only let him know what was going on.

The pebbled glass doors behind Jordan opened and some kid pushed through. Jordan knew him at once for a defendant. He had that sullen, hopeless look of someone who blamed everything on bad breaks. The kid's black T-shirt emphasized his skinniness. His cheeks were covered in black stubble, and his eyes were sunk in dark hollows as if he'd been up all night doing something bad for him. His eyes were downcast.

A sheriff's deputy pushed in behind him, holding the kid's

skinny arm, and Jordan saw that the kid's hands were hand-cuffed behind him. Jordan looked past him for the rest of the prisoners, in particular for the monster Jordan had been assigned, but there were no others.

Jordan stared as the deputy, a heavy Anglo man with arms twice as thick as the handcuffed kid's, guided his charge to the long bench at the back of the courtroom, and pushed him down onto it with no hint of gentleness. The prisoner didn't seem to notice his treatment. His eyes stayed lowered.

Jordan walked to the back of the courtroom. Behind him, the bailiff was also in motion. The deputy escorting the prisoner gave the bailiff a friendly one-finger salute, said, "Hey, Emilio," then noticed Jordan.

"Is this Wayne Orkney?" Jordan's question was freighted with doubt.

The deputy had deep, painful-looking wrinkles in his cheeks and iron-gray, curly hair at his temples. He looked as if he opened pecans by cracking them against his forehead. He glared at Jordan through amber lenses. "Who're you?"

"I'm his lawyer."

The deputy's eyes searched Jordan for worthy qualities and found none, but then he glanced past him and received some sort of affirmation, so he didn't block Jordan's approach to the prisoner slumped on the bench.

"I need to talk to him before the hearing. Would you mind removing his handcuffs?"

The deputy unclipped the keys from his gunbelt, weighed them in his palm, and walked away with them. Jordan rolled his eyes. He turned his attention to his client, who hadn't moved since being deposited on the bench. This was the scourge of Green Hills? It must be a featherweight town, because this guy looked less menacing than a banana peel on a staircase. He couldn't have been in the terror business very long either; Jordan doubted the kid was as old as the twenty years he'd been offered for his crime.

"Mr. Orkney?" No response. Jordan sat beside him. "Wayne? My name is Jordan Marshall. Judge Waverly appointed me to represent you. Understand? I'm your attorney."

He waited. Wayne Orkney finally muttered, without ever looking up, " 'Kay."

"Do you know what they're charging you with, Wayne? Has anyone told you? Attempted murder. They say you tried to kill this Kevin Wainwright." Wayne Orkney's head jerked, but he didn't form his reaction into words. Jordan continued. He found himself leaning lower, as if trying to talk to someone in a cave. "Now, the penalty range for attempted murder is two to twenty years. In the penitentiary. Understand? If you get sentenced to ten years or less, though, you'd be eligible for probation. Do you know what that is? Wayne, could you help me out a little?"

His client nodded, but in response to what, it was impossible to tell.

"Just lift your head a little, Wayne, okay? Look around you and see where you are. The judge is going to come out in a minute and tell you what your rights are and ask you to enter a plea. Say whether you plead guilty or not guilty to attempted murder. Now, I haven't heard your side of the story yet, obviously, but I've read the police report, and I think they've got you overcharged. I think it should be aggravated assault at the worst; that's only got a maximum of ten years. Understand? Now, I understand this Kevin Wainwright that you hit is a friend of yours, is that right?"

Wayne Orkney's eyes showed the first glimmer of light. He nodded.

"Well, that could be good or bad, I don't know. I'll need to talk to him. And to you. But we don't have time right now. For today just follow my lead and say 'Not guilty' when I tell you.

"Oh, one other thing. The DA's made an offer for you to plead guilty, a real preliminary offer, I'm sure he'll come down later on, but I have an obligation to pass the offer on to you. He's offered twenty years. Maybe eighteen, he said."

Wayne Orkney said his second word of the conversation. No, it was the same word. " 'Kay," he said, nodding.

"No, no. We're not going to accept that. That's a crazy offer. Just—"

"All rise."

Jordan was automatically on his feet at once. His client was slower. He didn't do anything until Jordan took his arm and pulled him upward. The defendant seemed without volition. If Jordan hadn't kept hold of his arm, Orkney might have kept rising, like a helium balloon.

It occurred to Jordan that the cops had done something to Orkney to zombify him. "How long have you been in jail?" he whispered as he led his client up the aisle to the front of the courtroom, but he didn't get even a shrug in reply.

Judge Waverly was standing beside his chair. In his black robe he looked no more formidable than he had in his office, but the robe seemed to make him hold his head higher and gaze more sternly. Jordan wished *he* had a robe to hide his stupid shorts and polo shirt.

The judge sat and immediately said, "We'll hear case number one two four CR, State of Texas versus Wayne Truman Orkney. Is the State ready?"

"Ready, Your Honor," Mike Arriendez said crisply.

"The defense?"

"Ready, Your Honor," Jordan said quickly. "Jordan Marshall appearing for the defendant."

He glanced at the court reporter to see if she'd caught his name. The court reporter was staring straight ahead at the side wall, her hands on the keys of her machine, her posture rigid. The other court personnel were stiff, too, all of them staring at the defendant.

Judge Waverly turned his attention in that direction as well. "Mr. Orkney, this is an arraignment, your first court appearance on this case. I have appointed Mr. Marshall to represent you. Do you understand?"

The judge's dark eyes were steady, their gaze almost palpable. They managed to do what Jordan had not: bring Orkney out of his daze. The defendant blinked in the strong light of the judge's stare. Orkney looked more alert. He also suddenly looked frightened. "Yes, sir," he said.

The judge went on to explain Orkney's rights as a defendant, all the while holding him in that stare, so that Orkney answered quickly when asked whether he understood.

All eyes in the courtroom stayed on the kid by Jordan's side—except the court reporter's, whose whole attention was focused in her ears—and the stares were hostile.

The judge was finishing reading the complaint, the document prepared by the district attorney's office detailing the accusation against Wayne Orkney. There hadn't yet been time for a grand jury to indict Jordan's client, but if the grand jury here was as compliant as most of those Jordan had known, when their indictment did come down, its language would be identical to what they were hearing Judge Waverly intone now: " '. . . intentionally and knowingly attempted to cause the death of Kevin Wainwright by striking Kevin Wainwright with his hands.' In other words, Mr. Orkney, you are accused of committing attempted murder. How do you plead to that charge?"

Silence. Jordan nudged his client with his elbow, then looked at him. The silence wasn't because Orkney had fallen back into his trance. He was staring at the judge, begging for the right answer or for a way out.

"Not guilty, Your Honor," Jordan declared.

The judge's stare settled on him. It was a heavy weight. "Is that the *defendant*'s plea?"

"Mindful of my responsibilities, Your Honor, I couldn't let him enter any other plea at a preliminary arraignment. We haven't even had a chance to confer about the facts of the case yet. The district attorney has made a generous plea bargain offer—"

The judge shot a look at the prosecutor, who held up his hands and shook his head. Jordan, watching the exchange, didn't pause a beat. "—but from my reading of the offense report it seems likely to me that the charge might be reduced as part of a plea bargain. There even seems to be the possibility the charge might be dropped altogether, since the defendant and the complainant are friends, I'm told."

There was a gentle stir in the courtroom, like a breeze that springs up on a summer afternoon and touches everyone on a city block but offers no relief because the breeze is as hot as the surrounding air. Jordan couldn't tell the source of the stir.

"Slim chance of that, Your Honor," Arriendez said.

"I'm sure all the possibilities are slender ones, but there are enough of them that we can't enter a final plea until after indictment. In the meantime, Your Honor, I don't know if bail has been set yet, but the defense would ask the court to set bail in a reasonable amount. I'm sure—"

"The State opposes bail in this case," Arriendez said hastily. "Your Honor is aware of the danger this defendant poses to the community—"

"*I'm* not aware of it," Jordan said, turning to him. "Is the district attorney offering evidence?"

"We—"

"I'm—"

The judge's gavel tapped its base. "Bail is set in the amount of one hundred thousand dollars," the judge said.

The amount told Jordan that the judge intended for Wayne Orkney to remain in jail. One hundred thousand dollars was at least ten times the amount of bail such an offense would normally require, but it was low enough that it would probably be upheld by an appellate court if Jordan bothered to appeal. On the other hand, it was probably high enough to keep Wayne Orkney where he was. A bail bondsman would make the bail if someone paid his fee of ten percent and put up property sufficient to pay the bail if the defendant went south before trial. In this rural county where the average income probably hovered around the poverty level, Jordan doubted anyone who held Wayne Orkney dear had ten thousand dollars cash and property worth ten times that amount.

"And I will set a hearing for motions for two weeks from yesterday. Mr. Arriendez, do you believe that will allow sufficient time for the grand jury to act?"

"Oh, yes, Judge. I'm sure."

"Mr. Marshall, will that date be convenient?"

"Certainly, Your Honor. I'll be here."

"Then this court is adjourned."

And they were done. The judge left so quickly his robe swirled. Jordan turned to his client.

"That's an awfully high bond, Wayne. Do you want me to file an appeal, try to get it reduced?" Shrug from the defendant. The judge's departure had removed even the slight animation Wayne Orkney had shown while court was in session.

"I'll try to see you before the next setting. And I'll need to talk to—anybody you can think of. Can you think of any witnesses who might help us raise a defense? Justification or self-defense?" Nothing. The eyes remained downcast. "Or maybe—"

Jordan looked up. The deputy with the iron face behind the amber shades was standing over him. He grabbed Orkney's arm and lifted him to his feet. "He's going back," he said flatly.

"Damn," Jordan said. "We were just beginning to bond."

He let his client, less substantial than the deputy's shadow, be towed out of the room. Then he realized he was standing in a courtroom in shorts and tennis shoes; what had passed felt like a dream. He turned to the prosecutor.

"This must be the fastest court in Texas. Two weeks from arraignment to motions setting? Is there something about this case that makes the judge anxious?"

"You're letting your regional prejudices show," Arriendez smiled. "All our cases go this fast."

Jordan didn't think so. This case had about it the strong odor of grease. The railroad tracks that descended from this courtroom to the state penitentiary gleamed with lubricant. Arriendez retained his little smile. He took everything in stride, except—Jordan had noticed—letting the judge think the prosecutor wasn't doing everything in his power to slam-dunk Wayne Orkney.

"I think I've figured out what's going on," Jordan said companionably. "Ol' Wayne there obviously isn't the terror of the county, so it must be everybody hates him because this Kevin Wainwright he beat up is so well beloved. What is he, the high school quarterback? The great white hope of the Green Hills Goliaths or something?"

There was an unexpected snort and Jordan turned to see that the bailiff was standing close by, frankly eavesdropping. "That little shit," he said, "never amounted to—"

" 'Milio," the district attorney said quietly. But his voice brought the bailiff to an abrupt halt. "Don't you have some work to do?"

The bailiff stayed to stick his finger into Jordan's chest. "Your little bastard of a client's going down hard," he said.

"Fine. You're breaking my heart, Emilio. Do I give a damn? What d'you think, he's my brother? Look," Jordan continued, transferring the complaint to the prosecutor as the bailiff lumbered away, "like I told the judge, I'm really more of a prosecutor still than a defense lawyer. I've seen guys that needed to be hammered harder than the offense report would indicate. I've tried for high sentences on cases that looked minor just because the defendant was such an all-around shit. I can see that. Just tell me what's going on. Maybe I'll help you out. He *wants* to plead."

"Then we shouldn't have any problem," Arriendez said. And that was all he said.

The beach sucked. It was the first time in years Jordan had been to Port Aransas by himself, and it was a bad idea. Oh, lying on the beach with a book was fine, and floating in the water by himself was okay, too. It was even nice that when he got bored with those things he could abruptly pack up and walk away from the beach without consulting anyone else's feelings, but that left him about twenty-three-and-a-half hours of the day to fill, alone. Lunch became the high point of his day, when he could grab something and take it back to the rented condo and have a beer to wash it down, but there is no good way to have dinner in a restaurant alone. He took his book along to restaurants, too, which filled the time between courses, but when the food was set before him, he had to put the book down, and then while he carefully chewed he had the options of acting like he was a real people kind of guy who got a big chuckle out of just looking around at the other diners or he could stare off across the room pretending to be absorbed by the fascinating thoughts inside his own head.

One of the things he'd thought just before he'd become single again was, *Wouldn't it be great to go some place by myself, some resort, maybe, and be free to stare and flirt and just go along with whatever romantic possibility offered itself?* Now he had an answer for that question: No, it wouldn't be. The only unattached women at the beach were college girls who roamed in packs, and it would have lowered his opinion of himself to hit on some flighty girl who probably didn't have a thing to say, when he was only attracted to her body and wanted nothing more than the kind of unbridled sexual romp that could only happen with someone perfectly disposable. He couldn't bring himself to do that—even if he'd thought he had a chance of success.

Jordan was no good at fantasies. Instead of reveling in freedom, he fantasized about being settled, as he should have been, in his life, in his work. Name whatever had been important to him, that's what he had failed at.

There weren't just high school and college kids at the beach, there were retired couples, there were families, there were real children. One afternoon Jordan watched a little boy, younger than two, who trundled around on pudgy legs, wearing a sunhat as big as he was, but not big enough to hide his smile that lit up like the sparkles on the waves every time he found a shell or a crab or a discarded beer can. Jordan wanted to grab the boy and hug him. He was stopped only by the certain knowledge that if he did he would terrify the boy and be arrested as a child molester.

So he cut the beach trip short and when he went home to San Antonio, he went home to his old house.

He didn't call Marcia first to see if it was okay. They were still in that tricky period when Jordan felt like the house was his, too, and Marcia hadn't yet gotten the locks changed or told him to shove off when he showed up unannounced. "Sure, come on in," she said at the door.

"Sorry to drop in, I haven't even been home yet, I've been at the coast, I just wanted to see Ashley before it got close to bedtime. Boy, the beach ..."

To disguise the way she hung on his every word, Marcia turned and walked out of the room. It didn't seem rude, it was intimate; in fact, she obviously expected him to follow her back, but Jordan stopped in the living room. The room looked just the same, so the way it made him feel must have emanated from him. The furniture hadn't been rearranged, nothing was missing, but looking around he couldn't quite remember living here, he couldn't place himself in the house. There was the furniture Marcia had picked out and he'd said, "Yes, that looks fine," the pictures to which he'd consented, the paint on the walls he'd agreed went well with the furniture, even the house itself that he'd liked well enough not to make an argument about buying it. It was a modern house, creating spaciousness by opening the rooms into each other. He could see into the dining room, over a counter into the kitchen, through a wide archway into the den, and he couldn't see any trace of himself. Yet he couldn't name anything that was missing except him. He'd been subtracted from the house without leaving any blank spots.

"Ashley, honey? Is she here?"

"Ashley," Marcia called. "Come see who's here!"

Marcia was in the bathroom, seated in front of the big mirror, creating her face. It was more formal than her first-thing-in-the-morning face, more emphatic, with darker eyebrows and more shadings of color. Both faces were lovely, but Jordan no longer imagined he knew what lay behind them. Being divorced from Marcia didn't seem strange—in some ways it seemed more natural than being married had been—but the speed of it still dazzled him. It hadn't been much more than a year since Jordan had realized there was a gap growing between them, a gap composed of their professional lives—that's all he'd thought it was—and when he'd tried to close the gap, Marcia had taken offense. When Jordan said no, she didn't understand, he wanted to keep trying, she'd said no, she didn't want to be an object of effort, and he'd said that's not what I meant, and she'd said she knew what he meant, so then there was no point in saying anything after she'd gone into her mind-reading act from which there was no appeal. Anyway, by that time, he'd been standing on the doorstep with a suitcase. It had happened so fast and so confusingly that it took Jordan weeks to realize that maybe Marcia's drift from him hadn't been unintentional. She seemed to thrive on being divorced.

He'd stood in the bathroom doorway too long, watching her, until she looked up curiously. He smiled awkwardly and called, "Ashley? Where are you?"

He found her in her room, having a tea party with her dolls, an important engagement apparently, because she couldn't look up from it.

"How are you, honey?"

"Fine."

Her name had been a bone of contention between him and Marcia; he hadn't liked it, but names take on a life of their own after they're imposed, so now he couldn't imagine her as anything else. He'd called her Ash a few times in a spirit of playfulness, but his daughter had cured him of that by not responding. At three and a half she knew what she liked, and she didn't like nicknames.

He reached out and touched her. It was difficult to find enough flesh to squeeze on her skinny frame. Ashley was pale like her mother, with surprising auburn hair that was still babyish, fine and curly, so that she carried her own aura.

"Give me a hug, baby."

"I will." A ploy she'd invented, pretending that a statement of intention was as good as the act. But she didn't move.

"Want to see what I brought you?" Jordan hated to resort to that, but he always did.

"Oh, yes," Ashley said, but her enthusiasm was polite, feigned. Jordan rocked back on his heels, puzzled, until he looked around his daughter's room. A net hanging from the ceiling sagged under its load of stuffed animals; the bed was covered with them, too. On a card table an elaborate circus was permanently set up, with roaring lions and a wirewalker that could slide down a long string. There was a small bookcase that couldn't hold all her books, two inadequate wall shelves for dolls, play makeup on the dressing table, costumes in the closet, a dresser bursting with T-shirts. There'd been more toys in the living room and dining room and den, too. The damned house was full of them. Jordan brought a toy every visit, but there were many he didn't recognize. Grandparents probably brought toys, too, maybe even a new boy friend of Marcia's. Everyone was trying to give the kid visible affection. They were drowning her in toys.

Marcia was standing behind him. She was wearing a lightweight summer dress, nothing fancy. It showed a bit of cleavage. He didn't say anything. "Just some people from the office," she said.

"You're taking Ashley? Would you like me to—?"

The doorbell rang. Jordan stiffened, not liking to be there when someone came to pick up his wife. Ashley jumped up and ran out of the room. Oh, great, she liked this guy.

"That's okay," Marcia said. He followed her out into the living room, wearing an indifferent face. Ashley flung the door open and screamed, "Poppy!"

The man in the three-piece pinstriped suit bent and picked her up, his face cracking in a big grin. "How's my baby?" he asked, and Ashley put her arms around his neck.

The woman behind the man hadn't been able to get in the door. She smiled indulgently, edged past, and cocked her head at a surprised angle. "Jordan!"

"Hi, Mom." He walked over and they pressed their cheeks together, leaving him feeling powdery.

"Well," his mother said, letting everyone know she wasn't going to pry. She wore an emerald green dress with a strand of pearls, and her tan was better than her son's.

"I just got back from the beach," he said.

"Jordan!" His father had just noticed him.

It seemed silly to shake hands with one's own father, and they weren't huggers, so what the Marshall men always did was approach each other as if delighted, then stop a few feet apart, smiling. "Hey, Pop. Just come from court?"

Emory Marshall laughed at the joke. The elder Marshall was a corporate attorney, the kind of lawyer who prospered without ever seeing the inside of a courtroom. Going to the courthouse represented a failure of his practice. Law clerks went to the courthouse to file papers.

Jordan had followed out of his father's footsteps, into law but then on a contrary, indolent course into *criminal* law— not precisely like being arrested oneself, but not something his father would boast about at the club either.

His father, holding Jordan's daughter who had run to him, looked every inch a grandfather, with his florid face and his stomach expanding the watch chain that crossed his vest. But he'd always looked like that.

"Are you two—" Mr. Marshall asked, not feeling his wife's elbow.

"No, no," Jordan said, thinking he heard Marcia echoing him. "I just dropped by. I just got back from Port A."

"Ah. Well." His father became hearty. "We're taking Ashley to dinner at the club. Show her off. Want to come?"

Jordan laughed. He was underdressed again. "What for, to clear tables? No, thanks. Listen, I've got to get going. I haven't even been home yet, and I've got work tomorrow."

They all made departure motions after that, but Jordan was the only one to actually leave. He kissed his daughter's cheek and she said, "Bye, Daddy," but didn't look up from her conversation with Poppy and Mamaw. Jordan remembered one of the reasons he'd hesitated at the idea of divorce was the thought of how terrible it would be to tear grandparents away from their only grandchild. But that hadn't happened. Only Jordan was gone.

There was no urgency at all to getting home. He sat in his car staring at the street until he realized Marcia might think he was spying on her. He started the car and drove aimlessly away.

The next day at the office there was only a short, undemanding stack of messages, mostly from a former client who was already back in jail. The message with the least familiar name and phone number he had difficulty placing for a moment until the pink message slip suddenly seemed to turn warm as he remembered standing in a small, unfamiliar courtroom dressed for a tennis game. It was nice to be wearing a suit and sitting at a desk with his diplomas on the wall behind him when he returned the call.

"Mike Arriendez, please," he said, and when the Madera County district attorney came on the line, Jordan said pleasantly, "I knew you'd be wanting to improve your plea bargain offer once you had time to think about it. Or did the grand jury balk at calling a little spat between friends attempted murder?"

He could hear the prosecutor grin through the long distance phone line. He could hear Arriendez lean back in his own desk chair, stretching out his pleasant sense of anticipation. "No, it's the other direction, actually," Arriendez drawled. "Now we've got a little elbow room to work with on the sentence. Kevin Wainwright died in the hospital."

bounced off him. They'd only be sure he'd do it if they beat him, but Jordan thought they not even that.

He just sat in anger. In the courthouse, together, one floor away, one judge was trying a traffic case. He thought of Kevin, cut off in mid-stream. The place would be filled with his whole tangle of life abruptly gone. Jordan realized there was also a cross-grained pain on many faces and a tragedy of deadlock in the city. The days would be centered in town if everyone was out in it, the pull of the courthouse and

3

The only mourner for Kevin Wainwright seemed to be his murderer, Wayne Orkney. "I asked to get out to go to the funeral, but they wouldn't let me," he said to his attorney.

Jordan just stared that down until Wayne said petulantly, "I didn't mean to hurt him."

"You said you intended to kill him."

Wayne shrugged. Before he could retreat back into his coma, Jordan asked, "What happened, Wayne? That day you jumped on Kevin."

The interview was in a cramped visitors' room where there was no room to pace, but Wayne was standing, turned half away from his lawyer. He said wonderingly, "Just what they say. I hit him, and—I must've . . ."

"Why, Wayne?"

There was no answer. Wayne seemed lost in his own world. *Need to get him evaluated,* Jordan thought, *and just ask around to see if Wayne had a reputation for being simple.*

The next time Jordan was having a nice chat with someone, he could ask.

"They said you had just jumped out of your truck, Wayne. Where were you coming from?"

His voice emerged from the fog. "Pleasant Grove."

"Is that a town? I've never heard of that."

Wayne turned to him. "The park," he said, softly as a curse.

"What happened there? What did you do there?"

But as if a timer clinked, communication ended for the day. Wayne sat and bowed his head. Jordan's questions bounced off him. *That's how he can stand to stay in this jail,* Jordan thought. *He's not even here.*

The jail was an annex to the courthouse; together they held down one side of Main Plaza, a grassy spot a city block in size, circled by Main Street. The plaza was equipped with trees, benches, some sort of monument, and two or three idlers who watched Jordan as he walked to his car. There was also a glass-fronted bank on Main Plaza and a couple of dead-looking stores. The plaza wasn't the center of town, it anchored one end, as if the bulk of the courthouse and jail had stopped progress dead at that point. Jordan looked up at the eyes of the courthouse and found the one unshaded window of Judge Waverly's office, but the window was mirrored by the sun.

Jordan drove slowly down Main. It was only after he crossed under the interstate to the other half of Green Hills that he no longer felt that courthouse stare on his shoulders. Low as it was, the red brick building, with its jail attendant standing at attention behind it, brooded over the whole town. That was how Jordan felt, but probably only because without the courthouse he'd have no business here.

Green Hills was cruciform in shape, with the interstate highway dividing it, and a few businesses that catered to passing motorists stretched along that highway spine. But just a block to either side of the interstate, the town changed character. It became older, slower, with Victorian houses right on Main Street and old-fashioned emporiums that depended on long-time customers. The hardware store's window was too dusty to entice customers inside with its window display, but that was just the sort of signal to attract a man interested in serious hardware.

Anchoring the far end of the town was the hospital, a three-story tower that was the most modern building in town, no more than fifteen years old, but with a built-in out-of-step look to it as if someone had sold the builder an old set of plans. The parking lot was only big enough to hold about thirty cars and was not full. Most of the cars were nuzzling head-in to the lone oak tree on the lot, like nursing kittens. Jordan parked in the blaring sun. The door handle of his car was already almost too hot to touch as he locked it behind him. He lunged across the parking lot, the waves of heat passing right through his back and head, then hitting him in the eyes as the heat rebounded from the asphalt. The sun killed thinking. All he wanted was to hear the doors of the hospital whoosh closed behind him and feel the blast of air-conditioning turning his sweat icy.

But the hospital doors were already standing open, and the only blast of air he felt was from a standing fan pushing hot air around the lobby.

"We're having a problem with the air-conditioning," the receptionist said as if she'd said it over and over, as if her only entertainment today were watching the disappointment of people stepping into that lobby where the air was so dead you had to keep walking in order to draw breath. Jordan just stared at her for a moment. The receptionist had her own little fan, mounted on the counter ledge in front of her, so that her hair was continually swept back. She looked like an oasis.

"Is Dr. Prouty in?"

"No, sir, he's in Cotulla today at his other office."

"Oh, good," Jordan said. "I'll come back some time when the air-conditioning's working."

But as he turned away he thought of having to drive back to Green Hills another day, and that thought was enough to turn him back to the happy receptionist. "Well, is there maybe someone else who was on duty when Kevin Wainwright died? Like a nurse?" A Dr. Prouty had signed the death certificate, but Jordan didn't have any deep medical questions.

Without consulting a record, the receptionist said, "I think Evelyn was here that night. Evelyn Riegert, the head nurse. She's on the second floor."

"Oh, no," Jordan said. Heat rises. "Is it hotter up there than it is down here?" The receptionist grinned at him. He must have been the most entertaining sufferer yet.

It didn't seem much like a hospital on the second floor, it seemed more like a cheap hotel, with the doors and windows of all the patients' rooms open, so that a sterile corner would have been hard to find. There were fans every few feet, whirring and throbbing at different rhythms. Jordan had shed his suit coat and didn't redon it when he found the witness.

"Evelyn Riegert? My name is Jordan Marshall. May I talk to you for a minute? I need to ask you about Kevin Wainwright. I'm an attorney, I'm looking into his death. No, no, I'm not that kind of lawyer. Judge Waverly appointed me to represent Wayne Orkney. The one who killed him? I just need to ask a couple of routine questions."

The nurse was the first person he'd met in Green Hills whose face didn't close down at the sound of Wayne Orkney's name, but then her face had just reopened after Jordan had seen the thought cross it that he must be a plaintiff's attorney sniffing for a lawsuit against the hospital. Compared to that possibility, a criminal lawyer defending a murderer was a welcome visitor.

"You need to talk to his doctor, Mr. Marshall, and Dr. Prouty isn't—"

"Ma'am, I've never yet talked to a doctor who knew as much about a patient as the nurse in charge did."

Evelyn Riegert looked at him skeptically just so he'd know she wasn't a fool susceptible to flattery, even though he *had* happened to voice one of life's universal truths.

"Well, there's not much I can tell you. I haven't seen the autopsy report, so I don't know the exact time of death. I wasn't on duty the evening he died, but the way Kevin was—he'd been in and out of consciousness ever since he was brought in—he could have lain there for a while without anyone's noticing he'd passed. We tried not to disturb him any more than—"

"He wasn't on a monitor?"

Ms. Riegert shook her head quickly. At first, as he'd approached her, Jordan had thought she looked like a kid. When he'd gotten closer and heard her talk, he'd thought she was older than he was, but he couldn't be sure. Evelyn Riegert was one of those women who move at the same speed their whole lives, whose skin has grown masked and crisp, so that she would look about the same for the next thirty or forty years before her close friends realized she'd gotten old. Everything she did was decisive.

"He didn't seem that dangerously close," she said briskly. "He was on a breathing tube the first day—no, the first two days—and he stayed on a glucose feed, but he was getting better." She was rattling off this information without consulting any record other than her memory.

"No one performed any new procedures on him that last day?"

She shook her head. "We'd set the broken bones the first day. After that there was nothing to do but change the dressings and see he got his rest."

"Did he have any visitors?"

"Oh, yes," Evelyn Riegert said. "Police officers in and out, of course, hoping to talk to him, but Kevin never came to enough to be any use to them. Somebody from the court to take a statement, but they didn't get any. His folks, of course, a couple of his friends, Reverend Abernathy."

"He was here what, five days?" She nodded. "And never got any better?"

"He *was* getting better." The nurse was standing with her arms folded, displaying a reined-in impatience as if she wanted to terminate the interview but correcting Jordan's misimpressions was more urgent. "He was showing gradual improvement—"

"Right up to his death."

"That's not uncommon, Mr. Marshall. Kevin was hurt very badly when he came in here. He had broken ribs, he had a crushed nose, he had abrasions and hematomas and cuts deep enough to require suturing, and he'd lost blood. You should have seen him, there was hardly a spot on his body that didn't require treatment of some kind. He *was* improving toward the end, but his body was working so hard to repair everything that his heart just gave out. Basically, he was dead when he got here."

He was just slow, Jordan thought, *like his friend Wayne.*

The air-conditioning inside his car welcomed Jordan back like a friend he'd brought from home. He drove back up

Main, and when he reached the interstate, he stopped. There was home, ninety miles north. He could be there in time for a late lunch. But he knew there was more he should do here.

Defending was a pain in the ass. No partner to chat about the cases with. The defense team was always Jordan and a defendant who, if he rarely struck Jordan as the incarnation of evil, seldom seemed bright enough even to understand what he'd done wrong. In the DA's office, cases had been delivered to him already worked up by police officers, and if he didn't know enough, he could send the case to an investigator for more work, or Jordan could call up witnesses who would be glad to talk to him, would usually come to his office. It was a cushy way to practice criminal law; he seldom had to leave the courthouse.

Now that he was on the defense side, what little investigation he cared to do was stifled from the outset by his necessary introduction to potential witnesses: "Hello, I'm representing a murderer/rapist/aggravated robber, I was hoping you wouldn't mind talking to me about the case." *So I can twist whatever you tell me into some devious defense and help my nasty client avoid the punishment he so richly deserves,* witnesses finished for him in their minds.

And it didn't matter how much he did, because they were always so damned guilty he was going to lose no matter what he did, and he didn't even feel bad about it. Already a couple of times he'd had clients who had made Jordan afraid of what they'd do next if he did get them acquitted.

Still, he had to keep up appearances. Impress the judge with his diligence, since this was his first appointment outside home base. Another hour ought to do it, he could be on his way home and only return once for the guilty plea. He sighed, drove under the shade of the interstate, and back into the heart of Green Hills.

"... Judge Waverly appointed me to represent him ..." Jordan realized he'd already made an invocation of this phrase. Not only did it make it sound as if the request were coming from the judge himself, but it allowed for a subtle undertone of *It's not my fault, I didn't ask for the case.*

"I know," the woman said. "You've already been in the paper."

"Really?" She pulled over a copy, which could have been hot off the press, since he was standing in the office of the *Green Hills Register*. He saw below the fold on the front page a headline saying "Accused Killer Arraigned" with a photo of Wayne looking as if he'd just awakened groggy from a night of feasting on carrion.

"But we wouldn't have a file," the young woman said. She was a skinny blonde with narrow cheeks and bright, almost colorless eyes that skipped around Jordan's face. She looked not long out of high school. "You're welcome to look through the last few issues, though."

"All right," Jordan said reluctantly. "I guess there'd be something on the sixteenth, the day after the beating."

He saw why she'd smiled, after she let him through the gate in the counter and set him at an empty desk with a very short stack of newsprint. The newspaper was a weekly, eight pages per issue. He wasn't going to have to scour a mass of data to find any coverage of Wayne's beating of Kevin Wainwright.

The *Register*'s first issue after the beating stood out. That day's headline screamed, "LOCAL GIRL MURDERED." Crime was more rampant in the little town than Jordan would have imagined. He skipped that story, which with pictures and sidebars consumed the whole front page and much of the second. By page three the paper returned to normal, reporting a farm to be auctioned off, crop prices, the formation of a civic betterment group, weather, a dance to be held at the VFW hall, and wire report box scores. Nothing about Wayne. Well, it hadn't been much of a story, only a fistfight on the street, no one had known yet it would be called murder, but an arrest had been made. Jordan would have thought that newsworthy, given the paucity of other news for the week.

He turned back to the first paper the young woman at the counter had given him, the one that supposedly carried Jordan's name. It was the only edition of the *Register* that had come out since the one he'd just perused; another would be due tomorrow. "Accused Killer Arraigned," Jordan read again, then skimmed the article looking for his own name. "An attorney of San Antonio, Jordan Marshall, was appointed to represent Orkney on the attempted murder accusation." Not much ad value there, obviously something the reporter had just copied from court documents later.

"Is this your byline ... Helen? You should have been there in person, then you could have mentioned my sexy appearance during the arraignment."

"I will in the next story."

"No, I mean—" But before he could explain his unorthodox dress at the arraignment, Jordan was struck by an incongruity. "Accused *Killer*," the headline had called Wayne. But this was last week's paper. At the arraignment Wayne hadn't been accused of killing Kevin; Kevin had still been alive. The reporter must have been psychic.

He went back and read the opening paragraph of the latest story more closely. "Wayne Orkney, formally charged in the beating of Kevin Wainwright and the prime suspect in the murder of Jenny Fecklewhite, made his first court appearance on Friday ..."

Jenny Fecklewhite? Jordan touched his tongue to his dry lips, put aside the latest issue of the *Register*, and pulled the earlier edition back in front of him. The headline seemed to have grown: *LOCAL GIRL MURDERED.* From the corner of his eye he saw Helen Evers watching him, saw that she knew he had made the connection. Then he was devouring the story.

There had been *two* beatings in Green Hills that day, one of them fatal. After Wayne's arrest for his very public assault on Kevin, police officers had found a body in a nearby park called—the cheerful name already sounded sinister with familiarity to Jordan—Pleasant Grove. The body, that of a local high school girl, showed the marks of blows and was dead from a smashed skull. It appeared to police that Wayne Orkney, set off by an unknown motive, possibly jealousy, had gone on a murderous rampage, first beating the girl to death in the park, then racing back into town to try to do the same thing to his old friend Kevin Wainwright.

There was a picture of a body under a sheet surrounded by trees and cops. Jordan read for details. He was accustomed to newspaper stories that lacked the clinical details of police reports and autopsy summaries, but that had more immediacy than dry official memos. This story, though, in spite of its sensationalistic headline, had an odd delicacy about it. The dead girl, "Jenny Fecklewhite, 17, had been seen in her usual haunts earlier in the day, chatting with friends, giving no hint of apprehension of danger." People had seen Wayne Orkney and Kevin Wainwright earlier, too, in a pizza restaurant. They'd been having an animated discussion, but no one had overheard it, and it hadn't ended in violence. Kevin had driven away, then Wayne. Somewhere between the pizza place and Pleasant Grove something had happened to turn Wayne homicidal.

The rest was speculation from witnesses and police officers. Jordan turned to one of the sidebar stories, headlined "Jenny 'Best of Us.' " Even before he began reading, Jordan had a tingle of understanding, like ice cracking under pressure. He was about to know why everyone in the courthouse hated Wayne Orkney even though they didn't care much about the man he had killed.

Jenny Fecklewhite. The names didn't fit together. And they didn't fit the high school yearbook photo that ran with the story that showed a lovely blond girl with high cheekbones, a bright smile, and a look about her eyes that said she knew something wicked about the photographer. Jordan studied the photo. Even through the grain and the dots of the newsprint, the girl's eyes sparkled. She was a girl who belonged on a float in a parade representing the hope of the future.

The story confirmed his impression. "If Green Hills had a golden girl," the story began, "Jennifer Fecklewhite was it. Everyone knew her as Jenny, and everyone knew her. When news of her death raced through Green Hills on Saturday, everyone who heard was shocked, saddened, and personally bereaved. Whether she was remembered for capturing first place in the Southern Region Interscholastic Speech Contest with no previous training, for her award-winning clarinet playing with the Franklin D. Roosevelt High School Band, or simply for the personality that made her everyone's friend, Jenny was remembered as, in the words of Mayor Harley Stephenson, 'the best of us, the best Green Hills had to offer the world.' "

Jesus. If the story was accurate, everyone loved Jenny, no one had a bad word to say about her, and her murderer, by implication, deserved to be dropped down the deepest hole in Texas and have hungry rats poured in after him. Some of Jenny Fecklewhite's accomplishments were ordinary enough—Honor Society, head cheerleader—but she was also captured in a couple of anecdotes that were out of the ordinary. "I remember I got Jenny to baby-sit my son Howard one afternoon," the local postmistress remembered. "Howie was five and he'd been having trouble in kindergarten with the alphabet. He couldn't even get started for some reason. By the time Jenny brought him back that afternoon, he could say it from A to G and knew how to spell his own name for the first time." Jordan could read the woman's tears through the lines of newsprint. "Jenny'd spent the whole afternoon taking Howie around town showing him things that started with the letters, and especially his name, so he finally understood what the letters meant. She didn't just write them for him, they went looking for letters, like a treasure hunt. And after that she kept coming back for Howie and taking him out until he knew the whole thing rock solid. Jenny wouldn't take pay for it, she said she enjoyed it. She was something, wasn't she?"

Jordan clicked his tongue.

"I could have filled the whole edition with stories like that," the reporter said. She was still halfway across the room at the counter, but she knew exactly where Jordan was in her story.

"This is beautifully written, you should submit this for awards."

The woman sniffed. "It's nothing special. You just think it is because it's about her."

Her eyes were slick. "Was she a friend of yours?" Jordan asked gently.

"She was everybody's friend. But she was more than that. Like the mayor said, if there was anybody in this town obviously going places, it was Jenny."

"Well—" It probably wasn't all that difficult to shine in a town like Green Hills, Jordan was thinking, where the competition was rather severely limited. "That's nice."

Helen Evers heard what he'd been thinking. "Screw you, big-city lawyer. Jenny could've competed with anybody you could think to put her up against. Like that speech contest? She didn't even take speech in school, she just one day thought of an idea for a speech she'd like to do, so she wrote it and went and delivered it for the speech teacher, who right away entered her in the next contest coming up, down at a high school in Corpus, and Jenny not only won that contest, she won first prize in the regional meet she went on to from there. She was going to state later this summer. Of course, some people say the judge helped her write the speech, but if you'd heard Jenny deliver it—"

"The judge? Judge Waverly? Why would people say that?"

Evers composed herself. She'd been in danger of falling forward off the high stool on which she was sitting. "The speech was about law," she said more calmly. "Jenny interviewed people to make sure what she was saying was accurate. But anybody who heard her give it knew what she was saying was her own ideas."

"She was interested in law?" Jordan glanced down at the story again: "Jenny, preparing for her senior year, had already distinguished herself at Roosevelt High. Only two months before her death she had been voted Queen of the Junior–Senior Prom, along with her escort Kevin Wainwright . . ."

"Oh," Jordan said, more like a moan than a word. When he looked up, Helen Evers was watching him expressionlessly.

"Was Kevin her boy friend?"

She shrugged; it might have been a small nod.

And Wayne was Kevin's best friend, so he would have spent time with them, maybe double-dated, been close to

Jenny Fecklewhite but perhaps not close enough. It must have been maddening to spend time that close to the golden girl but have her boy friend always in between.

Jordan glanced again at the news story of the murder, but it didn't have the information. He'd never known a reporter, though, not to have more news about a story than what had seen print.

"Was she raped?"

"Jenny wouldn't've let that happen," Evers said harshly. "She would have fought."

Which is maybe what had happened, a fight ending with a rock or a club to the girl's skull. She might have left marks on her attacker, too. Wayne had shown healing scratches the first day Jordan had seen him in court. He'd assumed those had come from the fight with Kevin Wainwright.

"So this Kevin Wainwright, he must have been the male best Green Hills had to offer. Why didn't you have any sidebar stories about him?"

"Who's this?" said an intruding voice that was short of breath but long on hostility. Bustling into the office from somewhere in back was an overweight woman with a mottled complexion and gray hair so thick it looked like a stage wig. She stopped directly in front of Jordan, glaring at him while her breath whistled in and out.

Helen Evers did not snap to attention. "This is Jordan Marshall, attorney of San Antonio, who's representing Wayne Orkney."

Jordan had risen to his feet before the sturdy lady, who folded her arms to make her disapproval more obvious. "I can't say I care for your taste in clients, Mr. Marshall. That's not my business, but your taking up space in my office is. We have a newspaper to get out by tomorrow."

"Mr. Marshall's trying to reconstruct the crime, Mom. I let him look at our last few issues."

"Oh, *Mrs.* Evers," Jordan said, coming around the desk.

"Mrs. Swanson," the gray lady said frostily. "I got a reprieve from being married to the scoundrel who—"

"Don't talk bad about Daddy, Mom," the younger woman said mildly.

"I'm not going to talk to this *stranger* about anything. This is a news-*gathering* organization, Mr. Marshall. If you have research to do, we have a public library."

"Well, thank you." Jordan walked back through the gate in the counter slowly, saying to the reporter, "What about Kevin?"

"I didn't do any sidebars on Kevin Wainwright because there wasn't any material for one. Kevin was common as dirt and everybody knew it."

"Except Jenny?" Jordan asked.

"Including Jenny. She wasn't dumb."

"But—"

"Look—"

"Could we maybe go to lunch?" Jordan interrupted. "There's a lot I'd like—"

Mrs. Swanson's voice cut through again. "We don't go out to lunch when we have a paper to get out, Mr. Marshall. Helen, let's get to work."

"No lunch," the young reporter said softly, giving Jordan a level, appraising look with no hint of flirtation in it. "But I would like to interview you."

"The feeling is mutual," Jordan said.

So he found himself back out in the sun with a bigger load of problems than he'd realized. At this end of Green Hills, he was in the figurative shadow of the courthouse. Two blocks away at the end of the street, the building's dark brick front shrugged off sunlight. At least it would be cool.

He found the district attorney in his office. On the desk blotter in front of him was a sandwich sitting on its plastic bag and a bag of nacho cheese-flavored tortilla chips. The sandwich was obviously homemade, dripping with juice, but the chips struck Jordan oddly. "I didn't think anybody who'd tasted real tostadas would eat those things," he said.

Arriendez picked up a single orange triangle and ate it with visible appreciation, as if filming a television commercial. "When I was in law school," he said, "living alone, I got used to the taste of plastic about my food."

Jordan nodded. "Or styrofoam."

"What can I do for you?" the prosecutor said.

"The question is what you will do for me, which I imagine is not much. I've found out what's really going on in this case."

The district attorney's face fell into such a bland, ignorant, easygoing expression it could have been represented by a happy face sticker. "Oh, is there something important? Tell me."

"Come on. I wish you'd quit playing me for a fool. This high-offer stuff isn't about Kevin Wainwright, it's about Jenny Fecklewhite. Nobody cares about him, it's *her* murder you want to get Wayne for. So why don't we just wait to do anything until you indict him for both of them, and then we can wrap the whole thing up."

"Without you putting too many more miles on your car," Arriendez said. "All right. How many years do you think your client would take for Jenny's murder?"

"No." Jordan almost laughed. "You make *me* an offer."

"Life," Arriendez said flatly.

Jordan sighed. "All right. Let's just wait. How long do you think it'll be until the indictment on that one?"

The district attorney hesitated. "The investigation is coming along," he said. "We want everything tight before we give some slimy defense lawyer a shot at it."

Jordan didn't take offense, but he hesitated. "That one's tougher to put together, isn't it?"

"Tougher, but not too tough."

Jordan would have bet otherwise. "No witnesses, at least as far as the newspaper reported, and I'll bet the newspaper reporter I met isn't too many steps behind the cops. And in a beating death you won't have a bullet to match to a gun or knife wounds to match to a knife. Tough case." Jordan nodded sympathetically. "No confession. Is there?"

Arriendez shook his head minutely, but Jordan's eyes narrowed. "I may have to file a motion for discovery," he said.

"You're not representing anybody on that case," the prosecutor pointed out. "No one's been charged with anything in Jenny Fecklewhite's murder."

"Oh, yeah. Lost my head. Okay, back to reality. What will you offer me in the one I *am* representing Wayne on?"

Mike Arriendez appeared to think over his answer carefully, but his answer belied that appearance. "Sixty."

"Is this local humor?" Jordan asked exasperatedly. "Or do you have local defense lawyers who actually go for this kind of thing?" Because sixty years was the exact equivalent of life imprisonment, the number the parole board used to calculate parole eligibility for an inmate with a life sentence, and life was the maximum penalty for a noncapital murder such as this one. The DA was offering Jordan's client exactly nothing in exchange for saving the State the work of trial.

"That's the offer," Arriendez said unemotionally.

"Be fair," Jordan said, which he didn't like to hear coming from his lips, because it was the same whine he'd so often heard from defense lawyers when he'd been a prosecutor himself. "This isn't a life case. This isn't even a thirty-year case. This kind of sudden passion barroom killing—"

"It wasn't in a barroom."

"Same thing. Look, I know you've got an outraged community to placate, but you can explain the difference between the two murders. Thirty years sounds like a lot of years to average citizens. Even twenty. Give me something I can live with."

Arriendez bit into his sandwich and chewed carefully. He started to speak, then stopped himself.

Jordan leaned toward him. "Look, I'm just here doing penance for a speeding ticket. I've got no stake in Wayne. My only worry is that some writ writer will get hold of him once he's in prison, and I'll end up in federal court trying to explain why I let my client plead to such a ridiculous offer. So let's just find some middle ground."

Arriendez thought awhile longer and finally said slowly, "I'll come down to fifty," and immediately looked pained as if he'd made a terrible blunder.

Jordan rolled his eyes. It was still a ridiculously high offer. "All right, I'll just have to wait until you have both cases ready. I don't want to plead him on this one and then have you come back and dump the other one on him, too. At least if we wait, he can get concurrent sentences."

The DA shook his head. He looked more sure of himself again. "That's not going to happen."

"It will if I wait. You'll have to—"

He stopped. Again he put himself in the prosecutor's place and remembered the pleasant feeling of not having to do anything. There was no statute of limitations for murder. Arriendez could sit on Jenny Fecklewhite's murder indefinitely, while the murder with which Wayne Orkney was already charged had to proceed through the system toward some conclusion.

Demonstrating that he understood this legal obstacle course as well as Jordan, the district attorney said, "When the judge asks you for an announcement on the case you've been appointed on, you'd better be ready to try it or plead."

Jordan raised his hands in small surrender, but he lingered. "This Jenny Fecklewhite, what was she like?"

Arriendez stared into the distance, into the past. "How would I know?"

"You called her Jenny."

The DA's gaze shortened to take in the defense lawyer. He looked angry for a long moment, then smiled slightly, reminiscently. "She was a good kid."

"How did you know her?"

Arriendez's eyes became less straightforward. "She was around here once in a while. The courthouse, I mean."

"In trouble?"

Arriendez laughed. "Not Jenny. Never."

"She was just interested in the law," Jordan said.

"I guess." Arriendez put a period to the conversation. "We're all so fascinating."

Jordan walked out of the district attorney's offices, momentarily distracted from the unfamiliarity of his surroundings by the familiarity of chewing over a legal problem. Knowing that a second case against his client was hovering in the near distance, any good defense lawyer would wait to dispose of both cases together, so the sentences could be served concurrently. Under normal circumstances, a prosecutor would be willing to accommodate him; prosecutors wanted to get rid of cases in clusters rather than individual units, too. But in this case, the district attorney was choosing to exercise every advantage he had, which were considerable in number. Arriendez could easily prove Wayne guilty of murdering Kevin Wainwright. If he could get a life sentence for that, Wayne wouldn't be eligible for parole for fifteen years. Then if they managed later to convince a jury that Wayne had killed Jenny Fecklewhite as well and obtained another life sentence, that sentence could be stacked atop the first one. Thirty years in prison before parole eligibility, that was effectively dead. That would be burying Wayne like a time capsule for a later generation to dig up.

But why go to the trouble? One high sentence should be enough to satisfy any prosecutor.

The sixty-year offer was a little bothersome, too. Any criminal lawyer knew sixty years was the same as a life sentence, but that wasn't well known among the general public. Sixty years was a very calculated offer, one meant to satisfy not some public clamor, but the district attorney's own desire. To Jordan it seemed strange for a prosecutor to demonstrate such a personal quest for revenge. Some small-town oddity. Maybe the dead girl had meant something to Arriendez as she seemed to have to others in Green Hills.

The district attorney's offices were in a nondescript building across the street from the courthouse. The noon sun sizzled his shadow down to nothing. The shade of the trees in the plaza was inviting, and Jordan crossed the street toward them. Still musing, he let his footsteps carry him to the plaza's most visible landmark, the monument circled by oak trees. When he reached it, Jordan found a pedestal as tall as his head, but it was untenanted. He walked all the way around the pedestal, finding no explanation. Puzzled, he turned away and noticed in the sliver of peripheral vision the dazzling sun allowed that Judge Waverly had also just entered the plaza, coming from the direction of the courthouse. The judge didn't seem to notice the heat. No, he encompassed it, as if he would ask, "Are you enjoying my day?" Even the loungers on the benches stood as the judge approached. Judge Waverly nodded to them, and they nodded back deferentially. As the judge and the woman with him resumed their progress across the plaza, the judge spotted Jordan, who approached the judge in the same respectful attitude as the idlers on the benches.

"Hello, Mr. Marshall." They shook hands briefly but firmly. The judge's hand was dry, almost crusty, and strong. "Have you met Laura Stefone, the court reporter in my court?"

"Not formally. Hello, Ms. Stefone."

She nodded. In the sunlight the court reporter looked less stiff than she did in court. She was in her early to midthirties, but Jordan could see laugh lines at the corners of her mouth, which looked as if it would twitch easily into a smile. At the sight of him, it did not.

"I'm surprised to see you," said the judge. "Were you coming to see me?"

Jordan noticed again how dark the judge's eyes were. They absorbed the light and reflected nothing.

Laura Stefone's eyes, on the other hand, were green. As tight as the expression on her face was, her eyes looked unprotected.

"No, sir, the district attorney. I heard about the upgraded charge against Wayne Orkney."

"Yes, I suppose we'll have to have a new arraignment. We'll keep you notified."

"I also wanted to know if my client was going to be charged with the other murder. With Jenny Fecklewhite's."

For the first time in Jordan's narrow experience, Judge Waverly looked unsure of himself. His eyes latched on Jordan's, his mouth opened, but he didn't say the first thing he'd thought. He turned away again, saying, "You'd have to ask Mr. Arriendez about that. Don't let us keep you from your appointment."

Jordan let the misimpression stand. The short conversation had communicated tension even to Jordan, who didn't know its source. Judge Waverly had been friendly in a formal way, but the court reporter was regarding Jordan as icily as everyone else in the courthouse had. Jordan watched the pair walk away, and it wasn't until then he noticed what was odd about them on this summer's day.

They were both wearing black.

Arriendez had been, too. It hadn't been so noticeable on him, because he'd been eating lunch at ease in his shirt-sleeves, but Jordan remembered the black suit coat hanging on the coat rack behind the district attorney's desk.

Jordan could understand a town saddened by the death of a popular local girl. But the *official* mourning for her and the concomitant courthouse hostility toward his client puzzled him. There was something else he should know.

It didn't matter, though. It wasn't his mystery. It wasn't his town, he'd be done with it soon. He tossed his jacket into the back seat of his car and drove away with gathering speed. It was strange the way the little town seemed so all-encompassing when he was standing in it, yet how inconsequential the highway made it. Green Hills was barely a speck on the map. Most drivers hurtled by it without ever knowing its name.

But curiosity continued to make Jordan's skin itch as he drove. It wasn't the case itself that nagged him, that was perfectly straightforward. It was the way no one would let him do his simple job. Transfer this case to the city, and it would disappear into the whirlpool of all the others. But in Podunkville they tried to blow it up into some earthshaking tragedy, so that even the out-of-town lawyer felt the pressure of the case's expansion.

As he pulled farther away, he began slowing down. Cars passed him. Back in that little town, people were laughing at Jordan. Or at least whispering about him. Something happened there when he left town.

He had no particular reason to rush back to San Antonio. No appointments until the next morning, no one waiting at home. He took the next exit, looped around, and picked up speed again, feeling foolish, but also feeling a certain satisfaction at the thought of making an abrupt reappearance, catching the town unawares.

* * *

"Get the paper out?"

Helen Evers came slowly toward the counter from the back room of the newspaper office. "Sure. Can't you hear the roar of the press?"

The sound was more like a clatter. Nonetheless, it signaled that her workday was done. "Like to get a drink?" Jordan asked.

Helen Evers wasn't much older than the college girls who'd made him feel so old on his solitary trip to the coast, but she had a face, she used her eyes on him; she made him feel interesting. That wasn't why he'd come back, though. He had spent the afternoon roaming around Green Hills, having lunch in a diner, dropping into stores, striking up what he hoped sounded like idle conversations. A couple of people had begun reminiscing about Jenny Fecklewhite, but all of them stopped to ask Jordan's interest, and as soon as he revealed that he was representing Wayne Orkney, the town's collective face had closed down. They weren't rude, they were just vague—adamantly so.

Helen Evers was the only person in town who had acted as if she wanted to tell him something. So he was back. But now she looked at him skeptically.

"This county is dry, Mr. Marshall. So the only way you can get a drink is to drive twelve miles to the county line, where just by coincidence there happens to be a liquor store just on the other side, then you drive back here and sit in your car and drink from the bottle inside a paper sack, making sure to drop it out of sight if a police car comes in sight. So, no, thanks, I don't think I'd like to have a drink. Why don't you just ask me whatever it is you want."

"Who is it, Helen? Oh." The self-sufficient older lady appeared in the back doorway, wiping her hands on a cloth. "Did you find the library, Mr. Marshall?"

"Yes, ma'am, thank you for the advice. It's simple," he continued in a lower voice. "I just want to know what everybody knows that I don't. The DA offers my client life in prison for what should be a ten- or twenty-year case. The courthouse staff treats me like some creature from the slime pit just because I had the bad luck to be appointed on the case. I understand this Jenny Fecklewhite was well liked and everybody thinks Wayne killed her. But what makes the case such a big deal at the courthouse? Why can't they treat it normally?"

Helen Evers's mouth had the closed look of consideration. It made her look much older. She opened it only slightly. "I'm sure Jenny had friends at the courthouse. She was in and out of there regularly, and she made friends wherever she went."

"Can you tell me anything about Mike Arriendez's personal life?" Jordan asked as if switching subjects.

The reporter was a little taken aback. "Mike? He's the most happily married man in town. Has four kids."

"Well, children don't necessarily make a marriage happy." Evers frowned. "What's your problem?"

"I'm just curious about the people I'm going to be working with. What about the judge? Married?"

"For thirty years."

"Happily?"

She hesitated and shrugged. "Who knows about people's home lives?"

"You knew about Mike Arriendez's."

Jordan waited for the reporter to answer, but she didn't have one. "Here's the thing," he said softly. "I have this suspicion. You'd probably just say I have a dirty mind, and maybe that's it. But I've asked around, and you're right, everybody loved Jenny. And the closer you get to the court-house, the better they seemed to know her. You said yourself she was in and out of there regularly. And that people suspected the judge might have helped her with her speech. And this ugly suspicion of mine, it would explain a lot of things."

"Why does it have to be ugly?" Helen Evers asked quickly. "You're never going to understand. Jenny was something special."

Jordan asked carefully, "Special to whom? Besides everybody, I mean."

"Helen," her mother said warningly from the back doorway.

"Maybe he ought to know what he's up against, Mom. Besides, somebody's bound to tell him." She hadn't taken her eyes off Jordan as she spoke over her shoulder. Evers was trying to read from his face whether she was doing the right thing in telling him. "You're right about what you're thinking, but not the way you're thinking. Jenny was special to the judge."

4

Not guilty, your honor."

Now everything made sense—almost. Once more appearing in Judge Waverly's courtroom, Jordan no longer had the feeling people were exchanging knowing looks over his head. Now he understood, too. Understood the glare the judge directed at Wayne Orkney and the way Wayne—Was he in on the judge's secret, too?—couldn't lift his eyes to the judge's. He understood the backbreaking plea bargain offer the district attorney had put on the table and the way Arriendez wanted Judge Waverly to know that this defendant wasn't going to get a good deal out of him. When a prosecutor spent every day in a particular judge's courtroom, it was part of the prosecutor's job to keep that judge happy.

"Does your client still find himself unable to speak for himself, Mr. Marshall?"

"Apparently, Your Honor. I certainly can't get much out of him."

Jordan felt more at ease now—in his suit, in on the secret. But in the first day after learning about Judge Waverly's relationship with the dead girl, he'd been a little panicked. He'd gone for advice to Jerry Ramirez, who had been Jordan's first lead prosecutor in a felony court and had preceded Jordan into private practice by several years. Jerry always seemed to know what he was doing, seldom had newsworthy victories in court, but didn't seem flustered by the losses. He was always midstream in the great river of days, happily aware of all the currents. "So your problem," he'd said when Jordan explained, "is that the judge who's going to judge your client hates him because the client—What's his name? Wayne. Of course—because Wayne also killed the judge's girl friend. Now you're sure about the relationship between the judge and the girl, the other victim?"

"Oh, yeah," Jordan had said. "Sure enough to be sure, if you know what I mean. Nobody'd say it straight out, but then they wouldn't, would they? But they'd tell me how the judge and the girl spent a lot of time together, which everyone seemed to think was perfectly natural since they were the two smartest people in town. And after Jenny Fecklewhite developed an interest in law, she started spending a lot of time at the courthouse because the judge was mentoring her, you know—"

"Yeah," Jerry had said knowingly. "You can get some serious prison time in this state if you start 'mentoring' a girl before she's seventeen. So your boy should've known better than to pick on the judge's one true love. So what's your problem?"

"Well, there was the bond deal, you know, it's just way too high. And so is the plea bargain offer, and I'm not going to get a better one, because the DA wants to please the judge by hammering my guy on the easy case, because they might not ever be able to prove the case everybody really cares about. And I can't go to the judge for punishment, needless to say. Plus I'm just getting out-of-town-lawyered to death down there. I go to the jail to see my client, and suddenly they've got visiting hours that they strictly enforce, even against attorneys. I can't get the case reset like I'd like to because there's this great rush on. It's just—"

"Yeah. And you think the judge is behind it all."

"Well, not necessarily telling people what to do. It's just they all want to please him, and they think the way to do it is to screw my guy to the wall and me with him. This Judge Waverly is something else, Jerry. Have you ever appeared before him?"

"Oh, yeah. Old stone face. Heart the same."

"Have you ever asked around about him? That's what I spent all yesterday afternoon doing. It's not like here, where most people on the street couldn't even name a district judge."

This conversation had taken place in one of the court-rooms of the Bexar County Justice Center in San Antonio, where Jordan and Jerry had met as they were just finishing up trundling clients back to jail. They'd sat in the courtroom chatting while Judge Sherman was taking pleas. Jordan had thought how different was this atmosphere from that of the small-town courthouse. Judge Sherman's court alone proba-bly disposed of more cases in a month than the only court in Green Hills handled all year. The San Antonio court was chaotic, lawyers running in and out, a jury box full of prison-ers, anxious family members rubbing shoulders with watch-ful victims. Jordan's memory of the Green Hills court was pastoral by comparison. In San Antonio he and Jerry could sit in the middle of court and have a perfectly private con-versation, not because their privacy was so scrupulously re-spected, but because no one gave a damn what they were talking about.

"This judge has been the judge in Madera County—the *only* district judge, civil and criminal—for fifteen or twenty years. Seems like he's touched every life in town. You know, anybody who's hurt his back in a slip and fall and wants punitive damages has been in Judge Waverly's court. He's sent people's uncles and brothers to the penitentiary and the victims remember that and are grateful to him. And the other people know he has that power. Sometimes he's put people on probation when they were young and he thought they were just stupid instead of mean. And then he's watched them like a hawk for ten years. He keeps track of everyone who's ever been through his court. He's married half the people in town, and he's divorced the only ones who're divorced—and a couple of times he's *refused* to grant divorces, like he was somebody's minister. One of those cou-ples is still together and *grateful* to him. Jerry, it's weird. He's got some kind of political influence, too, I don't know what that deal is, but it's damned important to the DA to keep him happy, I'll tell you."

Jordan had gotten a strange feeling while asking townspeople about the judge. In Green Hills Judge Waverly was a judge in the biblical sense, the leader of the community. His judgment extended beyond the courtroom. What had felt strange was that the information had confirmed Jordan's first impression: that the judge's vision took in everything. That the courthouse brooded over the whole town because the judge was inside it, watching.

"And everybody knew he had this girl friend?" Jerry had asked.

"No, not everybody. People saw them together, but probably hardly anybody would admit what it was. Those that did wouldn't call it by its right name. But the people in the courthouse, they'd damned sure have some idea."

"And nobody thought he was ridiculous, this old man with this teenage girl friend?"

"No, that's another weird thing. It was like everybody respected the two of them so much they thought it was natural, it wasn't even unexpected that they got together. The three or four people I thought must know about it didn't look inclined to snicker at all. I've never—"

"So you want to know what to do," Jerry had summed up, growing a little bored. Jerry had a broad, shiny face, always deeply tanned, as if he'd just come from a golf course, which was usually true. "Easy. You file a motion to recuse, you ask the judge to take himself off the case because he's prejudiced against your client. Think the judge would grant it?"

"Oh, no."

"No, of course not. So the motion gets heard in another court, probably one in the neighboring county where the judge is an old pal of your judge."

"You're so cynical."

Jerry had grinned. "You bring in witnesses to say Judge Waverly had this illicit sexual relationship with the dead girl. Think you could get someone to testify to that?"

"Are you kidding? They've all got to live there."

Jerry had nodded knowingly, as at a pupil with the right answer. "So you've got no evidence, you've just got this unsupported nasty allegation. Plus, your client isn't even charged with murdering the dead girl, that's not the case your judge is considering. Was your guy even arrested in the girl's murder?"

"They didn't have to arrest him for that, they had him dead to rights for killing this other guy."

"So no official record shows he's even a suspect in the girl's case and you can't prove that one's even connected to your case, so what difference does it make if Judge Waverly has some personal involvement in the other case. Right? So the other judge rules against you on the motion to recuse and you end up right back in Judge Waverly's court with him real fond of you now because you've smeared these rumors about him all over a public record. Does this sound like your best option?"

Jordan had sat mute, as Jerry expected.

"Or does your best option sound like letting your guy get what's coming to him and you get the hell out of Dodge and just make sure you're not appointed on the other case if he ever does get indicted for it?"

This time Jerry had sat waiting for an answer, which Jordan had been slow to deliver: "Yeah. Sure."

Jerry had laughed and clapped him on the shoulder. "So what's the problem?"

No problem. Jordan was just going to go through the motions, as he was doing now.

"Mr. Marshall, you've filed a motion to suppress evidence. Can you inform the court of the nature of the evidence?"

"I believe the defendant made some statements while in custody, Your Honor."

"Very well. Are you prepared to go forward on your motion?"

Jordan was nonplussed. "Actually, no, Your Honor. In light of the change in the charge from our last hearing to this one, from attempted murder to murder, I had expected we'd sort of ... start over, that I would just file motions today and have them heard at a later date."

Judge Waverly let him pick slowly through words to the end of his remarks, regarding him steadily, then speaking as if to a slow student. "This is the date the court had set to hear motions, Mr. Marshall, do you remember that? Were you informed of any reset to another day? No? As for the fact that your client has been indicted in the interval, it has been ten days since the grand jury handed down the murder indictment, as I see from the face of the indictment, so you have had your statutorily required ten days to prepare for *trial,* which this is not."

Everyone was looking at him. He felt again as if he were standing there in his shorts. Even the court reporter, Laura Stefone, glanced at him, her fingers poised to record whatever stupid excuse he made next. Jordan stepped forward, trying to make the exchange between him and the judge more private.

"Your honor, I'm prepared to argue the motions that don't require testimony, such as the motion for discovery."

The judge spoke just as patiently, just as coldly. "Mr. Marshall, today is a Thursday. As attorneys who have familiarized themselves with our local rules are aware, on Thursdays this court hears motions that require testimony. Motions merely to be argued are heard on Fridays."

"I'm sorry, Your Honor, I wasn't aware of that."

"Are you prepared to call witnesses on your motion to suppress?"

Jordan's lips rubbed together, but neither was moist enough to do the other any good. The answer was no, he was not ready. But if the alternative was to waive his motion altogether, which seemed to be the case, he could wing it.

"Yes, sir. I'll call Officer Wilcox."

He felt the heat dissolve as he took his seat. In a moment he'd be the one doing the questioning. Even if he wasn't as prepared as he would have liked, he'd questioned thousands of witnesses in his career, he could think his way through that, and he had read the police reports. He glanced aside at the district attorney, who gave him a small, comradely smile that showed no hint that Arriendez had been enjoying seeing his opponent reduced to an unprepared law student by the judge of their case. The small nod Jordan gave him in return acknowledged that they both knew who was winning this contest from the outset. *But just wait,* Jordan's confident nod said, *now you'll see me at my professional best.*

Nothing was happening. The bailiff still sat at his desk, his lip twisted as he watched Jordan. The clerk at her desk was openly glaring at Wayne. No one was doing anything to fetch a witness. Sweat beads suddenly popped out at the top of Jordan's spine, atop the ones that had just begun to dry. He looked up and saw that he himself was still the object of Judge Waverly's attention.

"Is your witness here, Mr. Marshall?"

Oh, shit. Jordan stood hastily, glancing at Arriendez, who was still giving him the same brotherly smile.

"Your honor, I had expected the State would subpoena the witnesses for the hearing."

The judge's eyes said this was the most curious statement he had ever heard. "Really, Mr. Marshall? For *your* motion?"

"Your honor, in the jurisdiction where I'm more used to practicing, the prosecution always subpoenas the witnesses for any hearing. Since the prosecution always has easier access to police officers, it seems to facilitate—"

"Here in the court where you are practicing at this moment, Mr. Marshall, our rules provide that the proponent of the motion is responsible for securing witnesses for the hearing."

Jordan coughed. "Your honor, could I maybe get a copy of these local rules?"

"I don't believe they're published anywhere, are they, Mr. Arriendez?"

"No, sir, Your Honor." Arriendez stood ever so slightly to speak, then sat again, hastily so as not to steal the spotlight from his adversary.

"Don't worry, Mr. Marshall," the judge said benignly, "we'll inform you of the rules as necessary."

As I violate them, you mean. Jordan again moved forward, trying to think on his feet. He had forgotten he had a client somewhere back there far behind him. Jordan seemed to be the only person on trial in this courtroom today.

As he came abreast of the court reporter's table, he

glanced at her, looking for a friendly face or even a smirk of human recognition. He received neither from Laura Stefone, but he noticed something unusual. The court reporter was equipped with the standard stenography machine, but there was no tape recorder on the table. Jordan frowned. When he spoke again it was very distinctly, still looking at Ms. Stefone. She stared back at him flatly.

"Your honor, I'd ask that instanter subpoenas be issued now. The only witnesses for the motion to suppress are two police officers, who I'm sure could be brought into court with very little delay."

The judge shook his head. "The court has set aside the entire morning of court time for your motions, Mr. Marshall. We do not propose to spend any more time."

"This is a formal request for a continuance, Your Honor. I'll find the witnesses myself."

The judge made no reply at all. After a moment of eye contact, Jordan spoke quickly. "I'll, um, I'll take that as denied. Then I would ask to carry the motion with the trial, Your Honor. After the appropriate testimony at trial I'll ask the court for a ruling before submitting the issue to the jury." There was another pause, but Jordan felt himself on solid ground at last. He stared back. "I believe that is my option, Your Honor, under the code of criminal procedure." Which takes precedence over your persnickety hometown rules.

"Very well, Mr. Marshall. That will be acceptable. What other motion do you have to present to the court today?"

"Uh, a motion to—no, a motion for discovery," Jordan said, returning to his table. He sorted quickly through his stack of motions, drawing out a couple that would require no testimony, only legal rulings from the judge. He skipped the motion for a change of venue. "A motion asking that the court reporter be directed to transcribe testimony, which I see she's already doing"—Jordan flashed his winning smile at her, but the smile had apparently grown bedraggled on the long drive south that morning—"but I would like to make it formal."

"That will be granted."

They disposed quickly of two more formal motions, and Jordan stopped. Judge Waverly could easily see that they hadn't nearly covered all the documents under Jordan's hand. "Other motions?" he asked with an edge.

"I believe any other motions I'll file at a later time, Your Honor, after I've had more time for investigation. I understand that any motions filed at least ten days prior to trial will be timely, and I can request any necessary hearing at the time of filing. Or does the court have any local rules providing otherwise?"

Their bland expressions were belied by the duration of the stares Judge Waverly and Jordan directed at each other.

"Very well," the judge finally ruled. "Any other matters? Mr. Arriendez? Then this court is adjourned."

Jordan remained on his legs, which grew a little shaky as the judge retired from the room. Jordan drew a deep breath, which only seemed to provide fuel for the shakiness. He saw the court reporter stacking her narrow reams of paper, their dots and bumps chronicling his humiliation. It was nice to be off the record.

Jordan began packing his briefcase. Wayne was watching him, too, but that stare Jordan could endure. "We'll talk in a minute," he said.

Arriendez was at his shoulder. "Sorry about that. You should have asked me what was going to happen today. I don't know what your rules are like in San Antonio."

"Yeah, right. Look." Jordan turned on him. Blood, which seemed under the judge's stare to have retreated somewhere south of Jordan's ankles, rushed back into his face. "I tried to be friendly about this, I told you we could work something out." His client was listening, but Jordan didn't care. "But everybody here would rather jerk me around than be professional about this. That's fine. I understand now. That's how we'll do it."

"Hey." Arriendez held up his hands. "I didn't do anything to you today, man. I just watched. If you want to work something out, let's talk."

"You mean your fifty-year offer is still on the table?" Jordan asked sarcastically.

And a new voice was heard from. It was Wayne's, hollow and scratchy. "I'll take it," he said.

Jordan barely turned toward him. "And you, shut up! You don't have a voice here. If you have something to say in court, it'll be *my* voice you hear, because I'm the only one who speaks for you. Understand?" He turned back to the district attorney, whose lips were pursed and his eyes questioning. "Maybe we can be done with this," Jordan said. "Let me talk to him, and I'll come see you afterward."

Arriendez shrugged. When Jordan turned back to his client, he almost bumped into the deputy with the amber sunglasses, who stood right at Jordan's shoulder and had his hand on Wayne's. "He's going back," the deputy said stonily.

Jordan put a peremptory hand on Wayne's other shoulder. "Not yet he's not. He has a right to confer with his attorney, which you've interfered with every step of the way so far. I am *going* to talk to him right now—or would you rather get the judge back out here, and I'll make the request more formal and let him know how you people at the jail have interfered with his attorney–client privileges and have the judge order you to let me talk to him?"

The deputy didn't back down, but when he spoke, it was in the snide tone of a bully whose bluff has been called. "So go ahead, talk."

"In private. Mr. Orkney and I'll go over by the wall. Why don't you sit over there by the door with your big old gun in your hand, and if he makes a break for it, you shoot him."

The deputy leaned into Jordan's face. "I don't need a gun to take care of a punk like him."

"Not if you could catch him. Come on, Wayne." As Jordan turned away, he caught a glimpse of Mike Arriendez smothering a laugh and the bailiff, past his shoulder, smirking at the stony deputy with the smoky glasses and the ample gut.

Wayne shuffled after Jordan to the far wall of the courtroom, where they sat on a bench under a tall wooden window with wavy panes of glass. "You pick a fine time to finally start talking," Jordan said. "So fifty years sounds

good to you? You want to plead guilty to murdering Kevin
Wainwright? You want to get the judge back out right now
and take the plea? That's fine with me. So you did intend
to kill Kevin, is that what you're saying?"

"I guess." Wayne Orkney had a strange young/old quality
about him, as if an old man had been deposited in a boy's
skinny body. His hands rubbed his cheeks and swept his hair
back from his forehead, moving slowly as if he were just
waking up.

"No guessing, Wayne. If you're going to admit you did
something, you have to know what you did. You know
Kevin didn't die that day, he died in the hospital days later."

Wayne nodded. "They didn't let me out for the funeral.
Did you go, did you see him?" Jordan shook his head.
Wayne fell into distraction again. "I wish I could talk to
him, I wish Kevin was here to tell me—"

"You should have thought of that before you beat him to
death," Jordan said unsympathetically.

"Not to *death*," Wayne denied emphatically. He leaned
toward Jordan. "I was amazed when the ambalance come.
You know I helped lift him into the ambalance myself? And
I rode with him to the hospital. That's where the cops arrested me. Before that, while Kevin was still lyin' in the
street, the last words he said to me (*Or to anyone*, Jordan
thought) was, 'It's okay, Wayne.' He tried to take my
hand . . ."

Oh, good, Jordan thought, *a deathstreet absolution. That'll
win the case for us.* But mad as he still was and in spite of
the cynicism defendants' reminiscences always aroused in
him, he could see the pain in Wayne's watery brown eyes.
His left hand was trying to close over a weak, almost life-
less hand.

"So you didn't intend to kill him," Jordan said quietly.
"You were surprised you'd hurt him badly enough that he
had to be taken to the hospital."

"Yeah."

"Then I can't let you stand up and say you committed
intentional murder. Not without looking at the law a little
more. Listen, Wayne, there's something else. I'm sure the

police questioned you about it. About Jenny Fecklewhite. You knew her?"

"Sure. Jenny was the best girl in this town. Ever'body knows that."

"They think you killed her, Wayne."

Wayne's head jerked up, and for the first time, his eyes were wide with astonishment. "That *I*—?"

"Did you?" Jordan asked, although the look on Wayne's face had already answered his question. Jordan's shoulders slumped at the sight. "You must have seen her, Wayne. You told me you were coming from Pleasant Grove Park when you attacked Kevin, and that's where her body was found, in the park."

Wayne's eyes were darting back and forth. Wonderment ruled his face. *This guy can't lie,* Jordan thought. *He doesn't have the face for it.*

"Listen to me, Wayne. This may be more important than the murder they've got you charged with. Did you kill Jenny?"

Wayne's baffled eyes reached his lawyer's face and stayed there as if he'd never seen Jordan before. Darkness began closing down again. Wayne looked wary in a way that was almost comic because it was so obvious.

"Tell me."

"No," Wayne mumbled. He could have been refusing Jordan's demand that he talk rather than answering his question, but Jordan already had his answer, and it made him feel very tired all at once.

Wayne stood up and motioned to his guard. Then he saw for the first time the two people who were still waiting in the courtroom. They'd been sitting patiently on the last row of the spectator seats. When Wayne waved to them, they stood and came toward him, the man shuffling, the woman walking more quickly.

"Mama and Dad," Wayne said. *Wonderful,* Jordan thought.

Mr. and Mrs. Orkney were only in their forties, but they looked old, as if they expected to have shortened lives. The man was thin like Wayne. He wore clean pressed khaki

pants and an embarrassed expression. His wife wore a flow-
ered dress out of which her heavy arms burst, taut as gourds.
She had a double chin and a small nose that flared when
she breathed. She gave her son a hasty hug. "We wanted to
see the way things happen in court," she said. "You want
us to get you a lawyer, Wayne? We talked to Mr. Piedmont,
and he seemed awful smart about things."

Wayne shrugged in Jordan's general direction. "This fella
seems all right."

If he thought that, he hadn't been paying much attention
while court had been in session.

"Mack Orkney," Dad said, shaking hands with Jordan. He
seemed glad to have someone besides his son to deal with.

"Pleased to meet you, Mr. Orkney. I'll let you folks have
a few minutes with your son, and then afterward, you and
Mrs. Orkney and I can talk."

Wayne's guard had stood up from his chair by the door
and was coming toward his prisoner. Jordan walked out to
the aisle, positioning himself between his client and the deputy. The deputy slowed to a halt, glaring. The only other
person left in the courtroom, Helen Evers, took the opportunity to approach Jordan.

"Evers of the *Register*," she said as if their previous meeting hadn't been official. "Well, that was something. We don't
often get to see big-city lawyers in action here in Green
Hills," she said without a trace of sarcasm in her voice.
"Most of our local attorneys try to play up to the judge
instead of antagonizing him. But I guess you have your
own methods."

"Yes, I usually try to make people think I'm so stupid
they can take advantage of me." Jordan squinted sagely. "I
think these people have fallen right into my trap, too."

Helen Evers said, "Have anything you want to add for
publication?"

Jordan thought of the headline he could make in next
week's *Register*. "Orkney Denies Murdering Jenny." But he
couldn't see any advantage in that publicity, not yet. "Maybe
I'll have something for you before your deadline."

"All right," Evers said and strolled away. She probably

already had her headline: "Big-City Lawyer Makes Fool of Self in Court."

"I'll be right back," Jordan said in the general direction of clan Orkney and hurried up toward the judge's vacant bench, then through the side door at the front of the courtroom that led to the court offices. He found the court staff—the bailiff, the clerk, and the court reporter—lounging in the clerk's office. At the sight of Jordan, their talk stopped abruptly. He thought he could still hear an echo of laughter in the air, but from the faces confronting him, that must have been an aural illusion.

"Excuse me for interrupting. Ms. Stefone, may I see you for a minute?"

"Yes," the court reporter said, not moving.

"Um, I'd just like to get a transcript of the hearing we just held. I want to see just how dumb I come across in print."

No one laughed. "All right," Laura Stefone said in a clipped voice. "I can have it ready tomorrow. But you won't be here then, will you? Are you on your way to the beach again, Mr. Marshall?"

"No, I'll be back in San Antonio. Could you mail it to me?"

He handed the court reporter a business card. She took it without glancing at it. All three were still watching Jordan, waiting for him to leave. "I guess at least you three are happy with me, since I gave you most of the morning off. If I'd been ready, you'd all be working now."

No one smiled. No one thanked him. Jordan appealed to the bailiff, who'd smirked at Jordan's upbraiding of the deputy guarding Wayne. "Is that deputy always that tough with prisoners half his size?" Jordan smiled.

"Yes," the bailiff said shortly and walked out of the office, bumping Jordan's shoulder.

The two women were still staring blankly at Jordan, obviously wanting nothing from him but his absence. "I'll mail the transcript to you," Laura Stefone said. "Was there anything else?"

Well, yes, I was looking for a little human contact, but I've obviously come to the wrong place. "No. Thank you very much." Jordan wasted another smile as he retreated.

That was the other piece of advice Jerry Ramirez had given him. "Try to make friends with somebody. Not a lawyer, somebody on the court staff."

"Those people don't make friends, Jerry. They're like three bricks in a wall."

"Come on, Jordy, you know there's no court in America like that. People who work together gossip about each other and get mad at each other and some of them are friends and some of them don't much like each other. Besides, people in courthouses love to talk. Somebody'll want to talk to you, trust me."

Yes, Jordan was on friendly terms with most of the clerks and coordinators and court reporters in the district courts in San Antonio. He hadn't deliberately cultivated their friendship, it just made doing business more pleasant to be friendly, to chat, to make requests rather than demands.

But apparently the court personnel in Green Hills already had all the friends they needed. They were better than air-conditioning. Jordan rubbed his hands for warmth as he returned to the courtroom.

His client and the amber-spectacled deputy were gone. Mr. and Mrs. Orkney were waiting for Jordan, who released an inaudible sigh. Talking to the families of clients was one of the great pains of defense work. They never saw the law operating in the practical terms with which Jordan had to deal with it. They always thought everyone was out to get their boy for no good reason. Mama would wring her hands and say, "He's always been a good boy, he's never been any trouble to us." They would look at Jordan like it was his fault that poor little Wayne was in trouble now.

"Hello, Mr. and Mrs. Orkney. You understand, don't you, that Judge Waverly appointed me to represent your son, Wayne, on this murder charge. Of course, he's free—or you're free if you choose—to hire a lawyer of your own choosing if you'd prefer." Which wouldn't be a bad solution, all around.

But the Orkneys had no response. Mr. Orkney was nodding along with Jordan; Mrs. Orkney was studying him sullenly.

"I practice in San Antonio, I don't have an office here. Perhaps we could go to the diner and have a cup of coffee while we talk if you like. Or they might let us use a conference room here if you'd rather."

Mrs. Orkney settled the question by plopping herself down on the first bench of the spectator seats. Her husband sat beside her, and Jordan pulled a chair up to face them. Before he could say anything, Mrs. Orkney folded her arms and glared at Jordan as she said, "Well, I always knew I'd be sitting talking to some damn lawyer about Wayne."

"Now hush," Mack Orkney said mildly.

"Well, it's true," she retorted. "At least as long as he hung around with that Kevin Wainwright."

"They'd been in trouble before?" Jordan asked.

"Not much," Mr. Orkney began, but his wife interrupted.

"No, but it was just a matter of time long as they stayed here. If they'd had the spunk to move to the city and get a job, they'd've been okay. But what's there to do if they stay here *but* get into trouble?"

Her eye stayed fixed on Jordan as if she expected an answer from him. Jordan kept his tone mild and professional. "Wayne didn't have a job?"

"Oh, he pumped gas at the Texaco," she said dismissively. "I don't think he was on his way to being chairman of the board, though, do you?"

"It was the best he could do for right now," her husband told her.

"Yeah, *here.*" She looked as if she were going to spit.

"What did you mean, Mr. Orkney, when you said not much? What kind of trouble *had* Wayne and Kevin been in?"

"Oh, you know, fights." Mack Orkney spoke understandingly, but it was hard for Jordan to imagine the older man's ever having harbored the passions that lead to fighting.

"When they were drunk," Mrs. Orkney added.

"Getting kicked out of the roadhouse, or once they were arrested driving home," Mr. Orkney continued.

"Drunk," his wife said again vindictively.

"Now hush, Charlotte, you'll make the man think alcohol ruled Wayne's life."

"No," Mrs. Orkney said, still simmering. "It's just that they didn't have anything better to do. Or the sense to get out."

"Had Wayne been drinking the day he attacked Kevin?"

"This time?" Mack Orkney asked courteously. "No, sir. It was the middle of the afternoon. I saw Wayne right after at the jail and he was sober as a judge."

There went that defense. "This time?" Jordan repeated. "They'd fought before?"

"Oh, you know, like boys will. Ever since they were kids. That didn't mean they weren't friends."

The courtroom was uncomfortably warm, as if the staff had shut off the air-conditioning when court ended. There was no one else in the room, which made the courtroom seem large and ominous, but Jordan felt peered at from behind cracked-open doors. "I'm sure you have things you want to ask me," he said.

"What's going to happen to Wayne?" Charlotte Orkney said immediately. Her eyes hadn't released Jordan once except when she rolled them in disgust.

"The district attorney wants him to go to prison for a long time. He's offered a fifty-year sentence. And Wayne said he'd take it."

"Idiot," she said. "Kevin wasn't worth that. Well, he wasn't. Besides, it was an accident."

"Well, that's not the way the law sees it, Mrs. Orkney. If you're beating someone up and he dies, that's murder whether you intended to kill him or not."

Mr. Orkney nodded again as if he already knew the law or was in perfect agreement with it. "Fifty years," he said sadly, shaking his head.

"It's much too high an offer," Jordan said. He hesitated and continued. "Somehow it's tied up with Jenny Fecklewhite's murder."

Mrs. Orkney nodded. "That was always the trouble, them being involved with Jenny. Now there was somebody who was already on her way out," she said admiringly. "After she went off to that state speech tournament, she might've never come back."

"She had to come back for her senior year," her husband said.

"Maybe. They got high schools other places. Any rate, she wasn't going to be hanging around here, like boys with no gumption."

"*What* was the problem with Jenny and Wayne and Kevin?" Jordan wanted clarified.

"That she was too good for them. Ever'body knew that. I always knew it would lead to trouble. Didn't think it'd be Jenny that got hurt, though," Mrs. Orkney added sadly, sounding sorrier for the victim than for her son.

Jordan let beats of silence pass while he thought. The Orkneys both sat straight and looked at him. "What are you going to do, Mr. Marshall?"

That was a good question. "Try to get the DA to come down on his offer." Hopeless. "We could plead guilty to the judge without accepting the State's offer and let the judge decide the punishment."

Jordan didn't know why he said that, since that was no longer a realistic option. Maybe he wanted to see how Wayne's parents would react. They both nodded. "The judge might know best," Mr. Orkney said, leading Jordan to believe the Orkneys weren't in on the town's secrets.

There weren't many more questions. Jordan promised to keep in touch, and the Orkneys left slowly, Mrs. Orkney talking vehemently, her husband making placating motions with his hands and his head. Jordan seemed to be watching them, but when the Orkneys turned aside, his stare didn't follow. It was distant with distress. His problem was that he had seen innocent surprise on his client's face at the suggestion that Wayne had killed Jenny Fecklewhite. Jordan never made the mistake of believing what his clients said, but he believed that astonished expression on Wayne's face.

Damn it, Wayne was innocent of Jenny's murder. And that was the one they were going to hammer him for.

* * *

Life reverted to normal when Jordan returned to San Antonio. He stopped being a displaced person. He had an office, he had a routine, he was part of a community where he was known, and he knew what to do. Familiarity was comforting, even when he was too busy or too idle, even when he was being pushed into trying a case he didn't want to try or when a prosecutor was being less than reasonable.

Not caring was a comfort, too. What Jordan's clients were usually guilty of was felony stupid, but even when he stood at the bench beside one who was genuinely evil, who took pleasure in hurting people, no one looked at Jordan as if he were the guy's codefendant. After the sentencing, the court coordinator would shake Jordan's hand and call him by name, and Jordan left the courtroom with a light heart while his client went out the other door in handcuffs. No big deal.

In the rush of his days, Green Hills receded into its rightful insignificance. But once in a while something reminded him of the case waiting there for him. He did research to be sure he was right in thinking that Wayne Orkney was guilty of murder even if he hadn't intended to kill Kevin Wainwright, and the dry legal opinions dissolved into the faces of Wayne's parents, attentively listening to Jordan talk, or into Wayne's watery brown eyes opening wide at the suggestion that he had murdered Jenny. Sometimes he saw again, in imagination, the newspaper image of Jenny. Jordan remembered that happy, knowing expression of hers, the look of a girl on her way out.

The week after his most recent visit to Green Hills, he was mentally teleported there again by the arrival in his office mail of a manila envelope bearing a slim burden of his own words. It was the transcript of the hearing, mailed to him by Laura Stefone, the court reporter in Judge Waverly's court. No note introduced the document, the envelope just contained the transcript in its clear plastic cover. Jordan saw his own name on the front page as the attorney appearing for the defendant.

The transcript was only a few pages. Jordan grimaced and settled himself to read. He'd read his own words in transcript before. He was familiar with the phenomenon of

words that had rung brilliantly in his own ears in a courtroom being reduced to ungrammatical fragments and non-
sensical drivel in a written record. But this time he wasn't
expecting to look good in print. He'd ordered the transcript
only to make sure he hadn't damaged his case. As unprepared as he'd been, he was confident that he hadn't let any
issues slip away permanently.

As he began to read, the scene came back to him but from
a new perspective. In the written record, Judge Waverly's
explaining of his court's local rules to the arrogantly unready
out-of-town lawyer sounded courteous, even kindly. Jordan
began to see the scene through Laura Stefone's eyes. Her
judgment sat on every page of the transcript. Judge Waverly
spoke in complete sentences with grammatical correctness
and a certain classical tone. The few sentences Mike Arriendez had injected into the proceeding were brisk and to the
point.

Jordan, on the other hand, sounded like the village idiot.
Laura Stefone had captured every "uh" and aborted sentence he had sputtered. Jordan had seen that in transcripts
before. One could read the court reporter's opinion of the
speaker by whether she bothered to clean up his speech
for him. Laura Stefone had done that for everyone in the
courtroom that day except the out-of-town clown. Jordan's
shoulders hunched as he read on. That's okay, hardly anyone reads transcripts. Especially transcripts from Green
Hills, Texas.

But Laura Stefone had done something more to him.
When Jordan reached the point in the transcript at which
he had formally requested a continuance to another day for
his motion to suppress evidence, there was no response in
the record from Judge Waverly. Had he spoken? Jordan
remembered the request had been denied, but he couldn't
remember if the judge had actively said so or if the implication had just been clear. Damn, he had fallen for that. If
the judge hadn't ruled on Jordan's request in the record,
there was nothing for Jordan to appeal if the judge's denial
of more time was erroneous, as Jordan believed it was.
Clever trial judges tried to avoid ruling on requests at all

for this very reason, but good defense lawyers forced them to do so. Judge Waverly had beaten Jordan on this one.

But on the next one it was the court reporter herself who had killed him.

After his request for more time had been denied, Jordan had saved himself and his motion to suppress evidence by asking the judge to let him raise the issue during trial. Judge Waverly had granted that request, Jordan remembered clearly. The evidence about Wayne's arrest and the admissions he'd made at the time would come up at trial. Jordan had asked that the judge rule, after hearing that evidence, whether the jury should be allowed to hear the statements Wayne had made. "... *before* submitting the issue to the jury," Jordan had said. He was positive of that.

But that's not what the transcript of the hearing said.

The transcript showed Jordan asking the judge, "After the appropriate testimony at trial I'll ask the court for a ruling submitting the issue to the jury." Laura Stefone had left out only one word—*before*—but it was the crucial word. As the transcript read now, what Jordan had requested and the judge granted was simply that the issue should be submitted to the jury. That *was* one of Jordan's options, but a stupid one. No lawyer with any sense ever let a jury hear evidence and then ask them to ignore that evidence if they decided it had been obtained illegally. Jurors never bothered with legal distinctions like that. They didn't put things out of their minds once they had heard them. Jordan knew that. He would never have said what the transcript had him saying.

It could have been an honest mistake. It was, after all, one word; the court reporter could have missed hearing it. But Jordan didn't think so. In every instance where his memory disagreed with the written record, Laura Stefone's record put Jordan and his client in a subtly worse position than they would have been in had the record agreed with Jordan's memory. In fact, the subtlety of the alterations amazed Jordan. They showed a keen grasp of criminal law. Mike Arriendez had not been Jordan's only opposing legal counsel in the Green Hills courtroom nor, perhaps, the best one.

He wondered briefly why the court reporter had tipped her hand so early but then realized she couldn't help it. Hers was going to be the official record of the legal proceedings against Wayne Orkney. She couldn't give Jordan one version of a transcript now and then change it before the case went up on appeal. That would give him some basis for challenging her record. As it was, there was no way he could. Laura Stefone, he remembered, hadn't used a tape recorder. Any challenge would just be Jordan's memory against Ms. Stefone's, and the person resolving that conflict would be the trial judge: Judge Waverly.

The result of this record was that Jordan's motion to suppress evidence was lost. So the statements Wayne had made after his arrest would come into evidence at trial. He had to think how to incorporate them into his defense.

But that wasn't his immediate problem. As Jordan reread the transcript, seeing himself appear even more buffoonish than he'd actually been, his hand tightened on the pages. He tore one corner as he turned the page. At the end he sat red faced, listening to his own breathing.

So the hicks from Hicksville wanted to play hardball, did they?

5

You might as well sit here inside the bar."

Jordan touched the lady's arm as he guided her inside the railing of Judge Waverly's courtroom. Mrs. Chambers wore a short-sleeved, knee-length dress of navy blue with white polka dots; not gaudy, but not designed to make her inconspicuous either. She was a very pleasant lady, he knew from past experience, with strong opinions and funny stories, but inside the courtroom, her demeanor was blank faced. She took one of the chairs just inside the railing and began setting up.

District attorney Mike Arriendez had been leaning casually against the State's counsel table. He stood straight to peer over Jordan's shoulder at Mrs. Chambers. "Who's this?"

"My bodyguard," Jordan said, sat down, removed papers from his briefcase, and folded his hands, placidly watching the judge's empty bench.

Other court staffers drifted in one by one. Each glanced boredly at Jordan, then looked past him and took in Mrs. Chambers, frowned, and went to confer among themselves. Arriendez joined them. The clerk, Cindy Garcia, left the courtroom. Laura Stefone took her place at her own table and began loading her stenography machine with paper, all the while glaring at Jordan and his cohort. When she was done, she sat stiffly, staring at the side wall of the courtroom.

By the time Judge Waverly entered, Jordan was deep in whispered consultation with his client. Jordan and Wayne were the first ones on their feet when the judge took the bench. Judge Waverly had obviously already been alerted to the presence of the intruder. He looked at Mrs. Chambers blankly, then frowned at Jordan.

"What is this?" he asked sternly.

Jordan again rose to his feet, this time slowly, as if he weren't sure he was the one being addressed. "Your Honor, my case hasn't been called, so I don't know if it's proper, under your local rules, for me to address the court."

When he spoke, Laura Stefone's hands moved briskly. So did Mrs. Chambers' on the keys of her own machine.

Judge Waverly's black eyes bored into Jordan, through Jordan's bland expression and innocent eyes, into the dark, squishy interior of the lawyer's brain, where evil schemes were hatched.

"This is the State of Texas versus Wayne Truman Orkney," Judge Waverly intoned. "Now, Mr. Marshall, what is going on?"

"This is Mrs. Chambers, Your Honor, a court reporter I've retained at my own expense, on loan from the 187th District Court of Bexar County."

"To what end? I'm sure you've noticed, Mr. Marshall, that this court has its own official court reporter."

"Mrs. Chambers is here to ensure the accuracy of the record, Your Honor." *Because the record for appeal is very important to me,* the judge could easily read in Jordan's expression, *since it's perfectly obvious my client isn't going to obtain justice here in the trial court.*

"Some people might admire your caution, Mr. Marshall, but it is a waste of this lady's time and your money. This court will have an official written record, therefore"—the judge was speaking more slowly than usual, glancing at Mrs. Chambers, whose fingers moved in rhythm with his voice— "your record will be redundant. Any discrepancies between the two records will be resolved by the trial court."

He didn't finish. He didn't have to. Of course if it became a matter of dueling records, Judge Waverly would decide in favor of his own loyal court reporter. Laura Stefone was being fairly successful at keeping her expression neutral, but

Jordan thought he saw a look of satisfaction flit across her face.

"And that ruling won't be overturned on appeal," Jordan said smoothly, "unless the appellate court decides the trial judge abused his discretion. The only way they could decide that is if the objective evidence"—he indicated the small tape recorder sitting on the corner of the defense table, its tape turning—"compellingly overrides the trial court's decision."

Judge Waverly sat silent for a minute, studying Jordan, who looked back innocently. "Approach the bench," the judge said. "Not you, young lady."

Jordan nodded to Mrs. Chambers. He picked up the tape recorder and took it forward with him, drawing another frown from the judge, who leaned forward and spoke more softly.

"This is an insult to the court."

"It's not intended that way, Your Honor."

"Then it's an insult to my staff."

"Not at all, Your Honor." Jordan and Laura Stefone were watching each other. Her hands seemed detached, going about their business in apparent neutral efficiency beneath the penetrating stare of her icy green eyes. "It's just that I've seen a lot of court records, and I think the court reporter's is the most difficult job in the courtroom. Am I speaking slowly enough for you? I know how garbled the record can be," Jordan continued. "That's why all the court reporters I've ever seen use a tape recorder to aid their memories in case something isn't clear to them on first hearing. I noticed that your court reporter doesn't use one, Your Honor, and I mean no disrespect to her at all, but I also have no idea of Ms. Stefone's competence, and this record is very important to my client. So I brought my own back-up court reporter to assist the court in the preparation of the record."

The judge turned to his own court reporter. "Ms. Stefone, do you feel you require assistance to record testimony?"

"No, Your Honor." Her fingers moved, recording her own words.

"Your offer of backup will not be at all necessary, Mr.

Marshall. As I don't like my courtroom any more crowded than absolutely necessary, I'll thank you to dismiss your Mrs. Chambers. Or I will be forced to hold you both in contempt."

His words were as stern as ever, but there was something new in Judge Waverly's tone. At least Jordan heard a subtle plea for compromise. And the judge was no longer staring into Jordan as if his stare were a weapon. He was studying him.

After a long moment Jordan said, "Very well, Your Honor." He turned and with a slight bow offered his tape recorder, its reel still revolving, to Laura Stefone. The court reporter opened a drawer in her desk and pulled out a small recorder of her own. She flipped up its cover, glanced at the tape, and pushed the Record button. She set her own tape recorder on a corner of her desk and she and Jordan traded enigmatic looks.

"Testing, testing," Jordan said in the direction of the tape recorder and carried his own back to his counsel table. In a few whispered words he dismissed Mrs. Chambers, who calmly packed her equipment and withdrew without having spoken a word to anyone.

"Now if we may proceed?"

"Yes, Your Honor. Earlier this week I had mailed the court and the district attorney a motion for change of venue and informed Mr. Arriendez by phone that I would be calling it to the court's attention this morning. This being a Thursday, I'm prepared to present evidence on that motion."

Jordan sat. The judge blinked. "Mr. Arriendez, are you prepared on the defendant's motion?"

"Yes, sir, Your Honor."

"Very well. Call your first witness, Mr. Marshall."

"The defense calls Rachel Lopez, Your Honor."

The hearing was unlike any Jordan could recall. It was his first change of venue hearing as a defense lawyer, but that didn't account for the difference. The difference was Laura Stefone. Jordan was no longer concerned about the record after his challenge and with two tape recorders spinning slowly. But the court reporter had injected herself into his attention. He not only chose his words more carefully, he watched Ms. Stefone for reaction. Jordan was accustomed to the flicker of eyes between lawyers in a courtroom or between lawyer and judge when one knows the other has scored a point. But in this hearing Jordan watched the court reporter as well. If he hoped for an occasional nod or expression of approval, it was a childish hope that deserved to fail. What he did see was Laura Stefone glance at him occasionally, following his words with her eyes as well as her fingers, an interest she had not shown him in previous hearings.

"Ms. Lopez, what county do you live in?"

"Madera," the young woman testified. She wore a simple dress that might have been the best she owned. When Jordan had met her, she'd been wearing a waitress's uniform. She seemed unfazed by the witness stand. The judge had smiled at her as if they knew each other.

"You remember my talking to you about this man next to me?" Jordan asked.

"Sure."

"Who murdered Kevin Wainwright, Ms. Lopez?"

She pointed. "Wayne Orkney did," she said matter-of-factly.

"Did you see it?"

"No, I was home that day. But lots of people did see it. Everybody knows who did it."

"You've talked to people about the murder?"

"Sure."

"And they're all agreed that Wayne Orkney is guilty?"

"Uh-huh."

"Answer yes or no, please, Rachel," Judge Waverly said gently.

"Yes, sir. Yes."

"I pass the witness."

Mike Arriendez said without pause, "You understand, Rachel, that Wayne Orkney hasn't been tried yet?"

"Oh, yes."

"And he's going to be found guilty or not guilty based on

79

what a jury hears in this courtroom, not on talk in the streets?"

"Yes, that'll be different," Rachel Lopez agreed.

"If you were on that jury, could you put aside what you've heard about the case and decide a verdict based only on the evidence you heard in court?"

"You mean pretend I didn't know Wayne did it? Sure," the witness said, "I could do that."

One of those exchanges of looks occurred. Jordan saw Laura Stefone raise her eyes to the ceiling. "No more questions," the district attorney said resignedly, and Jordan repeated the same phrase with satisfaction.

Jordan called three more citizens of Madera County and offered affidavits from five more, all to the effect that "everybody knew" that Wayne Orkney had murdered Kevin Wainwright. "He weren't exactly devious about it," one crusty farmer interjected to smiles from the bailiff and the clerk.

Laura Stefone did not join in the general amusement. Jordan had noticed before that good court reporters sometimes appear to go somewhere else while recording testimony. Ms. Stefone knew that route. She was again staring at the side wall of the courtroom, her expression muted and distant. Her fingers on the keys of her machine seemed to move independently of the rest of her. Jordan was glad he now had the tape recorder to rely on.

Mike Arriendez endured the parade of unknowingly adverse witnesses with good grace, smiling at his constituents and chatting with them as if they were standing at the counter of the hardware store. He only interrupted Jordan's questioning once, when Jordan asked one witness, "Do you know who killed Jenny Fecklewhite?"

"Objection. Irrelevant." The district attorney was on his feet fast.

"Sustained." Judge Waverly directed one of those stares at Jordan, both stern and questioning. The question renewed Laura Stefone's interest in the out-of-town lawyer as well. The tone of the whole courtroom glimmered into alteration for the next few moments as if magic, forbidden words had been spoken. The bailiff glanced at the clerk and at the judge.

"The defense calls Helen Evers."

The reporter for the *Register* hadn't expected to be called as a witness, but she came forward quickly from her spot on the front row of spectator seats. Mike Arriendez smiled at her but objected, "Your honor, this witness has been present for all the other witnesses' testimony."

"But no one invoked the rule," Jordan pointed out, wondering if the written record would back him up.

"I don't believe Ms. Evers would be influenced by what she's heard. Helen, do you swear the testimony you will give in this hearing will be the truth and nothing but the truth?"

"Yes, I do, Your Honor." Helen Evers lowered her right hand, which still held her reporter's notebook, and took her seat in the witness stand, pen poised over paper.

"We don't allow witnesses to take notes," Judge Waverly admonished her mildly.

"But, Judge, I'm covering this hearing for the *Register*. I wouldn't want to misquote myself."

The judge made no reply other than a slight shrug that Helen Evers could interpret as she would. She kept her notepad before her. Judge Waverly's control over the courtroom, which in earlier sessions had seemed absolute, had relaxed. He watched the witnesses attentively as if curious himself what the outcome of the hearing might be.

After establishing her name and occupation and that she had covered Wayne Orkney's arrest, Jordan asked carefully, "Did the *Register* report that Wayne was a suspect not only in the murder of Kevin Wainwright but in—another murder as well?"

"Yes."

"Has this been a big story for you?"

"The biggest we've had since I've been reporting."

"Splashed across the front pages, you might say?"

"It's been on every front page we've had since it happened," Evers agreed.

"Have you ever identified anyone other than Wayne Orkney as a suspect in the murders?"

She laughed slightly. "No."

"You reported that Wayne was arrested for the murder of Kevin Wainwright?"

"Of course."

"How many newspapers are published in this county?"

"Just the *Register*. We're the only one."

Jordan shifted in his chair to indicate a shift in the direction of his questioning. "When you were reporting on the story, Ms. Evers, did you speak to people who thought Wayne Orkney guilty of murder even though they hadn't seen the fight?"

The reporter frowned. "Well, when I was covering the story of the murder itself, I only spoke to eyewitnesses."

"It must make your job easier, Ms. Evers, this ability you have to distinguish at once between actual eyewitnesses and only rumormongers, so you speak only to the former."

"What do you mean?"

"I mean," Jordan said, a little annoyed to see that Evers had forgotten to keep taking notes, "didn't you, while looking for witnesses, talk to people who talked as if they'd seen the fight between Wayne and Kevin but in fact hadn't, who were only passing on what they'd heard?"

"Oh. Sure."

"And didn't you find that some of them had already formed impressions of what had happened even though they hadn't seen it?"

"Oh, yes. Everybody knew, long before we could report it."

"Make a note of that answer, Helen, that was a good one. I pass the witness."

Arriendez didn't ask many questions. Jordan knew the DA understood the law on change of venue when he asked, "Has the *Register* run any editorials about this murder, Helen?"

"No. We don't go in for editorials much."

"No stories saying something like, 'We all know Wayne Orkney did it, let's get him'?"

The reporter smiled at the joke. " 'Course not."

"How did you refer to the defendant in your stories?"

"As the accused. Or a suspect."

"The accused. Not the convicted. No more questions."

The hearing had seemed to be going all Jordan's way, but with those few questions and one prosecution witness, Arriendez disposed of the motion for change of venue. After Jordan rested, Arriendez called the registrar of Madera County, who came up from his office on the first floor of the courthouse to testify that the county held some nine thousand registered voters.

"Most of them Democrats?" Arriendez asked with a grin.

"Most of the living ones and damned near all the dead ones," the registrar replied in the same spirit. Jordan saw that Laura Stefone's fingers didn't move on the keys of her machine during this exchange, but he didn't register a protest.

The hearing was done and anyone who understood knew that Jordan had ably demonstrated his premise that Wayne couldn't get a fair trial in his home county, but they also knew how likely the judge's ruling was to reflect that fact. Jordan had presented through live testimony or sworn statements eight witnesses to say that Wayne Orkney could not get a fair trial in Madera County because everyone informed about the case believed him guilty already. But the district attorney had demonstrated that those eight people were only a pitifully small percentage of the possible jurors in the case. Jordan could have presented eight *hundred* witnesses and still failed to prove that a change of venue was necessary. This particular burden of proof was virtually impossible to carry. It was a matter strictly left to the trial judge's discretion.

So whether to move the trial to another county was entirely up to Judge Waverly, and Jordan had no illusion that the judge would permit the trial to travel beyond his power base. Jordan was merely doing what had to be done and, in the process, proving to the judge that he knew what he was doing.

"That motion will be denied," Judge Waverly said after brief arguments. "Do you have any others to present today, Mr. Marshall?"

Jordan did. But as the courtroom grew warmer, the pace of court proceedings slowed. Promptly at noon, Judge Waverly announced a recess for lunch. Wayne, who hadn't spoken a word all morning, was taken away to his jailhouse bologna. Mike Arriendez gave Jordan a sidelong look but decided not to speak. Helen Evers appeared suddenly at Jordan's shoulder.

"You're going to turn this into a *big* case, aren't you?" she said, eyes bright. "A—what-do-you-call-it?"

"Showcase?"

"I was thinking vendetta," Evers said slyly.

"I'm not mad at anybody. Excuse me."

Jordan hurriedly collected his tape recorder and briefcase and almost ran up the aisle to catch the briskly walking figure of the court reporter.

"Ms. Stefone, I want to apologize if I offended you. That wasn't—"

"No one has in mind to railroad your client, Mr. Marshall. Even if anyone were so inclined, it would be unnecessary, as he is so obviously, blatantly guilty. If you think he is going to obtain any less justice because this county is less populous than the metropolitan area you hail from, you are even dumber than you look in court."

"Who said anything about county size?"

"I have been in the San Antonio courts," Laura Stefone continued, not slowing the pace of either her voice or her steps. "And Houston courts. And Chicago courts. And let me tell you, the people in this courthouse are every bit as competent at their jobs as any—"

"Who said they weren't?"

She looked at him for the first time, a quick, scornful study. "It's been on your face ever since you first walked into the courtroom in your cute little tennis shorts."

"No, it wasn't."

" 'No it *hasn't been*,' " Stefone corrected him crisply, "if you're denying a continuing condition."

"What condition?"

"Your face." She saw Jordan's surprise and amplified. "It displays contempt for this whole town."

"That's not contempt, Ms. Stefone, that's bafflement. At the barrage I've been under ever since I got here just because I got saddled with defending the town schmuck. And the hostility that rains down on both of us."

Laura Stefone stopped and faced him. They were on the street corner in front of the courthouse—abruptly, it seemed to Jordan; he couldn't remember coming down the stairs. He hadn't even felt the glare of the sun yet. Only of Ms. Stefone's eyes.

"Maybe we're just not as blasé about murder here," she said. "Maybe we take it more to heart."

"Ms. Stefone, let me tell you a secret. Maybe I can make you, at least, understand. I don't give a damn about Wayne Orkney. I did not come here to defend him. What concerns me is ineffective assistance of counsel, which is what I'm going to be charged with if you keep distorting the record to make me look like a boob every time I—"

"A bigger boob."

"A bigger boob," Jordan agreed. "All I want to do is leave a clean record for appeal, put on the best defense I can, and wave bye-bye to Wayne Orkney as his bus leaves for Huntsville."

The court reporter looked him up and down again just as quickly but with a touch less scorn. Without an apology or an invitation, she turned and crossed the street. Jordan followed.

"I have never altered a record in my life," Laura Stefone said as he caught up.

"Then you have very selective hearing."

"Maybe you're just used to having transcripts cleaned up for you. Do the court reporters in San Antonio do that for prosecutors?"

"No." But the question set him thinking.

"Maybe you need an elocution class then."

"Perhaps," Jordan said distinctly, popping the *t*'s, "you—could—suggest—a—teacher."

She didn't laugh or smile. Maybe the set of her shoulders had softened as she turned away from him. He continued to follow where she led, even when she turned into an antique store, one that took up half a city block. The hardwood floor creaked beneath his feet. He smelled cracked leather and old wood. Confronting him, atop a dresser, was a portrait of a stern-faced pioneer couple.

"You came here spoiling for a fight. You shouldn't be surprised if people push back."

"I wasn't looking for a fight. I wasn't even looking for a *case*. I was on vacation."

"Yes, and you let everyone know that their little rinky-dink murder case was a waste of your important time."

"I'm not like that," Jordan said. Laura Stefone gave him a look over her shoulder.

In a back corner of the store was a tiny lunchroom, only five tables set for diners. That was Ms. Stefone's destination. Without quite realizing what he was doing, Jordan sat opposite her at the small round table. "I'm not," he repeated.

Stefone gave him a small, ironic smile, then widened it for the waitress who suddenly appeared. "Hello, Doris. I'll have the special."

"Uh—" Jordan looked around for a menu.

"Mr. Marshall will have Alpo on lettuce," Stefone added in the same pleasant tone.

Doris made a second note on her pad. "Iced tea with those?" she asked without looking up.

Laura Stefone raised an eyebrow at Jordan, who just stared back at her. "Please," the court reporter said to the waitress, who nodded and withdrew.

The joke in the midst of fighting with him struck Jordan silent. He looked at Laura Stefone more closely. She was not the remote, officious lady he'd offhandedly pegged her; that was just her court persona. Ms. Stefone was about his age, somewhere in the broad range of thirties. This was the first time he'd looked straight into her face, and he noticed something unusual. Her face was not quite symmetrical. When he saw her in profile, as he had all morning in court, or when she tilted her head, it wasn't noticeable, but as he looked at her full on he saw that one cheekbone was ever so slightly higher than the other, and the eyebrow on that side quirked marginally higher when she raised them. She was a pretty woman in profile, but in full face she was something more, she looked thoughtful and quizzical and as if sadness hovered near her, waiting until she was tired enough to let it touch her.

This kind of thing happened to Jordan once in a while lately, he saw something in a woman—maybe a woman he'd known for years—he'd never seen before and had the sudden feeling he knew a part of her no one else knew. He could imagine Laura, for example, studying her face in the mirror until the imperfection became the most obvious thing about it, until she couldn't realize that no one else would even notice, until she thought herself disfigured. In the rush of the insight, true or not, Jordan wanted to take her hand, kiss her cheek, tell her she was beautiful, and reveal something about himself he'd never told anyone.

Luckily, he'd restrained the recent impulses of this kind, and he hadn't told anyone about the phenomenon. He could imagine what any of the jerks he knew would say: "You've only started having these bursts of sympathy for women since you got divorced, right, Jordie?" But he knew what he felt. He had to shake off the feeling to go on talking easily to Laura Stefone.

Casting about, he asked, "Have you lived in Green Hills all your life?"

She laughed. "It's not the kind of place you move *to*." When Jordan renewed the question with a look she added, "Yes, except for two years at court reporter school in Chicago. I was planning to stay there, but then the judge's old reporter retired, he offered me the job, and—" She shrugged.

Jordan said, "Sometimes you get—" but was interrupted by the return of the waitress, who set a lettucy concoction in front of Laura Stefone and something steaming in front of Jordan. "You people really know how to run with a joke," he said, because the plate in front of him held small meatballs in brown gravy ladled over wedges of toast.

"No, no, Doris," Laura Stefone said concernedly. "I said Alpo on *lettuce*. Mr. Marshall is dieting."

"Please, don't be so formal," Jordan said, taking in both

of them with the invitation. "Call me Bozo." He looked down at his plate and back up at the waitress. "It's fine like this."

"Okay, enjoy."

Laura Stefone took a delicate bite of her salad and did not appear to be watching him, but she didn't resume conversation either. Jordan realized his two options: He could refuse to eat and look like a jerk, so stupid he thought a restaurant would actually serve him dog food at Laura's instigation, or he could eat heartily and look like a jerk when he discovered that what they'd called Alpo and looked like Alpo actually *was* Alpo.

He took a bite, heavy on the toast but also including one full glob of meat. The meat had an ever so slight grittiness, a resiliency that hamburger always had, didn't it? Jordan made a tight-lipped smile. Laura Stefone returned a broader one.

Either what he was eating was a chunky hash with actually a very nice brown gravy or he had a hitherto unsuspected taste for dog food.

"Thanks for ordering me the good brand," he said.

"We like to put our best foot forward."

The tiny lunchroom was filling up, and Jordan realized he knew half the patrons. Laura smiled past his shoulder at the bailiff and the clerk taking seats nearby. They glanced at Jordan quizzically, then at Laura as if she'd brought a stranger to the speakeasy. As he turned back to his food, Jordan caught a glimpse of Deputy Delmore. He had sneaked up on Jordan just as he had on the highway. Delmore was eating with a city police officer, both of them clinking with gear, both of them looking at Jordan as he bent to his food.

"We hear Wayne wants to plead guilty," Laura said suddenly. She saw Jordan decide not to answer and added, "And that you won't let him."

"That's just for the time being." If he'd had a defense, he would have kept it to himself, but the nothing he had could be shared. "I imagine it'll end in a guilty plea one of these days," Jordan said offhandedly.

Laura was waiting for more. When it didn't come, she added, "Mike Arriendez says you used to be an assistant DA in San Antonio."

"Yes," Jordan said flatly.

"But you decided defense work appealed to you more?" the court reporter gently interrogated.

There was absolutely no reason to tell her the story. She was a complete stranger who'd already demonstrated hostility, if anything, toward Jordan. But there was something about the way Laura Stefone sat opposite him, waiting, hands in her lap, that drew Jordan. Her expression was touched with sadness, as if she already knew he had a story—and the nature of the tale.

"I was very happy in the DA's office," Jordan said abruptly, surprised by the harshness of his voice. "I would have stayed there forever, probably."

In the pause, Laura Stefone said, "But there was this case—" Jordan glanced at her sharply, attuned for ridicule, but he saw none in her expression.

"It was a capital murder case," he said. "Really ugly. These gang guys robbed a convenience store and killed the nineteen-year-old clerk, kind of as an afterthought—or for fun. It was one of those cases that get under your skin for some reason. But it was hard, too. I didn't have any witnesses, not to the shooting. I was working on this one kid, the youngest one. I wanted him to testify, and his lawyer was helping me convince him. I got the kid indicted for capital murder, and that chance of a death sentence did it for him, put the fear of God in him."

Jordan stopped, wondering if his voice was too loud. Delmore and the other cop were glancing at him. Laura Stefone was watching him attentively so that he felt embarrassed at his fervor. He shrugged. "The one I really wanted was the gang leader, I was sure he'd done the shooting. The kid I had indicted finally agreed to testify against him for a reduced sentence. I let him plead to robbery and promised him a twenty-year sentence if he testified."

"And?" Laura said.

"And then I went on vacation," Jordan said. *In a last*

attempt to save my marriage, he could have added, but that was the story of a different failure, one he had no intention of sharing with anyone. "Just for a week. A week," he repeated, feeling the anger creeping over him again. "And when I got back the gang leader had agreed to testify, too, and had gotten an even lower sentence than I'd given my kid. So the whole case had gone to shit and I'm left to explain to the convenience store clerk's parents that the guy who killed their son's going to be walking around loose in a few years."

Laura said, "It was just a question of one hand not knowing what the other was doing?"

"Maybe," Jordan said, realizing he was going to tell her his final speculation, the one he hadn't shared with anyone else. "But the gang leader'd been real smart, he'd hired a lawyer who'd just happened to have been the district attorney's campaign treasurer in the most recent election. And people said the DA—my boss—owed him other favors, too. I'm not saying the DA told anyone to drop the ball, but just maybe he assigned the case to someone who didn't care about it as much as I did. Who didn't want to go to the trouble of putting together a difficult prosecution. Maybe. Or maybe it was all just coincidence and sloppiness. But the end is the same. It just turns into a case, into backstage maneuvering, and nobody remembers that it was a crime. That there's these two old parents looking at me with these—" He stopped abruptly.

He felt again those sad eyes on him. When he glanced up, he saw that they were Laura Stefone's eyes. For a moment hers looked like those wells of sorrow he still saw in his worst moments.

"So you quit," she said.

"I quit."

"And became a defense lawyer."

"Criminal law is all I know, Ms. Stefone, and there's only two sides to it. If you quit doing the one, you've got to do the other. But the point of this story is"—there must have been a point to the story, or rather to his having told her the story—"that I'm not some fighting young defense lawyer who got into it because I want to rescue innocents from an unfair system. I know they're all guilty. I know *Wayne*'s guilty. I'm not running a crusade here. I've just got a small problem with the sentence your district attorney is offering. I understand what's behind that, too."

Laura Stefone did, too, he was certain of that. Her asking seemed only a courtesy. "What's that?"

"He thinks Wayne killed Jenny Fecklewhite."

"And you don't?"

"I just don't know. And as people keep reminding me, that's not my case. But it keeps intruding into the case I do have."

After another silence, as if she were helping him think, Laura said, "You've got a problem, all right."

Jordan nodded. "Even worse than the court reporter hating me."

Laura shook her head. "I'm sure people have to get to know you a little better before they start hating you."

When Doris brought the check, Jordan reached for it, but Laura was quicker. "My order," she said and laid bills on the slip of paper. "Thanks, Laura," the waitress said as she gathered it up. "Come again, Bozo," the waitress added without a glimmer of humor. But Laura laughed.

"Can we assume I don't have an ulterior motive and that I'm just telling you this to be helpful? Just as a hypothetical. So listen to it hypothetically and see if it makes sense."

"All right," Mike Arriendez said, but his face didn't say it. His face was an image of skepticism.

"All right," Jordan said, standing in front of the DA's desk as if it were the jury box and talking as intently as if he faced a jury. "Wayne didn't kill Jenny. You need to—"

"He confessed to you that he didn't do it? Aren't you violating his attorney–client privilege by passing this on to me?"

"It's not just that he *said* he didn't do it, it was the way the whole idea came up and his reaction to it. You think Wayne Orkney is a great actor?"

"He's had plenty of time to prepare how to react. Did he tell you who *did* do it?"

"No," Jordan admitted. "I don't think he knows. I'm just telling you, because the cops will listen to you, they'd better keep digging. There's a murderer walking around free here. It's your town, it's not mine, I'd think you'd be concerned."

"Thanks. I appreciate that," Arriendez said, and Jordan knew there was no point talking any more. The DA had that little smile that was almost habitual with him. "Just to follow up on your hypothetical, wouldn't it be good for your case—hypothetically—if we did turn up another suspect. Not one we could prove, understand, but just suspicious enough to divert attention from your client. Something you could bring up at trial, a diversion."

"I know the temptation to make things simple," Jordan said. "You've got two murders, one obvious murderer, the easiest thing is to assume he did them both. But I'm telling you, it's not that simple in Jenny's case."

Arriendez terminated the interview by standing up. "Don't worry, it's not a closed case. Half the cops in town are still putting in overtime on it. Who knows, by the time your case comes up for trial, we'll probably be able to prove that Wayne killed Jenny, too."

Jordan sighed. Halfway down the stairs, in the briefly sheltering dimness of the landing, he stopped to think. *Let it go,* was what he thought. Everybody wanted Wayne in prison, Wayne wanted to plead his way there. Let it happen. Because the alternative was a lot of work to no purpose. The alternative was that he had to investigate Jenny's murder and uncover her murderer himself. With no help and no one inclined to talk to him.

As he started down the stairs again he grimaced, realizing that he was doing it, too, doing what everyone in town did: calling the dead girl by her first name as if he knew her.

"Good-bye, darling. I'm glad you came to see me. I love you."

Ashley probably didn't hear the last sentence. She'd jerked the door handle up almost before Jordan stopped the car and was flying across the yard toward her mother, who stood in the open doorway. Maybe Ashley had muttered, "Bye, Daddy," but what she clearly screamed lovingly was "Mommy!" She ran like a freshly released kidnapping victim.

It was Sunday evening, the end of Jordan's weekend with his three-year-old daughter. They'd been to two playgrounds, an amusement park, and a pizza place, but Ashley had barely cracked a smile. Now there she went, his contribution to the future, and she didn't give a damn about him. We like to think our children will become our private biographers. But Jordan had no future. He would live in no fond memories.

He followed Ashley more slowly, carrying her suitcase. Marcia gave him a sympathetic look, to which Jordan returned a shrug. It wasn't as if he'd lost anything, he reflected as he drove to his own silent home. Even if his marriage had continued, Ashley wouldn't have been a big part of his life. She never had been. By the time he got home from the courthouse, it was almost her bedtime. Weekends he tried to reserve for her, but Marcia had built up so much more time with the girl that Ashley often acted as if Jordan were intruding on the day she could spend with her mother. Divorce had just sealed the relationship—the lack—Jordan already had with Ashley. He should just let her go, stop embarrassing both of them.

But in the middle of that night he went flying back home; that is, to Marcia's house. He almost threw himself into the windshield with the suddenness of his braking, then ran barefoot up the dark, dewy lawn to the front door, which opened into dimness like a gap in a smile.

"Are you all right? Where's—"

"Shh," Marcia said. "She's fine, she's still asleep."

"Where did you hear it?"

"From the window. Same window. But Jordan, this time I thought I heard somebody in the backyard, too."

"Are you okay?" Jordan barely touched her. Marcia stood hugging herself. She was fully dressed in T-shirt and jeans. Her skin felt cold.

"I'm fine. Nothing happened. It was just like before, just that little scratching. I'm sorry, I panicked."

"That's all right. Show me."

She led him into the bedroom, where a lamp burned, making a countryside of the rumpled bed. "This window?" Jordan asked. Marcia nodded. He parted the blinds to look out but couldn't see anything. "Where's the gun?" he asked. Silence made him turn.

Marcia's head was lowered slightly, waiting for his chastising. "I don't have it any more. Jordan, the damned thing scared me. I knew somebody'd kill me with it before I could make myself pick it up. It wasn't—"

"Damn, Marcia, I'm not here, and if you can't—"

"I know, but—"

"All right, never mind. Maybe I'll get you something that would just make noise."

She was still hugging herself. She was no longer quite so pale. The T-shirt and jeans were both tight, enough that he could see she wasn't wearing anything under them, she had just pulled them on.

"Let's turn out the lights," he said. "See if they come back."

Snapping off the lamp, Marcia said, "I'm sure it's just kids, Jordan. You remember it was summer when it happened before, like now."

"Damn kids," Jordan said. In the dark there was only their voices, they might have been lying in bed.

"I shouldn't have called you," Marcia said.

"Yes you should. You did exactly the right thing. Whenever you need me, I'll come, don't ever stop to worry about me."

After a long wordless pause in which their breathing sounded loud, she said, "Jordan, I didn't call you because I wanted—"

"I know." He walked to the doorway. "Go back to bed. You need your sleep. I'm not leaving. I'll be in the living room. Later on I'm going to slip out and see if they've come back."

"Thanks." Marcia sounded sleepy. "I won't bother you again, Jordy."

"You'd better." She was still standing, she wasn't going to start undressing until he left. Jordan walked down the hall, back to the living room, where he turned out the lights, waited until his eyes grew accustomed, and peered out the window. There was nothing on the lawn but pale moonlight. He walked back down the hall and into Ashley's bedroom. She'd kicked off the sheet. He pulled it up and let his hand rest on her chest. The girl's heart throbbed. He brushed her hair off her face. Tears sprang to Jordan's eyes, but it wasn't love that made his hand tremble, it was rage. The house felt fragile. A window might shatter at any moment, a door burst open. Next time Marcia might not have time to call him. He imagined being called to the aftermath of a crime, finding them. He would go insane. He would kill anyone who hurt his child. He would track them down and strangle them.

Later, when the house had stood dark and silent for an hour, he walked outside, all around. The windows seemed secure. It probably *had* just been neighborhood kids, trying to do exactly what they'd done, scare somebody. But how could Jordan sleep at home the next night, wondering? But he couldn't spend every night on Marcia's couch either, and he couldn't keep Ashley with him for the rest of her life; she wouldn't stay. It was terrible to have this portion of himself out in the world, without him close by to protect her.

The police reports did not tell him much, except that small-town cops knew the same jargon as big-city ones. The reports reduced the tragic events to bland observations. The officer who had discovered the body, Jordan was surprised to find, was his own Deputy Delmore. Pleasant Grove Park was outside the city limits of Green Hills but inside Madera County. As a county sheriff's deputy, Delmore occasionally patrolled the park. On the hot July afternoon he was drawn to a wooded area because of a car parked nearby; "upon investigation this officer discovered the body of a white female aged approximately 17 years of age, known to this officer as Jennifer Fecklewhite." After calling in the find,

Delmore had investigated like a mad thing (knowing, Jordan surmised, that he would soon be superseded by a detective who would take over the case from Delmore, a mere patrol officer), noting in his remarks that the victim was fully clothed, though one red tennis shoe was near her foot rather than on it. "The victim's face was marked by premortality abrasions. Signs of a struggle abounded, including crushed leaves and disturbed gravel beds." Delmore also noted the root on which the victim's head lay.

Though the park was outside the city limits, no one had seemed to object when city cops involved themselves in the investigation. The first of these was one Officer H. L. Briggs, who had turned up a witness of sorts, someone who had seen Wayne's pickup truck racing into town from the direction of Pleasant Grove Park. So officers had already been looking for Wayne for questioning when they discovered he'd been arrested at the hospital for beating up Kevin.

So Wayne had been the best suspect in Jenny Fecklewhite's murder from the beginning, but there were no witnesses to what had happened in the park. Jordan sympathized with the district attorney's problem proving Wayne had murdered Jenny as well.

The police department and the sheriff's office were both housed in the jail, next door to the courthouse. When Jordan emerged into the plaza, it was after eleven on a Friday morning. He looked up at the brick courthouse, wondering if it was worthwhile to go inside. There was no one he needed to see. The one he was thinking of—was the one emerging from the courthouse door, tossing back her hair and exhaling as if it had been a rough morning. She hurried heedlessly across the street into the shade of the plaza, head down so that she was almost upon Jordan before she noticed him. When she did, she pulled up sharply. Jordan saw her think about veering aside as if she'd had trouble enough for one day.

"Mr. Marshall," Laura Stefone said. "Are you lying in wait for me?"

"Can you tell me," Jordan said quickly, taking her arm

to guide her, "what the deal is with this empty pedestal? I don't see construction going on, but it's obviously not finished."

They stood looking at the pedestal with no statue, as if erected for a hero not yet born or at least not yet proclaimed.

Laura Stefone's voice remained cool but with an unmistakable undertone; she enjoyed telling a story about her hometown. "City council two years ago received a bequest to build a monument and got so excited they started right in before they'd decided who—whom—the monument should honor. The deceased had wanted it raised to the Confederate dead, but that didn't go over."

"No, I guess not."

"Some people wanted Juan Seguin, some wanted a memorial to Vietnam war dead. City council realized they couldn't do anything without offending a bunch of voters, and the thing just died. Or as they say at City Hall, debate continues. So are you here researching a history of Green Hills, Mr. Marshall?"

"I'm investigating my case. I just got distracted."

"I hate to tell you," she said, "but this isn't the scene of the crime. It happened a few blocks east of here."

"I know. But that's not the crime I'm investigating."

"Oh?" She stood as if he were detaining her.

"I'm looking into Jenny Fecklewhite's murder. They seem connected, you know."

Laura nodded abstractedly. Even in the heat of the day, her pale face looked cool in the shade. Jordan looked for the slant of her cheekbones but couldn't see it today.

"I thought I might go talk to her parents," he continued slowly, "but I hate to. Can you tell me anything about them?"

"Yes. They won't be home in the middle of the day."

"I was hoping for something a little more personal."

Laura studied Jordan, who stood with his hands in the pockets of his suit pants. Suddenly she appeared to make up her mind. "Come on. Where's your car?"

"Over this way."

"I hope you parked it in some shade," Laura said impatiently.

From the perch of his courthouse office, Judge Waverly watched his court reporter run into the San Antonio lawyer in the plaza, continued watching as they talked, and stared at them as long as they were in sight. His profile was so hawklike he would have looked at home perched on the ledge outside his window. Even alone as he was, he let his face betray nothing.

Where Laura took Jordan was Franklin D. Roosevelt High School. It was a sandstone building with a tall facade and two-story wings that spread in both directions from the entrance. Carefully tended trees were arrayed across the building's front, all of them young and slender as if something had killed their predecessors all at once only a few years ago.

When they got out of the car, Laura looked at Jordan critically. "Take off your jacket, look like a normal person."

Jordan did as he was instructed. Under her continued scrutiny, he rolled up his sleeves, too. Laura's lips remained pursed. Finally she shook her head hopelessly and led the way inside. Jordan looked down at his white shirt and paisley tie, wondering what it was about him that Ms. Stefone found hopelessly inadequate or ostentatious.

"Does Jenny's mother work here?" he asked, hurrying to catch up.

"No. But if you want to get to know Jenny, this is where to start."

In an otherwise empty classroom they found Christine Cavaletti. She was eating a sandwich at her desk while reading a paperback by Anne Tyler. On the blackboard behind her was written in authoritative cursive: "Romeo and Juliet: Inevitable or Accidental? Why not Juliet and Mercutio?" Laura introduced Jordan to her, adding, "Chris teaches freshman and sophomore English. Getting ready for school to start again, Chris?"

"At my own pace." Ms. Cavaletti leaned forward to shake

hands. "Keep the Christine to yourself, please. We guard our first names from the students, just the way we don't let locks of our hair or our fingernail clippings fall into their hands."

Ms. Cavaletti was perhaps a year or two older than Jordan, but she had an air of long experience. Her face was barely lined, but her dark-rimmed glasses made her look as if she didn't give much thought to her appearance. She sat waiting for him to explain himself as if she had just called on him in class.

"I'm a lawyer, Ms. Cavaletti, Judge Waverly appointed me to represent Wayne Orkney."

The teacher's expression said that that didn't answer her question. "He wants to know about Jenny, Christine," Laura Stefone said from the side.

"What about Jenny?"

"Well—"

"He doesn't know anything, Chris. He's just starting to find out about her."

Laura sounded unaccountably angry, as if Jordan could be blamed for his ignorance of the dead girl's life. Her voice had gone higher than her normal tone. Jordan gave Laura a look, and she subsided, turning her back on him to pace away, making the classroom suddenly look confining.

"I see," Ms. Cavaletti said.

"Whatever you could tell me about her would be helpful, Ms. Cavaletti. She was a good student?"

"She was a pain," the teacher said distinctly.

"Excuse me?"

"Oh, she was a good student, the best I ever had. She was *too* good."

"She got bored in class?" Jordan asked.

"I suppose she did, but the form her boredom took was to challenge me."

"For control?"

"Challenge my assumptions," Christine Cavaletti said. Her arms were folded. She watched Jordan as if waiting for him to catch up. "She would ask why did we read these books when others were better, why did certain essays get included in our textbook, who made the decisions? For example—let me think. All right. When we were doing the romantic poets, when we came to the Brownings, Robert and Elizabeth Barrett. I took my approach pretty much from the textbook, talking about what a team they were, how rare it was to find two such talented people so deeply in love, how fate, you know—

"And Jenny suddenly chimed in that maybe it hadn't been fate, maybe it had been mutual advantage. Maybe Robert Browning had aimed himself at Elizabeth Barrett because her family had money and marrying her could give him the leisure to do what he really wanted. And maybe Elizabeth accepted that because after all she was this pathetic, almost crippled woman, she probably didn't exactly get the cream of the crop in suitors.

"Then this other girl"—Christine Cavaletti stood up and pointed, directing a reenactment of the scene—"who had never said a word in class before unless it was dragged out of her, suddenly burst out, 'You're crazy, they were in love. Read their poems: "How do I love thee? Let me count the ways. I love thee to the depth and breadth and height my soul can reach—" ' And she wasn't reading the poem, she had it memorized. So then Jenny came back, 'Yes, listen to it. It sounds like a Hallmark card. I bet she got paid by the word to write it.' And then this boy I could always count on to smart off under his breath said, 'But look, they didn't *have* Hallmark cards then. Hallmark is ripping off Elizabeth Barrett Browning, not the other way around.' And kids started wondering if we'd have a whole different tradition of romance if not for some of these old dead poets. We got completely off the track of my prepared lesson."

"So she was a troublemaker?" Jordan asked.

"No! Well, yes, but always to good effect. She made good trouble. The year I had Jenny I started rewriting lectures I'd given for ten years. And the next year I wrote fresh ones again. She—I'd be more of a burned-out shell than I am if not for Jenny."

Laura Stefone had retreated into the rows of student desks. She might have been remembering her own youth in this high school. Here and there she touched a seat back or desktop as if the object held specific memories, as if Laura might find her initals carved somewhere in this room.

"Well," Jordan broke that brief silence. "That sounds great. But I read in the paper about how well liked she was by all her teachers, and it seems to me that this kind of thing wouldn't go over all that big with a lot of teachers. Did some of them—?"

"Rare students get famous among teachers," Chris Cavaletti said with a smile. "I asked around about Jenny, and I found out she wasn't like that with everyone, in most of her classes she was just a quiet good student. At the end of the year I told her I was glad she'd taken such a lively interest in English literature, and she said"—the teacher paused as if she didn't want to part with this tidbit—"Jenny said it wasn't just interest, that she acted the way she did in my class because she knew I could take it. You know, in fifteen years of teaching I can't think of a better compliment I've had."

The teacher's eulogy was punctuated for Jordan by the flash of Laura Stefone's green eyes as the court reporter strolled around the classroom in the background but turned to Jordan periodically with a sharp glance that asked whether he got it, whether he was capable of understanding.

"Thank you, Ms. Cavaletti, that helps me understand her. Oh, by the way, did you ever have Kevin Wainwright as a student?"

"Oh, sure. Somewhere in the back of the room."

"I won't take up any more of your time. Thanks again."

"You should have heard her on *Oliver Twist*," the teacher recalled suddenly.

"She hated it?"

"Loved it. She said it wasn't just a great book, it was a good mystery. Her view was that Oliver wasn't an orphan, he just didn't know who his parents were. He spent the whole book trying to find them. She got the other kids trying to figure it out, too."

Christine Cavaletti was chuckling to herself as Jordan and Laura left the classroom. They walked under the pressure of silence until in the sunlight Jordan admitted, "Sounds like a nice girl."

Laura didn't answer. She got into Jordan's car, where the vinyl seats made their clothes stick to their backs, and directed him to a road that led out of town. "Of course, some kids have more advantages than others," Jordan said. "Early start means a lot."

At a crossroads, Laura Stefone said, "The road to Pleasant Grove." Her voice was harsh.

Jordan glanced left. He didn't turn down the road, but the scene exerted a pull on him as he drove away.

"There's the Fecklewhite estate," Laura said a few minutes later. Jordan slowed and stared. It was a country house, ramshackle, with a short uneven front porch and an old roof. The people who lived in the house probably thought of its color as white.

The house was small, possibly three bedrooms, maybe only two. It was about a week away from looking abandoned.

"You should see Jenny's bedroom," Laura said, looking ahead down the road. "Going through her doorway was like stepping through a space warp."

"You've been in her bedroom?" Laura didn't answer, since the answer was obvious. "You really befriended her, didn't you?"

"No," Laura said tonelessly. "Jenny befriended me. People took her in hand because *she* gathered *us* up. She collected people wherever she went."

"She was rather a courthouse favorite, wasn't she?"

Laura didn't seem to hear the significance of his question. She was staring out the windshield. Her mind might still have been back in the high school they'd left. Laura's expression led Jordan suddenly to wonder what her own school days had been like. From the looks of her, she wasn't dwelling on a happy memory.

"The judge took her under his wing, didn't he?" Jordan asked more explicitly.

"No more than lots of others," Laura said. "Like Chris Cavaletti back there."

"Yes, but . . ." Jordan let the topic die. Judge Waverly's court reporter wouldn't confirm his suspicion for him. Jordan had already seen how protective of her judge Laura was.

She turned to stare at a house they passed and didn't turn back until two or three minutes later, when she pointed suddenly.

"Now there's who you need to talk to," she said. "Stop here."

He stopped at another wooden frame house, not quite as dilapidated as the Fecklewhites', but just as tiny. The prettiest thing about the house was the white picket fence that staggered around the perimeter of the yard. In the side yard a lady who could have been eighty years old or only two-thirds that age was hanging clothes on a line. Laura guided Jordan through the creaky gate, saying softly, "Mrs. McElroy knows everything.

"Mrs. McElroy, I'd like you to meet somebody. This is a lawyer from San Antonio."

"Jordan Marshall, ma'am. I'm—"

"I know who you are." Mrs. McElroy, a tall, thin woman wearing a shapeless housedress, barely turned to glance at him. Secondhand information had already given her all she needed by way of Jordan's biography.

"I want to talk to your neighbors, the Fecklewhites, but I haven't gotten a chance yet."

"Good, decent people. Always mind their own business."

Mrs. McElroy finished hanging a sheet. Its flapping wafted bleachy tendrils toward them. She stopped as if unwilling to expose the rest of her laundry to Jordan's view.

Jordan cleared his throat. "Yes. If it wasn't such a terrible shame about Jenny, I wouldn't have to—"

"Good girl. Helped me plant my garden." Laura and Jordan looked over their shoulders at a few leaning flowers in the cracked soil beside the front porch. "Smart to talk to, too. Always worth hearin'. Can't say I thought much of her taste in boyfriends, but that's the one part of anybody you can't predict, can you? We all go haywire over somebody."

The sudden laughter in her eye made Jordan want to see Mr. McElroy.

He asked a few more questions, unable to think of anything in particular he needed to know. After five minutes, Mrs. McElroy turned back to her laundry, and Jordan thanked her for her time.

"You didn't half plumb that well," Laura said in the car.

Jordan responded in the same rural vein. "Well, ma'am, I was afraid of getting in over my head."

"Straining your attention span, you mean." He was never going to get in the last word with Laura Stefone.

What Mrs. McElroy had confirmed for him was the general opinion that Jenny had been much too good for Kevin Wainwright. Maybe Wayne had thought so, too.

The violent end to the uneven romance seemed almost preordained. Jordan remembered girls from his own school days who had seemed so bright, so pretty, and never went out with anyone worth their time. It was inexplicable to observers, the way most romances are.

But sometimes they wised up, those smart girls hooked up with losers.

6

It was the weirdest case. Every time Jordan left town and went home to San Antonio, he felt as if he'd peeled off another layer of himself and left it back in Green Hills.

"Objection, Your Honor, calls for hearsay."

"We're not offering it for the truth of the matter asserted," the prosecutor protested.

"Then it's irrelevant."

"Sustained," Judge Sherman said offhandedly. Jordan allowed himself a fleeting smile, invisible to the jury. It was a brief triumphant moment during a losing cause in San Antonio. Jordan didn't have a prayer of winning the trial, which was okay, the defense always lost, it was expected. What was so pleasant about the trial in San Antonio was his confidence that he was in command of all the facts, and his confidence as well that when the judge ruled against him he would do so impersonally, with no animus toward either side. In Green Hills, everything was personal.

"Mr. Marshall . . . Mr. Marshall? Your witness."

"Oh. I'm sorry. Thank you, Your Honor."

In sudden memory, Jordan had been transported back there, to a dusty crossroads that now seemed populated, where it had been empty when he'd seen it. The road to Pleasant Grove Park wanted to tell him something. Almost as soon as his San Antonio guilty verdict was announced, Jordan was driving south.

He was sure he had the right spot, a small, densely treed copse that afforded privacy from the rest of the park; the trees provided shelter not only from the sun but from the sounds of other park patrons. A trickle of running water nearby softened the air. When a breeze came, it was a cool breeze. This might have been the spot that had given the park its name. But no one would ever find it pleasant again. Kids would come to whisper and dare each other. Lovers would startle at the sound of a soft footstep.

It was a fine and private place where Jenny Fecklewhite had met someone or come across someone or someone had caught up to her. The trees were cedars, their narrow leaves hanging like curtains. Jordan imagined the girl leaning back against the crumbly bark, invitation in her stance, or imagined invitation. The ground was rocky, and roots stuck out of it hard and cracked like old men's knuckles. If there'd been a fight, there were impromptu weapons close at hand.

Leaves made the wind moan. The ghost might already be afoot here. Jordan stopped, suddenly chilled in the hot afternoon. His shoulders prickled. He turned, terribly slowly, but he was still shocked at the sight of the face growing out of the tree. Jordan gasped an inarticulate cry and stepped back, losing his footing. The face came forward through the leaves. It was dark as the tree bark, dark with tan and the rush of blood. Finally Jordan saw the face was mounted atop a six-foot body that still looked rather treelike except for its blue uniform. The cop's face had a thick brown moustache and eyebrows and a clamped mouth that widened when he opened it.

"What're you doing here?"

"I have to have an explanation? Isn't it a public park?" Immediately Jordan regretted the smart response. "But this part is special, isn't it?" he added.

The uniformed officer was younger than Jordan, taller, much sturdier. He knew what his appearance was good for, too; he advanced on Jordan without speaking.

"You're Officer Briggs, aren't you?" The cop didn't answer, but he wore a nameplate. "You were the first officer on the scene."

"Second."

"That's right, second. Deputy Delmore was first. You got

here in a hurry, though, didn't you? Why did you come to the scene when it was outside your jurisdiction?"

"We share a radio frequency with the sheriff's office. When I heard the call, I wasn't thinking about jurisdiction. The last murder we had in Green Hills was before I joined the force. Murder's something special here."

"People keep talking to me like I'm jaded," Jordan said with sudden heat. "Nobody close to me has ever been murdered. If they were, I'd take it goddamned hard. Just because we have more murders than you do doesn't mean we get used to them."

Briggs's expression didn't even soften to skepticism. "You got here before the ambulance?" Jordan asked.

"Yeah."

"Delmore'd gathered all the evidence by then, right? He wins efficiency awards, am I right? Did you notice anything in particular? Besides the body?"

One of Briggs's thick eyebrows twitched. He turned away and looked at the ground for the first time. "She was stretched out here, full length, like she'd fallen back, but her hands weren't flung out, they were folded on her chest."

"Ready for burial."

Briggs looked back over his shoulder. "Yeah."

"What killed her?"

"Fist." Briggs clenched his own for demonstration. It looked to be the size of Jordan's head. "And this root helped."

He still knew the very one, a gnarled cypress root the thickness of a baseball bat lifted up from the ground. "Maybe broke her neck when she fell back across it. I don't know, you'd have to ask the doctor."

"Anything else?"

"You've read my report," Briggs said truculently.

"Yes, but we're here now. It's so much more vivid."

The officer shrugged. "Boot prints all around. Some tennis shoe prints. Nothing complete, though. Ground's too rocky. And no tellin' who'd been here before."

Jordan nodded. "Did you arrest Wayne Orkney?"

"No."

"But you already knew he was in custody when you got the call about the body here in the park."

"Yeah."

Jordan hesitated. "Did you know Miss Fecklewhite?"

Officer Briggs's eyes squinted momentarily as he wondered what the question meant, but he answered simply. "Yeah."

"Yeah," Jordan echoed. "Did you like her?"

Briggs nodded sadly. "Everybody did."

"Can't you afford an investigator?" Laura Stefone said.

"I thought you wanted me to get the right slant on things," Jordan cajoled. They were standing on the courthouse steps, where Jordan had been waiting for her. She looked off over his head and put her hands on her hips as if exasperated.

"But you've probably got to rush off home," Jordan said. "Do—? Are you married?"

She made a face as if to an invisible friend beside her. "No."

"Me neither," Jordan said.

Laura nodded. "You're divorced." Jordan looked down at his hand, thinking he was still wearing the ring, but it was long gone; even the mark it had left on his finger was gone. He frowned. He didn't like being so easily pegged.

"I guess everybody's divorced."

"Not me," Laura said.

Her self-satisfaction was annoying, too. Jordan snapped, "It must be terrible to go through life unloved."

Laura laughed, walking past him. "I guess it would be."

As she led the way to his car, she said, "I was in San Antonio last weekend. I saw the Dance Theater of Harlem. Did you see them? I didn't see you there."

"No, I didn't hear about that."

"You really missed something," she said. "They stretch the possibilities. You should have gone. How often do you think they come to Texas?"

Jordan rolled down the windows as they half-circled the plaza and headed out of town. Laura's hair blew back. She closed her eyes. In her lap her hands stretched. Jordan looked at her long, unmarked fingers.

"Where were they?" he asked.

"The Carver Cultural Center. Great old theater."

Jordan frowned. "Yeah, but kind of a tough neighborhood. When I was in the DA's office, half my cases came from within a few blocks of there. I hope you didn't go alone."

Laura spoke ironically at his concern. "No, I had a friend with me."

"She like dancing, too?"

"No, but he endured it for my sake."

Jordan fell quiet. In only a few blocks they passed the edge of town, and the countryside unscrolled before them. The horizon was far, far away, the view of it unimpeded. The trees that stapled the ground to the bedrock were mostly mesquites, low twisted shapes with few leaves, like wire sculptures of trees.

"So you're a big dance aficionada?" Jordan asked idly.

"*Real* dancing," Laura Stefone emphasized. "I don't get to see it very often. Have to go to Houston or Dallas sometimes. What passes for dancing now is like—well, you know the road show of *Cats* that came to the Majestic Theater? Now, that's the kind of commercial thing that by comparison—"

"Sorry, I didn't see that either."

Laura cocked an eye at him. "Why do you live in the big city, Mr. Marshall?"

"Hey, I take advantage of the cultural opportunities. I subscribe to the full cable package, not just the basic. And every December—"

"What?"

I go to my daughter's preschool Christmas pageant, he'd started to say.

"What?"

"I think you could call me by my first name by now, couldn't you, since you feel so free to criticize?"

Laura thought it over. "I don't know if I could."

"It's easy, it's just like a last name anyway."

"That's true." She didn't extend a reciprocal invitation.

Jordan took his foot off the gas and let the car drift to the shoulder of the road. The shoulder extended indefinitely. When the car stopped, dust closed over it like a giant clutching hand.

"What's the matter?" Laura asked, concerned by Jordan's puzzled expression.

He got out of the car and she followed. It was after five o'clock, but thanks to daylight saving time, the landscape would be popping and sizzling until nine o'clock that night. Jordan looked back the way they'd come, still frowning.

"Green Hills," he said.

"Yes?"

He extended his arms to encompass a small portion of the flat landscape that extended for miles in every direction. "Where are the hills?"

Laura shrugged ironically. "Where's the green?" she responded. "The first mayor gave it that name in 1882. He thought it was more alluring than what the trail drivers had called it, which was Mule Droppings. He hoped to lure new settlers here and the railroad. Worked great, you can see."

Jordan nodded bemusedly at the explanation. "So even here in the gruff, honest heartland, nothing is what it seems."

Laura laughed shortly. "Everything's *exactly* what it seems. We've just got different names for it. Have you driven down Flowing Springs Boulevard?"

"No, I've missed that."

"Yeah, it's easy to miss. They've got the birdbath closed for repairs."

Her words were joking, but her tone was almost angry. Jordan wondered if he had done something to offend her again. Back in the car, he asked, "So you're a student of local history?"

Laura shook her head. "You'd be surprised all the things you hear in court testimony."

Jordan whistled. "You mean court reporters listen? That's scary."

* * *

The Fecklewhites were a joint anomaly. Oh, they fit their house perfectly, they were just as ramshackle. What Jordan couldn't picture was Ed and Joan Fecklewhite as the parents of the golden girl.

Laura Stefone had wanted to wait on the porch, but Jordan had insisted she come inside. "You give me legitimacy, you make me look less like a vulture." So Laura had introduced him, but after that she stayed in the background, arms folded.

"Like to sit down?" Ed Fecklewhite offered. He was a balding man wearing a once-white undershirt that showed off his paunch. Mrs. Fecklewhite—Joan—gestured to the couch. Jordan studied her more closely. She had a sunken quality that made it hard to picture her youthful. She might have been pretty once, with effort, but she could not have been striking. Both the Fecklewhites were only in their late forties at most but seemed already old, as if they'd decided, Why fight it?

"Thank you. I hate to intrude on you, Mr. and Mrs. Fecklewhite, I really do, and I'll keep it as brief as possible. Do you know where Je—your daughter had been that day or who she'd been with?"

Ed Fecklewhite was slow to respond, but his wife shook her head quickly. "It was summer, Jenny was on her own. I asked her to be home by three to take care of the younger kids when they got out of day camp, so when I called and she wasn't here, I knew something was wrong, because Jenny wasn't never late, not without phoning me. Ed works over in Kenedy, he's pretty much out of reach during the day"—her husband looked a little startled at appearing in her narrative; it took him a moment to nod—"so I knew she hadn't called him. I work at the Food Mart here in town, and after I'd called home, people started comin' in and we started hearin' about what had happened, about Wayne jumpin' on Kevin, so I thought maybe she'd gone to the hospital. That's what I thought, that if Jenny wasn't where she was supposed to be, it was because somebody *else* was in trouble. Even when the police officer walked into the store, even when he came up to me, I figured it was something to do with Kevin."

Her mouth stopped and twisted on itself as if a key had been turned in it. Jordan asked quickly, "So you didn't know she was going to be at the park?" Joan Fecklewhite shook her head quickly, her husband more slowly.

That was all he could think they could contribute toward the solution to their daughter's murder. But he didn't expect to be coming back, he wanted to get all the hard questions out of the way in this interview. "How long had she been seeing Kevin Wainwright?"

The Fecklewhites glanced at each other. "That fall?" Ed offered.

His wife nodded. "Just that year, her junior year," she amplified. "Kevin was already graduated, but they had a homecoming football game in—Was it October?—that he asked her to go to with him. We thought it was kind of funny, but then they kept going out."

"Did Jenny date anyone else?"

"At first she did, but not after a while."

"Had she ever been out with Wayne Orkney?"

He seemed to have slipped the name past them without the Fecklewhites being consumed by sudden rage or terminating the interview. They looked more puzzled by the question than angry. "Just doubling with Kevin," Joan said.

"Wayne never called her or showed up here or asked her out?"

They looked at him as if this hadn't crossed their minds before. "Not that I know of. Ed?"

The husband said, "I never saw 'em together except with Kevin."

"Maybe Wayne could've talked to her after school or this summer. We both work," Joan Fecklewhite said with a touch of pleading. "And we trusted Jenny so much, we knew we didn't have to worry about her." Her eyes moistened again; her husband looked uncomfortable.

"Did you approve of her going out with Kevin?"

It was Ed Fecklewhite who spoke up, stubbornly, as if at the end of an argument. "Kevin was all right."

"We certainly didn't tell her not to," Joan Fecklewhite said, patting her husband's hand. "But we thought sure she'd meet somebody she liked better, maybe after she went off to school. We hoped she didn't get too serious about Kevin in the meantime."

"Do you know if she was interested in anybody else or whether anybody was asking Jenny out?"

Jordan heard Laura Stefone rustle behind him. Ed Fecklewhite glanced up over Jordan's shoulder. But Mrs. Fecklewhite just smiled at the question. "Our phone rang all the time," she said, "and Jenny was usually the one who answered it. School projects and volunteering and girl friends. She didn't tell us about anybody else." She gave a slight emphasis to "us" as if she knew she had already lost her role as her daughter's primary confidante.

There was a bang so sharp and sudden it made Jordan think someone had fired a gun. When he turned, he saw that the sound had been of the screen door swinging shut. Laura Stefone was no longer backing him up. She was gone.

Jordan cleared his throat. This was the point where, as a prosecutor, he would lean toward the victims and reassure them not to worry, that he'd do everything in his power to satisfy their craving for justice. He still wasn't sure in his role of defense lawyer how to end such an interview. But as he rose, he thought of a variation of his old closing. "I've only talked to a few people, but they've given me a real sense of how extraordinary your daughter was. I'm very, very sorry."

Joan Fecklewhite gave him a smile that was small, sad, grateful, embarrassed. Her husband's lower lip became more prominent.

Jordan hurried through the good-byes. The Fecklewhites didn't rise to see him out, so on the porch he found himself alone. Laura wasn't in the car or by it. That wide, flat landscape seemed to have swallowed her. She must have kept walking with the same force that had carried her out the door, perhaps annoyed at Jordan's prying.

But when he approached the car, passing the corner of the house, he saw her. Laura was kneeling in the dirt of what might have been intended as a garden, but it was even more of a failure than Mrs. McElroy's. Laura's shoulders were hunched inward. Her hair almost trailed along her arms, shielding her face. When she heard Jordan, she rose quickly, holding a handful of the dirt. She let it trickle out of her hand, creating a thin curtain.

"God, this place is an eyesore," she said harshly, though she wasn't looking at it. "We should've gotten together some volunteers and come out here one Saturday with some paint."

"Why not now?" Jordan asked.

When Laura turned and looked at him, he saw that the thought hadn't even crossed her mind. Trying to cheer up the Fecklewhites' drab lives now would be a waste of time.

In the car, they didn't speak for a mile. Jordan had been reminded by the sound of her movement when he'd asked about other love interests of the dead girl's that Laura was not his partner; she had an interest of her own to protect.

"I felt a sense of relief back there," he finally said.

"I'm sure you *were* happy to get that over with," Laura said. She was staring out the side window.

"No, I mean *their* relief. I know, I know they're very sad over their daughter, but I felt, too, like there was a little bit of relief that it was over, that they didn't have the responsibility for her any more. They don't have to see if all that promise is going to work out or if she would have . . ." He trailed off. Laura's silence seemed hostile. "But what do I know?" he added.

"There is that," she said flatly.

Jordan dropped her off at the edge of the plaza, which was deserted now. "I'll wait until you get to your car," he said.

"Nobody here's going to hurt me," Laura said. "Go on."

She waved him away and he drove off. Once his car was out of sight, Laura looked up at the courthouse. She saw the lowered blind in the judge's window, saw one of its slats raised. She looked up at it for a long moment before turning away.

* * *

Jordan had more parents to do, Kevin Wainwright's, and he thought he'd better get it over with the same day. He had Kevin's home address from the police report. No one answered the phone, but when he drove by, he found Swin Wainwright, Kevin's father, in his side yard breaking an engine out of a Chevrolet. He found, too, the anger he'd been expecting at the Fecklewhites.

"I'd like to talk to you and Mrs. Wainwright together if I could. Is she—?"

"She's dead," Swin Wainwright said. "Eight years."

"Oh. I'm sorry."

Swin Wainwright shrugged sullenly as if it wasn't Jordan's fault, but he would take a swing at him if he brought it up again. Mr. Wainwright appeared a man of more than vigorous middle age. He wore a navy blue work shirt with his name over the pocket and the sleeves rolled up, exposing his thin, sinewy arms. He was grease streaked and abraded, but he didn't seem to notice anything of physical discomfort, including the heat. Apparently he wasn't familiar with the phrase "shade-tree mechanic," because his block and tackle were set up in the barren, blazing miniplain beside his tract house. A cigarette lay on the fender of the car he was working on, burning down to ash. Between the cigarette and the sun, Jordan felt certain they were both going to be scorched by grease fire before the talk was done.

"Judge Waverly appointed me to represent Wayne Orkney, so I have to—"

"Poor stupid idiot," Mr. Wainwright said bitterly. "I hope they fry him. But he's not the one that killed Kevin. That girl killed him."

Jordan was taken aback. "Jenny Fecklewhite?"

"Yeah. First she jerked his life out from under him, then she killed him. What business'd he have with her? Everybody knew anything knew she was just playing with him. What for? She could've had anybody, man or boy in this town, what'd she want with Kevin? Not for her my boy'd still be alive, he could've gone somewhere, done something. He could've joined the navy, he could've seen Australia. But no, he had to stay around here making a fool of himself, being the prom king"—he spat—"because he thought he could get into the prom queen's panties. And that's all he spent his time trying to do.

"She wasn't his first girl friend, you know. He'd had girl friends ever since he knew there was such a thing. Sometimes two at a time. Because they weren't so all-fired important to him, you know, they didn't rule his life. If he had to get tough with 'em, he got tough, or if he didn't think it was worth the trouble, he'd walk away. He'd never had a girl throw him crazy before like that one did. You could see her thinking, that little minx face, it was writ all over her. 'What can I do to him he's never had done before? How can I make 'im think something that's never crossed his mind before?' "

"You think she pursued him?"

Mr. Wainwright gave him a disgusted sidelong look as he took a wrench to a bolt. "Not any normal way. But she kept 'im on her string. Had 'im actin' ways he'd never acted before. Sneaking around, hangin' around the high school so he could see if anybody else talked to her. They kicked him out of there half a dozen times. I told him, 'Stay away, do something else with yourself.' But why would he listen to me? And the really sad part—what'd you say your name was?"

"Jordan Ma—"

"The really sad part, Mr. Jordan, was that it would've all been over soon anyway. Everybody knew she was gonna drop Kevin sooner or later. Him actin' jealous was bringin' it on sooner, probably. It would've been all over and he could've had his heart broken and gone on with his life. Instead he—"

Here was a defense he hadn't thought of, though it should have come instinctively to him if he'd been a long-time defense lawyer. Blame the victim. If you couldn't find another defense, make the victim seem deserving of killing. Here was his witness for that purpose.

Sure. He could see the stony faces of an imaginary jury, with the very real rock face of the judge beside them, as he tried to put across the idea that the golden girl had really been some trampy little flirt who'd gotten what was coming to her.

So Jordan discounted everything he was hearing from Swin Wainwright, but he stayed for half an hour to listen to him, partly because he thought no one else had. The man had had a vehemence of words dammed up in him, now gushing out and pooling around Jordan's feet.

And Jordan found himself oddly touched. Everyone else he had talked to dismissed Kevin as an inconsequential sidelight to the story of Jenny's death. But at least one person grieved over Kevin alone. No grave should be without a mourner.

"So you think the fight between Kevin and Wayne was over Jenny Fecklewhite?"

"Hell, yes. What else did they have to fight about?"

"Well, I heard they'd fought before, it was almost—"

"Kid stuff. Shoving each other around. Even when they were boys, Wayne'd be sleeping over here, and I'd have to go in an' tell 'em to knock it off with the pillows or I'd put 'em in the garage."

Mr. Wainwright sniffed abruptly, buried his head under the hood again. He emerged with his harshness restored. "But this, fighting to the death, you can bet there's a girl in that. Wayne had eyes for her, too. Course he did. She'd twitched it at him, too, bet your life on that. She couldn't stand the thought of somebody not makin' a fool of himself over her."

It was some time later before Swin Wainwright wound down. There were fresh grease stains beneath his eyes that did not make him look clownish. "I'm very sorry, Mr. Wainwright," Jordan concluded. "You know I'm representing Wayne in the trial. But I—"

"Do a good job for him," the dead boy's father said. "Wasn't his fault."

It just went to prove, Jordan thought as he drove away, that there are no universal opinions. If you kept looking long enough, you could find another angle.

For the first time, he saw the possibility of a jury in this case's future. If he could make vivid the jealousy, the pressures of small-town life that could lead one old friend to kill another—

Listen to him. *Him* make *them* understand.

He spent that night in Green Hills, his first, or rather he spent it in the motel twenty miles down the interstate, the closest accommodation for strangers. His room seemed depressingly familiar as soon as he stepped into it: linoleum floor, window-unit air conditioner, worn chenille bedspread, painted pasteboard dresser bolted to the wall. That night, his Dairy Queen cheeseburger lodged somewhere between his throat and stomach, nothing on the six cable channels, he got up suddenly from the bed and drove away. It was ten o'clock at night, but it seemed later. Main Plaza was ghost-ridden. Its empty pedestal, looming in the moonlight, looked as if the statue had walked away on business of its own. The courthouse, which seemed to absorb sunlight during the day, was now giving it back, glowing faintly. One office light had been left burning; it was lonely downtown, where no other lights kept the night at bay. Nothing was open, of course. Rolled up the sidewalks was right; even the gas station looked abandoned. He drove through the residential neighborhoods, but even there, he could see no signs of life except the flicker of blue lights leaking through screens.

He found himself at the high school and got out to walk around. The air was dead and humid, but a little cooler since the sun had gone down. Jordan was wearing shorts and a T-shirt and felt comfortable. Maybe kids were having a late-night drama rehearsal or conferring in their cars in the parking lot. Maybe he could find someone to ask about Jenny or Kevin or Wayne.

But it was summer, no kid would be caught dead near the school. Jordan sat in the shadow moonlight cast under the facade, lingering until a fake nostalgia overtook him. When he drove away, his car took him to Pleasant Grove Park. If it was ghosts he was seeking, why not go to the source?

He parked close to the death grove and walked toward

it, skin prickling, but before he reached the darkness of the trees, he was blinded by a spotlight. He froze the way a brainless deer would have. As he gathered his legs to spring away, a voice shouted, "Halt!"

"Halt?" Jordan said, turning and shading his eyes.

He walked toward the squad car, its outline barely visible behind the spotlight. But Jordan was sure it was a squad car because of the light mounted on the driver's door and because of the command.

"Delmore?" he said. "Is that you?"

"Stand back! Raise your hands."

"I will if you'll take that goddamned light out of my face." The driver's door opened, swinging the light to the side. Jordan blinked. "I knew it was you, Deputy."

"What are you doing here?" Deputy Delmore asked harshly, putting a hand on Jordan's chest and pushing him backward.

"What're you? Why aren't you out on the highway harassing tourists?"

Jordan said it lightly, but Delmore didn't accept the banter in kind. The deputy was stiff as a fence. "That was you trespassing at the high school, too, wasn't it?" he bristled.

"My God, what a security system you people have here."

He heard the note of pride when Delmore spoke again. "I heard the squeal on the radio. But by the time the city P.D. got there, you'd fled."

"Fled? Wasn't me, Deputy. There must be a high-speed chase going on right now; you're missing out on it."

"What *are* you doing here?" Delmore's voice softened a trace but still admitted no nonsense. He looked at Jordan as if he'd caught him in the church graveyard. "What are you messing with?"

"Isn't the evidence all tucked away by now? You were the first officer on the scene, weren't you, Deputy? You found her."

They were standing close enough that Jordan saw the deputy's eyes shift to the side, looking into the dark grove, where moonlight strangled in the treetops and never reached the ground. "Yes," Delmore said softly.

"Was she dead?"

"Of course. Otherwise I would've called for an ambulance."

"Had she been dead long?"

"You'd have to ask the doctor."

"Didn't you touch her?"

He saw Delmore's Adam's apple move in his throat. "She was still warm. It was July."

"What killed her?"

"Mark here." Delmore touched his left cheekbone. "Bad mark, almost a gouge, but it hadn't come up a bruise because she didn't live long enough after it to bruise. I figured that was the one that did it."

"Who did you suspect?" Jordan asked quietly. The deputy seemed almost hypnotized by the darkness and the sight of the fatal grove. Jordan had the feeling he could get anything he wanted out of him if he didn't break the spell.

He was wrong. "My speculations are none of your business," Delmore snapped. "Get over there, put your hands up on the car, and spread your legs."

"The boy friend, didn't you? Isn't the boy friend or the husband always the first suspect? Or the wannabe boy friend. Terrible waste of pretty young flesh, wasn't it, Delmore?"

"You shut your fucking mouth!" The deputy grabbed Jordan's arm and slung him around.

But Jordan jerked free. Delmore's fist came back but stopped. Jordan looked at it. "Is that your response when you don't get what you want?"

The moment froze, then slowly leaked away. The deputy lowered his fist. "How did you happen to be the first officer on the scene?" Jordan asked.

"I got a call of two vehicles speeding near here. Didn't find them, but when I cruised the park I saw the other car, the victim's, and went looking."

"Does your dispatcher keep a record of those calls?"

"It was anonymous," Delmore said, looking at him dead on.

"Did—?"

"Get over here. I told you to assume the position."

"What are you going to call it this time, Delmore, trespassing? In a public park?"

"Park's closed."

"Really? You should have the hours posted."

"Everybody knows. I've warned enough—"

"But I'm a stranger here, Deputy." They both hesitated. "Do we have to talk to the judge about this?" Jordan added.

"You get the hell out of here. *Now* you've been warned. Next time—"

The deputy shoved him again. Jordan let himself be ordered out.

As he drove, the squad car followed him. Jordan kept carefully five miles under the speed limit, smiling for the benefit of the rearview mirror, until the squad car impatiently pulled out and roared past him, spraying small rocks. But when Jordan reached the interstate, he saw the car waiting, crouched under an overpass. He didn't see it pull out to follow him, but he had the strong feeling that Deputy Delmore knew where he slept that night.

He had a court appearance the next day, but not until later in the morning. On an impulse, he drove by the Fecklewhites' house again, saw no stirrings, and went on past it to the white house down the road. When he saw Mrs. McElroy on the porch shaking out a rug, he stopped. She didn't return his wave, but when he came through the gate, she asked, "Tea?"

"I don't—yes, ma'am, please."

So they sat on the porch drinking iced tea at nine o'clock in the morning. The first thing Jordan said was, "Think if I'd hung around the high school a few minutes longer, they would have arrested me?"

"None of my business," Mrs. McElroy said, not looking at him. But added, "If Tom Delmore arrested everybody he'd like to, the jail'd be full and the town empty."

Jordan smiled in satisfaction. Mrs. McElroy seemed satisfied, too, at having beaten back his challenge.

"I met the Fecklewhites yesterday," Jordan said.

"Nice people."

Jordan nodded. "Everybody sure loved Jenny."

"She was something special," Mrs. McElroy agreed.

"Do they have other children?"

"The twin boys that'll be twelve before school starts and a little girl, Edwina." By keeping her tone perfectly neutral, Mrs. McElroy invited criticism of the name.

"Are they all something special, too?"

"Not that anybody's noticed. Not even 'specially troublesome."

"Well, they've got a big reputation to live up to. Still—"

"What is it?" Mrs. McElroy asked, letting her keenness show.

"I'm just having a little trouble putting it together. After I heard so much about Jenny, I made some offhand remark about how she must have started with advantages, and then Laura Stefone took me—"

"Laura was giving you the tour, was she?" Mrs. McElroy said enigmatically.

"Yes, ma'am. It was like she deliberately took me to meet the Fecklewhites to show me I was wrong, Jenny started off no better than anybody else. And when I met Ed and Joan— well, they seem like nice people, like you say—"

"Oh, yes, after Ed's one little stint in jail, he settled right down and made a pretty good husband. Good as husbands get, I guess."

A hint of amusement crept into Mrs. McElroy's voice at the sight of Jordan's startled look. But Jordan chose to stick to his topic.

"Yes, but nice as they are, it's hard to see Jenny coming from them. I didn't see a book in their house, and everybody tells me what a great student their daughter was."

"You'd've found some books if you'd gone into Jenny's room, I 'magine. Ed finally built her a case when they started falling off their stacks."

"Well, but he wasn't the one who encouraged her to start reading, was he? You know, and I couldn't even see her in their faces. She didn't even look like them."

Mrs. McElroy decided it was time she could release a tidbit. Casually. "Oh, didn't you know? Jenny wasn't theirs."

"What?"

"No, no, she was adopted. Yes, I remember, Jenny just showed up at their house one day when she was a baby. Nobody'd even known Joan and Ed were looking to adopt. Joan never would say where she came from, but everybody knew. Joan's kid sister had come from Midland to visit them one summer, and everybody saw what a wild girl she was. Pretty, though, and had a smart mouth on her, but just out of control. Joan spent the summer dragging her out of one man's car or another. So when a year after that Joan showed up with a baby girl all of a sudden, everybody knew it was the sister's from Midland. Parents probably couldn't handle the sister, and the sister wouldn't've wanted a baby to raise—"

"Did she come visit?"

"No, sir. She was wild right up to the end. Got killed in a car wreck years ago when Jenny was just a girl. Jenny never knew who her real mother was, I guess."

Unless somebody had been kind enough to let her in on her family history. Even without such knowledge, she might have sensed that her parents treated her with a certain delicacy. Waiting for that wild streak, her inheritance, to display itself in Jenny's character. The way she turned out must have been a wonderment to Ed and Joan Fecklewhite. They must have watched her grow like an exotic plant brought back from a foreign clime, wondering what strange fruit she would bear.

Having dropped a big mossy rock into his mental pond, Mrs. McElroy paid Jordan the courtesy of letting him sit and roil in thought. The heat of the ascending sun brought Jordan to himself. He glanced at his watch. "I'm sorry, Mrs. McElroy, I'm due in court. You make a nice glass of tea. May I come back for another some time?"

"I don't know the answers to everything," she chuckled. "But you come back and visit."

He stopped on the porch steps. "Oh. Ed. He served time in jail, you said? When was that?"

"Oh, Lord, Mr. Marshall, ancient history. It was right before he and Joan got married or about the same time. Twenty years ago?"

"What was it for?"

She wrinkled her nose. "What is it you lawyers call beating somebody up real bad?"

"Assault?"

"That's it. Why can't you folks say what you mean?"

Mrs. McElroy had given Jordan more to think about than she probably realized. So Jenny had been a changeling child, not the biological child of Ed and Joan Fecklewhite at all, or even of Green Hills. How many people in town remembered ironically that "the best Green Hills had to offer the world" had actually been transplanted from outside?

And Ed Fecklewhite, her ostensible father, had a history of violence. Had the violence continued in the private confines of the family? Jordan remembered Joan Fecklewhite patting her husband's hand, lovingly or calmingly. He'd seen wives who stayed with abusive husbands, denying for years what was clear to everyone on the outside.

The courtroom was twenty degrees cooler than the air outside. Heat rose to its high ceiling. The atmosphere was unpressured today, too. Apparently the previous hearing had ended earlier than expected; the court personnel were taking their ease in the quiet of the airy room. While he was setting up at the defense table, Jordan was surprised to hear someone speak to him.

"How'd you like your antique food?"

Jordan looked up. *You talkin' to me?* The bailiff, Emilio Arroyo, clearly was. He lounged back in his chair, grinning.

Laura Stefone emerged from the court office, carrying a stack of fresh paper. Her pace didn't falter when she saw Jordan, but she didn't have the woodenness he'd observed in her before either. She seemed pleased with her work as she prepared her machine for the hearing.

"I'd say it was the best antique store lunch I've ever had," Jordan answered the bailiff. "I like my beef well aged."

On his other side, Mike Arriendez chuckled. "On the hoof or in the can?" he asked.

While the DA and the bailiff appreciated their own wit uproariously, Jordan watched Laura. She wore a private smile, one in which Jordan felt included, though she obviously hadn't sheltered much of their encounters in a cloak of privacy.

Jordan smiled along. When the laughter died, it left a conversational atmosphere in its wake. "We get lots of San Antonio lawyers," the bailiff said, "but we never saw you down here before. Don't you get out much?"

"Maybe I should travel more," Jordan speculated. "Right now I'm just getting my practice established, I've only been out a year."

"Take anything that comes or just criminal?"

"I wish more did come." Jordan adopted the bailiff's lounging attitude. "Right now I'm doing almost nothing but criminal cases and a few divorces. I'd like to get into more P.I."

The bailiff sounded genuinely interested. "Private investigation? That pays more than being a lawyer?"

The silence was embarrassed as Jordan tried to think of a kindly way out. It was Laura Stefone who chimed in.

"He means personal injury, 'milio. He means trying to drive some poor company bankrupt because some clumsy moron tripped in their parking lot."

"Oh, a lawyer hater," Jordan said to her.

"Just certain kinds of lawyers," she came back.

"Yeah, I'd like to get into some P.I. work on the side," Emilio mused. "You need some investigation, Mr. Marshall, you keep me in mind. I know everything happens in this county."

Jordan's and Laura's mouths twitched simultaneously. For a moment their eyes spoke until she turned away.

"Your Honor, I believe this date was set for me to file the remainder of my pretrial motions. You have them before you, including a motion to suppress evidence."

"I believe we've already heard your motion to suppress, Mr. Marshall."

"This is a new one, Your Honor, based on new facts uncovered by the defense."

Judge Waverly sorted through the stack of paper before him and plucked out the motion to suppress. His dark eyes seemed to take it in at a glance, but Jordan knew that the motion was couched in such vague terms that it gave away nothing of its factual context.

"We'll hear this in one week?" the judge asked blandly.

"That would be fine, Your Honor."

"We will also assign this case now a disposition setting," the judge said. In his tone was the threat he knew was communicated by the words. *This game has a time limit.*

"Thank you, Your Honor. The defense requests a jury trial setting, and we would ask for the court's consideration in making it a special setting, since I have to travel to be here and some of my witnesses will have to come from out of town as well."

A special setting would be a day on which only one case was set for trial. Such settings were given only to cases that very probably *would* go to trial. Jordan knew he'd surprised Judge Waverly—and the prosecution as well; he could almost smell the consternation from the State's table—but the judge's face revealed nothing. "Very well, Mr. Marshall. Shall we say four weeks from Monday? Mr. Arriendez?"

"The State will be ready, Your Honor."

"Then are we concluded? If—"

"There's one more thing, Your Honor. I'd like to renew my request for a bond reduction."

"That will be denied."

"Your Honor, in order to prepare a defense, I need free access to my client, and I'm not getting much cooperation at the jail."

"Mr. Marshall is to have unrestricted access to the defendant, Mr. Arroyo," the judge said to his bailiff. "Pass that information along to your colleagues. Anyone who violates it will be in contempt of my court. Will there be anything else, Mr. Marshall?"

"Thank you, Your Honor, that will do it for now."

"Then we are dismissed."

"All rise," Emilio said swiftly, then upon the judge's exit, the bailiff strolled up to Jordan. "Thanks loads," he said.

"Hey, I thought you'd be grateful, gives you a chance to boss old pit-face around."

The bailiff cracked a grin and sauntered away. Jordan turned to the State's table but found the district attorney already gone. But he managed to catch Laura before she exited. She looked down ironically at his hand holding hers and withdrew it.

"Your Mrs. McElroy told me something interesting."

"She's not my Mrs. McElroy, and I wouldn't take everything she says for gospel either." There was a natural combativeness about Laura that let her accept nothing at face value, but her tone was pleasant, even friendly.

"This should be a matter of public record," Jordan said. "She said Ed Fecklewhite had an assault conviction."

"Ed? Really?"

"Long time ago. You would've been just a child." Laura laughed. "Where would a twenty-year-old record be kept?"

"Basement, I think," Laura said lightly. "I'll ask Cindy."

"Thanks, I'd appreciate it. I'll come see you."

In parting she gave him a fleeting, sidelong look. If she'd been mad at him, she'd gotten over it.

Jordan turned back to his table and remembered his client. Wayne had been a minimalist presence during the brief hearing, sitting dead silent, not even letting his eyes roam. "We need to talk," Jordan said.

No response. Wayne didn't even raise his head. ". . . later," Jordan continued smoothly, which did catch his client's attention. "Right now I've got something to check on here, and I'd better do it while they're willing to help me. I'm going to come see you in a few minutes, and you're going to tell me something important."

"What?" Wayne asked.

Jordan liked his curiosity. He let it remain intact as the deputy took Wayne away. Jordan found the clerk, Cindy Garcia, in the court office. "*How* old is the record you want?" she asked petulantly. Laura, standing in the corner, smiled at Jordan at the tone of Cindy's voice.

"Could be twenty years, maybe more."

"Well, we wouldn't have something that old in the computer," Cindy said, flicking her fingers across her keyboard for confirmation. "No, *nada*. No Fecklewhites."

"That's good to know. Where would the old file be?"

"Laura says in the basement. The judge would know, but I don't want to disturb him now. I don't even know who would have a key, and Emilio's gone to the jail."

"I could come back after lunch if that would make things easier."

"All right," the clerk acquiesced with the obvious hope that one of them might be hit by a big truck over the lunch hour.

"What's the special today?" Jordan asked Laura.

"Oh, you'd like it. Kitty kabobs." They smiled at each other. Jordan wouldn't give her the satisfaction of asking if the imaginary meal was composed *for* kitties or of them.

"Would you—"

"I, unfortunately, have a previous engagement, so I can't join you."

"Oh. Well—" The court reporter looked regretful, but Jordan didn't trust any of her expressions.

On his way to the stairs, a voice called his name. Mike Arriendez leaned against the table in the small conference room/law library across the hall from the courtroom. "See you a minute?"

Jordan stepped inside and closed the door behind him. Arriendez was watching him minus the lazy smile. "I've got to hand it to you," he said, "you sounded deadly sincere when you asked for a jury trial setting."

"I was. I'm getting some interesting breaks in the case. And I've got a theory why your local cops haven't broken the Jenny Fecklewhite murder."

"Uh-huh." The DA didn't bother to ask. "Here's the thing. You're right, I was a little hard-nosed. I've reconsidered my offer. I'll go thirty." Arriendez frowned. It hurt him.

"Gee, you're almost in the realm of reason. By trial—"

Arriendez shook his head. "This is as good as it's ever gonna get, and it's good for one week only. At our hearing next week it's gone, we're back to fifty."

Jordan had said things like that himself as a prosecutor. But he could have returned Arriendez's sincerity compliment. The DA's face was flat and hard, not eager to plead the case away.

"Pass it on to Wayne," the DA said.

"That's a good deal," Wayne said thoughtfully, as if thought were occurring. "I'll take it."

"It's a suck deal, Wayne. But Arriendez's got you pegged. He thinks you're stupid enough to take it, and he's right."

"It's none of your damned business!" Wayne shouted. Even rising, his voice sounded muffled in the acoustic-tiled jail visitors' room. "I'd be out in what, ten? I could do ten." He snorted. Ten years in prison: How did that differ from his normal life?

"Wayne, look. Things're not the same as when Jimmy Cagney was making movies. Even a year in prison could be a death sentence if you get fucked in the ass by somebody who has AIDS."

Wayne's fist clenched. "That won't happen."

As gently as possible, Jordan said, "Wayne, you might be the toughest guy you've ever seen or heard of. But there are guys in prison who make you look like a two-day-old kitten. Guys so mean they could kill you by looking at you and who have a hate-on for everyone in the world. Listen, you'd better start making plans. What gang are you going to join in prison?"

"I don't need no damned gang."

"Yeah, right. Well, when it's rush week, and you get an invitation, you'd better turn 'em down real gently. There's no Switzerland in prison, Wayne. They don't allow neutrality."

Wayne's fist was still clenched but as if to keep his hand from trembling. He was staring into space. Jordan had managed to give his client a taste of panic, which had been his goal.

"Maybe you *should* take the offer, Wayne. Maybe it's the best you can do. I don't think the case is worth thirty, but I can't guarantee anything better."

What Jordan had thought on the way from the DA's office to the jail was that it might not matter what Wayne decided. The prosecutor's generosity might have been prompted by a break in Jenny's murder. If they could pin that one on Wayne, it *would* be a life case, no doubt about it, the murder of Kevin Wainwright would just be a tag end.

"What was it you wanted to ask me?" came Wayne's quiet voice. "Something important, you said."

Jordan leaned close to him. "There's only one important question in your case, Wayne. Who killed Jenny Fecklewhite?"

Wayne bit his lip.

"You were coming back from the park when you attacked Kevin, weren't you, Wayne? Was it you? Tell me, it won't go any farther than this room."

"No."

"Then who, Wayne? You saw, didn't you?"

Wayne nodded dumbly. The blackness under his eyes was creeping down his cheeks. He mumbled.

"Who?"

"Kevin killed her," Wayne burst out. He looked up hopefully at his lawyer as if his troubles were over.

"Damn it, Wayne, why didn't you tell somebody that before she was buried, when they were still collecting evidence?"

Wayne looked surprised. The answer was obvious. "I didn't want to get Kevin in trouble."

That's right, Kevin had lingered for almost a week after Jenny's death. Wayne had beaten him to death, but they were still friends.

Jordan sighed. "You saw it?" he asked. "Or Kevin admitted it to you?"

Wayne shook his head. "I knew he was meeting her at

the park, and when I went there and found her dead, I knew it was Kevin had killed her. I went crazy after that, I guess."

That fit the bare facts. Someone had seen Wayne's pickup driving fast into town from the park. But that fact also fit the prosecution theory that Wayne had killed both Jenny and Kevin. And when Wayne had found Kevin in the street on Wayne's return from the park, they hadn't had a discussion. The only recorded words preceding the fight were "I'm gonna kill you." Jordan sighed again.

"What's the matter?"

"There's no evidence. *We* can't even be sure of what happened, and we damned sure can't prove anything."

"What do you mean?"

"You didn't give Kevin a chance to explain, did you, Wayne? You just found her dead and you assumed he did it."

"So?"

"Maybe that's how Kevin found her, too."

Wayne's mouth stayed open. His eyes were wide for the first time in Jordan's memory. As realization began to crowd in on him, Jordan turned away. His client's face was too pathetic to watch.

"You know the last time anybody was down here?"

"Last time you had a hot date, Emilio?"

The bailiff made a startled chuckle, laughing and frowning at the same time. "Boy, you got a mouth on you. You remind me of her."

Jordan didn't have to ask who the other smart mouth was. "Really? Two of a kind?"

The bailiff regarded him pityingly. "This'll be fun. Next time I see you you'll have this little whipped puppy look, 'cause she's sliced off a little piece of it." He held up his little finger to demonstrate.

Jordan snorted. "You small-towners, you've got to make soap opera out of everything."

Emilio still spoke pityingly. "You've got it all over you, son. You watch. I will."

Jordan hesitated. "Does she have somebody special?"

The bailiff grinned. "Everything in pants's taken a run at her. Some of 'em caught her, too, but nobody could pin her down. Laura wants something more than she'll ever get."

From this town, Jordan thought. He said, "You take a run at her, too, Emilio?"

The bailiff laughed good-naturedly. "I like 'em a little meatier, man. Listen—"

They were in the dead, dank basement, where the only air-conditioning was provided by the fact that they were underground. At the bottom of the stairs they'd encountered the gate of a wire wall that closed off the whole basement. The bailiff opened it and spun the key on its ring.

"—I'm supposed to lock you in here. It's the rule. Can't have you running off with our files."

"You'd be killing me, Emilio. I've got claustrophobia. Being down here's bad enough without being locked in."

The bailiff considered. "Maybe the gate won't click. But you get me in trouble, it'll be worse trouble for you, understand?"

"Yes, sir."

Jordan stepped inside the wire cage, trusting as a child, then heard the gate swinging shut, much too fast. He turned, almost catching the gate in the face, and just before it latched, the bailiff's hand caught it. Emilio walked away grinning.

Immediately Jordan felt hot. He shed his suit jacket. Rows of metal shelves stretched before him, taller than his head. He felt something lurking in the stacks with him. The heat. The files shedding dust. And contained in the files, the lives that had turned to dust themselves.

The files had been organized by someone who had taken the secret of the system to the grave. They were arranged by years mostly and alphabetically occasionally, but there were clusters of cases that someone, some time, had known were related.

An hour later Jordan was still among them. He had a smear of muddy dust across his forehead and growing circles under his arms. One reason he had taken so long was that he had succumbed to the inclination to snoop. Having so many lives arrayed before him had proven too great a temptation. He had found an Arriendez with a criminal conviction, no telling if he was a relative of the current district attorney. No Waverlys, no Fecklewhites yet, but he had found a Stefone. It turned out not to be a criminal case, though, it was a divorce. Lewis and Pamela Stefone had dissolved their marriage of six years with a minimum of paperwork, but in the decree Jordan found one child of the marriage, Laura, aged five. Eyes stinging from the dust in the basement, Jordan suddenly felt even dirtier and thrust the file back among the others.

He found Ed Fecklewhite soon after that, twenty-one years back in time, where Ed was imperfectly preserved as a younger, fiercer man who had attacked someone who was a stranger to Jordan. He had been hoping the conviction would drop a piece into place, that the victim would be Joan or Swin Wainwright, one of Wayne Orkney's parents, some name that would lead him somewhere, but it wasn't; the complainant was a plain Henry Smith, and the facts were vanilla. After a couple of days spent in jail, Ed had pled guilty and been given probation, which, as far as the file showed, he had completed without incident.

Jordan was about to replace the file in disgust when a name did leap out at him. He reopened the file to the judgment, signed by a county court judge with an unfamiliar name, but declaring that the defendant had appeared "with counsel Richard Waverly."

Jordan was struck by how hard it was to picture. Twenty-one years ago Richard Waverly had just been a young lawyer, about Jordan's age now, representing petty criminals. He hadn't yet been elevated to the title people used on him as if it were a hereditary position: "the judge."

Jordan wondered if Waverly had had that obsidian stare even then.

7

Where do kids go on dates around here?"

"Gee," Laura laughed, "as I remember, the old mill used to be a nice spot, but it burned down when I was in—"

"I mean nowadays, old-timer."

"Nice talk. They teach you this technique in law school?"

"Come on," Jordan said, managing not to wheedle. "You're not the only master of all the local lore. I could take my business elsewhere."

"Oh, and my days would become so empty." Laura leaned back against the top of the last pew in the courtroom, where Jordan had stopped her on her way out. Up front, the judge and lawyers had cleared out, but Emilio and Cindy were finding business to keep them at their desks.

"It's hard on kids here," Laura said seriously. "The movie theater closed even before John Wayne died, the closest other one's thirty miles away, and if the girl's parents won't let her leave town, that pretty much just leaves school dances."

"Where do they go *after* dates?" Jordan probed.

"Well, the few teenage couples *I've* followed around," Laura said archly, "always seem to end up at the Pizza Hut. Where if the boy's really ingenious, he's got something to slip into the Pepsis, and the girl pretends to be outraged or not to see. I've sometimes thought a boy could save himself the trouble and expense of liquor if he just got hold of a flask. Those girls'd get just as giddy on watered-down Dr. Pepper as they do on bourbon."

Jordan was standing close to her, so their voices were soft.

He had no business in her court today, so he'd spent time deciding what to wear. A suit would set him apart from most Green Hillers, but not from the lawyers Laura saw every day. He'd settled on pressed khakis and a blue sport shirt and now felt a tad dweebish.

"And where do adults go on dates?"

Laura looked at him with amusement in her posture and her cheeks but still with contemplation in her eyes. With the heat of August a constant threat just beyond the windows, she still looked cool, her skin fine as milk.

"Everybody's married here, Mr. Marshall, so anybody having a date would be sneaking around, and they haven't let me in on where they meet."

"I thought we said Jordan."

Laura smiled. "And I said I'd have to work on it."

"Could we practice over lunch?" He hated the way he had to force the words through his tight throat as if her answer mattered. "Before I hit the dusty investigation trail again? I'm being a P.I. today instead of a lawyer."

Laura laughed. The snappy banter had given her time to think. She took that time and a little more before saying, "All right."

"Today I'm going to order for myself," Jordan said. "I've heard the lunchroom serves something called prairie oysters, and I want to find out where they get seafood this far inland."

Laura laughed again. He felt the nearness of her arm as they went down the stairs.

"I understand Swin Wainwright's feelings," Christine Cavaletti said. "Of course he'd like to think that Jenny had somehow kept Kevin hanging on, so what happened was her fault. But he's just wrong. Jenny wanted to be rid of Kevin, but she was being too gentle about it. *He* was the one desperately hanging on."

Desperate because he thought he was losing her, Jordan thought. To whom? Had Kevin known about Jenny's much more important relationship—with Judge Waverly?

He wanted to ask Chris Cavaletti some variation of that

question, but in the quiet of her classroom it seemed inappropriate. The teacher was watching him more than attentively as if she were probing Jordan's mind while he questioned her.

When his hesitation continued, Ms. Cavaletti went on, "None of us understood that attraction in the first place. Kevin's for Jenny, I mean. What he saw in her was obvious. I think—Jenny gave more of herself to Kevin than she intended.

"Not that way," the teacher added hastily. Jordan hadn't thought his expression had said anything lascivious. His eyes widened innocently.

"I mean she couldn't do anything halfway," Cavaletti continued. "Even the way she walked. She turned heads when she walked down the hall, and not just boys' heads. I know male teachers in this school who made sure to be standing at their doors every day at a certain time." She paused, obviously wanting to add something but afraid that Jordan would misunderstand again. Jordan just stood, leaning slightly toward her, face empty and receptive. "She was going to be head cheerleader her senior year, you know," Chris Cavaletti finally continued. "That's an elective position, very competitive, and you don't get one vote for good grades or being nice. You have to—"

Look good in the sweater and the little skirt, Jordan finished for her silently. He could picture her, and he remembered his first impression of Jenny from the grainy newspaper photo—that glint in her eye that had seemed to speak to him.

He wasn't the first grown man to have thought that about Jenny, was he?

"And when Jenny was enthusiastic about something," Cavaletti hurried on, "when she laughed and her eyes lit up— Kevin was mesmerized by that glow, I think. He thought it was for him. He didn't understand that it was just a part of Jenny, it was what happened when her heart beat."

"And what kept Jenny with Kevin?" Jordan asked gently.

Chris Cavaletti shrugged. "We all want to be loved, and

it was obvious Kevin loved Jenny. Especially at that age, it's hard to reject somebody who loves you. Isn't it?"

She paused as if the question weren't rhetorical. When Jordan didn't have a ready answer, she continued, "There were certainly other perfectly nice boys she could have gone out with. Boys more her peers."

"Some of them actively hoping for Jenny to throw Kevin over?" Jordan asked, hoping for another suspect.

"Maybe," Chris Cavaletti answered calmly. "But I only ever saw one who seemed to be actively in the hunt to succeed Kevin."

"Who was that?" Jordan wondered why she made him ask. Ms. Cavaletti was studying him as if thinking maybe she shouldn't tell him.

"Your client," she said. She seemed to admire Jordan's surprised expression before she continued. "Oh, yes. You didn't have to see the three of them together very often to catch Wayne staring at Jenny. And if Kevin happened to interrupt the stare, Wayne's look would change dramatically. Yes, I'm sure," she answered Jordan's not-yet-asked question. "Besides, I broke up a fight between the two of them one time, Kevin and Wayne, and since the fight happened here at school, one could imagine its object."

If one were inclined that way, Jordan thought. But Chris Cavaletti didn't sound or look like a small-town gossip. She appeared to take no delight in the information she'd conveyed. What she said next confirmed that impression.

"I'd appreciate it if you could avoid calling me as a witness."

"If things go well, there won't be any trial," Jordan said. "And I can't think of anything you've told me that I'd want you to repeat from a witness stand."

"So you'd drive around with Kevin, following her?"

"Yes, sir," Wayne admitted, "like a couple of spies, like she was selling state secrets."

As he talked to his client, Jordan remembered Kevin's father. "All anybody thought of Kevin as any more was Jenny's boy friend," Swin Wainwright had said, anger darkening his face, anger that was supposed to ward off tears. "If he'd've lost her, he'd've lost everything. He wouldn't've been able to show his face in this town again."

Now Kevin's best friend was saying the same thing. "Kevin wasn't nothin' when we was in high school. But then he kept hangin' around, until he got to seem like an older man, you know, and he got this second go-round, with Jenny." Wayne shook his head. "Kevin wasn't no Einstein. He thought—he thought you could change things."

"Like what?"

"You know, live your life over. Or he thought if he caught Jenny at something, he could change *her*, make her stay with him. Poor stupid old Kevin, he was the only one didn't see he couldn't hold her. No way."

Jordan was looking at Wayne's hands. They were healing, only one scab left on one knuckle. Wayne looked like a skinny kid, and like many easily provoked men, he seemed unusually mild when sober and unaroused. But his hands promised pain. Wayne and Kevin's fights, Swin Wainwright's dark face, Ed Fecklewhite's assault conviction. There was an undertone of violence to the whole town. People thought fighting no big deal, just part of the landscape, until it ended worse than anyone had expected.

"Who did you see her with?" Jordan asked.

"Not hardly with any boys from her own class," Wayne reminisced. "We'd see her talking to grown men. Like Kevin had just been the first step up, she was still moving on. Jenny didn't even look like a girl any more, you know, and she damn sure—she wasn't no flighty kid. She knew what she wanted."

Jordan listened for the sound of jealousy in his client's voice. He wasn't certain he heard it, but he certainly heard the tone of admiration—of longing?—when Wayne talked of Jenny.

"Who did you see her with?" Jordan asked again flatly.

Wayne's eyes shifted. "That cop."

"Deputy Delmore?"

"No." Wayne frowned as if Delmore were one he should have known about. "That city cop. Briggs."

The officer who'd rushed outside his jurisdiction to be at the murder scene.

"Jenny said she was getting another speech ready," Wayne continued. "About law enforcement. She said she had to do research. Kevin just went nuts when she'd tell him things like that."

"Who else did you see her meet, Wayne?"

Wayne looked shifty, but did it so poorly he looked like a bad actor portraying shiftiness.

"Help yourself out, Wayne, tell me the truth."

"Don't you know?" Wayne finally said.

"You say it."

But Wayne wouldn't.

Jordan had to: "The judge."

Wayne nodded, not looking at his lawyer. "That's right."

"So you know what the judge thinks of you now, Wayne. You know what that does to our chances."

The boy looked startled. "What?"

Jordan shook his head disgustedly. He sat down at the small table so that for the first time his face was close to his client's. "Listen, Wayne, there's not much point in my doing more investigating if you're going to take the DA's offer. Thirty years. I'd be so embarrassed I wouldn't even tell anybody I'd let you take it, but maybe you're right, maybe it's the best way. You're the one has to decide."

Jordan wondered why he cared. Usually when he put a plea bargain offer to a defendant like this, he was silently praying for the jerk to take it. *Spare me any more of this grimy case.* Whatever Wayne decided, Jordan knew he wouldn't like it.

"Tell the man."

Wayne looked up meekly from his troll-like posture at the defense table. "I'll take your offer, Mr. Arrendez." As well as the district attorney seemed to have known Wayne, Wayne had never learned to pronounce Arriendez's name.

The prosecutor's face did not light up. "Thirty years?" he said insistently.

"Yes, sir." Wayne lost his resolve and looked down again.

"All right. I'll get the plea papers ready." His face giving nothing away, Arriendez glanced into Jordan's disgusted eyes as he turned away. Jordan dropped into the chair at his idiot client's side. Well, at least the damned thing was over, which was always a relief. Having a client plead *not* guilty was a terrible responsibility. The plea was also a relief because if Wayne was willing to plead guilty, it probably meant he *was* guilty—of both murders, so Jordan could be done with them all, with the whole case, the whole town. *Be guilty, Wayne. Let me out of here.*

Wayne didn't speak. He'd decided, but he didn't like his decision, but he thought it best. He'd have a long time to wonder.

Jordan half-turned away from him and glanced around the courtroom. The witnesses he'd called for his now-not-to-be-heard motion to suppress, Officer Harry Briggs and Deputy Tom Delmore, were sitting shoulder to shoulder in the audience. Arriendez had gone to give them the good news that they wouldn't be testifying after all. Delmore's lip lifted in a wretched simulation of a smile aimed at Jordan.

Jordan turned away. "Look around," he said to his client.

"What?"

What are you doing? Jordan thought to himself. But his voice went relentlessly on: "Look around at who you're making happy by taking the plea. Somebody in this town's going to heave a sigh of relief, because this will close out their books. Once you plead, everyone will be sure you killed Jenny, too, or Kevin did, and somebody's going to know they got away with something. Maybe somebody in this building."

Wayne was looking back. "One of them two?"

Jordan shrugged. "One was the first one to officially find the body, the other one was lurking close by. One of them you saw with Jenny, the other one almost punched me when he lost his temper."

There was a low hum of idleness in the courtroom. The district attorney was rapidly filling out the guilty plea papers, everyone else knew what he was doing, knew that in a few more minutes a short ceremony would bring the case to a close. The news had already reached the judge's office, Jordan was sure.

"It won't make any difference to you," he said easily. "They probably won't ever be able to prosecute you for Jenny's murder. But everyone will know you did it."

Wayne was still watching the cops, who looked back at him contemptuously. Jordan, surreptitiously watching his client, saw Wayne's eyes turn suspicious. A few minutes later the district attorney approached their table.

"Your attorney can explain these to you," Arriendez said. "When you're ready, I'll—"

Wayne stood. "I'm sorry to have put you to the trouble, Mr. Arrendez, but we're not going to take your offer after all."

Arriendez frowned at Jordan, who looked innocent. "Did he tell you the offer is only good for today, after this we go back to the original fifty-year offer?"

"Yes, sir, he did."

"All right. It's your decision."

Jordan was thinking how stupid defendants were. "*We're* not going to take your offer," Wayne had said as if Jordan would be accompanying him to prison at the conclusion of the trial. That was how defendants sometimes got, they began to think of themselves as a team with their lawyer. But the lawyer and the defendant always left the courtroom by different doors after a guilty finding. Jordan felt suddenly hollow. He had tricked Wayne out of years of his life.

Wayne was sitting there with his head bobbing slightly, pumped up, more emerged from his shell than Jordan had seen him. Jordan suddenly felt immensely sorry for him. Poor fool, he didn't know what was coming.

Why had Jordan goaded him into withdrawing his guilty plea? Jordan wasn't sure himself. The shoving match with Green Hills was over. When Jordan had encountered blockades, he had fought back on automatic pilot, but that response was long since dead. He would have been happy if Wayne had persisted in pleading guilty. That would have meant he was guilty, as all defendants are—Hadn't Jordan said that, or something like it?—and the case would end as every criminal trial should, with the defendant on his way to prison.

But Wayne wasn't guilty, not of the murder that mattered. Jordan was convinced of that now, and he felt the weight of his knowledge. It was the first time he'd experienced feeling responsible for the fate of an innocent client, and he didn't like it a bit.

But Wayne sat there looking eager for the proceedings to begin. Jordan could hardly bear to see his client's confidence.

He hoped Wayne hadn't invested any hope in the outcome of the hearing on Jordan's new motion to suppress evidence, because the hearing went quickly as if toward a predetermined conclusion. Judge Waverly brought testimony to an early halt.

"Mr. Marshall, is it going to be your legal contention that all evidence from the investigation of Miss Fecklewhite's murder should be suppressed because one or more of the investigating officers was outside his jurisdiction?"

"Yes, Your Honor, that's my basic premise."

"Can you show that any evidence obtained in that investigation is going to be introduced against Mr. Orkney in the case in which *he*'s charged?"

"If I may develop that issue, Your Honor."

As Jordan resumed his questioning of Officer Briggs, he watched the judge. Waverly looked remote, watching a distant wall or sorting through papers on his bench rather than watching the witness. The judge had other cases to get to, other lives to weigh. He bore his responsibilities casually, the same way those responsibilities had been conferred on him by public accord. Power over people's lives appeared the judge's God-given right when in fact *he* was the one who deserved to be investigated. Jordan had listened for hesitation or distraction when the judge mentioned the dead girl but had heard none.

"Your motion to suppress evidence will be denied," the judge said soon afterward.

"Thank you, Your Honor.

"Just what I was expecting," Jordan added to his client

before the deputy took Wayne away. Wayne nodded, but his eyes had lost their sustaining anger. He looked bewildered.

"Gonna make me work for it, huh?" Arriendez said, but Jordan didn't feel like joshing. "May I talk to you for a minute?" he asked Laura Stefone.

"You want a transcript of this one, too?"

"No. I have a different kind of problem." He led her aside, which had the effect of focusing the attention of everyone remaining in the courtroom—Emilio, Cindy, Harry Briggs—on the two of them. Jordan turned his back on them.

"The Austin Ballet's coming to San Antonio, did you hear?"

"The *Austin* Ballet?" Laura's mouth relaxed into humor.

"I know, I know, it's not the Joffrey, but they have this one number that's supposed to be more modern dance than—"

"The gangsterish number."

"Yeah, so you've heard of it. Me, too." He was talking quickly. "So as soon as I heard they were coming, I ran out and got tickets, like a fool, before I realized I didn't know anyone who'd really want to go as much as I did until I remembered you." He paused and regained his composure, although it wasn't her face that helped him do so. "So would you like to go?"

"Yes," she said deliberately.

He smiled, but Laura didn't, and his suspicion of her reasserted itself. "With me, I mean," he added.

Laura hesitated a long time. "If that's part of the package," she finally said, beginning to smile.

His relief was out of all proportion, much greater than any emotion he'd felt over the hearing he'd just concluded on behalf of his client. "Great. It's on Sunday night, is that okay?"

"Mm huh." Laura still smiled, but she had grown reserved. They were different with each other now that Jordan had revealed himself.

"In San Antonio," he stressed.

"Yes, you said that. Um—I'll meet you there."

"Oh. All right." Jordan felt as if he'd grown taller, was looking down on her from a great height. They made plans. He wanted to touch her hand, maybe even her cheek, but Laura grew more businesslike as their conversation wound down. When she walked away and he turned to follow her, he saw that people were still in the courtroom watching, people he didn't have to see again but whom Laura worked with every day. Of the observers, only Emilio the bailiff gave Jordan a friendly look, one of pity. He held up his little finger.

"She said to me once, 'Mama, what's going to become of me?' "

"You think she sensed—trouble coming?" Jordan asked.

On his way out of town, he had returned to Jenny's house hoping to find only Mrs. Fecklewhite at home this time, and he'd gotten his wish. Not only was Joan Fecklewhite home alone in the midafternoon, but her cordiality remained intact. She welcomed Jordan into her home almost as if he had a right to enter at will, as if she lived in a crime scene or a museum.

What Jordan was hoping for was some hint of tension between Jenny and her father, but he couldn't bring himself to ask the question. Instead he asked if Jenny had kept a diary, and Joan Fecklewhite had said indulgently, "She kept it secret from me if she did. But you're welcome to look."

So they were in Jenny's room. It wasn't perfectly preserved as Jordan had expected. In a small house with three other children, someone else, the younger daughter, had already inherited the room, so that the room was undergoing transition. It was still Jenny's room in spots, but it didn't have the eerie atmosphere of a room in which no one lives any more. A pile of dresses lay on the twin bed. Stuffed animals were scattered on the floor nearby.

"No," Joan Fecklewhite said patiently. "Not trouble. Not this kind. She meant life, Mr. Marshall. She was seventeen years old. She was trying to imagine how her life was going to be."

She folded her arms suddenly, and her face tightened.

Mrs. Fecklewhite was standing in the doorway of her dead daughter's room. Jordan was moving slowly, touching objects at random. In the bookcase were a couple of volumes from a popular teenage series, some Nancy Drew, some popular novels, and a host of classics, mostly nineteenth century—Dickens and Twain and Emily Dickinson—and a few books Jordan was sure hadn't been on the school curriculum, such as Virginia Woolf's *Orlando*. But nothing that looked like a diary, and he didn't want to pry any more.

"And I couldn't help her," Joan Fecklewhite said. "When she asked me what she was going to do, I wanted to tell her, 'Honey, I never had the problem of scoring 1480 on the SAT. I didn't have to decide whether I'd rather go to Princeton or Stanford.'"

Jordan crossed the braided rug to glance at the items atop the dresser: small vials of makeup, a program from a play, and imbedded in a glass paperweight the head of a white unicorn, its horn raised questioningly. "Could she perhaps have been talking about Kevin?" he asked.

"That's what I thought next," Joan Fecklewhite answered, her voice brightening, "and I wanted to tell her—well, I did tell her, I said, 'Jenny, things will work out between you and Kevin.' She shook her head, like I didn't understand, but I did, I said, 'I don't mean whatever problems you two're having, I mean it'll work out when you leave. You're gonna have a whole different life. Kevin'll—well, he'll have a good life, too, but it won't be like yours.' I thought maybe I was saying too much, so then I said, 'Unless you want to stay with him. If you do, you'll find some way.' She smiled at me then, like I'd helped, but it was the saddest smile you've ever seen."

Mrs. Fecklewhite sniffed but otherwise didn't move, remaining on the threshold of the room. Standing among the dead girl's belongings wearing his suit, his late-model car waiting outside to take him back to the big city, Jordan could picture Jenny Fecklewhite's sad smile perfectly. It was as if he made eye contact with the dead girl past her mother's shoulder. Jordan understood the sadness: Joan Fecklewhite had described for Jenny not only how her relationship with Kevin could shrivel and fade but that the ties to her parents could do the same. Jenny was poised to have a life completely removed from all those in her hometown. It was what everyone expected of her; it had probably been what Jenny had hoped for herself, but the expectations must also have made her very lonely at times.

"Then he showed up," Mrs. Fecklewhite said.

"Who? Kevin?"

She nodded. "He did that sometimes, like he knew when she was thinking letting-go thoughts about him. We were in here with the college catalogs spread out on Jenny's bed when I heard this banging on the front door, and when I went to open it, I saw Kevin through the screen door wearing this old hat that must've been his dad's from before Kevin was born, with a piece of cardboard stuck in the hatband that said 'Press.' And he tips the hat to me like we've never been introduced before and he says, 'Hello, ma'am, I'm Joe Feeblemeister'—something like that—'I'm a press photographer for the *Weekly Reader,* and we heard there was a photo opportunity here.' "

She chuckled, shaking her head. Reliving the story, seeing Kevin, Joan Fecklewhite had regained her footing. She walked away, and Jordan followed her down the hall. "Jenny had come out behind me, and when she saw Kevin, she put on this—"

Superior smile, Jordan thought.

"—this look she gave him sometimes, but Kevin just barged right in and says, 'Hello, miss, you look like you must be the college girl. Could we maybe get a few candid snaps for our readers who can't read?' Jenny started laughing, too. Kevin was acting like he was a real pro, he was squinting around here like he wanted to line up the perfect shot. 'Maybe with your trophies,' he said. 'Ain't you got any trophies? Bowling trophies maybe? Or a beauty crown. Ain't you ever won a beauty contest?'

"Jenny started getting into the spirit of it. She said, 'Wait, wait,' and she ran and cut off a long strip of butcher paper and wrote on it with a black marker 'Miss Agricultural By-product,' and when she came back with that for a sash,

Kevin said, 'Oh, perfect.' He snaps her picture and says, 'Now when you're at Harvard or Yale and they say you didn't have no culture where you come from, you can show 'em this.'

"The kids were here, too," Joan Fecklewhite continued, "Edwina and the boys, and they came running in to see what all the excitement was about—they always gathered around when Kevin was here—and he said, 'Oh good, little people. Let's have a picture of you thanking the little people who made it all possible.' And we all go running around putting together a beauty contest costume for Jenny. She got a paper towel tube for a scepter and—What did we use for a cloak? I don't remember, but she—" Mrs. Fecklewhite's laugh stopped abruptly. The picture had become too vivid for her. Jordan stood with his hands in his pockets, watching her face, which had gone from pale to splotched with red, from middle-aged to youthful to suddenly aged.

"Jenny was having as good a time as any of us," she continued more quietly. "One time she looked at me and shook her head like 'What an idiot,' but before Kevin got here, she'd been blue, and after he came, she was smiling. She was running around, and Kevin snapping pictures every two seconds, and the kids jumping around her like she was about to do something magic."

Like vanish, Jordan thought. Disappear like the out-of-place creature she'd been.

He followed Joan Fecklewhite out onto the front porch. She wasn't dismissing him, she was still reliving the past day. "They came out in the yard," she said, "and see that tree stump? They used that for a throne. Jenny sat there with her chin so high you could barely see her eyes, and they were all bowing and scraping to her. Then she made Edwina the princess and took off all her stuff and put it on Edwina, who just about got lost in the cloak and the—the stuff, but she was grinning so big, she loved it when Jenny included her.

"Jenny starts shouting, 'Where's some crops? I want a picture of all of us with some crops. Where's some cotton?

And get the house in the picture. And Mom—' " Joan Fecklewhite stopped again, her hand lifted in a wave. The smile that had been starting on her face froze in midformation. Her eyes were distant and deep.

Looking at her daughter, Jordan suddenly wondered, had Joan Fecklewhite also seen her lost sister, Jenny's mother? Jordan remembered with a shock that the Kevin he'd just heard described as so lively was dead, too. So much death encompassed by this tiny house and yard: the transformer of every memory. Mrs. Fecklewhite would never be able to remember her daughter with unalloyed pleasure. Jordan turned away from the sight of her face to survey the empty yard that sounded so silent. The tree stump looked abandoned.

"Thank you for your time, Mrs. Fecklewhite." He had to repeat the sentiment to bring her out of her trance. He left her still staring across her front yard. Driving away, Jordan felt a little displaced himself. When he came to a crossroads he sat there for a long minute, trying to remember which way to turn.

"Kevin hit him, too, right, I mean there was some give and take, like any fight?"

"Not that I saw," the hardware store owner said calmly. "Kevin reached out for Wayne, like to grab him, and they both fell down once, so Wayne might've got a little scratched up, but Kevin never took a swing at him. 'Time I went to help, Wayne just had him down on the ground, punching."

Jordan grimaced but was careful to thank the man. Before he left, he tried another probe. "You know about—Jenny Fecklewhite and the judge?" he asked Hiram Lester, as if Jordan already knew, as if he were just challenging the store owner's knowledge.

"Know what?" the hardware store owner said. "That he helped her with her homework, maybe lots of times? I know what some old busybody women would say."

He knew. Jordan hadn't been able to get anyone to say it, but some people obviously knew what Jordan had figured out: that Jenny and Judge Waverly had been lovers.

*   *   *

"They were in here. Perfectly friendly, too," the Pizza Hut owner said of Wayne and Kevin. "Kind of intense, but not mad."

"Which one left first?"

"Kevin. Wayne just sat over there in the corner booth for a while, talking to himself, but I didn't get close enough to hear. Then he suddenly jumped up and left, too."

"Looking mad?" Jordan asked.

This wasn't the first time the Pizza Hut manager had been questioned. He had his story down pat. Dale Hines was a youngish middle-aged man, with a florid face and a gut that looked as if he enjoyed his own product; he had retired early from something else, probably the military, before buying the pizza franchise. "No, sir, he wasn't mad. Said good-bye when he left, like always."

"And this was how long before you heard about the fight and the murder?"

"Oh, an hour maybe, I'm not sure. Late lunch shift, then it was three or later before some kid came in talking about Jenny. I thought of Wayne right away."

Jordan kept his face neutral. He'd had practice by now. Better the witness drop this observation now than by surprise from the witness stand. "Why? I thought you said he didn't look mad when he left."

"No, but the way he and Kevin'd been talking, so serious, then when Wayne left he looked—not mad, but like he'd made up his mind."

The hospital's file on Jenny included, surprisingly, a color photo, the first time Jordan had seen the girl in living color. It wasn't a preautopsy photo, it was a candid snap of the girl laughing, just turning toward the camera, a green-eyed blonde so pretty and so young it was heartbreaking to think of her growing old—or dying.

"I put that one in," the nurse Evelyn Riegert answered Jordan's surprised expression. "Jenny had volunteered here a few times, and once we got pictures of the staff at a kids' day we had. After they brought her in, I had a copy made for the file. For contrast."

Ms. Riegert kept her chin from trembling by closing her mouth firmly. Jordan studied the picture. "I need copies of everything," he said quietly. "I can get a subpoena if you—"

"No, I know you're entitled." She took the file from him, then the photo. "I'll have that one copied for you, too."

There was no one in Green Hills who was going to let Jenny be reduced to lifelessness.

Dispatch records showed that Officer Harry Briggs had been on solitary patrol, his last recorded call more than an hour before he raced to the scene of Jenny Fecklewhite's murder. And Deputy Delmore had been coming off a late lunch, which he'd reported eating alone in his car, when he'd received the call that had supposedly led to his discovery of the body. Either of them could have been in Pleasant Grove Park earlier than he'd reported.

As Jordan left the law enforcement annex to the courthouse, he knew that word of what he'd obtained there had spread through the building before he reached the front door.

Dr. Wyntlowski said judiciously—as much as an unshaven man rubbing a hand across his eyes could appear judicious— "There definitely could have been an event in the hospital."

"An event," Jordan said. "Like a calf roping, you mean, or a bake sale by the ladies' auxiliary of the VFW."

"I love to hear a lawyer tell me I'm being obscure," the assistant medical examiner grinned. "It's so entertaining. You know what I mean by an event, or were you not listening all those times I testified for you?"

"Not during the gory parts." They were in Bob Wyntlowski's glass-walled office at the morgue, with gory parts on display just behind him if Jordan turned his head, which he resolutely refused to do.

"An event, meaning your boy here—What was his name? Kevin?—didn't necessarily just go into decline and not recover from the beating. Possibly something else happened in the hospital to contribute to the cause of death."

"Something criminal?"

"Not necessarily. Bubble in one of his tubes. Choking on food—but he wasn't eating solid food, was he?"

"No. These other possibilities aren't mentioned in their autopsy summary or the death certificate?"

The assistant medical examiner hesitated. Dr. Wyntlowski remembered Jordan only as a prosecutor, when they'd been more or less on the same team. Jordan hoped that ever so slight sense of cameraderie—as much as could exist between a doctor and a lawyer—still prevailed. He knew that ordinarily Wyntlowski wouldn't be nearly as forthcoming with a defense lawyer.

Wyntlowski held up the autopsy report on Kevin. "This summary from their local doctor just reeks of who-gives-a-damn. Or of aw-we-all-know-what-happened. They don't seem to have explored all the possibilities."

"And you can't tell from their findings? Or the hospital records?"

"No. But you know, they were probably right. Beating victim dies, you don't look real hard for the cause when you can see it all over him."

Dr. Bob glanced past Jordan's shoulder and held his head up curiously as if something interesting had happened out there at one of the tables. Jordan stiffened a little more. "What about this other one?"

"Now this one they did a good job on," the medical examiner said, flipping open the file on Jenny. He brushed past the color photo of the living girl and went straight to the autopsy report. "I don't have any quarrel with their conclusions, and I don't see anything they didn't look for."

"Broken neck," Jordan said, and the doctor murmured affirmatively. "Does it look like it was intentional?"

"Some day I'm going to have to get one of you real smart lawyers to explain to me how to read somebody's mind just from looking at the wounds he inflicted."

"Well, I mean, it was the root that broke her neck, right? Not the blow itself."

Wyntlowski said, "If you want to try out your defense on me, go ahead. Yeah, he might not've meant to kill her. Accidents happen when you start punching people in the head. But the law doesn't call them accidents, does it, Jordy?"

Jordan stood, thinking of the gauntlet of corpses he had to run to get out of here. He reached for his files, but Dr. Wyntlowski still had the Jenny one open to the preautopsy closeup photo of the girl's damaged face. Jordan had to narrow his eyes to look at it.

"Interesting mark here," Wyntlowski said. "This is the blow that cracked her cheekbone, probably knocked her over backward. Look at the impressions it left."

Jordan did. "Big knuckle?"

"I'd say a ring. Definitely a ring. Either that or he used a club with a small knob on it. But I'd say from the surrounding indications that it . . ."

By concentrating on the mark, Jordan could put her face almost out of his mind. The impression was deep and pocked with details. It might have been a closeup of a crater on the moon.

"You know what you're telling me on both these cases," Jordan said. "You know what I'm going to have to ask for now."

"Yeah," Dr. Wyntlowski said, managing to hide any concern he felt for the lawyer's problems.

Jordan felt like a cigarette ad. In his dark suit and silk tie, standing on the mezzanine level of the old Majestic Theater, he felt so sophisticated that **all** that was needed to complete the picture was a cigarette or a martini glass. Some vice was definitely called for.

"Hello, Judge," he greeted a passing county court judge, who smiled back at him so graciously it might have been campaign time. He nodded across the room to an older couple, friends of his parents. He hadn't been to the Majestic Theater in a long time, almost since it had stopped showing movies and been renovated for stage productions, but he felt at home in his native city. He watched alertly for Laura, hoping she hadn't had any trouble finding her way.

But he got distracted by familiar faces, by couples looking elegant or goofy, by beautiful women at their most beautiful.

He was watching one, wondering if the deep shimmers of her dress were green or black, wondering what sort of underwear she wore to keep herself upheld like that, when he realized it was Laura. He had never seen her shoulders before. He hurried down the stairs, watching not to lose her, and reached her side just as she turned.

"Hello."

She only smiled, but Jordan read a lot into her smile: her pleasure at his thoughtfulness in arriving early, the way his familiarity made him stand out from the background of the entire foreign city, her slight relief that he had not only appeared but looked appropriate to the surroundings and to her.

"You found it."

Laura kept her smile. "Last year I had season tickets."

"Oh. Then you show me around."

She took his arm. Jordan remembered that this was his first date in how many years, but the thought didn't make him nervous. He no longer had a date mode, that high-octane tense phoniness that had kept a variety of girls from learning anything about him. He felt at ease with Laura as soon as he'd seen her.

"What was the best thing you saw last year?"

"Here?" She thought. "*Guys and Dolls,* I suppose."

"But it wasn't like Chicago, was it?"

She turned her head as if she'd seen someone she knew. "I didn't get out much in Chicago," she murmured.

Jordan stopped close to a pillar so that she would turn toward him. He liked everything he saw about her. The way she wore her elegant dress and makeup not as if they were costume and disguise, but as if she were comfortable in them; yet he could still see her daily face as well: the slightly upturned nose that invited a kiss, the bright eyes startling beneath the brown eyebrows, the quizzical look produced by the ever so slightly raised cheekbone. When he looked at her cheek, he was reminded of that other cheekbone, the shattered one in the autopsy photo.

"What's the matter?"

"Nothing. If I'd realized how beautiful you are, I would have asked you out sooner."

She said wryly, "I try to keep it under wraps so men will be attracted by my simple homely virtues instead of my dazzling looks," but her eyes glittered at the compliment.

"Tell me what to watch for in the ballet."

"Oh, I'm the expert? Well, if someone falls off the edge of the stage, it's probably not a good sign."

She did tell him a few things, but it was wasted breath, because Jordan couldn't afterward have related any details of the performance. What he enjoyed was touching Laura protectively as they found their seats, joking with her, seeing the look of anticipation she turned on him when the lights went down. What he watched was her hand dangling from the armrest next to his, her profile in the dimness, her collarbones that the dress left bare.

"Drink?" he asked at intermission.

"Sure. Some wine would be nice."

"White?"

"Only if there's no alternative."

"Two red wines," Jordan said to the bartender, then stood around holding the two plastic glasses, feeling married again and not disliking the feeling, until she returned from the ladies' room. They clinked their glasses softly. Laura sipped and made a face.

"I was wrong about it being nice."

"I swear I told him red," Jordan grimaced. "This tastes more brown. So, did you just drive in tonight?"

"No, I came with Chris Cavaletti. The teacher? We drove in yesterday. Chris had some friends to visit, and I wanted to go to a real mall."

So Laura had been in town last night, Saturday night, while Jordan had sat like a lump at home, watching a crummy rented movie. If he'd gone out, he might have run into her somewhere, they might have spent the evening together.

But maybe Laura had a friend in town, too. Season tickets, she'd said.

For the second act Laura suggested they move up from

what Jordan had thought were their good seats to the relative emptiness of the balcony to get a different perspective. Up there, unsurrounded, they could comment on the performance, which made it worthwhile to Jordan. The perspective put him closer to the bewitching ceiling of the Majestic, too, which was decorated with the skyline of a Moroccan village, with a night sky overhead studded with stars and clouds passing faintly behind them. Looking up, he felt alone in the galaxy with the woman beside him.

"I'll bet we could find some better wine without much trouble," Jordan said in the lobby afterward.

"I'd better be getting back," Laura said.

Jordan touched her hand very lightly. "Not yet."

Laura hesitated, looking away. Then she looked at Jordan, and he saw rejection. Laura looked as if she felt herself out of place for the first time. But she took an extra few moments to study Jordan's face, and when she spoke she said, "I'll have to call Chris."

They walked, not far, to the bar of the St. Anthony Hotel, where Jordan liked to think of the picture they presented except when he remembered that they were downtown and their clothes made them look worth robbing. But the bar was well lighted and quiet and Laura looked at home in it. He couldn't think of what to say to impress her, so instead he asked a question.

"Oh, it was good," Laura said. "I hate to criticize dancers, I know how hard they work."

"But everyone can't be Baryshnikov, otherwise we wouldn't have known how good Baryshnikov was."

"Did we?" Laura teased.

"I saw him once. In New York. My wife dragged me. I was stunned when I was actually impressed with him."

"The leaps," Laura said.

"I admit it, I'm shallow. The only way a dancer can impress me is to do something I don't think Lynn Swann could have done."

"But could Baryshnikov have caught a football at the top of his leap?"

"If only I'd had one with me."

The night was giving them some shortchanged version of time, the hour that dissipated in only a few minutes. Jordan had the bad luck to see the clock mounted above the bar and felt the hated pressure of a new week starting soon.

"Are you driving back tonight?" he asked.

Laura nodded. "Unless Chris wants to get up very early in the morning. She doesn't have to be back tomorrow, but I do."

"I'll take you," Jordan said impulsively.

Laura looked at him indulgently. "Remember where we are?"

"It's okay, I have to be in your court in the morning anyway," he lied.

"Jordan, you don't have to—" she said, laying her hand on his.

"I want to. And Chris will thank you."

"That's true. But it's a long drive."

"I have to make it anyway. Now or in the morning."

"Jordan," she said seriously. "There's no reason for it."

"Except that I want to."

She gave him a long unsmiling study, while Jordan tried to look innocent or sincere or whatever she wanted.

"All right," Laura finally said.

He touched her hand.

"I have to go by and get my things."

"Me, too. I'll get the car."

He rose quickly and hurried out without giving her a chance to change her mind, but it was a long walk to the car. He had a strong feeling she'd be gone when he returned. The night felt menacing. The sound of his heels seemed to carry.

But when he drove up in front of the bar, Laura was waiting just inside the door. They hardly spoke on the drive to the house where Laura had been staying with Chris Cavaletti's friends. Jordan hoped the silence wasn't a harbinger of the long drive to Green Hills.

"This is close to my apartment," Jordan said when they reached their destination. "I have to pick up a few things, too, I'll be right back."

"All right."

"Laura—" He got out of the car and caught her hand on the sidewalk. She looked at him as if he'd announced a major intention. "Before we change, before the date's over," Jordan added, "could I—"

He leaned close, hoping he wasn't surprising her. Her eyes seemed to grow bigger, then their lips met. Hers were soft with a faint taste, sweet breath held behind them. He was still holding her hand. Her lips remained soft and parted only slightly, but her hand clutched his.

"I'll be right back," he said again briskly, down to business, but in the car he was thoughtful. The taste and feel of her mouth stayed on his.

Once again back at the unfamiliar house, he said, "All set?" and put her suitcase in the trunk, next to his. He was sorry that she had changed, but the evening dress hadn't been traveling clothes, and her skirt and short-sleeved blouse made her look even fresher.

As they left town, they talked more about the dancers, but that topic was exhausted before they reached the city limit. "*You're* a dancer," he said to make it personal.

Laura laughed ruefully. "I used to dance a little."

"But you gave it up."

"No, I'm still the finest dancer in Green Hills."

It was Green Hills she wouldn't give up. Jordan didn't understand her. He'd gotten to know Laura well enough to think she was too smart for her job, too wide-ranging in her thoughts to be happy in the little town. But she'd suffered some failure of nerve in her youth. "Why did you go all the way to Chicago for court reporting school?" he asked.

"Because I wanted to get far away. You know how rinky-dink you think your hometown is when you're a teenager. But I found out I was a small-town girl. I hated the big city. I hated waking up in the morning and knowing I wasn't going to see anybody I knew, all day. And the traffic scared me, of course, and the crime."

"But you lasted two years."

She nodded. "But then the job opened up in Green Hills for the judge, and it seemed like a sign."

"Are you glad you did?"

"Some things don't have anything to do with happiness, you just do them because you feel like you have to. Like destiny." She was staring out the window into the night, looking as if the life she hadn't had had become precious. Laura drew a short breath and seemed to change the subject. "Like you being a lifelong prosecutor."

"But that turned out not to be my destiny."

"That's what I mean. That's what you thought you were, but your life took a different course without you meaning it to."

Jordan shook his head. "I made up my own mind. I quit."

"But would you have if you hadn't felt like you had to?" Jordan couldn't answer. As he sank into his own thoughts, he again felt Laura consciously change beside him, change her tone. She said lightly, "Listen to the master of his fate. Where were you born?"

"San Antonio."

"And where do you live now?"

"All right. But maybe you should have gone to law school instead. I've seen how well you understand the law. Doesn't it gall you sometimes to listen to some stupid lawyer and think—"

Laura shrugged. The resignation in her voice was so old it had lost its bitterness. "That would have been three more years of school on top of college that I never had. I didn't want to take that time. Besides, fifteen years ago . . . It didn't seem like an option."

Jordan let the subject drop. They were out on the uncrowded interstate, the car's headlights piercing the night, but the darkness prevailed on both sides, unbroken to the horizons. They could feel its soft weight. Jordan and Laura talked in the darkness of the long distance night as if they were disembodied spirits. But in fact, he was aware of her legs stretching forward as if the legs were propelling the car. He wanted to touch her again as they'd casually touched hands throughout the evening, but in the close confines of the car, casualness wasn't possible.

"Have you given your daughter dancing lessons?" Laura asked.

"We've talked about it. I told Mar—my ex-wife that it's up to them. When Ashley asks me for something, I don't know if she really wants it or if she's just testing me to see if I'll do it for her."

He felt uncomfortable discussing his family, but Laura turned to him with a concerned expression and he soon found himself pouring out his worries about his daughter withdrawing from him, voicing discouragement he'd never told anyone else.

"Sometimes I think it might be better if I just let her go. A father should be there every day. The way things are—"

"You keep trying," Laura said with surprising fierceness. "That girl is your responsibility, Jordan, and you trust me, a girl needs her father, no matter who else she has in her life. Even if she doesn't think so. She won't ever forget you."

Jordan remembered what he had learned from his snooping in the files, about Laura's parents' divorce when she was young, and he was too embarrassed to pursue the subject. So he almost shifted to business again. "Did Jenny get along with her father?" he asked.

"I guess." Laura looked out the window. "They weren't the kind of people to let everybody know their business. But police never got called to their house if that's what you mean."

"What about Kevin, what did they think about him?"

"What did anybody think about him? He wasn't much. He was a long way from the best Jenny could have done, even in Green Hills, and she knew it. She asked me once what I thought of him. She must've asked everybody."

"What did you say?"

"I was very careful to say he seemed like a nice enough boy. Let her take that any way she wanted. I wasn't going to give her advice and then get blamed for it later."

Jordan was thinking of the photograph from the hospital file, the one that showed the living, smiling girl. "You know, this case isn't like any other one I've had," he said quietly. "I feel like I've gotten to know this girl. Sometimes I forget why I'm asking people about her, and then it's a shock to remember I'm never going to meet her."

Laura crossed her arms and reverted to the beginning of the conversation. "You know the best thing Ed and Joan did for her?" she said, staring out into the dark. "They called her Jenny. Her name was Jennifer, but now every other girl in the world is named Jennifer. Just by giving her that silly old-fashioned nickname they made her distinctive."

Jordan couldn't think of anything to add to that. He didn't want Laura to think he'd offered to drive her home so he could wring more information about the case from her, so he changed subjects. They talked about their childhoods and about high school, the universal equalizer; comparing their experiences, they made the astonishing discovery that they'd both felt alienated as teenagers.

They'd been in the car an hour, and the night no longer seemed so unpopulated. Her hometown lurked not far ahead. Jordan thought about his suitcase in the trunk, about driving up to her house after midnight.

"Were you ever serious about being a dancer?"

Laura's laugh sounded hollow as if forced or unpracticed. She stretched. "Oh, yes, I took lessons for years, I even started giving them when I was in high school. I took lessons from Mrs. Jensen, who'd been as far as Dallas, so we thought she knew everything."

"She had a studio in Green Hills?"

"Yes, it was an old laundromat, from when we'd had more than one laundry in town. It had stood empty for so long the bank let her have it for next to nothing. Mrs. Jensen put in some mirrors and a barre and didn't change anything else. It still had the big plate glass windows, and she didn't even curtain them. Mrs. Jensen thought it was good advertising to let people see our practices."

"I'll bet you drew some attention."

"You should have seen me then," Laura admitted. "I was in fine shape, I'm not ashamed to admit it. Boys'd come around to make fun, then they'd hang around outside. We'd be inside in our leotards bending to the barre and raising our thighs to our chests. Those boys' faces were just like newsprint, you could see them thinking about the possibilities. Nudging each other. Really crushed my respect for manhood to see how all alike they were."

"Did any of them ever make use of the possibilities?"

Laura stared hostilely at him. "What business is it of yours?"

"None."

That was the only answer that could have placated her. She looked out the windshield again and said lightly, "That's the sad, pitiful thing. Some of them came after me because— they said—I seemed like something special. I knew what they meant. But the one or two that ever got close, it was just the same old grope and thump, always in or near a pickup truck."

Jordan said carefully, "Well, your prospects were a little limited."

Laura laughed at him. "Oh, right, you big-city boys had all the technique, right?"

"Not me. But I heard stories—"

"We had the same stories, Jordan. Sophistication is overrated."

"What about now? Is there someone in your life now?"

"Yes," she said, but unconvincingly, he thought.

"Home," Jordan said as he took the exit for Green Hills. But they still seemed to be the only people alive in the night as he drove slowly down Main Street, turned past the dark courthouse, and followed Laura's directions to her street, which he laughed to see was Flowing Springs Boulevard. Jordan turned off the headlights as he swung into the driveway in front of a pretty white house with a front porch and dark shutters.

"Tired?" Laura asked.

Jordan shook his head. "I feel like the road's still moving."

"I guess you deserve a cup of coffee or a drink," she said.

Minus the sound of the engine, the night seemed very quiet. He thought he could hear people breathing in the surrounding houses as he carried Laura's suitcase up the walk. She looked at him speculatively as she opened the door.

Before she could turn on a light, he took her arm and said, "Could we repeat the—?" and kissed her again.

Laura seemed suspicious, but after a moment, she put her arms around his neck and gave herself up to the kiss. It was as good as the first time, her lips still soft and this time a little more responsive. And he thought he could feel her thoughts.

"Well," she said after a minute. "Let's get out of view of the neighbors. Do you always ask?"

"Yes, ma'am, I'm very polite."

The living room was small, and the furniture looked as if it had lived there for a long time. Laura dropped her keys on an end table, took the suitcase from him, and disappeared long enough to let Jordan look around. There were two tall wooden bookcases full of novels and a few serious works of anthropology and history, no popular nonfiction on how to please a man or improve your working relationships. There was barely room on the shelf for one picture, of a middle-aged woman not used to smiling, who looked a little like Laura.

"I keep that there to placate her when she comes over."

"She's still alive?"

"She's only sixty, Jordan. Lives a few blocks from here in the same old house. I see her every Sunday and usually three or four other times a week, we can't help running into each other." The words were harsh, but Laura said them indulgently, forgiving both herself and her mother for being fond of each other.

"I sensed you'd prefer a drink to coffee," she said, handing him a short glass tinkling with ice cubes. The taste of scotch and water erased the feel of her lips from his, and he wanted to restore the feeling. She looked at him over the rim of her own glass as if she knew what he was thinking.

They resumed their conversation, but when Jordan put down his empty glass some time later, Laura didn't offer to fill it. She looked at him and said with a flatness he understood, "It was nice of you to bring me home."

"Thank you for letting me," he said.

At the door they kissed again, gently, exploring. He put

his hand on her arm and reveled in its roundness and smoothness. Much as they'd told each other about themselves during the long night, it was as if they hadn't known each other at all until they touched, and as soon as they did, they recognized each other. When they pulled apart, she stepped back. "I hope you don't think I've led you on," Laura said, "but I'm not looking for romance." Her voice sounded as harsh as the first times she'd spoken to him, but Jordan wasn't sure the anger was directed at him.

"Me neither," he said.

He stepped out onto the porch, feeling regretful but somehow relieved. But his feelings changed as soon as he began to walk away. He turned back and frowned.

"Does this seem right?" he asked.

He didn't pursue his arguments, he just let his face speak, wondering if she was having the same thoughts. *Does this seem right? Me leaving, both of us being alone?*

Laura looked at him a long time, not melting. When she spoke, her voice wasn't very friendly. "Would you do me a favor? Would you move your car some place, please? I've got neighbors."

For a long time they just talked. Jordan talked about still feeling the burden of his father's expectations, about disliking the practice of law but not being able to leave it, partly because he couldn't make as much money at anything else, partly because he was good at what he did but had never accomplished what he thought he was capable of doing. Laura talked about the contrary burden of having no expectations. "You don't realize how far in the world I've risen," she said. Jordan wanted to ask about her childhood but was afraid to return to the subject of her father, so he asked about everything else he could think of. He knew her well, he knew her attitudes; the questions were just filling in details.

"And when you came back, was everything changed?"

"No, only me. I wanted to cry at how familiar it all was, but it was as if I was just visiting. For a long time I was waiting to leave again."

"Are you still?"

She regarded him. *Who are you, trying to ferret out my secrets, stranger?* "Only on weekends."

It grew late, until they stopped paying attention to time. When Jordan went to the bathroom, he passed through her dim bedroom. He saw more shelves, keepsakes, a four-poster bed. The bathroom was very feminine and old-fashioned, bottles with gracefully curving necks sitting on a mirrored tray, a wicker shelf holding powder and potpourri. He looked around the bathroom, a strange place with which he might become familiar. He wondered if he would get to know the room well, if he would impose his masculinity on the white surroundings.

When he emerged, Laura was waiting and went in after him. Jordan stayed in the bedroom, barefoot, having discarded his shoes some time earlier when she did. Laura had turned on one old-fashioned lamp in the bedroom with a wonderfully dim bulb. When she came out of the bathroom and saw him waiting for her, she looked at him with the same suspicion he'd seen cross her face before, but the suspicion could have been of herself.

"Should I leave?" he asked, not seriously.

"Yes," she said.

She stood without moving while he crossed the room. He kissed her cheek and her eyelid before she lifted her mouth. But when she kissed him, she folded her arms in front of her chest, and after a moment, she thumped her fist against his chest with surprising force. Jordan held her, feeling her sigh. Her arms went around him slowly, starting with her hands on his waist, drifting softly up his back. He stretched his fingers along the backs of her shoulders, kneading gently. His tongue touched her lip. Her hands descended again.

Her blouse slipped down her arms before he was sure he'd gotten all the buttons. He stroked the round firmness of her stomach. Her breasts were against his shirt. When he stepped back so he could see, he smiled slightly. "You wear a one-piece bathing suit."

Her chest, which had seemed pale, was darker in the dimness. The tan line went across the tops of her breasts. The breasts were pale, so that the reddish nipples looked dark, but her stomach was pale, too, as much of it as he could see.

"Shh," Laura said. "Don't comment."

She put her hand inside his shirt, touching the top button. She stared at the button as if it were something she'd never encountered, until Jordan unbuttoned it himself. He started to finish the job, but she brushed his hand away and undid the rest of the buttons herself, stepping close to him, so that when she pulled open his shirt, her breasts brushed his chest. He pulled her closer. His hand slipped inside her waistband, but at the same time his mouth found hers and he marveled again at her lips. She seemed to be speaking to him in murmurs too soft and too important to be heard.

"Laura." He said it again because he liked the sound of it. "Laura." She murmured in reply.

She had been busy with her hands, his pants began to fall. He found the button of her skirt and opened the waistband so wide that it fell down around his hands. They had to step aside out of the tangle of clothes. Laura looked down, lightly touched his thighs, looked up at him with her seriousness finally beginning to give way. Jordan's hands kept searching for new smooth skin to delight in.

When they moved toward the bed, he cleared his throat and said, "I keep thinking what you said about what disappointments your old lovers were. It's intimidating."

She laughed. "I won't hurt you."

In the four-poster bed, she didn't make an athletic contest of it, but he remained aware of her strength. When she stretched she seemed as tall as he. Her legs might have been able to pin him if she'd tried. Her legs were wonderful, smooth and firm and supple. Laura liked to move, she didn't lie still for long. Some undeterminable time later, as she turned, she cried out suddenly. "Ah. Ah! Wait, wait."

Jordan tried to hold her. "What is it, are you—"

"It's all right, it'll—ah!"

"God, I'm sorry."

"It's okay, it's not your fault, I just turned the wrong way."

She reached to massage her leg. Jordan helped. "Guess I should have warmed up," she said ruefully.

"I thought we had."

They laughed, holding each other so that he could feel her breasts shaking, laughing comfortably and for longer than the mild witticism deserved. Laura fell against him, hair in the hollow of his collarbone.

After a while Jordan said, "When you first screamed, I thought, God, I've never heard a woman so passionate."

Laura chuckled again. "Passion and pain, darling, they're so close."

She began stroking his chest. He kissed her shoulders and her breasts; she reached for him. When she cried out again some time later, when they both did, there was no pain in the sound. Jordan held her for a long time in the dark after Laura had turned off the lamp, until he expected the windows to be lightening. He touched her, remembering the sight of her body, her face inside the bar and in the dashlights of the car, her mouth when it spoke and when it touched his. It was amazing that he had found her.

She stayed in his thoughts all night. In his dreams she lay wakefully beside him, studying him.

8

Good morning."

"God, didn't you sleep?"

"I slept like the dead," Jordan said. "Then when the sun came up, I was resurrected."

Laura put her hand over her eyes. "When the sun came up? What time is it?" She looked at the clock, looked uncertainly at Jordan standing across the bedroom from her, holding one of her books. "What have you been doing to entertain yourself?"

"For a long time I just looked at you."

"My God." She pushed her hair back.

"You looked beautiful so many different ways as the light changed."

She put her face back in the pillow. "At least your vision's lousy," she said. "I can be thankful for that."

"Then I started snooping through your things," Jordan said. Laura reemerged. He bent to kiss her. Her kiss had recognition in it but not much enthusiasm.

"What's that, my yearbook? You *were* desperate for entertainment."

"You went to school with Deputy Delmore?"

"Yeah. Ol' Tommy. Class treasurer. We knew he was too straight to steal."

"And Evelyn Riegert, the nurse at the hospital. Isn't this her? Her name was Busby then."

"Yeah. Me and T. J. and Evelyn, we were about the only three too dumb to get out."

The old class photos made Jordan feel out of place by

167

reminding him that these people had histories to which he'd always be an outsider. "For my best friend," was written across Evelyn Busby's photo in a flowing graceful script. "Stay as sweet as you are."

"Were you sweet then?"

"She was being satirical," Laura said.

"Is she reliable? I may need her for a witness."

"Oh, yes, you can count on whatever Evelyn tells you."

Jordan hovered uncertainly over her. Laura looked up at him with a gentle smile but showed no inclination to get out of bed. "I have a couple of errands before I go to court," Jordan said. "Is there some place we could have breakfast?"

Laura shook her head. "Let's take it a little more slowly before we start being seen having breakfast together."

"I forgot your reputation." He touched the sheet she was holding to her chest. "You're modest this morning."

"Sorry if in broad daylight I'm not the wild wanton you're used to."

He sat on the edge of the bed and kissed her, meaning it to be light and quick, but she put her arm around his neck and nestled against him. She said softly, "You're a sweet man, Jordan. Men don't even like to hear that, do they?"

"I—"

"Shh. Don't say something stupid. I'll see you in court."

He carried her last touch with him as he walked down her street to where he'd moved his car during the night. As he drove, he felt that soft weight on the back of his neck, that touch on his cheek. He found he was driving at random and had to think about where he was going.

Jordan was sitting quietly in the spectator seats of the courtroom when he saw her enter from the office. Without thinking, he rose and put out his hand to help her even though he was twenty feet away, because Laura was walking with a cane. She saw Jordan and rolled her eyes.

Emilio, from his bailiff's desk, said, "What happened to you?"

"It's just a little sprain," she said irritably as if she'd explained too many times already. "I just stepped off a curb the wrong way."

Jordan laughed. Laura grimaced at him. He had forgotten what it was like to share intimate looks with a woman in public.

"You!" came an angry voice. "You're crazy."

Mike Arriendez was stalking toward him, crushing a sheaf of papers in his outstretched hand.

"It's just a motion," Jordan said mildly.

"It's a sacrilege!"

"Look, I just filed it today, I don't know when we'll take it up. We can talk—"

"No, we'll settle this today." Arriendez's face was flushed redder than brown.

When he turned away, Jordan called after him, "I hope you're not going to have an ex parte communication with the judge."

"I'm going to talk to Cindy," the DA said tightly. "You can follow me if you like."

Jordan didn't. He shrugged at Laura, who was looking at him wonderingly. Emilio was looking back and forth between the two of them.

"Mr. Marshall, you filed a motion this morning?"

"Your Honor, my case is not on your docket this morning, my client isn't present, and I'm not ready to present evidence on the motion," Jordan said.

"We're only taking it up in chambers, Mr. Marshall." The judge was in his shirtsleeves, black tie pulled tight. The office felt congested with the two lawyers standing before the desk and Laura transcribing on her machine. Her face was blank; she looked at the far wall. Judge Waverly looked even more predatory than usual in the narrow space, as if he could reach out and choke one of them at any moment. "I'll allow you to summarize the evidence you expect to present. The district attorney is anxious to have the matter settled, and given the nature of the motion, the court agrees. Now, you are asking for an order that would permit you to exhume two bodies?"

The phrasing made Jordan feel grubby. "To allow additional autopsy studies, Your Honor. I've consulted an outside medical examiner who feels further study of the bodies of Jennifer Fecklewhite and Kevin Wainwright might reveal further cause of death information."

"Might?" the judge said mildly.

"No!" Mike Arriendez almost shouted, no longer able to remain quiet.

"The State opposes the motion?" asked the judge.

"Vigorously, Your Honor. Those two victims of this man's client deserve to rest in peace. Thinking of the horror those children's parents would feel when they hear that we're going to dig them up and pry their coffins open and spill their remains out onto another table—"

"Jesus," Jordan said, then more loudly, "Your Honor, I'm sure the procedure would be done with dignity. If the original autopsies had been complete—"

"What exactly would you expect further autopsy to prove?"

"In Jenny's case, Your Honor, the doctor I consulted noticed a deep mark on her face that he thinks could be matched to the murder weapon. So we could conclusively—"

"Weapon?" Judge Waverly asked with mild surprise. "You have a weapon with which to compare this mark on the victim's face?"

The DA waited for the answer, too. Jordan saw that the prosecutor had trapped him. In order to argue the motion, Jordan had to reveal, before trial, whatever pitiful shreds of defense he had. "No, Your Honor," he said miserably.

But he continued arguing. As he did, he watched the judge. Jordan's appeal was emotional, not legal. Didn't Waverly want to know definitively who had killed his girl friend? Hadn't he cared about the girl? The judge's face was less stony than usual. He waited with obvious concern to hear evidence Jordan didn't have to give him.

"At any rate, it would be irrelevant to this case," Arriendez said firmly, interrupting Jordan's plea.

The judge looked at Jordan sympathetically. "He's right,

Mr. Marshall. As for exhuming the victim in the case in which your client is charged—?"

He reoffered Jordan the floor. But Jordan had lost steam. He talked about the incompleteness of the autopsy on Kevin Wainwright, but he was anticipating the prosecutor's argument, and he had no answer for it.

Arriendez unkindly let Jordan speak without interruption until he had wound down to nothing before the prosecutor responded. His anger was under control again. His words were clipped and hard. "Pure speculation," the DA said. "The defense has no evidence of any 'event' occurring in the hospital to cause Kevin Wainwright's death, nor any proof that an additional autopsy would even uncover such an event. For example, an air bubble in a blood line would only result in the kind of heart failure that's already documented in the completed autopsy report, isn't that so, Mr. Marshall?"

"That's my understanding," Jordan admitted.

"For the court to authorize this grisly exploration—" Arriendez began, regaining his fervor.

"All right," the judge said calmly. "The court doesn't require argument. The motion is denied."

Jordan, looking into the dark eyes, saw something in their depths, some knowledge, a mind working over a problem not at all legal in nature. He and the judge stared at each other for a long moment.

"Thank you, Your Honor."

Laura caught up to him in the courtroom, almost falling as she grabbed his arm and pulled him around. Jordan reached to help her and she stiffened, standing tall, the cane dangling from her hand. "Are you intent on having everyone in this town hate you?" she said angrily.

Not you, Laura. "No, but it doesn't matter if they do. At first I was just pushing back because that's what I do when I get pushed," Jordan said sadly. "But then I found out something about myself I didn't know: I don't like seeing someone get jerked around. I never thought I minded that, but I do. Poor stupid Wayne, he may be innocent of the girl's murder, but no one cares about that, they're going to get him for it anyway. Because they're not willing to look at what's really going on. And here I am, Laura, and what am I going to do? I didn't want the case, but it's mine. I'm not going to just stand by and let it happen. That was my plan, but now I find out I can't do it." His voice turned abruptly bitter. "And I hate it a lot more than you do."

Laura was taken aback. She studied Jordan, her face softening a little, but her eyes still angry. "You don't know what in the world you're talking about. Aren't you the one who told me everyone charged with a crime is guilty?"

"Hell, Laura, we're all guilty, aren't we? But that doesn't mean we have to live in prison."

She looked startled. Jordan shared her surprise. He wanted to share with her, he wanted to change the subject, but the place and the timing were all wrong. He had to just shake his head and walk out, feeling torn in every direction.

A week later he parked a block from her house and walked down Flowing Springs Boulevard, the late afternoon almost pleasant when he passed under the shade of oak trees. Labor Day had passed and with it the worst of the summer's heat, though even when the sun went down the air was nothing like autumn. But something about the street softened the air. A sweet scent teased him. Jordan felt like he was in a movie, walking along a picture-perfect small-town street, past houses with wide front porches, screen doors, and open windows, such a place as he had never believed existed. Occasionally a house even had a white picket fence.

He passed one where the scent of flowers or a flowering tree was stronger and stopped to examine the garden.

"Come through the gate if you want a better look," said an unexpected voice. "I don't keep the prize-winners close to the street where kids and dogs can trample them."

"Hello, ma'am," Jordan said to the plump old woman sitting complacently on the porch as he took her suggestion. "It must take a lot of water to have a garden this pretty in this climate."

"Mrs. Johnson," said the woman, with a sort of stern smile.

"Nice to meet you, Mrs. Johnson. I'm—" He changed his mind. "I'm just passing through town on my way to the coast."

"No you're not," she said, not even annoyed. "You're that San Antonio lawyer's defending Wayne Orkney."

"I've got to subscribe to this service," Jordan said.

Mrs. Johnson's smile remained complacent. "Tea?"

"Thank you, ma'am."

She had an extra glass and a pitcher handy. Jordan joined her in the shade.

"Going to see Laura Stefone?"

"I do have a few questions for her. She's preparing a transcript for me."

Say whatever you like, the old lady's pleasant smile invited him. "Laura's a nice girl."

"She seems to be. Have you been her neighbor long?"

"As long as she's lived here," Mrs. Johnson said, "this time around."

Jordan wanted to ask a wealth of questions, but he didn't want to confirm the old lady's suspicions. He gave Mrs. Johnson a sidelong glance. She looked like Mrs. Santa Claus, iron gray hair pulled back from a red and white forehead. Her cheeks were rosy, her plump mouth was pursed in certainty, and her blue eyes, which were supposed to look kindly, were instead glistening and pale and treacherous as waistdeep seawater.

"That's right," Jordan advanced in spite of himself. "Someone told me Ms. Stefone moved away from Green Hills for a while."

"So many do."

"I suppose. But she couldn't stay away, could she?"

"Oh, maybe she could have," Mrs. Johnson said. "Laura wasn't like some of the kids who tell everyone they can't wait to get out, then come skulking back to town a few weeks later. Laura was different. She didn't brag about what she was going to do, but people who knew her knew this town wasn't going to hold her. Nothing much for her to stay for. Her mama didn't have anything to give her, she was barely getting by with sewing and Avon selling herself. And Laura had something, she was a smart girl and she suddenly got ambitious some time in high school. When she went away to Chicago, we thought that was the last we'd see of her."

"But she came back," Jordan said, implying the question.

Mrs. Johnson gave Jordan a sly glance and took pity on him. "Well, she owed the judge a big favor for one thing."

"Judge Waverly?"

"Yes, sir. Laura worked for his wife part-time while she was in high school, cleaning house and whatnot. Let me see, the judge wasn't a judge yet then, but everybody knew he would be, he just had to wait for old Judge Pearsall to die or retire. Anyway, that's when Laura got interested in the law. From talking to the judge."

"Judge Pearsall."

"Judge Waverly," the old lady said impatiently. "I think he had an office in his home back then, so he was around when Laura was helping his wife. They'd get to talking. Mrs. Waverly'd laugh and say they were both over her head. The judge must've seen something he liked in Laura, too—"

So he's had a long-time interest in teenage girls, Jordan thought cynically.

"—because finally when she finished high school, he was the one paid for her to go to court reporter school in Chicago."

"But she came back."

"Well, after a year or two, the judge had become judge, the old judge's court reporter wanted to retire, too, and there was nobody to take her place. So Laura came back."

"Returning the favor," Jordan said. "So Laura and the judge go back a long way."

"That's how small towns are, Mr. Marshall. There's only a few of us out here on the frontier, every time you reach out, you bump the same people. Everybody's got more than one connection."

"I guess every place is a small town in that regard," Jordan mused.

"That so? Mmm. What's Laura's connection to your case, by the way?"

"Oh, well," Jordan stammered, "just trying to get to know the players, you know."

"Mmm huh. So you're from San Antonio, is that right? You have a family there, Mr. Marshall?"

Jordan realized his obligation, and he fulfilled it. He'd used up some of Mrs. Johnson's store of gossip, and he owed her a refill. But he kept Laura's name out of it. Not that he expected her to be spared the gossip mill's workings.

"I've found out where adults go on dates around here," he announced at Laura's front door a few minutes later. "A place called Barney's, just across—"

"—the county line." To Jordan's knowing look, Laura said high-mindedly, "Well, one has heard stories."

"And just so your reputation won't suffer besmirchment, I've brought us a pair of cunning disguises." He handed Laura Groucho Marx glasses and stuck a bright red clown nose on the end of his own.

Laura laughed appreciatively. "But they'll still know you're a lawyer," she said.

"Come on," he urged.

Laura looked down and swallowed. "Listen, Jordan, I've been thinking . . ."

Such an announcement always precedes bad news. Jordan was instantly somber. "Don't," he said.

Laura pressed on stubbornly. There was a sheen across her eyes. "This isn't a good time for us," she said.

"No, but if not for all this, we wouldn't have met at all." Laura shook her head. Jordan found his voice going higher, out of his control, saying things he hadn't thought. "Look! I don't care. I know it's bad timing. I know it might not work out! Let's find out. Hurt me if you want to. Break my heart. But don't back away because you're afraid."

He thought the challenge would stir her. But Laura just stared at him, her expression turning from sad to angry to, perhaps, fond. He saw her turning inward again, and he reached for her hand.

"That would have been touching," Laura said, "if not for this."

She reached and pulled the clown nose off his face.

"It gives me a touch of mystery, doesn't it?" Jordan said, striving for a lighter tone.

Laura smiled. It wasn't much of a smile. She only did it for him. "I—" she began but didn't seem to have any idea where the sentence was supposed to go. Jordan remembered the rigidity of her face the first time he'd seen her in court. If he hadn't lived through the last few weeks, he wouldn't have known this was the same person. Laura struggled to compose her face and failed.

"Come on," Jordan said quietly. "You have to eat. Keep your strength up."

He pulled at her hand very gently, but standing undecided on the cusp as Laura was, that was all it took.

Barney's offered chicken-fried steak and long-neck beers. There were other items on the menu, but the waitress didn't approve of anyone's ordering them. There was a separate dining room, but Jordan and Laura sat in the main room, a big room, mostly dance floor. Along two walls were booths, dark under an overhang; across the room was a long bar for people who wanted to drink under the lights. At seven o'clock on a Thursday night there were only three or four people at the bar, men in work shirts and plaid shirts and work boots and cowboy boots, but the booths were pretty well filled. There were rustlings all around them, and the waitress spent longer at the other booths than she did at Laura and Jordan's, joking with regular customers. Laura looked around and took a deep breath. The familiarity of the scene seemed to restore her.

"So you met Mrs. Johnson? She must know everything then."

Jordan shook his head. "I covered very well. You're doing a transcript for me."

"And we needed to discuss it over Lone Stars."

"She doesn't know where we went," Jordan protested.

Laura laughed pleasantly.

"Well, we'll just have to come out in the open then," Jordan said easily. When Laura didn't respond, he switched subjects. "What's new in town since my last visit?"

"They fixed the birdbath."

"The spring flows. I had more in mind court news."

Laura shrugged. "What could be new?"

There were three couples on the dance floor, standing out like as many ants on a windowpane. "You do partner dancing, too?" Jordan asked.

Laura glanced contemptuously at the floor. "Oh, please."

"Come on, earn your chicken-fried steak." He pulled her out of the dark booth, looking at the men in their hats holding puffy women close against their chests. "As long as it's not—"

Just as they stepped onto the floor, the band finished the slow song and started a two-step. "Oh, hell," Jordan said.

"What's the matter?" Laura called over the noise. "Can't do it?"

They stepped. Two-stepped. He got to hold her but not close, and he had to pay too much attention to his feet to enjoy it. But Laura's enthusiasm made up for his lack. Her face shone. At the end, the scattering of applause was for her. They fell back into their booth, Jordan gratefully, to find their food growing cold.

"The two-step," Jordan grumbled. "The most unromantic dance ever invented."

"This is Texas, pal. Dancing's for exercise, not romance."

More beer improved Jordan's disposition. By nine o'clock the food was long behind them, the dance floor was more than half full, people moved from booth to booth. If Laura wasn't a regular at Barney's, she was certainly a community favorite. Jordan was introduced to three couples from Green Hills, including the mayor and his wife, and said hey to a few people he'd interviewed. They were much friendlier when he was off-duty, or did Laura legitimize him? He wished she weren't quite so popular. He wanted to hold her hand across the table and talk quietly. He watched the side of her animated face, saw her glance his way, saw her smile expand a notch, and he brightened with the hope that some of her animation was for him. Between dances and visitors, they did touch hands lightly.

"Tell me about the judge," Jordan said. "Is he—?"

"Here's a slow one," Laura said, pulling him out of the booth. Jordan decided not to talk business. But business was all he knew about her. Asking about anyone else in town could be construed as related to the case. Instead he breathed the scent of her hair and murmured her name. When she looked up at him, he only said, "I'm glad you came back. From Chicago."

When they returned to the booth, there was a man behind Jordan's beer. "Excuse me, I think you're in my seat," Jordan said politely before he realized Laura had stiffened beside him.

"Funny, that's what I was gonna say to you," Harry Briggs said. Man, he had a voice like he was speaking from the bottom of an oil drum. Jordan realized liquor had deepened it and wondered how long the cop had been in Barney's. Jordan hadn't recognized him at first because he was out of uniform, wearing a short-sleeved blue shirt that let the forest of hair at his neckline breathe freely.

"Woncha sit down, Laura?" Briggs rumbled, looking at her intently.

Laura, still holding Jordan's hand, tugged at it. "Let's go have a drink at the bar," she said quietly.

Jordan didn't even see Briggs's hand move before it was clamped on the lawyer's wrist. "No, me 'n' your frien' here have to talk," Briggs said.

"Did you think of more details of the investigation you wanted to share with me, Officer?"

" 'Not an officer right now," Briggs said, standing, which he had to move out from under the overhang to do. "I wanta talk to you man to man. 'Course"—looking over Jordan's head, Briggs smiled down at Laura, who looked away—"you might need to get somebody to hold up your end."

"That's amusing," Jordan said. "We'll pass that one on to the folks at the bar." He tugged ineffectually at his captive arm, which seemed to have the effect of pumping blood into Harry Briggs's face.

"You don't understand," Briggs said, leaning into Jordan's face. "*You're* leaving. She's staying here."

"Oh, is that what this is about?" Jordan stepped back, lifting his hands. Briggs let him go. Jordan made an offering gesture in Laura's direction. "Take her."

Briggs looked puzzled and suspicious. Laura's reaction was more verbal.

"What?! Just who the hell do you think you are?" she said to Jordan. "You're not *giving* me to this jerk or anybody else. If you *own* anybody around here, I don't know who it would be. You don't even—"

"See?" Jordan said amiably to Harry Briggs. "What's the point of you and me fighting? Suppose you win, suppose you beat the hell out of me? You can't win her, she's not a prize. If she doesn't want to go with you, she still won't. Suppose I get in a couple of lucky punches and *I* beat *you* up? And say Laura liked me better, but she doesn't like seeing me fight over her? But she still doesn't like you either, so she walks out on both of us. Then where are we? Both sore and got nothing to show for it. You show me where the advantage is in it for either one of us and I'll fight you. But until then, what's the point? Scuffling around like kids on a playground. I ask you."

As Laura had fallen silent, Briggs had transferred his bewildered attention to Jordan. Jordan spoke more confidently as he saw that the big cop was still mad but was growing sullenly immobile under the flow of the lawyer's words. Jordan stopped with a reasonable, questioning expression.

"Laura?" Briggs said.

"No, Harry," she said firmly. Briggs returned his attention to Jordan, looming like a leaning wall.

"You're right," Briggs said. Jordan smiled. "No sense fighting you over her."

Jordan didn't even see his fist draw back, so it was like a sudden attack of appendicitis, the pain blossoming in his stomach, growing like a fuel-fed fire, spreading to his throat, making him feel as if his limbs had dropped off, pain an amazing, all-consuming, never-ending presence in his body. Jordan was down on his knees, trying not to vomit, before he even realized that Briggs had punched him.

"That's just for being a fucking smart-mouth lawyer," Briggs snarled down at the prostrate form. Then in a little-boy voice, "Laura?"

Laura pushed him out of the way. Jordan grew vaguely aware that she was beside him on the floor, touching him hesitantly, afraid to hurt him. "It's okay," Jordan mumbled but ran out of breath, and when he tried to draw more, the pain in his abdomen drew fuel again.

It had been years since he'd been struck and never by a grown man. It was amazing what adult muscle and fury could do to unprotected flesh.

"That's the trouble with being a silver-tongued devil," Jordan said in the parking lot as Laura helped him toward the car. "When somebody can't keep up with your wit and logic, he has to respond some other way."

"We'd better go to the hospital," Laura said worriedly. "You might be hurt bad. He might've ruptured your stomach lining or something."

"Yeah. Maybe I can't straighten up. Maybe I'll need a cane to walk. You still got your cane?"

"Shut up." But then Laura started laughing. "Just shut up about my cane."

They leaned together against the trunk of the car. Laura's face was close to Jordan's. "I can see why somebody'd want to slug you," she said fondly.

"I don't think hospitalization will be necessary," Jordan said, putting his hand on her cheek. "Maybe if you just keep me under observation for the next twenty-four hours or so."

Laura laughed while she kissed him, a pleasant rumble of lips. They tumbled into the car together. Jordan protested when Laura insisted on driving, but that turned out okay, it let him lie with his head on her lap. Occasionally she stroked his hair back from his hot head, and when he murmured appreciatively, he could feel her leg vibrating along with his throat.

"Mrs. Johnson'll love this," Laura said.

"I'm kind of enjoying it myself," Jordan agreed.

"This is where I come those times when I'm not in San Antonio," Jordan explained as he drove down Green Hill's Main Street with Ashley in the carseat beside him. She looked around sleepily, lower lip outthrust.

It was Saturday, the heavy shopping day, they had so far seen five people on the streets. Jordan couldn't have explained why he wanted to bring Ashley to Green Hills on his weekend with her. He would have said it was something different, like a living amusement park, if she could only see the possibilities of the town. But the way he felt, as he pointed out the hardware store and the antique store and Main Plaza with its statueless pedestal, was as if he were bringing his daughter to see his old hometown.

"That's where I'm going to be working," he said of the courthouse as he parked close by. The old red courthouse looked avuncular and unthreatening on the weekend. "Remember when you came to see me at my office in the courthouse in San Antonio?"

"No," Ashley said a little petulantly, as if he'd put something over on her.

"Well, you were"—he counted—"eight months old."

He walked with his daughter back up Main Street, enjoying the feeling. A couple of older women and a man in overalls said grave hellos; Jordan didn't think they would have spoken if he'd been alone. The man knelt and shook Ashley's hand, and afterward Ashley opened it to display a quarter.

"Magic," Jordan said.

"No, that man gave it to me."

The old farmer, a stranger, winked at Jordan as he walked on. "Honey," Jordan said, "when a stranger gives you money for no reason, that's magic."

They strolled to the antique store to find that its lunchroom was only open weekdays, but Ashley stayed to admire a handmade rocking horse and a child-sized table. Stepping back, Jordan almost bumped into a man who, as they both excused themselves, revealed himself to be Judge Waverly.

"Mr. Marshall."

"Hello, Judge. This is my daughter, Ashley."

Waverly didn't stoop as the old farmer had done; he gave Ashley an initial once-over but then fastened his attention on Jordan. "Pretty girl," he said perfunctorily.

"Thank you. She doesn't get it from me. Do you have children, Your Honor?"

"Mrs. Waverly and I were never blessed."

Before asking the question Jordan had glanced at the judge's hands and noted the simple wedding ring. On his right hand the judge wore a more elaborate ring, something like a class ring. Jordan wondered if it represented membership in some quasi-secret society.

"I've seen a great many children pass through my courtroom, though," Judge Waverly continued. He was watching Ashley intently now, with a more kindly air and a note of longing in his voice. The child found the judge less interesting than the rocking horse. "In person or on paper. And I see what happens too many times afterward, the father just abandons them. I've never understood how a man could rest at night, knowing his child was growing up somewhere in the world without him."

Jordan had to swallow his sudden anger. "That would be hard," he said tightly.

"Well." The judge nodded politely, reached as if to touch Ashley, then turned away. Jordan wondered, seeing him retreat, if he would have guessed the tall silver-haired man in short sleeves and wrinkled pants was a judge, and thought he would. There had been an added dash of humanity in the judge's Saturdayness, though. Even through his sudden anger, Jordan had felt that the man might be on the verge of opening up to him. Instead, he'd offered advice.

Jordan was eating with Ashley in the diner—she'd reluctantly agreed to try the fried chicken and french fries, and Jordan's hamburger had grown cold as he pulled the chicken into boneless bites—when Laura came in. She stood at the counter in profile to him and asked the cook by name for an iced tea. Jordan hadn't phoned to tell her he was coming. He'd hoped to run into her just like this, catch her unawares in her native habitat, but now he had another reason for talking to her. "Ms. Stefone," he called softly.

She turned, not surprised to hear her name called, but surprised and pleased to see Jordan, then frowned slightly and shot a glance across the booth to see, he thought—wondered, hoped—if he was with another woman.

"Well, this must be Ashley."

"No, this is Ashley's evil twin, Hepzibah."

"No, I'm not," Ashley said. "Hi." Laura was the first person in Green Hills she'd spoken to.

"Hello," Laura said pleasantly, her voice not changing from its usual timbre. "How's the chicken today?"

"It's okay. Want some?"

Laura didn't glance at Jordan until there was a natural pause in her conversation with the child, then she raised her eyes. "Hello, Mr. Marshall."

"Hello, Ms. Stefone. I brought Ashley to see your town."

"I hope she approves. Well, I'll get my tea."

"I'll be right back, darling." Jordan followed Laura to the counter, where he said in a suddenly harsh voice, "I really don't appreciate you talking to the judge about my personal life."

"What?" Laura looked utterly baffled.

"I saw him just now. He seemed to know I was divorced and that I might not be as close to Ashley as I want. I didn't tell you that so you could pass it on to him."

Laura shook her head. She didn't get mad in return, but there was a sudden reserve about her. "I haven't said a word to the judge about your marriage or your child."

"Then how did he know? You're the only one I've told."

"Are you sure?"

Jordan had to wonder. Had he mentioned to Mrs. Johnson that he was divorced? Had Mrs. McElroy gotten it out of him without his noticing, or Helen Evers? "Maybe he just figured it out," Laura added. "You don't wear a ring."

"Some married men don't. And he wasn't studying my hand." But Jordan was no longer angry. He was curious.

Laura said firmly, "I don't talk to people about you, Jordan. I let them talk." He shrugged an apology. Laura softened. "Beautiful little girl, Jordan."

"She's smarter than she is pretty."

"Sorry, I didn't mean to insult her."

Jordan looked sheepish. He still had some undirected anger to work off. "I don't know if pretty is even any good for a girl," he said.

Laura smiled. "But smart is?" She reached for him but stopped. "So I guess you're driving back to San Antonio soon?"

"Yes. I have Ashley until tomorrow." He waited. "But I could come back after that."

"That would be nice."

"If you asked me," Jordan concluded, suddenly wanting more from her than smiling acquiescence.

Laura's eyes were suddenly moist and so warm and lonely and honest that he thought she'd reached out and held him. "Didn't you hear me ask?" she said.

It was the first night Laura opened her windows. She got up and stood beside one of the bedroom windows, looking out into her backyard and the fields beyond. "They said we're going to get an early cool front," she said. She laughed. "I think I feel it."

She was dressed perfectly to appreciate any stray breeze, in nothing. Jordan rose on his elbow and watched her. Moonlight turned her into a classical statue, illuminating her face and chest and long, strong legs and leaving dark hollows beneath her breasts and below her navel. When she rested her hands on the windowsill and lifted her head to cool her neck, he appreciated the play of muscles in her back and the confident curve of her buttocks. He muttered an appreciative blasphemy.

Laura might not have heard him. Jordan joined her at the window, moving so swiftly she didn't have time to turn. His hands insisted on enfolding those curves. He kissed the junction of her shoulders and neck. She leaned her head back against him, and when she turned, he felt moisture on his temple.

"My God, what's wrong?"

Her cheeks were streaked with tears. She smiled at him, her smile looking very bright with the wetness of her eyes. "Nothing," she said. "Nothing."

"Is it—?" He didn't feel quite intimate enough with her to ask about the time of the month. "Are you—?"

"It's nothing," Laura insisted, laughing. "I'm just happy, Jordan."

"I can tell."

"I'm *too* happy. I hate being happy, then you have nowhere to go but down."

"God, that's a wonderful philosophy."

She sat on the windowsill, legs spread, and pulled him close. "Are *you* happy?" she asked teasingly.

He thought about it. "I am. I'm ecstatic. This is terrible. You know we might both be at the peak of our lives right this minute, and any second we'll start sliding down."

"That's right." She was still smiling. "So let's prolong the moment," she said with a strange emphasis that made him laugh nervously. "Can you waltz?"

"The question is whether I can move."

She slid off the sill, against him. Jordan held her tightly as they circled the room, Laura humming. The ceiling fan hummed along. They could feel the currents it stirred. They felt the length of each other's bodies. Jordan lifted Laura to kiss her, then held her there, hands under her thighs, her arms and legs around him. He felt her nipples tighten against his chest. Laura kissed him, hard, reaching. She was no longer crying.

Later, as he lay in bed beside Laura, their hands entangling or falling softly on each other's legs, the thin curtains puffed inward with the first breath of fall that had traveled so far to reach south Texas. Jordan felt the brave little breeze on his chest.

"There it is," Laura said, "the cool front. My goodness, isn't it refreshing?"

Jordan could picture the front of Laura's house, with the narrow porch behind its railing and the dark green shutters. He could picture the street, the town, the countryside, as if he belonged there, as if he'd spent his whole life among them. It felt right to be there.

But tomorrow they would all be arrayed against him again, because tomorrow the trial started. And he still didn't know anything he needed to know.

"I guess you were one of the first people to hear about Jenny's death," he said, an intrusive observation in the soft dimness. But Laura answered easily.

"No, I wasn't even here. We closed the court early that day, a case that had been supposed to go to trial settled at the last minute, and I went to Corpus Christi to take a deposition."

"They don't have court reporters in Corpus?"

"It was for a local lawyer, Don Myers, and he wanted to show up with his own court reporter, make himself look important. You know the type."

Jordan smiled and knew she was smiling with him. It hadn't even crossed his mind to suspect Laura—the killing had been too physical—but somehow he was comforted to know she hadn't even been part of the scene the day of the murders.

"Jordan," Laura said, rising on her elbow, "what are you going to do?"

For answer he pulled her across him. There was a spot on her neck he hadn't yet kissed. A tender, delicious spot. "I thought we might get something to eat," he said, mouth so close to hers she must have felt his voice, "keep our strength up, maybe have a shower together, then end up right back here."

"I meant tomorrow," Laura said indulgently. Her legs moved across his.

"Tomorrow, too, if you want," he said.

9

Yeah, nuke 'em, that's right, Emilio. They're not all in Iraq or Iran, you know."

"What's he saying?" Cindy Garcia asked, coming in from her office.

Jordan filled her in. "The political scientist here thinks we should just nuke the Mideast out of existence."

"Just take care of all of 'em at once," the bailiff emphasized.

"But you can't, that's what I'm saying. They're all over the world, Emilio. Some of 'em are right here, and what do you think they'd do? Like to see the Mercantile Building go up in smoke?" Jordan was naming the tallest building in Green Hills.

"Aw, they wouldn't come here," the bailiff said. "Maybe blow up a few New Yorkers, but how bad is that?"

"Emilio!" Cindy exclaimed. "That's racist."

"That's not racist," Emilio defended himself. "Hating Mexicans is racist, 'cause I have to be a Mexican. Nobody has to live in New York."

Laura was there, too, but she wasn't joining in. Jordan thought she was looking at him the way a mother looks at her child on the first day of school. He wished he had some way to reassure her that he knew what he was doing.

He needed to reassure Wayne, too. He could feel the uneasiness of his client beside him as he listened to Jordan bantering with the court staff, including the prosecutor a few minutes ago. Wayne surely didn't understand that making friends with one's adversary was sometimes part of the job.

Jordan leaned over and whispered to him, "You know your part?" Wayne nodded, but Jordan explained again. "We won't get to you today, you just have to listen. And if you hear something that doesn't sound right to you, write me a note. And for God's sake, don't get mad. Getting mad is what got you here today."

"Okay," Wayne said tightly. It probably hadn't been real to him until today, the idea that he was going to be judged. He was very stiff in his white shirt and tie. His eyes stared even when there was nothing to see.

Jordan didn't stiffen until the jury panel was brought into the room. That's when the case becomes real for the lawyers. One second the lawyers could be joking with each other and with the judge, but when the civilians came trooping in, the lawyers were on duty. Their chairs were turned to face the potential jurors, who came into the audience section of the courtroom expectantly or nervously or irritably.

Judge Waverly's voice came over Jordan's shoulder, welcoming the potential jurors and immediately beginning to instruct them. Jordan had heard judges who fawned over jury panels, which after all were composed of registered voters. There was none of that in Judge Waverly's voice. They were in his courtroom now and they would all do as he said, everyone within the sound of his voice, which fell with particular heaviness on Jordan's ear.

But the jury panel was not what he would have expected three months ago when he first thought of their threat. They were not the unitary, unfamiliar entity Jordan had pictured. Among the thirty-two prospective jurors, he knew one or two, he had met them while investigating. One stood out vividly; Jordan winced at the sight of her. Other faces were vaguely familiar. Jordan wasn't one of them, but he was no longer the total stranger in town either. A few of them studied him frankly. Behind them, Evers of the *Register* gave Jordan a welcoming smile.

When the individual questioning began, however, it soon became clear that this trial would hark back to the early days of trials, when the only people who could serve on a jury were those already familiar with the case.

"Sure," was the most common answer when each prospective juror was asked whether he or she had heard of the murder of Kevin Wainwright. When asked the follow-up question, whether they had formed an opinion as to who had committed the murder, the consensus was summed up by one rail-thin man with his shirtsleeves rolled up who appeared surprised by the question but waved a long finger at Wayne and said, "Well, it was him, wasn't it? Isn't that why he's here?"

It began to look as if Mike Arriendez might not be able to get a jury, but he managed to "rehabilitate" most of these prospective jurors by explaining the presumption of innocence and getting them to agree, sometimes reluctantly and with their sincerity in doubt, that they could put aside whatever they'd heard and render a fair verdict.

Jordan questioned them further on the subject, but that only got their backs up and made them declare even more adamantly that they wouldn't pay any attention to the stories they'd heard. Sure they could be fair. The written record that Laura was compiling behind him would show no reason why these panelists shouldn't serve on the jury, but some of them had gleams in their eyes. They'd put one over on the big-city lawyer.

Finally Jordan came to the centerpiece of the jury panel. She smiled confidently at him, serenely awaiting his questions with her hands in her lap.

Jordan didn't ask any of the standard questions. He began abruptly with a question that killed her smile. "Can I trust you, Mrs. McElroy?"

He didn't wait for an answer. "I'm not singling you out, I'm using you as an example. You've heard stories about this case, haven't you? All of you have. Do you understand that those stories count for nothing now? That before you can be a juror in this case, you have to understand that you don't know anything yet? Because those stories aren't evidence. They only become evidence when someone gets up here on this witness stand and swears to God to tell the truth and then tells you what he or she saw. Not heard, saw. And even then it's not evidence unless you believe the person. Unless you believe that he was able to see what he says, that his opinion hasn't been distorted by what he heard later or what he thought he *should* be seeing."

Jordan paced in front of them, making individual eye contact. They were very quiet, perhaps with the first realization that before they got to judge anyone they were going to be under the microscope themselves.

"Because we know what stories are worth, don't we? They get passed from person to person and the story changes a little bit every time it changes hands, sometimes just accidentally and sometimes because one of the people passing on the story *wants* to put a little different spin on it, because of the way he or she feels about somebody in the story, because of something that happened years ago. Or maybe just because people want a story to be good."

That was something they understood well. The certainty in their eyes changed subjects.

"So all that is garbage," Jordan said fiercely. "What you have to understand and be able to say is that everything starts anew in this room. Nothing has happened yet. We don't know anything. Because before you can be a juror, you have to take an oath, too. You have to swear to God that you won't consider anything except what you hear people say from this witness stand and any physical evidence we bring you. Can you do that, Mrs. McElroy? Can I trust you to do that?"

"You certainly can," the old lady said righteously. "If I was on this jury, I'd want to know the truth, not just what people say."

Jordan smiled at her. To his surprise, it had begun to happen—something that hadn't happened to him since he was a prosecutor. Jordan felt the power descend on him. The power expressed itself physically—in the deepening of his breath, in the way his suit seemed to fit tighter, and his peripheral vision was improved—but that wasn't its source. The wellspring of the power was his sudden certainty that he was right. That he had justice on his side. The sense of moral clarity both energized and calmed him.

Jordan spoke carefully, aware that this sense of power had played him false in the past. He was his own best audience: He always convinced himself if no one else. Behind the jury panel, across from Helen Evers, he saw Wayne's parents. Mrs. Orkney watched him shrewdly. She knew perfectly well that the out-of-town lawyer had no particular interest in her son. She could only hope that something about the case would inspire him in spite of his disinterest.

"Let me ask you something else, Mrs. McElroy. Have you heard anything about the murder of Jenny Fecklewhite?"

"Objection. Irrelevant."

Both lawyers turned toward the judge. "The two cases are inextricably entwined, Your Honor."

"I don't believe so, Mr. Marshall." Judge Waverly spoke without emphasis, apparently unconcerned.

"In the public mind they are, Your Honor."

"The objection is sustained."

Jordan resumed his seat. Mrs. McElroy had an eager-to-help expression if he could only get to her.

"Have you heard about another murder," Jordan asked, "that took place here in Green Hills the same day as Kevin Wainwright's?"

"Objection."

"Sustained."

Jordan drummed his fingers. "Let me put it this way, Mrs. McElroy. From what you've heard and read, do you believe that the same person killed both Kevin Wainwright and Jenny Fecklewhite?"

"Objection. It's not relevant."

"May we approach the bench, Your Honor?" Jordan was already doing so, walking stiffly. At the bench they all leaned their heads close, including Laura, to make the record. Jordan's first words were fierce. "Your Honor, this trial will be a foregone conclusion if I'm not allowed to ask these questions. In order to intelligently exercise the defense's peremptory strikes on the panel, I have to know which of them already believes that my client is a double murderer.

If they've already convicted him in their minds of Jenny Fecklewhite's murder, it won't matter what the evidence in this trial shows."

Judge Waverly leaned forward and spoke as if giving comfort. "At the conclusion of the evidence, I will instruct the jury to consider only the evidence in this case."

"You'll instruct them, Your Honor, but the question is whether they can obey that instruction. That's what I need to ask."

Still Jordan looked for a sign in the judge's face. *Don't you want to know yourself? Don't you* want *me to solve Jenny's murder?*

"That's denied," the judge said kindly.

"I object."

Judge Waverly's face dropped into its habitual sternness. "Did I make a mistake, Mr. Marshall? I appointed you to this case because I thought you were an experienced trial lawyer. You led me to believe you understood the law."

Maybe you did make a mistake, Jordan thought.

His questioning of the jury panel was perfunctory after the bench conference. Wayne leaned over once to say, "That guy hates me, he's owed me twenty dollars for two years." Jordan made a silent mark on the jury list. No other words passed between him and his client.

In the end, he didn't have the nerve to leave Mrs. McElroy on the jury. She was too strong a personality; if she turned against him, she'd lead others. When Cindy called out the names of the jurors who had been chosen, and passed over Mrs. McElroy to name the woman behind her, Jordan looked at Mrs. McElroy in surprise, as if to say, *Gee, I guess the other side must have struck you.* Mrs. McElroy remained huffily in her seat when the unchosen panelists were dismissed with the court's thanks, and the lawyers turned their chairs around to face front.

"How do you plead?"

Wayne stood straight, but his voice was shaky. "Not guilty, sir."

"Mr. Arriendez, do you have an opening statement?"

The district attorney spoke earnestly and at some length,

explaining what he expected his evidence to prove and what he did not have to prove.

"That's right," Jordan said when it was his turn. "The State doesn't have to prove motive. But if they don't, what have they proven? The defendant is charged with murder, which means he intended to kill someone and he did it in what we used to call cold blood. If he had a good reason for what he did, then it wasn't murder. If he was so consumed with rage that he couldn't help himself, for good reason, *that's* not murder. If he had no intention of killing anyone, that's not murder either. So if the State doesn't show you something of what was in Wayne Orkney's mind when he attacked Kevin Wainwright, they haven't proven their case."

Jordan hurried on. "Wayne's state of mind is one of the defenses we expect to bring up. We also intend to suggest that someone else might actually have killed Kevin Wainwright after he was supposedly safe in the hospital. And remember, the defense can throw out as many theories as we want. Because we don't have the burden of proving anything. The State does. Their case has to tie up all the loose ends; it has to satisfy all your questions. Otherwise what's left is reasonable doubt, and your verdict will have to be not guilty."

The jurors listened politely. The district attorney began his case.

"Where were you, Joyce, when you first saw the defendant here that July fifteenth?"

"I was getting into my car in front of the Kwik Wash," the twenty-eight-year-old math teacher said precisely. Perhaps she had felt compelled to come to court as a clichéd version of her life in a prim print dress buttoned to the neck and harsh dark-rimmed glasses. The glasses turned her pale eyes into huge aqueous doorknobs. "I was still standing with my car door open when there was a screech of brakes and I almost choked in the dust. Wayne Orkney had just stopped his pickup right behind me, sideways, blocking my car, and he jumped out."

"How did he appear?"

"I thought he was going to hurt *me*. His face was red, the cords were standing out in his neck, and he screamed, 'I'm going to kill you!' I thought he meant me, and I ducked into my car."

"What happened then?" Arriendez asked.

"Oh, he just ignored me. That was when I noticed that Kevin was passing on the sidewalk. He was the one Wayne had screamed at."

"Kevin—?" Mike Arriendez asked easily.

"Wainwright. Wayne's friend. Actually I relaxed a little when I saw Kevin, because I knew he and Wayne were friends, and I thought for a minute they were just playing around, the way boys do, but then Wayne ran up and hit Kevin very hard right in the face. Kevin fell back against the wall—I was afraid he was going to go through the plate glass window of the Kwik Wash—and then Wayne hit him again."

"Did they exchange any words?" the prosecutor asked.

Joyce Livingston shook her head doubtfully, not liking to let imprecision creep into her testimony. "I don't think I heard either of them say anything else after that, but they were rolling around on the ground on top of each other, and other people were running up and there was shouting ..."

"Did you see the defendant hit Kevin again?"

"Oh, yes."

"How many times?"

"At least five or six. Probably more."

"Hard blows, like the first one you saw?"

"Very hard," the teacher said, wincing with the memory.

"Your witness," the DA said with what Jordan thought was a note of satisfaction.

"Hello, Ms. Livingston, my name is Jordan Marshall, I'm representing Wayne Orkney here—"

"I remember you, Mr. Marshall." She smiled warily, politeness prevailing over apprehension.

"Good. Now, Ms. Livingston, if I don't make myself clear, please ask me to repeat or put the question differently. I don't want to confuse you."

"All right."

"Now, while this fight was going on, did you stay in your car?"

She blinked hugely behind the lenses. Her arms moved, trying to recreate her actions. "I believe I did. It happened so quickly. I got out some time to see if I could help, but I believe that was afterward."

Jordan asked kindly, "So you saw the fight through your windshield or a side window of the car?"

"Yes, sir. The windshield."

"Were you wearing your glasses?"

There was a faint collective sigh from the audience, relief that Jordan had asked the obvious question. Jordan half-turned surreptitiously and saw out of the corner of his eye that the jury panel had been replaced in the spectator seats by a small crowd that more than half-filled the benches.

"I always wear my glasses," Ms. Livingston said. "I can't see three feet without them."

"All right. But you were looking through the windshield, you said, over the hood of your car, so once Wayne and Kevin fell to the ground and were—What did you say?—wrestling around?"

Joyce Livingston nodded.

"—you couldn't see them any more, could you?"

The witness blinked again perplexedly. "But I could," she said. "I can still picture it."

"You can imagine it," Jordan said patiently, "but how could you actually have seen it? Once they had fallen below the level of the car hood, your line of sight—"

"I understand angles," the math teacher said sharply, because Jordan was intruding on her thoughts. He let her sit and try to work it out, hands moving vaguely as if shifting playing pieces around a board. "I suppose," she finally said slowly, "that's when I got out of the car and came around to the front."

"Are you sure?"

"It must have been," she said, "because I saw it."

"All right." Jordan didn't press her, he just let the jury see her uncertainty. "From the portion of the fight you did see, Ms. Livingston, did you see Kevin hit back at Wayne?"

"No, I never did."

"Never?" Jordan asked. "You never saw him hit Wayne at all? Was Kevin unconscious then, from the first punch?"

"No, sir. He stayed on his feet for a while, and he put up his hands but only to try to protect himself."

Jordan was not altogether displeased with this testimony. It sounded so unbelievable it called the rest of Joyce Livingston's answers into question. At least that was the defense lawyer's reaction.

"Let's go back to the very beginning, Ms. Livingston. What were the exact words that you heard Wayne shout when he first pulled up?"

" 'I'm going to kill you,' " Ms. Livingston said distinctly.

"Have you ever threatened to kill anyone, Ms. Livingston?"

"No, sir."

"No?" Jordan said amazedly. "Aren't you a teacher?" There was a titter behind him. Judge Waverly's stern eyes sought its source, and the titter died.

"Yes, I am," Ms. Livingston said.

"And you've never said, even to yourself, 'I'm going to kill that kid if he smarts off to me again'? Or words to that effect?"

"No, sir."

"You have remarkable patience," Jordan said and before Arriendez could object hastened to say, "I just want to take up one more topic, Ms. Livingston. You said Wayne screeched his truck to a stop. Which direction was it coming from?"

Joyce Livingston's hands moved again. "From the west," she said confidently.

"You were on Main Street about two blocks from where we sit today, and Wayne was coming from the opposite direction, is that right? What lies in that direction, Ms. Livingston? Where might Wayne have been coming from?"

"Objection," the prosecutor stood to say. "Calls for speculation."

Testing, testing. Some lawyers got too nervous during trial to object or couldn't think fast enough. Mike Arriendez was obviously not one of those. Jordan rose and said innocently, "I'm just trying to set the scene, Your Honor. So the jury can picture it."

The judge studied Jordan untrustingly. "Briefly," he said.

"What landmarks lie in the direction Wayne was coming from, Ms. Livingston?"

The witness had had time to compile a mental list. "Well, the Texaco where Wayne worked sometimes. The interstate. Any number of places. The hospital, the park."

"Pleasant Grove Park?" Jordan seized on the answer, and Mike Arriendez gathered his feet under him. "Do you know what had happened in Pleasant Grove Park earlier that afternoon?"

"Objection, Your Honor. Irrelevant."

"It's relevant to the defense," Jordan said testily.

"Sustained," was Judge Waverly's only reply.

They let Ms. Livingston go on her way. Jordan thought he had done a nice job of undermining the reliability of her recollection of the fight, but he had a lot more undermining to do, because as the prosecution called witness after witness, it began to appear that Wayne had beaten his best friend in front of half the population of the town. Joyce Livingston had not been the only person getting her laundry done on a summer weekday afternoon. Mike Arriendez called three other women who'd been inside the laundromat and seen at least part of the fight. He called shopkeepers and shopkeepers' customers, the people who'd watched the beating and the men who had broken it up. And all of their testimony agreed, more or less, with Joyce Livingston's.

"How many times did you see Kevin hit back at Wayne?" Jordan asked.

"Not any," said Hiram Lester, the hardware store owner.

"Now, Mr. Lester"—Jordan let exasperation be apparent in his voice—"have you seen very many fights?"

"A few." Lester looked quite at ease in the witness stand, as if he were sitting around his store.

"Have you ever seen another one like you've just described, where a man just let himself get beaten up and didn't try to defend himself?"

"Don't believe I have. It was unique. 'Course, I didn't catch the beginning of this one."

But witnesses who had caught the beginning of this one claimed not to have seen Kevin throw any punches either, though, as is always true, the eyewitnesses didn't agree on details. One man said he'd seen Kevin get in a punch or two. One woman thought she'd seen him claw Wayne's face. But Jordan had his client's arrest photo in the file before him, and though Wayne had looked disheveled and dusty, he hadn't had a mark on his face. After a while, after Jordan's questions had raised the issue, Mike Arriendez thought of introducing the photo to show just that. Jordan objected, but the photograph of a relatively undamaged Wayne was admitted into evidence.

After the first witness, Judge Waverly no longer let Jordan "set the scene" by asking what local landmarks lay in the direction from which Wayne had been driving just before the beating, but Jordan continued to ask each witness whether he or she knew what had happened in Pleasant Grove Park earlier that afternoon. After the third time the district attorney's objection was sustained, Jordan approached the bench in a huff. He kept his voice down, but the ferocity of its tone might have carried to the jury. "Your Honor, I have to object to the court's not allowing me to get into this perfectly relevant line of questioning."

Judge Waverly asked mildly, "Is this going to be a lengthy, heated objection?"

"Yes, sir."

"Then we'll do it in chambers." Raising his voice, the judge ordered a ten-minute recess and in a rapid swirl of robe led the procession to his office. Mike Arriendez and Laura carrying her transcribing machine followed quietly in Jordan's wake. Jordan didn't offer to help Laura. He'd scrupulously avoided casting any significant glances in her direction since trial had begun. Laura wouldn't have caught them anyway. Her face had been turned resolutely to the far windows, wearing its mannequin blankness. Her only animation was in her fingers.

"Your Honor," Jordan began reasonably once the judge's

office door had closed behind them, "this line of questioning that you won't let me pursue is essential to the defense. It goes to the defendant's state of mind. What Wayne Orkney found in Pleasant Grove Park was the sole cause of what he did to Kevin Wainwright."

"There's no evidence of that," Mike Arriendez said.

"I'll provide the evidence. It's not going to promote court efficiency to have to recall all these witnesses after I do. Furthermore," he added hastily before the judge could rule, "because the court prevented me from asking the jurors during voir dire whether they thought my client guilty of Jenny Fecklewhite's murder, I now have to prove to their satisfaction that he did *not* kill her."

Silence followed the sudden stopping of Jordan's voice. Jordan had turned his attention solely on the judge, who sat slightly slumped behind his desk. His eyes were on Jordan. Jordan saw in the dark eyes shadings their blackness had never revealed to him before. Memory tugged at the judge. His right hand closed on something invisible.

"Can you?" Mike Arriendez asked quietly.

"Prove that Wayne didn't kill Jenny? Yes, I can." Jordan's eyes were still on the judge. *If you let me,* he tried to make his face say. *If you really want to know what happened to your girl friend.*

Judge Waverly was the cause of the silence. He understood that, but didn't let silence goad him. The line of his thin lips pursed, straightened. His eyes were lost in thought.

He recovered himself abruptly. The judge's eyes were as penetrating as ever when he turned them on Jordan. "Mr. Marshall, you promise me as an officer of the court that the testimony you want to elicit is relevant to the defendant's state of mind and that you will demonstrate that relevance?"

"Yes, sir, I do."

"Then I will let you get into it. But we're not going to have two murder trials in one. I'll let you develop the circumstances of the other case just so far as they're relevant to this one. And if your proof fails to show your client's innocence of Je—of the other murder, remember that you're the one who wanted to bring in the extraneous offense, Mr. Marshall. Is that clear?"

"Yes, sir." Jordan was standing stiffly. "And now I have something else to say to the court. In private."

"No privacy during a trial," the prosecutor scoffed.

"It's a private matter between Judge Waverly and me," Jordan said to the judge, ignoring Arriendez. "I promise it has nothing to do with the case."

"I don't care if it's about a shortcut back to San Antonio," Mike Arriendez said more heatedly, feeling left out of the silent exchange between Jordan and the judge. "During trial—"

Judge Waverly's stare at Jordan was not threatening. It was curious at first, then for a moment Jordan could have sworn it was frightened. But the judge's voice was perfectly calm and authoritative when he spoke to the prosecutor.

"I believe you can trust me not to receive an ex parte communication concerning this case, Mr. Arriendez. If anything comes up the State should be informed about, I'll let you know."

No one moved until the judge glanced sharply, surprised, at Mike Arriendez, and the prosecutor closed his mouth tightly and abruptly stalked out, leaving the door open.

"Off the record," Jordan said.

Laura didn't protest the way the district attorney had, but for the first time since trial had begun, she became something other than an automaton. She stood slowly and looked at the judge, obviously willing him to do something or at least to understand something. Judge Waverly didn't turn to receive her look.

"Thank you, Ms. Stefone," he said.

Laura hadn't looked at Jordan, but as she left the room, her shoulder brushed his back. Jordan felt the threat in the contact.

The door closed. Judge Waverly turned his mild and exclusive attention on Jordan, who found his mouth dry.

"I wanted to warn you, Your Honor," he croaked, swallowed, and went on, "I've investigated this case rather thoroughly, and some things have come to my attention that ordinarily I would just dismiss as none of my business. But where the information is relevant to the case I may have an obligation to introduce it into evidence."

The judge sounded unintimidated. "What are you talking about, Mr. Marshall?"

"There's a popularly held notion in some quarters, Your Honor, that there was a—a special relationship between you and the victim. The other victim, Jenny Fecklewhite."

Silence. The judge didn't move. He still leaned back in his chair, looking vulnerable or confident. Jordan looked at Judge Waverly's hand resting on the desk. The hand was spotted but strong, strong as the aging profile.

"I didn't want to sandbag you, Judge, I didn't want to spring it on you during trial. But it plays a part in what happened, and I have to—may have to bring it up. If you'd like, I could file a motion to recuse, we could still have the trial moved—"

Judge Waverly shook his head. It seemed like a request for silence, and Jordan obliged. Suddenly he saw the judge's posture for what it was: exhaustion. Secrets are heavy burdens. When the judge began speaking, his voice was soft with tiredness, too. He seemed to be talking to himself.

"I made an inappropriate marriage," he said.

Jordan, while fascinated, suddenly didn't want to be in the room.

"It didn't seem so at the time," Waverly continued. "Margaret was a beautiful, affectionate girl, and she so admired me she could hardly speak. I felt like a god when she listened to me talk about the law. This was years ago, I was young and full of myself, I thought that's all a man wanted of a wife. But after a few years of that, I no longer felt adored, I felt—as if I lived alone."

The judge sighed. He wasn't looking at Jordan and might have been only dimly aware of his presence. But confession has momentum. The judge had waited a long time to unburden himself. He continued, animation suddenly making him sit up straighter.

"And then after what seems a long time, someone else comes along, and you realize this is the one. This is your other half, the one you should have waited for. A girl with spirit, not just admiration. Who can talk back, who's bright and quick and lovely. It's very hard—not to reach out for that."

Caught in the uncomfortable oddity of hearing the judge confess his love for the dead girl, Jordan suddenly realized that this was why the judge had impulsively appointed him to defend Wayne Orkney: Because Jordan was a stranger, he wouldn't care anything about the case, and if he did learn anything, he would take the knowledge away with him, Judge Waverly would never have to see him again.

The judge had wound down, he was now undoubtedly as embarrassed as Jordan. But he stood manfully and looked the defense lawyer in the face.

"So you do what you have to do, Mr. Marshall. I won't recuse myself, and I won't exclude any relevant evidence. You just ... be careful, and remember the lives that are involved."

"I will, Your Honor. Thank you."

It was as Jordan watched Judge Waverly struggle to redon his aloof authority that Jordan saw the older man's humanity most clearly. Inappropriate marriage he could understand, and the futile attempt to hang onto youth or to relive it. In the moment before they left the office, Jordan felt perfect compassion for the judge.

It was a shame he had to destroy him.

10

It was Mike Arriendez who introduced the defensive evidence. Jordan winced when he heard it coming. It was just what he would have done when he was a prosecutor.

"What happened after you helped pull the defendant off Kevin Wainwright, Mr. Stimmons?"

"He just stood there, he wa'n't no problem after that." Judging by appearance, Wayne Orkney couldn't have given Hal Stimmons much of a problem. Stimmons was a black man in his late thirties, very heavy in his shoulders and upper arms, with legs that looked as if they would stand wherever he planted them, no matter what. He had a broad face, a quiet voice, and watchful eyes.

"Did Wayne say anything?" the prosecutor asked.

"He said something like, 'Oh my God, did I hurt him?' and he said Kevin's name."

"Did Kevin answer?"

"He couldn't."

"What did you men do next?"

"I said let's not move him, we don't know what's happened to his back. So we just got a sheet and held it over 'im to keep the sun off, and one of the ladies gave him some water and we waited for the ambulance. It didn't take long."

"When the ambulance came," Arriendez asked thoughtfully, "did you help lift Kevin into it?"

"Yes, sir. After they got him onto the board."

"Did anyone else help?"

"He did." Stimmons gestured with a broad, two-tone thumb.

"The defendant?"

"Yes, sir."

"Did Kevin say anything then?"

"I think so, but I couldn't hear. He might've heard." Stimmons looked at Wayne as if expecting him to join in.

"Did *Wayne* say anything, Mr. Stimmons?"

"He kept shakin' his head, shakin' it and shakin' it, and saying, 'I'm sorry, I'm sorry.'"

There was the defensive theory of unintended harm, presented as neatly as Jordan could have wished, without his even having to call Wayne as a witness. But the reason a prosecutor puts on evidence like that—before the defense can offer it to the jury—is in order to destroy it. Mike Arriendez was nodding in apparent sympathy. He said, "Mr. Stimmons, have you ever known a man to do something he had every intention of doing and then be real sorry about it afterward?"

"Objection," Jordan said, not caught unawares. "Your Honor, what may have happened in other instances is not relevant to this one. And this witness has not been qualified as an expert on the defendant's state of mind or anyone else's."

"Your Honor," Arriendez said smoothly, "the defense has already announced its intention of showing that the defendant didn't intend to harm the deceased. How can I disprove that claim except by the testimony of people who saw how he behaved? I can't reach into the defendant's mind. And if experience of life isn't relevant to this issue, what is?"

Judge Waverly paid the two lawyers careful, if abstracted, attention. "Overruled," he said.

"That means you can answer, Mr. Stimmons. Do you think just because a man is sorry afterward, that means he didn't mean to do what he did?"

"No, sir. I've seen some people do some mighty ugly things, and you could tell by their faces that's just what they wanted to do, and afterward cry like a baby over it. I've done it myself."

"Did you see Wayne Orkney hitting Kevin Wainwright?"

"Yes, sir, some of it, before I could get across the street to stop him."

"Did it look to you like Wayne knew what he was doing?"

"His eyes were burnin'," Hal Stimmons said. "He wasn't missing where he was aimin' to hit either. Sure looked deliberate to me."

"From the way he hit Kevin, should he have expected to hurt him?"

Hal Stimmons's voice remained as mild as it had been. "'F I hit a man that hard that many times, I'd expect him to be dead afterward."

"Your witness," Arriendez said.

Like hell. Mild-mannered, trustworthy Hal Stimmons was a prosecution witness all the way. Jordan sat there wondering what use he could make of him.

"Did you see Kevin hit Wayne, Mr. Stimmons?"

"Naw, sir. Kevin was down and pretty much out of it by the time I come runnin'."

"So you didn't see whether Kevin hit Wayne earlier. You didn't see what started the fight."

"No, I didn't."

Jordan was struck by inspiration. "Was this the first time you ever saw Wayne Orkney and Kevin Wainwright fighting?" he asked.

"Oh, no," Hal Stimmons said immediately as if he'd been hoping for that question.

"You sound like a fight between Kevin and Wayne might've been a common occurrence. Was it?"

Stimmons shrugged. "I been seein' those boys since they was little boys. Seems like they was always fightin'."

"Kevin hitting Wayne and Wayne hitting Kevin? That's how their fights went?"

"Yes, sir."

"Did you take them very seriously?"

"Naw. Just boys fightin', you know."

Feeling much better about the witness, Jordan passed him. Mike Arriendez immediately asked, "Did you stop any of those other fights, Mr. Stimmons?"

"Naw."

"Why not?"

Stimmons shrugged those heavy shoulders again. "Nobody gettin' hurt too bad. Just regular fights, both of 'em givin' as good as they was gettin'. No reason to interfere."

"But you interfered in this one. Why?"

Hal Stimmons's face darkened with memory. "This was somethin' different. Kevin's just down on the ground, not fightin' back. And Wayne, he was hurtin' him."

Arriendez let the testimony sink in while he wrote an elaborate note to himself. "Pass the witness," he finally said.

Damn, Jordan was thinking. Mike Arriendez was good: smooth, alert, always one step ahead of the defense so far. He could see the effect on the jurors' faces of the prosecutor's last short questioning. Here was big Hal Stimmons, a man used to violence, casual about it, who had been so appalled by this particular beating that he'd felt compelled to intervene.

All right, if it was bad, make it even worse. "How did Wayne look while he was hitting Kevin, Mr. Stimmons?"

"Like I say, his face was beet red. I thought *he* was cut at first, but it was just blood rushin' to his face. He looked crazy. Looked like his head'd pop off his neck. And his eyes buggin' out like a crazy man's."

"Was he shouting?"

Stimmons nodded. "Somethin', but I couldn't catch it. 'Did you?' I think was what he yelled once, but I couldn't tell what he was talkin' about. It was just crazy yellin'."

Jordan wrote a note of his own and shifted gears.

"Mr. Stimmons, do you know what happened in Pleasant Grove Park earlier that afternoon?"

Mike Arriendez was on his feet quickly. "I object to any hearsay."

Judge Waverly looked at Jordan with an invisible shrug. The prosecutor was right. The judge turned to the witness. "Hal, if you know from your own experience what happened in the park, you can testify to it. But you can't just repeat what you heard someone else say."

At that Hal Stimmons turned back to the lawyers and

said, "You mean about the other murder, I guess, but I don't know anything about it except what I heard."

"Thank you, sir," Jordan said, frustrated. He had already won this round in chambers, when Judge Waverly had ruled that evidence of Jenny's murder would be admitted. But the prosecutor wouldn't let him seize the victory.

The day ended abruptly. *Is it over?* Jordan wanted to ask, like a boxer awakened long after the fight. Judge Waverly walked out without a glance back at the courtroom. Laura emulated him. Jordan's only companion was the one beside him, whom he had almost forgotten.

"Need to confer?" sneered the deputy with the amber glasses. Jordan looked at his client. Wayne looked back at him expectantly. "Wayne," Jordan began earnestly but couldn't think of anything to add. He turned his attention instead to the iron-faced deputy. With a beguiling smile Jordan said, "We do need a minute, please, if that's not too inconvenient."

The deputy retreated but only after a manly snarl. "Anything you want to ask me?" Jordan said.

"I'm not lookin' too good, am I?" Wayne said quietly.

"Right now, Wayne, my strategy is to make you look as bad as possible. Everybody knows you beat up Kevin, we can't refute that. What we have to show is that you were so mad you couldn't control yourself. So Mr. Stimmons's testimony actually helped us in that regard." Difficult as that might have been for a layman—or anyone else, including the jury—to understand.

"So what're you going for, insanity? Maybe I could help with that."

Jordan instantly knew the voice of Wayne's mom at his shoulder, though it had been weeks since he'd heard it.

"No, ma'am," he said quietly. "Not insanity, voluntary manslaughter." Into the silence he added with a trace of the whine he'd tried to keep out of his voice, "Which is a lot better than murder for Wayne."

"Hmph," Mrs. Orkney said, which Jordan recognized as a prelude to speech and interrupted.

"Will you excuse us for just a minute, Mr. and Mrs. Orkney? I'll talk to you right after Wayne and I go over a couple of things."

Mrs. Orkney repeated her syllable, and her husband led her away.

"Just one thing, Wayne. What were you screaming while you were hitting Kevin?"

Wayne didn't even search his memory. "I don't know. I didn't know I was. Somethin' about Jenny, I guess."

"Good," Jordan said. "Those are both good answers."

He signaled to the impatiently waiting deputy and joined Wayne's parents at the back of the now-empty courtroom. "I wish you wouldn't say things to discourage Wayne, Mrs. Orkney," he began.

"You want to keep that job for yourself?" she snapped back. "If I was settin' where Wayne is, this trial'd be depressing hell out of me."

"Now, Ma," Mr. Orkney said mildly.

"What?! You seen anything different from what I have? I don't see this fellow here thowin' his whole heart and soul and lungs and pancreas into his job. Looks to me like he's just here to prop Wayne up so they can get a better shot at him."

She was a head shorter than Jordan but outweighed him. He couldn't have moved her out of his path if he'd tried. But that wasn't why he felt compelled to answer her charges. He felt his face flushing as he tried to keep his voice level.

"We haven't gotten our turn yet, Mrs. Orkney. The State's case always looks good when the defense hasn't put on its evidence."

She stared Jordan straight in the eye and lowered her voice for the first time. *"This* good?" she said.

Laura answered his knock at her door immediately and stayed in the doorway, arms folded. "I'm not going to ask what you said to the judge," she said.

Feeling the lostness of his cause, Jordan said, "I told him I might have to introduce evidence about him and Jenny."

He almost flinched, but Laura hadn't moved. It was only her eyes flaring. "What about them?"

"I think you know," Jordan said quietly. "Other people do, and they're not as smart as you." The compliment passed her as if he hadn't spoken. Jordan continued. "Jenny and Judge Waverly were lovers."

Laura looked stunned. But her blank expression turned quickly to even deeper anger. "People are so stupid!" she said. "People have to have drama, they have to make nasty stories out of, of—"

"You don't believe it?"

"It's not true," she said icily. Her sincerity shook Jordan's confidence in his theory.

"But some people believed it," he said slowly. "That's why it's important."

"On what possible theory?" Laura asked harshly. "You're not trying Jenny's murder."

"But the judge said I could get into it, remember? Because it goes to Wayne's motive." A pause. She still hadn't moved. "Can we talk about this inside? Or at Barney's? I could sure use a drink."

She turned her head as if away from his touch. The long line of her neck struck him as peculiarly vulnerable and peculiarly strong. "No," Laura said quietly, the anger gone from her voice, but the resolution still holding it firm. "I think we both need our rest tonight. Don't you?"

Jordan nodded. He didn't ask anything else because he didn't want to make her decision more far-reaching than it was. She stayed in the doorway; he felt her watching him as he walked away.

"Oh good, we can get our exclusive interview," Helen Evers said brightly. "What do you think of our local juries, Mr. Marshall?"

"They seem like fine, intelligent people. I trust them to do the right thing," Jordan said by rote. "Ask me if I still think that after the verdict. Y'all're working late." He'd been surprised to see lights in the offices of the *Green Hills Register* as he'd driven by, and sudden inspiration, not a pleasant one, had brought him to a stop.

"We're putting out a special trial edition," said the editor and publisher, suddenly appearing from the back room as Jordan remembered her doing from his last appearance at the newspaper. Mrs. Swanson was actually wearing a green eyeshade and reading a long roll of paper without glancing at him.

"So we can use a couple of good snappy quotes," Helen said brightly. "Do you want to give me some, or do you trust me to supply them?"

"In a little while, okay, Helen? Right now I need to talk to your mother."

Mrs. Swanson looked at Jordan in surprise, and Helen turned the same expression on her mother. "I'm not a witness to anything," the older woman said.

"I'm pretty sure you are," Jordan said.

Still watching him, puzzlement turning suspicious, Mrs. Swanson said, "Helen, why don't you go get us some sandwiches."

"Are you kidding?" Helen said, but her mother cut her off without even a glance. The reporter gathered up her purse and went out with a glare at Jordan.

"To what am I a witness?" Mrs. Swanson asked, not offering Jordan a seat or entry behind the counter.

"You tell me. I've developed a theory about Judge Waverly and Jenny Fecklewhite. I want to know if it's true."

"We don't have a gossip column, Mr. Marshall. Even if we did—"

"I don't want gossip, I want the truth, because I may have to put on evidence of their relationship in the trial, and I'm not going to do that unless I'm damned sure it's true."

Mrs. Swanson didn't say anything. After a long moment's study of Jordan's expression she seated herself at the desk. Jordan came around the counter and sat in front of her. "Ask," Mrs. Swanson said.

"They spent a lot of time together. People have said he was just teaching her about the law, but I think there was something more. Is that true?"

Jordan had come for confirmation, because Laura's emphatic denial of the relationship between Jenny and the judge had made him wonder if he was wrong. But then he had remembered how protective Laura was of Judge Waverly, how much she owed him. She would deny anything that cast him in a bad light.

He had remembered, too, that Judge Waverly had as good as admitted the relationship to Jordan.

If Mrs. Swanson had seen anything like lascivious interest in Jordan's face she would have glared him out of her office. It was his seriousness that started her talking. "I never saw them in a car or a motel room," the newspaper editor said slowly. "But I saw them together, and if looks and touches mean what I've always thought they do, yes, they were in love."

"In love?"

"Yes," Mrs. Swanson said firmly. "Love. That's not what you asked, is it, but that's what I saw. The two of them saw each other almost every day. Look out our window, see our view." Jordan knew the view; it was of Main Plaza and the courthouse. "Jenny made no secret of it. She'd go to the courthouse every day after school, like going home. Sometimes he took her to dinner or lunch on weekends or during the summer. Sometimes somebody else would go with them, like Laura Stefone, but sometimes they didn't bother with that. He wasn't discreet at all. People in this town said he was teaching her, that he was just fond of her. Nobody wanted to acknowledge what was right in front of their eyes. But I know love when I see it."

Jordan looked into the ungainly, at-least-twice-married editor's face, with its ruddy complexion and snapping eyes, and felt no desire to challenge her knowledge of romance. "Did you ever see them when they were together?" he asked quietly.

Mrs. Swanson shot a harsh glance at him, but Jordan's expression mollified her by telling her he wasn't enjoying asking the questions. "Yes, sir. Of course I spend time at the courthouse, or I might've been in the diner the same time they were. In a town this size—"

"I know."

"Judge Waverly'd put his hand on hers or give her a quick hug, that kind of thing. Are you sure this is evidence?"

"The judge has already given me permission," Jordan said. "I told him I might have to."

Mrs. Swanson's eyes widened, then narrowed. "Then you understand what it was," she said harshly. "It wasn't something dirty. It was beautiful in its way. That middle-aged man, that young girl, they loved each other. People like you have to make something dirty out of that, I know, but it wasn't. There were the little touches, like I said, but that wasn't where you could see it. You could see it in the judge's eyes. The way he looked at her. It was plain as day, he loved her and was proud of her and proud of himself for being with her. I've seen him just sit and listen to her, smiling, and you couldn't find one other person in this world Judge Waverly could stand to listen to for very long."

"So—" Jordan said slowly but had no finish. He sat thinking and Mrs. Swanson let him, watching him.

"And you're going to use this?" she finally asked.

"I hope not," Jordan said resignedly. But he owed no loyalty to the judge.

He had a room at the motel for appearance's sake, he had hoped, but it turned out to be reality, the harsh reality of bare linoleum and unfiltered light. He could hear two people talking desultorily outside his window, and when they went away, they took his hope of sleep with them. Feeling hopeless, feeling stupid, he pulled on a few clothes and got into his car. He rolled his window down; the night air flowing across him was pleasant after the stuffy motel room. Besides, he wanted to smell the magnolias on Flowing Springs Boulevard.

He saw only one other moving car on the streets of Green Hills, and they sneaked by each other guiltily. Laura's street was dark and still. Mrs. Johnson's porch was empty, her windows unlighted. He slowed to a crawl, then to nothing, coasting to a stop across the street from Laura's. Her car was in the driveway. The front of the house was dark, but he thought he saw a fraying glow of light from the back bedroom. He wondered if she had her windows open. When the house had first come in sight, Jordan had suffered a gladness of heart, a sense of homecoming. But as the house remained tightly contained, it seemed to be consciously excluding him. He thought he sensed a dark presence behind the front window, but he would have felt that whether it was true or not.

"You look tired."

"I hear the note of accomplishment in your concern, Miguelito," Jordan said to the district attorney, "but it's strictly a result of a bad night's sleep." To Arriendez's studied silence he added, "I don't recommend the motel's beds. But to give you your due, you certainly didn't help me rest. Are you going to finish up today, or does this parade go on forever?"

The DA just smiled and withdrew. Jordan turned, looking for his client, and saw two witnesses in the front row. Surprised, he approached them. "Hello, Ms. Riegert, Dr. Prouty." He turned his attention to the nurse. "Are you going to be a State's witness, Ms. Riegert? I'm the one who subpoenaed you."

He had to resist an inclination to call her Evelyn. After all, he knew her past; he had seen her high school yearbook photo.

There was nervousness in Evelyn Riegert's manner as she smiled. "No, I just got a ride with Dr. Prouty. I thought I'd watch some of the trial before it was my turn."

"Oh. Well, I'm very sorry, Ms. Riegert, but you can't do that. We have a rule that witnesses can't hear other testimony. If you watched some of the trial, I wouldn't be able to call you to testify."

"I'm sorry," she said, rising hastily. "I didn't know."

"Not your fault. I should have told you."

"I'll just—" She gathered up her purse and a file folder, then regarded a small cardboard box doubtfully. "These are the other things you asked for. Kevin's effects that his father never picked up. Should I keep them with me or—?"

"Um—I guess I'll keep it, so you won't have to lug it around. I am sorry about this, can I—?"

"It's perfectly all right," the nurse said, regaining her

poise. She eyed the door at the front of the courtroom but instead left through the back spectators' door, leaving Jordan to gather up the box, which he touched gingerly as if it were Kevin's remains.

"And how are you doing, sir?" he said to Dr. Prouty, a corpulent, balding man with a pugnacious nose, who sat with his arms folded.

"Getting tired of waiting," the doctor said. "I have other things to do than wait on lawyers and clerks."

Mike Arriendez called the busy doctor as his first witness of the morning so Dr. Prouty could more quickly get on with his life. His testimony was brisk and brusque. Quickly reducing Kevin Wainwright to a corpse, he spoke of him as he would have to a medical seminar.

"Broken ribs here, here, and here, one of which was in danger of puncturing the lung when he was brought in, but we took care of that. Cracked cheekbone, but that was superficial. His nose was broken. There was internal bleeding. Multiple abrasions and contusions. Shall I detail those?"

"Please," Mike Arriendez asked graciously.

As the doctor hurried on, Jordan turned slightly to see that the spectator seats were more filled than they had been the day before. On an aisle near the back he saw Swin Wainwright, sitting very straight, his face rigid.

"What was the cause of death, Dr. Prouty?"

"Coronary arrest," the doctor said at once. "Might have been a blood clot that broke loose and blocked the major artery, might have been just the strain of trying to recover from all that damage. He was never really on the road to recovery from the time he was brought in."

"In your capacity as medical examiner, what was your ruling as to the cause of death?"

"Homicide," the doctor said.

When it was his turn, Jordan stared at Dr. Prouty for a long moment, until eyes turned toward Jordan curiously. Jordan was thinking of asking the doctor no questions at all.

"You treated Kevin in the hospital, didn't you, Dr. Prouty?" he said.

"Yes."

"So you were told how his injuries came about?"

"Yes. It was part of his file."

"Did you find his injuries consistent with what you were told?"

"Absolutely." The doctor answered quickly, displaying no curiosity about the questions.

"And you didn't really expect him to recover, is that the effect of your testimony?"

"I wouldn't say that. Someone else in his condition might well have recovered. But this boy never showed much improvement in the few days we had him."

"So then, let's say, his death was no surprise to you?"

"No, sir," the doctor said in the tone of someone seldom surprised.

Dr. Prouty had reduced Kevin Wainwright from victim to statistic. With his last witness, Mike Arriendez corrected that impression.

"How old are you, Jason?"

"Eighteen."

"You're a senior this year?"

"Yes, sir."

He looked like he was probably a linebacker for the football team, maybe a lineman if it was a light team. A pale boy six feet tall, with big-knuckled hands, a head like the rounded top of a telephone pole, a face that looked as if it would break easily into a grin, but uneasy and serious now on the witness stand.

"Did you know Kevin Wainwright and this man here?"

"Yes, sir. Hello, Wayne."

"Did you see the last fight they had on July fifteenth?"

"Yes, sir. I was driving by, and when I saw Wayne's truck pull up so sudden, I thought something was up, so I stopped, too."

"How did the fight start?"

"Well, Wayne yelled that he was gonna kill Kevin, and Kevin stopped on the sidewalk and just looked at him."

"Did he look frightened?"

"I wouldn't say that," Jason Merritt said. It appeared

Kevin's expression had left an impression on him. "He just looked kind of blank, like he couldn't place Wayne."

"Then what happened?"

"Then Wayne went runnin' up, and it was perfectly obvious he was gonna punch him, but Kevin didn't do anything to duck or block it. He just stood there, and Wayne ran up and hit him with his fist right in the face. That's when I came across the street to watch."

"What happened then?"

Jason's hands had crept closer to each other on the railing in front of him, but they didn't touch. They gripped the rail as if in a terrible attempt to stop their movement. "Kevin's head snapped back against the glass and his eyes went like—" Jason demonstrated, lifting his head back and fluttering his eyes. "And then Wayne hit him again in the nose. The blood spurted out, it went all the way up Wayne's arm and all across the sidewalk, out to the street."

"Did Kevin fight back?" Mike Arriendez asked quietly.

"Aw, no, sir. But I don't think Wayne even noticed, he was screaming, screaming names, you know, and he punched Kevin in the stomach and Kevin fell down on his hands and knees. When Kevin fell down, Wayne looked like he was going to punch the wall. I looked at Kevin. He was still awake, but he was spitting up; spitting up, you know, blood and—I think he was choking because he was tryin' to get his breath at the same time. Then Wayne kicked him."

Jordan felt immobilized. He wasn't listening as a lawyer, he was just letting the scene unfold before him, watching Wayne's merciless beating of his best friend. Gradually another sound intruded itself and he became aware of the boy beside him. Jordan turned and saw that Wayne was breathing heavily as if he couldn't get enough air. His eyes were wet. His Adam's apple moved as he gulped. Wayne's hands had turned to claws on the table before him. He was on the verge of crying.

Jordan turned slightly and saw Swin Wainwright again. The older man, darkly tanned, face creased, looked very similar to Wayne in his posture and expression: a man holding it in but barely.

"Mr. Stimmons got there ahead of me," Jason Merritt was saying in answer to another question. "I was standing right there, but I couldn't move. It was just—I was afraid to touch Kevin at all for a minute."

The district attorney sat quietly for a moment before asking, "Have you been in fights, Jason?"

"Oh, sure. Yes, sir."

"Have you been in any since you saw this one?"

"No."

The boy's hands had finally come together. They gripped each other, making his arms bulge. But his face looked like a little boy's, bewildered by his helplessness. "And I got cut from the football team," he added. "Coach says I don't hit hard enough any more."

Jordan felt rather helpless himself when Jason Merritt was passed to him for cross-examination. Mike Arriendez's cunning had not been better displayed than in this, his last witness, a callow high school boy who had been so traumatized by witnessing the fight that he could no longer smash into opposing linemen. Jordan didn't think he could do anything to make less vivid the picture Jason Merritt had painted, even for himself. He asked his usual questions about how crazy Wayne had looked, how remorseful he'd been afterward, whether Jason had ever threatened to kill anyone himself, but the boy still looked shaken. Just before he was going to pass him away, Jordan was struck by an idea. It might have been a bad idea, because it required him to revisit Jason's most horrifying testimony, but there was no time to dissect the idea.

"The first punch you saw Wayne throw," Jordan asked, "where did it hit Kevin?"

"Right in the face," Jason repeated. He lifted his fingers to his right cheek, then changed his mind and made it the left. "Here."

"A hard punch?"

"Oh, yes, sir. Kevin's head spun around and the other side of his face hit the window."

"Thank you, Jason." Jordan received some curious looks

by ending there. He felt them on his back, on his own cheek. He kept his head down.

"The State rests," Mike Arriendez said.

And a good rest they deserved. The case the DA had put on against Jordan was the equivalent of the beating Wayne had given Kevin Wainwright. Judge Waverly mercifully broke for lunch before requiring Jordan to call his first witness.

For the first time since trial had begun, Laura looked at him as she left the room, as if she wanted to say something. Jordan wondered if she had seen him drive by her house the night before. But he knew she wouldn't say three words to him now.

He found his way out of the courtroom blocked, and the sight of the person in his path brought Jordan to a dead halt. He hoped he hadn't flinched broadly enough for anyone to notice. But Harry Briggs didn't look angry; he looked nervous. His tall face looked softer than it had the night in Barney's, softened by the conflict of its emotions.

"I came to say I'm sorry," he said. He rushed forward, making Jordan step back. "I was drunk and stupid and it wouldn't've happened without both. What you said was right—what I remember of it. What happened with Laura and me, you didn't have anything to do with it."

"Okay," Jordan said, and stopped, remembering the effect lengthy speeches had on Officer Briggs. He started to brush by, but Briggs stopped him, realized he might have been squeezing the lawyer's arm too hard, and released him.

"But what's this?" he asked, holding out a piece of paper.

"Surely you've had subpoenas before."

"Not from the defense," Briggs said perplexedly. "What's up?"

"You are," Jordan said. "My first witness, right after lunch."

Harry Briggs still looked puzzled, tempered by sullen suspicion, on the witness stand. He even said, "I don't know anything about this case," drawing a reprimand from Judge

Waverly, because the remark wasn't in response to a question.

"I want to ask you about the murder you did investigate," Jordan said. "The other murder committed that July fifteenth. Do you remember that one, Officer Briggs?"

"Of course."

"Who was murdered?"

"Jenny Fecklewhite."

Mike Arriendez was half-turned away as if to exclude himself from this unorthodox portion of trial. But he was listening intently.

"Did you find her body, Officer Briggs?"

"No. I was the second officer on the scene."

"What scene was that?"

"Pleasant Grove Park."

Briggs's bare hands were clasped across his knee, apparently at ease. Jordan studied the hands. They tightened when he asked, "Would you describe the position of the body, please?"

Briggs did succinctly: Jenny on her back, head at a wretched angle on the cypress root, her hands at rest.

"Who put her hands together, Officer?"

"I don't know. They were like that when I got there."

Jordan knew that Ed and Joan Fecklewhite were in the spectator seats behind him. As trial had progressed, the crowd had grown and grown familiar. Mrs. McElroy had retained her good seat for two days, anger at being passed over for the jury giving way to curiosity. Swin Wainwright remained, all alone. Today was the first appearance by the Fecklewhites, who must have gotten wind that their daughter's name was going to come up. Jordan no longer gave a thought to how word like that spread through the little town. He only accepted that it would.

He asked, looking down, "That wasn't your first visit to Pleasant Grove Park that day, was it, Officer Briggs?"

Briggs's alertness increased. "Yes, it was," he said firmly.

"Jenny was a friend of yours, wasn't she?" Jordan asked in the same quiet, knowledgeable voice. Laura Stefone glanced at him from her position behind her machine.

And Briggs looked at Laura. "Jenny was a nice girl," he said. "Everybody liked her."

"You and she had worked on a project together, hadn't you? A speech?"

Briggs actually smiled. "Jenny must have interviewed every law enforcement officer in the county for that speech. It's too bad we never got—"

He'd started to make a joke, a pleasantry, but it died along with his smile. Officer Briggs swallowed hard.

"Have you arrested a suspect in her murder, Officer? Has anyone?"

"No, sir."

"Why not?"

Briggs shrugged. "Best suspect was already in custody. Now he's sitting right there beside you."

"You mean Wayne Orkney. And why did you consider him the best suspect?"

Briggs shrugged again. "Two people killed the same day, both beating deaths, you tend to think the same person did 'em both."

"That's it?" Jordan said. "Do you have any evidence to connect Wayne to Jenny Fecklewhite's murder?"

Briggs thought hard. His hands were on the railing. "He was seen in the vicinity," he finally concluded.

"He wasn't the only one, was he, Officer?" Jordan said and let a scornful beat of silence pass before he added, "I pass the witness."

Arriendez favored him with a short glare, an expression that said, *I'm not going to play your stupid game.* "No questions," he said.

"Call your next witness," Judge Waverly instructed.

Jordan took a deep breath. *Here we go.* "The defense calls Dr. Bob Wyntlowski."

Mike Arriendez gave Jordan his first satisfaction of the trial by leaning over to say, "Who?"

11

"At my request," Jordan asked, "Did you examine an autopsy report and accompanying evidence concerning the death of a young man named Kevin Wainwright?"

"Yes, I did," Dr. Wyntlowski said. He was a friendly man; he favored the entire room with one quick, bright smile, apparently not noticing that no one smiled back. Jordan had established the doctor's credentials as an assistant medical examiner of Bexar County who had performed thousands more autopsies than the local doctor. Wyntlowski had been accepted as an expert, but no one, from the judge on his high seat to the interested parties in the audience, had any idea what Dr. Wyntlowski was doing in their courtroom.

"And do you agree with Dr. Prouty's stated cause of death, coronary arrest?"

"I certainly agree that his heart stopped," Wyntlowski said easily. "That's all coronary arrest means. And his lungs stopped pumping air and his blood stopped flowing. But *why* those things happened is an open question."

"You can't determine cause of death from the observations included in the autopsy summary?"

"Not to *my* satisfaction," the doctor said.

"What's left out?" Jordan asked.

This was the tricky part, the part where Wyntlowski had to criticize a fellow doctor. He tried his best to avoid it. "The report is fine as far as it goes. It covers the standard, vital areas of inquiry. There are just maybe a couple of things I would have looked for if I'd conducted the autopsy."

"Such as?"

Wyntlowski shifted his weight. "Dr. Prouty undoubtedly already knew the circumstances of the injuries, which I don't. I'd be starting with a clean slate. So I would want to know why the patient died, as opposed to how he got injured. Because these injuries, although serious, were not necessarily life-threatening."

"Are you suggesting that something happened to him in the hospital to cause death?" Jordan asked.

No, Dr. Wyntlowski wouldn't commit to that. "Every patient is different," he said earnestly. "One will die of something another would walk away from without treatment. We're not machines, you can't confidently predict that if you do A to us, B will always result."

"But does this autopsy report *exclude* the possibility that something happened to Kevin Wainwright *after* the beating, something that resulted in his death?"

"No."

Mike Arriendez had rejoined the party. He was not only facing forward again, he was leaning across his table, eyes narrowed as he studied Dr. Wyntlowski.

Jordan heard murmurs at his back as well. Judge Waverly tapped his gavel lightly. The judge was also studying Dr. Wyntlowski, no longer hostilely.

"What would you have looked for, Dr. Wyntlowski, to determine whether something like that had happened?"

"Anything that would have increased the strain on his already weakened heart. Suffocation, for example. If someone had held a pillow over the patient's face or even a large hand cupped over his nose and mouth. Someone wouldn't have had to cut off his oxygen long enough actually to suffocate him, just long enough to increase the strain on his heart, which was already weakened by his injuries. A minute of that, maybe less, could have resulted in a fatal heart attack, especially if no assistance was called in."

"And how could you have told if that happened?" Jordan asked.

"I would have examined the insides of the lips," the doctor said, indicating his own with his finger. "If something had pressed down on the mouth hard enough to shut off breath, the teeth should have left impressions on the lips. An impression that wouldn't have faded if the patient died immediately afterward."

"Did Dr. Prouty check for that?"

"Not according to his report," Dr. Wyntlowski said as charitably as possible.

"Any other possibilities for death-causing events in the hospital?"

"Several. Some could have been detected by autopsy, some not."

"If the defense had been allowed to exhume the body," Jordan said, directing the question at the judge, who understood perfectly, "so that you could have conducted a second autopsy, could you have found indications of what actually caused the death of Kevin Wainwright?"

"Possibly," the doctor said. "I could have looked at least."

Jordan passed the witness while he collected his thoughts. Mike Arriendez only asked one question. "Dr. Wyntlowski, your examination of Dr. Prouty's autopsy report doesn't suggest any actual evidence that anything other than the beating he suffered killed Kevin Wainwright, did it?"

"No, sir."

"Pass the witness."

Jordan had pushed one file away and pulled another toward him. He spread the contents before him as he began quietly. "I asked you to examine another autopsy report, didn't I, Dr. Wyntlowski?"

"Yes." The medical examiner opened another file himself.

"One concerning Jennifer Fecklewhite."

"Yes, sir."

Jordan felt the winds of stirring at his back again, and not only at his back. Mention of Jenny's name seemed to cast a spell on the people of Green Hills, or to break one.

"What did you think of this autopsy report, Doctor?"

"Very thorough," the medical examiner said with satisfaction. "It lays out the injuries and the probable causes very clearly."

"What did Jenny Fecklewhite die of, Dr. Wyntlowski?"

Mike Arriendez rose to say, "I object to this entire line of questioning as irrelevant. No one is being tried for Jenny Fecklewhite's murder."

"Overruled," said Judge Waverly. His mild tone did not match his appearance. The judge was sitting at attention, one hand under his chin with the index finger crossing his lips, sealing them.

"What killed Jenny, Doctor?" Jordan asked again.

"She died as a result of a broken neck. From the supporting evidence, the offense report, the death scene photographs, it seems clear that what happened is that she fell backward, her neck fell across a tree root, and her head struck a rock. Either of those injuries might have caused death, but in my estimation it was the broken neck that did."

Dr. Wyntlowski was speaking clearly, briskly, but he understood that the victim might be represented in the courtroom by people who cared about her, which lent his voice a sympathetic tone. A much less sensitive man than the doctor would still have noticed the stillness of the room as he talked about Jenny. Jordan looked at Laura and saw that her hands were still moving purposefully, but Laura's head was turned and cocked as if she saw something in a high corner of the ceiling.

"Were those her only injuries, Dr. Wyntlowski?"

"No. She also showed marks from being struck."

"By a hand?"

"Yes," Wyntlowski said positively. "Dr. Prouty noted traces of someone else's skin in one of the wounds. Also the shape of one of the bruises on her shoulder indicates fingers squeezing very hard."

Jordan's voice was quiet, too, but he kept it audible. He didn't want anyone to miss anything. Particularly the judge. The testimony was having an effect on Judge Waverly; his head was slowly bowing as he listened. His normally sharp eyes had softened in distraction or distress. The judge's head jerked ever so slightly as Jordan asked, "Was she hit very many times?"

"No," Dr. Wyntlowski said. "It wasn't a beating. It was probably, in fact, a very unlucky punch that knocked her down, and she had the very bad luck of landing on the tree root and the rock at just the right angle to break her neck."

The medical examiner was displaying a preautopsy photograph that showed the marks on Jenny's face. Jordan was looking at another photograph in his file, the blown-up hospital file photo of Jenny. What a pretty girl she had been. There was such confident expectation in her cocked head, her knowing smile.

"Is there anything distinctive about her death you can tell us from the photos, Doctor?"

"That the person who hit her was wearing a ring."

The silence of the courtroom broke. Murmurs swept forward, a wave breaking over the trial participants. The judge did nothing to quiet them. Dr. Wyntlowski sounded matter-of-fact and Jordan the same as he asked his witness how he knew about the ring.

"I blew up the photo of her face," the doctor explained, "and examined this one deep gouge to her cheek. In the blowup you can see the tears of the skin, sharp cuts that a hand or a knuckle wouldn't make. The depth of the wound, too, indicates that the person who hit her was wearing something on his hand."

"Do you think from these photos you could identify the ring that made the marks on Jenny's face?"

"I believe so. Normally I wouldn't think I could, working just from pictures, but in this case the impressions in the wound are very clear. The ring should match up obviously enough for identification. Not like a fingerprint, but I could certainly tell you there's a high probability of a particular ring's having made the wound."

This was the moment at which Jordan had aimed all his trial strategy. He had wanted the case heard by another judge. When that failed, he wanted to understand Judge Waverly's motivations precisely. In that attempt, he had noticed something else about the judge, leading him to a theory he hadn't been able to test until this moment.

"May I approach the bench, Your Honor?" Jordan walked stiffly, feeling hollow. He had never done anything like what he was about to do, nor had he ever heard of anyone doing anything similar.

"Your Honor," he asked loudly when he stood directly under the judge, "may I please borrow your ring?"

The judge stared. But there was a roomful of witnesses at Jordan's back. Judge Waverly couldn't refuse. Slowly he brought his hands together.

"No, sir, not your wedding ring, the other one, the heavier one."

In front of the bench, Jordan was standing beside Laura. He felt her, though he didn't look anywhere but into the judge's face. He thought Laura had frozen like everyone else in the courtroom. But the record of what he was doing wouldn't matter.

With icy eyes, the judge removed his ring and silently handed it to the defense lawyer. It was a heavy lodge ring, black in its crevices. The crown was red-faceted glass with crossed gold swords. Jordan carried it gingerly the few steps to the witness box and handed it to the medical examiner.

"Is this the ring that caused the cut on Jenny Fecklewhite's face?"

Dr. Wyntlowski accepted the ring and bent over it, turning it, running his fingers over its crown, looking from the ring to the blown-up photograph of Jenny's wounded face. Jordan found he'd been holding his breath and let it out in a long, ragged exhalation.

Dr. Wyntlowski looked up and handed the ring back to Jordan. "No, sir," he said.

"What?"

"That's not the ring that caused the cut on her face."

"Are you sure?"

"Positive. I may not be able to identify the ring that did it with absolute certainty, but I can definitely exclude some, including that one. The markings don't match up."

It seemed like a long, long time that Jordan stood stock still at the front of the courtroom. The ring was warm in his hand. He turned and handed it back to the judge, who accepted it grimly. "Thank you, Your Honor."

Jordan's fingers moved across each other, but he no longer

wore a ring. Turning to go back to his seat, he saw Mike Arriendez's wide eyes and then the district attorney's hands splayed on his table. "May I borrow that, please?" Jordan asked, hoping the note of desperation in his voice was one only he could hear.

"Is this the ring?" he asked the doctor, who barely glanced at the DA's class ring before dismissing it with a shake of his head.

Still moving in a daze, Jordan returned the prosecutor's ring and saw a flash of light at the bailiff's desk. Before he even took a step in that direction, Emilio was holding a heavy gold ring out to him with an almost eager expression as if they were playing bingo. Jordan conveyed the ring to his witness, waited for the ring to be exonerated, and returned it.

Next he moved out into the audience, like a mindreader's assistant. "Sir?" he said to Swin Wainwright, but then noticed that not only was Kevin Wainwright's father not wearing a ring, but he was missing most of the ring finger on his right hand. Jordan passed on and came to Ed Fecklewhite in his aisle seat. "Mr. Fecklewhite, may I borrow that ring?"

Fecklewhite gave up his class ring reluctantly, growing red-faced as the ring stuck for a moment. Jordan's hope rose as he carried the heavy ring to his expert. He remembered Ed Fecklewhite's assault conviction and the fact that Jenny had not been his biological daughter.

"What about this one, Dr. Wyntlowski?"

The doctor took his time. It was going to be all right, Jordan thought, beginning to recover his equilibrium. In fact, he was going to come off looking like Perry Mason.

"No, sir," Wyntlowski said, shaking his head.

"No?" Jordan was starting to hate his witness.

"No," the doctor said mildly but emphatically.

As Jordan returned the ring to Ed Fecklewhite, he talked to his witness. "So it couldn't have been just any ring?"

"No, sir, it would have very distinctive markings."

Jordan stood in the audience, casting around. Harry Briggs, excused as a witness, was sitting near the back, but Jordan had already noticed that Briggs didn't wear a ring and didn't have a telltale white band announcing one's absence. When Jordan glanced at him, Briggs held up his hands. Jordan gave him a tight nod. He had considered Briggs a suspect, given his closeness to the dead girl and his haste to make the murder scene, outside his jurisdiction. But the absence of a ring had cleared the police officer in Jordan's mind.

He saw no other suspects in the audience. Two or three of the men followed Harry Briggs's example, holding up their hands. Jordan nodded again authoritatively and marched back to his seat. Judge Waverly was staring at him with a curious expression composed of hatred and hope.

"So," Jordan said, having regained the defense lawyer's knowing tone that so often, as it did in his case, masks utter ignorance, "Dr. Wyntlowski, you feel confident you would know this murder ring if you saw it?"

"Pretty confident," the doctor said easily.

Jordan looked at Arriendez as if the ball were now in his court. "Pass the witness," he said, never so glad in his life to utter the phrase.

Arriendez smiled at the doctor, who smiled back. "I have no questions," the prosecutor said.

Judge Waverly leaned down to say to Wyntlowski, "You're excused as a witness, Doctor, with the thanks of the court.

"Call your next witness," the judge then commanded Jordan in a tone from which the warmth had instantly fallen out.

Jordan stood. "Your Honor, in light of this new evidence, the defense requests a continuance in order to pursue further investigation."

Judge Waverly stared at him, trying to gauge the depth of the defense lawyer's insincerity. Finally he said, "We will recess until tomorrow morning at nine."

"Your Honor, I don't know if one afternoon will be enough time."

"Try," said the judge and left the room.

Around Jordan, the stir that had been waiting to break out did so in full force. Spectators talked to each other loudly, making suggestions, dismissing possibilities. Even the jurors were talking until Emilio ushered them out.

But Jordan was watching only Laura. She gathered up her day's papers with her customary efficiency, and as she turned to leave, her eyes snagged on Jordan, apparently by accident. She stopped for a long moment that made Jordan take a step as if she had called to him, but his movement hardened her face and propelled her out of the room, her back stiff.

"Mr. Marshall? . . . Mr. Marshall?"

"Sorry, Wayne. What is it?"

"Where's the ring?" his client asked plaintively but with an underlying confidence that Jordan did not wish to dispel.

"The great thing about being the defense, Wayne, is that we don't have to produce any evidence. We just point out where the State didn't do its job. And when you testify tomorrow and people see that you're not wearing a ring"— Jordan checked hastily to make sure of that; Wayne's hands were grimy with ground-in dirt, his knuckles were scarred, but his fingers were mercifully bare—"then we'll have cleared you of Jenny's murder. That's a big step, that'll help—"

On punishment, Jordan had started to say, but it was bad form to confide to a client while the guilt-or-innocence phase of trial was still going on one's certainty that it would be followed by a sentencing phase.

"But—" Wayne said, but then his guardian, the angry deputy, appeared, producing an unheralded first in the deputy's career: Jordan was glad to see him. He didn't want to answer any more of his client's questions.

"I'll come see you later," he said to Wayne.

The courtroom was gradually clearing in little talkative clumps, the way people leave church. Mike Arriendez remained, leaning back on his table. "Very dramatic," he said.

"Thanks. Now if you can find that ring, you'll have a case against the real murderer, and you can leave my boy alone."

"Thanks," Arriendez replied in turn and walked away at a pace that showed no inclination to launch a major investigation.

Helen Evers was inside the bar. "Can we talk now?" she asked, pen poised over notepad.

"It's not a very good time."

In my life, Jordan meant. He slumped into his chair, shaky from the ebb and flow of adrenalin. He'd had a perfect case until he'd tested it in front of the whole town and it had collapsed.

So where was the damned ring?

The bailiff returned, grinning. "Thanks for clearing me, man."

"No problem. You know all the rings in town, don't you, Emilio? Where's the one I'm looking for?"

It was a rhetorical question. Jordan began slowly gathering up his materials. He had to do something. He couldn't think exactly what.

Atop his files was a small cardboard box he didn't recognize. When he shook it, it rattled like a Cracker Jacks box. He turned it over and found an address label. Mercy Hospital. Oh, yes. It was the box Evelyn Riegert had given him, Kevin Wainwright's leftover belongings. Idly, Jordan broke open the flap. The contents of the box spilled out onto the table in front of him. A cheap watch that might have an inscription. Should have been returned to the boy's father. Three dollar bills and some change, a wallet.

But no one was looking at those things. All three of them—Helen Evers, Emilio, Jordan—were staring at the gold ring that had gone skittering across the table. Jordan gathered it up, almost afraid to touch it, and held it in the palm of his hand.

"There it is," he said reverently.

"That's it, all right," Emilio agreed casually. "How'd it get in there?"

"These are Kevin's things from the hospital," Jordan explained.

"Yeah, I know," Emilio said. "But that's not Kevin's ring."

"Now how do you know that, Emilio? Maybe he'd just—"

Emilio was shaking his head sagely. "Kevin never wore a ring. His daddy lost a finger in an engine because his ring got caught on a fan blade. You remember that, Helen, or were you too young?"

"I remember," the reporter said tonelessly, staring at the ring in Jordan's palm.

"No, Kevin wouldn't wear a ring," Emilio continued knowingly. "They scared him. Ever'body knew that. That one, that's Wayne's ring. Pretty, isn't it?"

It was the tackiest thing Jordan had ever seen. The face of the ring was a jagged chunk of raw gold, as if it had just been panned out of a stream. The sharp points and ridges looked lethal. Its crevices were crusted by something black. The ring seemed to sink more heavily into Jordan's palm at the bailiff's remark.

Jordan didn't have to ask for explanation. "Remember when Wayne came back from Mexico with it?" Emilio was asking Helen Evers. "That time him and Kevin went to Nuevo Laredo. He was showing it off to everybody, remember?"

"Uh-huh," the reporter said. "How did it get in with Kevin's things?"

They all mused over the possibilities. But Emilio was thinking about something else. "I think Mike'll want to see that ring."

"Maybe Wayne slipped it onto Kevin's finger in the ambulance," Helen suggested, "knowing, you know, that it might be incriminating."

"Oh, Mike'll definitely want that ring," Emilio said.

"I think I'll just—" Jordan gathered up the things and put them back in the box, but when he reached for his open briefcase, the bailiff's hand clamped on his wrist with a grip that surprised Jordan.

"No, I'll take it now," Emilio said.

"This is mine, Emilio, she brought it in response to my subpoena."

"We'll let the judge decide," Emilio said easily. He was not in the habit of being intimidated by lawyers. He took the box and walked away with it.

"You be careful with that," Jordan called.

Of course, there'd been no chance of keeping the ring

secret, not with a law officer and a newspaper reporter standing right at his shoulder when the discovery was made.

"Maybe now Wayne will confess," Helen Evers said helpfully.

A long, slow time passed, during which Jordan would have said that he was thinking, but in fact he just sat like a lump, stunned at the thoroughness with which he'd destroyed his own case. He had insisted on bringing the other murder into the case, then he had provided the evidence that would allow the prosecution to prove that Wayne was guilty of that one, too. Brilliant work if he'd been on the other side. Jordan felt too stupid to do any more thinking.

Some part of his brain must have been doing its job, though, because when he resurfaced, it was with an idea clenched firmly in his teeth.

He made a couple of phone calls, then he went to pay his client the promised visit in the jail. In the small jail conference room he found Wayne animated by a new spirit—his mother's spirit.

" 'Course it's my ring!" Wayne almost screamed. "Everybody knows that! *You*'da known it if you'd ever talked to me!"

"Talk to me now, Wayne. Tell me how—"

"Jesus, what'm I doing?" Wayne said to himself. He stood like a man all alone, hand to his face, eyes scraping the walls of the room. "I must've been crazy." He brought Jordan back into the conversation. "To let you talk me out of takin' that thirty-year offer. What do you think this jury's gonna give me? Can they give me anything more than life?"

"It's not that bad, Wayne, it's—"

"Not? Where's the good part?"

"I couldn't get you to talk to me, Wayne," Jordan said nervously. "If you'd—"

Wayne whirled on him. Jordan thought he was seeing the last face that Kevin Wainwright had seen. The veins were standing out in Wayne's neck. His face was dark, his hands clenching spasmodically. Here was almost the creature the witnesses had described. "Why should I've talked to you? I didn't know you, you were just some *lawyer* they run in on me. The stupid part was when I *did* start to trust you. Like a baby, lookin' around for somebody to be on my side and thinkin'—"

"I am on your side, Wayne."

Wayne stilled him with a glare. "Why?"

Because I have to be, Jordan thought. *Because the judge assigned me to you.* "Because I don't want them to run over you, Wayne. Because I want to do what's right for you."

The only change in Wayne was that his lip curled. His fist was still clenched.

"Because your mother'll kill me if I don't," Jordan said.

Wayne's shoulders started to shake ever so slightly. He burst out with a belated chuckle, then he was crying. "Oh man," he started saying. "Oh man, oh man, oh man."

Standing there straight and slight, hands going limp, the shakes moving from his shoulders down his chest. Jordan went and put an arm around him self-consciously.

"It's okay," he said. "It'll be okay." Hoping Wayne didn't ask him to explain how. Jordan felt more strongly than ever the weight of this defense. His perspective abruptly shifted. He saw the situation as someone else could have seen it all along: this wounded boy depending on him because he had no other choice, and Jordan more concerned with his own life, his reputation, looking for nothing but a good way out.

"Let's talk about it," he said. "About your ring."

A long talk with Wayne sent Jordan back to the Pizza Hut for a second interview. By evening he knew a little more than he'd known that morning, but he still didn't seem to be on the road to solving the central problem of his case, which was clearing Wayne of the murder with which he was charged—Kevin's murder. When Jordan grew tired of thinking and of being alone, he let the Bonneville do what it wanted. The houses turned familiar.

Laura answered the door at once and stood with her hands on her hips as if he were late. "I didn't expect to see *you,*" she said stonily.

"Where else would I go? Do you want to hear what I was thinking?"

"Is that what you call what you do? Well, get in here, we don't have to put on a show for the whole neighborhood."

He walked in, dropped his jacket on the sofa, and was unconsciously comforted by the smell of her house, the subtle fragrance of her houseplants or the peculiar dust produced by old furniture and books, maybe blended with a scent of Laura herself, not perfume but her shampoo, the lotion she used on her skin.

Jordan said, "It all fit so well. Judge Waverly was in love with Jenny—"

"I told you that was garbage," Laura said. She had changed out of her court uniform into casual slacks and a knit striped top with three-quarter-length sleeves. Her hair had been freed and she'd done something to make herself look fresh as morning again.

"Yes, but the facts told me otherwise," Jordan continued. "Anyway, there he is, older man, young girl, situation that just cries out for jealousy to rear its ugly head. He was possessive of her, it must have galled him to see her running around with a young idiot like Kevin."

"He wouldn't have cared about that."

"Okay, you know everybody better than I do, but I know how men think. Anyway, I'd already talked to my medical expert, I knew that Jenny's murder probably wasn't even intentional, probably just a result of the kind of sudden spat that lovers have. Plus I knew about the ring, and I'd seen a heavy ring on the judge's hand one day. Then when you told me that court had ended early the day Jenny was killed, I knew he'd been free to meet her. Maybe in the park."

Laura was shaking her head. "Took somebody real smart to come up with as dumb an idea as that."

"Thank you."

He understood suddenly how furious Laura was; she showed it abruptly. "I've never seen someone with such gall!" She tilted her head upward as if condemning Jordan to the gods. "You drive in here out of nowhere and think you understand *any*thing about *any*one when you don't know the first thing about anybody on this planet, let alone people who—" Her reddened face seemed suddenly to stopper her voice. She recovered quickly. She looked as if she would slap Jordan. "How could you think such a *stupid*—"

He yelled louder than she had. "Because I'm an IDIOT!"

It was probably the only thing that could have diminished Laura's anger: the sight of Jordan's equal rage directed at the same target. "You're right, I don't know anything! So who put me in charge? Was it my idea? Did I ask for this? Everybody's treated me like a moron since I got dragged into your courthouse, and that's how I've been acting! Because I don't know anything and nobody will tell me anything. If I—"

He had exhausted himself. Laura still sounded belligerent. "If you knew *any*thing, you'd know the judge could no more hurt that girl than you could—"

"Well, it was a good theory."

"These ain't theories, these are real people."

Laura's face was a study. She was angry, no question about that, and sad. When her anger diminished, her shoulders began to slump. Jordan was suddenly very glad to see her. He'd forgotten why he'd come to see her. The reason was no reason: He'd just had to see her. Being in her house was like coming home.

"Now I know you're not really mad any more," he told her, "because you only say ain't when you're straining for effect."

"Oh, what do you know?"

"I know a lot, darling." He wanted to brush one stray strand of hair back from her cheek. "I know the noises you make when you sleep—"

"Shut up," she said, but he saw her eyes change. He'd almost surprised one of those abrupt laughs out of her. Laura tossed her head, shaking the stray hair back off her face.

"I know how you turn your head ever so slightly when you're working, like you're a radar turning toward whoever's speaking. And I know what you think of some of those people even though you try to keep your face blank as a mannequin's. I know what you eat for breakfast out in public, and I know what you *really* like for breakfast, which is Rice Krispies with a little syrup poured over them."

Laura smiled ever so slightly at hearing herself described. Jordan had been smiling, too, but as he continued, he lost the smile and only stared at her as if, even while describing her in minute detail, he realized he had never seen her before. He was standing stock still in the middle of the room, and he felt a chill in his shoulders as if someone were pointing a gun at him.

"I know what you look like when you close your eyes and let the shower water pour over your face."

"When did—?"

"I know which of your clothes fit you best and your favorite color. And where you got that little scar on the side of your knee that doesn't even show except when you get a tan. I know—Have you ever noticed this?—how you start to make a gesture with your hand sometimes but you stop yourself. Then a second later you go ahead and do it as if you're saying, Oh, what the hell. I know the place you have in this town, the way you know everything about it but don't really quite fit in yourself. I know how you've never really felt at home here, and you feel like your real home is somewhere else, but you can't tear yourself away from this one-horse backwater because ..." Jordan was speaking more and more slowly. It seemed unnecessary to speak at all, because surely Laura knew everything he was thinking. But what he finally said was a surprise even to him. "I love you," he said.

Laura's slight smile blossomed. "Well don't say it like it's an irritating skin disease."

But that was how it felt. It was like a lump he'd just discovered. When he realized that he loved Laura, he also realized he'd never been in love before. He understood for the first time what love was: an invasion. He was afraid to move for fear he might injure her. Her welfare took precedence over his own. Jordan had felt a different version of the same emotion the first time they'd put his daughter into his arms in the hospital. Afraid to hold her until he did, thereafter he hadn't wanted to let her go, not to a nurse, not to his wife. "Careful," he'd said as he'd finally handed the baby back at Marcia's insistence. "Careful." His hands had hovered under the baby.

He wanted to hold Laura so carefully that no one else could reach her, nothing could hurt her. At the same time, he was afraid to touch her.

She came to him very slowly, smile turning questioning. He touched her cheek. It felt just as he'd remembered. She held his hand in place there, closing her eyes.

Why was she so short? Jordan realized it was because he was wearing shoes and Laura wasn't. He kicked his off, which was better, but picking her up was better yet. He could encompass her then, all of her, she was all there in his arms. They kissed softly as children. They celebrated. Everything seemed new. Jordan loved Laura's smile, her hesitation, her house, her breast. His joy was so world-filling it seemed that she loved him, too. But that didn't matter as much as holding her did, as getting to know her even more completely.

A long time later he realized that night had fallen and that Laura might be hungry, but he couldn't stand the thought of sharing her. He asked, "Is there some place in town that delivers pizza?"

Laura laughed. "Where d'you think you are, son, Chicago?"

"I don't know."

She laughed again. "I can make us something."

She rose from the bed and picked up a short robe from its foot, but Jordan took her wrist and shook his head. Laura rolled her eyes and let the robe fall. "I hope all the shades are down," she said.

She started out of the bedroom, Jordan following, but only got as far as the doorway, which was where he caught up, wanting to stroke the skin of her shoulders and legs again. Laura turned, a little startled by his touch but put her arms around his neck and held up her face to be kissed. Jordan just wanted to look at her, though. Laura's expression turned slightly alarmed. "I look a wreck, don't I?"

"Haven't you had enough compliments for one day?"

"There's no such thing as enough," she said. Then she made a sound that in a younger girl would be called a squeal as Jordan gave her a knowing look, bent to nuzzle her neck, and lifted her to him.

It was Laura who reintroduced reality later in the kitchen. Jordan by that time felt a little embarrassed at sitting naked in a kitchen chair, but the sight of Laura moving confidently as a nudist around the kitchen, peering into cabinets, bending to check the refrigerator's crisper, more than made up for any discomfort of his.

"I do have pizza," she said, "but I hate to turn on the oven." She glanced at Jordan. "I wouldn't want you to risk injury."

"That's why I love you, you're so considerate."

"I guess a chef's salad? That's what I call it when I dump all the leftovers from the fridge into a bowl and pour blue cheese over it."

"Sounds great."

When she brought the bowl to the table, she handed Jordan a napkin, which made them both laugh; seeing her laugh made him want to kiss her again.

"So Wayne did kill Jenny," Laura said. Not to Jordan's surprise, she had heard about the discovery of the ring before Jordan got to her house.

"Who cares?" he said. "Sorry, I know, a lot of people care. That's not what I mean, I mean—let's forget it for a while."

"It's a hard time to do that. The judge only gave you until tomorrow morning, and look how much of your time you've already wasted." She smiled in acknowledgment of his expression, but she was serious about her questions. "What are you going to do?"

Jordan hadn't wanted to talk about it, but the problem enmeshed him, too. "I've got something that might help. But I still don't—" He mused. "Maybe I need to switch to proving who really killed Kevin."

Laura gave him a curious look. "But everybody knows Wayne did that."

"Everybody might be wrong. No, it could have been somebody in the hospital." But why? Maybe Kevin knew something someone didn't want him to tell. "I wish he'd said something before he died." But Kevin hadn't. He hadn't made a statement to the cops or to the representative of the court. Something nagged at Jordan, but he didn't need this shit any more. He needed to go to the beach with Laura for a month.

"What are you going to do?" she asked again.

"There's only one thing to do." He set his napkin on the table and leaned close enough to reach for her in a moment. "When the jury comes back with their guilty verdict, you write 'not guilty' in the record. Would you do that for me?"

Her eyes moved around his face. "Of course."

12

The next morning in court Jordan waited anxiously for trial to start, anxious not because his case was ruined and he was about to put on his most crucial testimony, but because he hadn't seen Laura in an hour. What if something had happened to her on her separate way to the courthouse? He didn't relax until Laura came out of her office and took her place at her small desk. She gave Jordan no look at all as she crossed in front of him, which was a look in itself. The way she held her shoulders communicated to him.

"Am I going to be first?" Wayne asked.

"No, Wayne, last. The defendant always goes last. That way you can hear everyone else's testimony before you have to give yours. I don't mean you should change your story to fit theirs, but at least you'll know." Jordan had explained this the night before when Wayne had finally told him all the circumstances of Jenny Fecklewhite's last day. All the circumstances Wayne knew, anyway.

After Laura had taken her place, all the other court staff appeared as well: bailiff, clerk, prosecutor, the judge. There seemed to be electric communication among them. Jordan felt it but couldn't hear the message. With elaborate courtesy, Mike Arriendez presented Jordan with the box of Kevin Wainwright's belongings. "I'm sure you'll need this for your presentation of evidence," he whispered.

"Call your next witness," Judge Waverly said in a voice that conveyed nothing but authority.

"Thomas Delmore, Your Honor."

Deputy Delmore didn't like being there; he particularly

Chapter Eleven

"Faith!" Pearl exclaimed when Faith returned to the bakery. "Your face is so... Are you alright?"

"It's probably wind burn," Faith mumbled, avoiding her friend's eyes as she hung up her shawl. She couldn't disclose that she'd wept so hard on the way back from Ruth's house she had to dismount her bike three times because her lungs ached from inhaling deep, sobbing gasps of the arctic air.

"Even so, you ought to take the afternoon off," Pearl urged. "You don't want to get sick right before *Grischtdaag*. I'll stay here until the last customers collect their orders. Truly, it's not a hardship, especially since I'm taking the day off tomorrow to meet our *kinner* at the van depot."

It didn't take much to persuade Faith to go

home early: her eyes were nearly swollen shut, her stomach ached and she couldn't imagine being attentive enough to ring up a purchase or follow a recipe. Feeling as if there were an ox cart hitched to her bicycle, Faith slowly trundled along the winding roads leading to the farm.

"What's wrong?" Henrietta asked when Faith traipsed into the kitchen. "You look terrible."

"I *feel* terrible," Faith replied.

"Go straight upstairs and gather fresh bedclothes while I put on a kettle for tea and draw a bath for you," Henrietta ordered, and Faith complied.

But when she reached her room, Faith was so chilled and the bed looked so inviting she burrowed under her quilt and didn't stir again until nearly five o'clock the next morning. Her first thought upon waking was of the conversation she'd had with Hunter, and she would have begun weeping again if she had any tears left to cry.

She felt like a fool. All this time, she thought he was her friend—in fact, she even wondered if he wanted to be more than friends, considering his comments about her hair and her laughter. At the very least, she believed he cared about her and respected her goals as a businesswoman, just as she highly esteemed him and his interests. She assumed he understood how much her relationships meant to her. Come to find out, he saw her as vain and worldly, as someone who was interested only in her appearance and her business.

I'd gladly gain fifty pounds if it meant I could have a bobbel, *and I dare say I'd give up the bakery if I had to, too*, Faith thought. Hunter had no idea what was important to her, and she was appalled to think she'd been on the cusp of sharing her most intimate secret with him. If his opinion of her was that low before she confided about her condition, what would he think of her once he knew?

She'd be polite to him, but beyond the usual pleasantries, she had nothing more to say to him. Didn't Ruth mention she was getting her cast off next week? Faith hoped Hunter would leave town as soon after that as possible. The past two months had been grueling, but Faith looked forward to starting the new year afresh.

To her surprise, as she was tucking her shawl around her waist, Henrietta approached her in the kitchen. "Your nephews couldn't rouse you for supper last night. I checked on you, but since you didn't have a fever, I let you sleep. How are you today?"

"Better now," Faith said, hoping her sister-in-law wasn't going to try to persuade her to stay home. Pearl was taking the day off to pick up her daughter's family from the van depot, and Ivy couldn't be left on her own.

"I woke Reuben to take you to the bakery. He'll pick you up, too."

Grateful for Henrietta's nurturing gesture, Faith promised her sister-in-law she'd bring home special treats for dessert. She slogged through the morning, and by dinner break, Faith was exhausted. She knew she'd have to tell Ivy about the cannery closing, so in order to get her accustomed to the idea, she presented her with a little gift: a pair of blue oven mitts, Ivy's favorite color.

"Remember, you must never get them wet except to wash them," Faith instructed.

"But you said no more baking."

"I've been thinking about that, and if you'd still like to bake, Pearl and I can give you lessons," Faith said. Then she explained about the changes that were to occur at the cannery.

"Ruth Graber isn't coming back to the shop?" Ivy repeated.

"*Neh*, but she'll come into town to visit," Faith explained. "And she'll invite you to her home and you'll see her at church, too."

"Did Hunter Schwartz tell her I ran away on his first day?"

"Oh, Ivy, Ruth isn't angry with you. She just

needs a change in pace. She's getting older and she needs to take care of her health."

"But her leg is mending."

Faith decided to switch tactics. "Ivy, don't you want to continue working with Pearl and me? We really need your help."

"I dropped your applesauce cake."

"That's alright. I made another applesauce cake."

The timer went off in the back room. Sighing, Faith rose to check on the rolls. She wondered if she'd made a mistake by telling Ivy today instead of waiting until after *Grischtdaag*. She didn't want to spoil the holiday for the young girl. Her own holiday already felt ruined by her rift with Hunter.

"Listen, Ivy, I have an idea," Faith said when she came back into the storefront.

The room was empty.

Wearily, Faith glanced toward the coat pegs in the hall. At least Ivy remembered to take her shawl. Grabbing her own garment, Faith turned the ovens off and locked the front entrance before exiting through the back door. Until that moment, she'd forgotten her bike was at home, so she fled for the pond on foot. By that time, Ivy had taken a significant lead and Faith lost sight of her.

For an instant, her thoughts turned to the day

she and Hunter pedaled down the same lane, and her lips twitched at the memory before she blotted it from her mind. *I'd better get used to solving problems on my own again*, she thought. *Or at least, solving them without any help from Hunter Schwartz.*

After spending a sleepless night of ruminating on his mother's words, "I've witnessed how deeply you and Faith cherish each other," Hunter's concentration was lagging. He had just finished refreshing the horse's water when his balance was thrown off by a small dip in the floor. Spreading his arms, he tried to steady himself, but he floundered backward against a stack of baled hay. It knocked the wind out of him and pain coursed through his hips and back, but his landing was less damaging than it could have been. As Hunter lay supine, trying to catch his breath, Proverbs 16:18 came to mind: "Pride goeth before destruction, and an haughty spirit before a fall."

The truth of Scripture seared Hunter's conscience, and he finally acknowledged he'd have many more falls, both literally and figuratively, if he continued to act in such an arrogant manner. Furthermore, his pride wouldn't just destroy his own body and future; it would damage his relationships, as well. Hunter knew he had a long list of people to apologize to, including his aunt and mother, Joseph, the staff at the hospital and Faith. Especially Faith. But first he needed to ask the Lord's forgiveness.

Please Gott, *forgive my disdainful attitude and with Your grace, help me to change*, he prayed, and then propped himself up on his elbows. Was that a car door he heard nearby? The doctor paid Ruth a visit the day before—was he back again? As Hunter pulled himself upright, James Palmer appeared in the entryway.

"Hello, Hunter," he said. "I hope you don't mind me paying you an unexpected visit. I looked for you at the cannery, but it was closed. A man named Joseph told me I could find you here."

"Wilkom," Hunter replied. "What can I do for you?"

"I'm wondering if you might be able to refinish more furniture for me," James requested. "You did a terrific job on the chair and my wife was thrilled. We've been storing an antique dining table and chair set in our attic for years. I'd like to have the furniture redone as a Christmas gift for Marianne. Obviously, I don't expect you to finish them—or even begin them—in the next two days, but if I have your word you'll start them soon, I can wrap a big bow around one of the chairs and set it in the dining room on Christmas morning as a symbol of what's to come. Marianne will be delighted."

She's not the only one! Hunter thought, amazed. Here was a provision to his financial needs he hadn't had to strive for one bit: the Lord literally delivered it to his doorstep.

"I'd be glad to," he said, without hesitating to consider the project would extend his time in Willow Creek.

After James left, Hunter hobbled to the house as quickly as his makeshift cane enabled him. Expressing sincere regret for his recent surliness, he promised his aunt and mother they'd see a changed man from now on. Then he told them about the restoration project.

Ruth beamed. "Your *onkel* would have been pleased you're using his workshop."

"And your *daed* would have been pleased, too," his mother said. "He was always proud of your skills at the factory and of your handiwork, but he thought you were especially good with numbers, too. I think he always imagined you'd run your own business one day."

"Who knows, maybe he might yet," Ruth suggested with a wink.

Hunter ambled back outdoors to look at the supplies in his uncle's workshop. Recalling how happy Faith was to tell him about her order from Marianne Palmer the day of the accident,

Hunter wished he could share his good news with her. As much as she may have wrongly blamed herself for his accident, Hunter wanted Faith to know it was actually her customer who played a role in God's provision for him.

He was so lost in thoughts of her he imagined her calling, "Please come back. I need to talk to you. Please."

Then he realized, he *was* hearing her voice. He exited the workshop and surveyed the landscape. Down the hill at the pond, he spied Ivy ducking into her usual hiding place beneath the bridge. Perhaps the ground there was especially muddy or slick, but a moment later, she reemerged and sauntered across the snow-and-ice-covered pond as nonchalantly as if across a field.

"Ivy!" Faith hollered from a distance behind. "Stop right there! You're walking on the pond! The ice isn't strong enough to hold you!"

Hunter darted into the stable, grabbed a rope and started for the pond just as a tremendous crack reverberated through the air like a gunshot, paralyzing Ivy in place.

"I'm coming, Ivy. Stay right there," Faith commanded.

Loping down the hill, Hunter trained his gaze on both of them as Faith shuffled toward where Ivy was standing. When Faith was within a few feet of the girl, she tossed one end of her scarf toward her.

"Hold on to that, Ivy," she instructed, her voice carried by the crisp winter air.

Ivy whimpered as the end of the scarf fell at her feet. When she crouched to lift it, the ice shifted again. Apparently startled by the sound, Ivy bolted past Faith back to solid ground, leaving the scarf behind. Faith cautiously rotated toward the embankment, leaning from side to side, as if trying to establish her balance. But the ice cracked a third time and down she plunged, the water closing over her head. Hunter didn't so much run as hurtle himself forward.

"Kick!" he remembered the *Englisch* swimming instructor urging him the summer Mason, Noah, Hunter and Faith fell into the creek. After the accident, their fathers enrolled the children in a special swimming clinic for Amish kids. Although the Amish rarely swam recreationally, after the footbridge mishap, their parents wanted the children to know what to do if they ever found themselves submerged. *Pretend you're a frog and kick*, Hunter willed Faith as he reached the edge of the pond.

She must have remembered the instructor's directive, too, because suddenly she surfaced and took an enormous gasp of air before bobbing back under. As Hunter looped the rope around a nearby tree and began inching toward where she'd fallen in, Faith surfaced again, thrashing at the water. This time, she stayed afloat and Hunter could hear her breathing was fast and furious. Knowing her hyperventilation would subside within a minute as her body adjusted to the cold, he tossed the rope toward her, but it was too light and fell short. Faith continued to tread water until her breathing normalized, and then she flung her arms over the ice and pushed her torso upward, but the edge broke off and she nearly went under again.

"Hold on, Faith, I'm almost there," he shouted as he worked the end of the rope into a bulbous knot.

A second time she tried to lift herself but Hunter could tell the ice was too slippery and she couldn't heave her lower body from the water. Her arms wobbled, and she disappeared again. Hunter crept precariously close to the fractured ice, praying for the Lord to save her. When she came up again, he adroitly lobbed the rope straight to her. "Grab the rope, Faith, and wrap it around your wrist!" he coached.

Faith clumsily grasped the knobby end and managed to stretch her upper body over the ice as she wound the rope twice around her wrist.

"*Gut*, that's *gut*! Now, on the count of three, you're going to kick as hard as you can so your legs rise behind you, like a swimmer's," Hunter commanded. "You need to make yourself flat and straight so I can pull you forward. Ready? One…two…three!"

As Faith vigorously thwacked her legs against the water, Hunter heaved with all of his might until Faith's body jerked forward, out of the water and atop the solid ice. Hand over hand, he reeled her closer and closer until she lay not a yard from him and he swept her into his arms. By the time they reached the shore, her teeth were chattering so hard she couldn't speak.

As Hunter lurched toward his house, he didn't register his own pain or the cold, nor could he fully process the words Ivy was screaming—all he noticed was Faith's bluish pallor. He held her body close to his to try to subdue her shaking.

His mother and aunt must have heard the shouting and seen what had happened, because they were ready with blankets and dry clothes. Ruth directed him to lay Faith on the bed in her room and for Ivy to put on a pot of tea. Then the women shooed him from the room.

As he headed outside to get more wood for the stove, Hunter beseeched the Lord, using the simple petition he often uttered in regard to his own health, "Please, *Gott*, make Faith well again."

* * *

Drifting in and out of lucidity, Faith had the impression she was sinking—not into water, but into sleep—and she felt unable to fight the enticing pull of its gravity.

"She's dry now, but we can't let her doze off," Iris was saying. "Let's get her back on her feet."

Even with Iris and Ivy supporting her, it took all of Faith's strength to rise from the bed. She was fatigued when the day began, and her icy dunking drained the rest of her energy. She could barely move under the weight of the quilt wrapped around her shoulders. The three slowly made their way to the parlor, where Iris and Ivy settled her into a rocking chair positioned near the woodstove. Ruth placed her hand over Faith's forehead.

"That tea was enough to warm you but not enough to give you energy. You need sustenance," Ruth decided, doddering toward the kitchen. "I've heated some soup. Ivy, *kumme* give me a hand."

"I don't know if I could lift a spoon," Faith mumbled, but the words felt funny in her mouth.

"Let's warm your toes," Hunter's mother said. Cupping Faith's foot by the ankle, Iris slowly guided it onto a stool in front of the fire. Then she did the same with the other foot.

"Whatever will I do if I'm sick when I live alone? How will I manage?" Faith tried to say, but the words were barely audible. She was so sleepy.

Ruth gave her a gentle nudge and handed her a mug without any spoon. Faith's hands trembled as she lifted the piping liquid to her mouth and blew on it. "It's *gut*," she said after her first swallow. She hadn't realized how hungry she was.

She was slurping the last noodle from her second serving when Hunter tentatively stepped into the parlor as if unsure whether he was allowed to enter. His arms were full of firewood. "I thought I should stoke the stove," he proposed.

"If I get any warmer, I'll start to sweat!" For some reason, the notion amused her, and she giggled.

"I think she's still… She's still thawing out," Faith heard Iris comment to Ruth.

"*Jah,*" Ruth confirmed. "She'll be back to herself in another hour or so."

"I'll go wring out her clothes," Iris replied.

"*Gut* idea. *Kumme*, Ivy, you ought to have some soup, too," Ruth instructed. "Hunter, keep an eye on Faith for a minute, will you?"

Hunter unloaded the wood into the bin beside the stove and then clapped the debris off his sleeves before turning toward Faith. He scrutinized her, rubbing his thumb against the cleft in his chin. "Are you feeling better?" he asked.

"*Jah*," Faith answered. Vaguely recalling her last conversation with him, she wondered if thanking him for coming to her aid on the ice would be well received. Would he brush her off, the way he'd done when she tried to thank him for helping her keep her business? Regardless, she figured saving her life merited an expression of gratitude. "*Denki* for rescuing me, Hunter," she said simply but ardently.

Hunter's voice was tremulous and his countenance astonished as he confessed, "I'm so relieved the Lord gave me strength to pull you out. I wasn't sure I could."

Fearing he'd further injured himself from the effort, she replied, "I'm sorry if carrying me put a strain on your back."

Hunter frowned. "*Neh*, I didn't mean that. I meant—"

"Excuse me," Iris interrupted as she bustled in with Faith's clothes and a wooden drying rack. "I need to hang these in front of the fire. Hunter, would you take Ivy back to town? She feels terrible about what happened and she wants to be helpful, so she's volunteered to tidy the bakery before closing it for the night. If you leave now, she can finish by the time Mervin arrives to pick her up. When you return here, perhaps Faith will be warm enough for you to take her home."

Hunter promptly agreed, although he lingered where he was standing, as if there was something else he wanted to say. But when Ivy entered the room a moment later, he simply remarked, "I'll go bring the buggy around," and exited the house.

Wrapping her shawl around her, Ivy announced, "I'll make sure the goodies stay extra fresh overnight."

Faith smiled benignly. "*Denki*, Ivy."

"I won't eat anything, not even a cream-filled doughnut," she promised solemnly. "You don't have to worry about that."

Her expression was so earnest that Faith couldn't allow herself to laugh. Aware her young friend felt guilty about Faith's icy plunge and was doing her best to make up for it, Faith said, "I trust you, Ivy. But since the cream-filled doughnuts don't keep well overnight, I'd appreciate it if you'd take them home to share with your *groossdaadi*."

Ivy's eyes went wide. "Really?"

"It would be a big help to me if you would."

"Oh, I will, Faith," Ivy said, nodding fervently.

After she left, Faith leaned back in the chair

and closed her eyes. How cozy it was to be bundled in a quilt, her insides warm from sipping homemade soup, and her mind at ease because her friends were tending to the bakery on her behalf.

"You're not dropping off on us, are you?" Ruth asked, limping to the sofa.

"*Neh*, I was thinking about how blessed I am to have such *gut* friends," Faith explained. Then, for the umpteenth time, she reminded herself she didn't need a man in her life. She had her friends as well as her family, and she was going to be fine, just fine—wasn't she?

When Ivy was situated in the buggy beside Hunter, she asked, "Are you angry at me?"

"*Neh*, I'm not angry, Ivy. But you did give us a scare. You have to stop running away when someone hurts your feelings."

Ivy sniveled.

"I know it's not easy," he confessed. "Sometimes when people hurt my feelings, I want to run away, too."

"But you can't because you use a cane, right?"

"I guess that's one of the reasons," Hunter replied, chuckling. "From now on let's both try not to run away when someone hurts our feelings? How about if we tell them, 'You hurt my feelings and I'd like to talk about that'?"

"Okay," Ivy agreed. Then, without missing a beat, she said, "Hunter, you hurt my feelings and I'd like to talk about that."

Hunter smiled again. "I'm sorry I hurt your feelings. What did I do?"

"You don't want me to sell jarred goods anymore. You didn't think I was doing a *gut* job. That's why Ruth Graber is closing her shop."

"I understand it might feel that way, Ivy, but it's not the truth. My *ant* Ruth closed the cannery because she's getting older and she has to take care of her health. Her decision has nothing to do with your abilities." As he spoke, Hunter realized his assumptions about Ruth's decision were as ridiculous as Ivy's. He added, "Ruth's decision doesn't have anything to do with my abilities, either. In fact, I don't think she ever would have closed the shop if she thought working there was the only thing you or I could do. She would have kept it open to make sure we had employment."

"I have a new job now," Ivy said. "In the bakery. Faith Yoder and Pearl Hostetler will give me baking lessons. Faith bought me blue oven mitts."

"See? You've got so many talents you get to do something else now!" Hunter exclaimed. "But no matter where you are or what you're doing, I hope we'll always be friends."

"We'll always be friends," Ivy repeated.

The two of them decided to keep the shop open for any last-minute sales while Ivy wrapped up the baked goods and Hunter swept the floors. They were halfway through their tasks when Henrietta arrived to pick up Faith, saying she'd sit in the storefront until closing time. Hunter took her aside and told her what had happened at the pond.

"I knew I shouldn't have allowed her to *kumme* to work today!" Henrietta asserted. "She looked absolutely miserable when she arrived home early yesterday, and she slept straight through supper. I should have insisted she get more rest."

As Henrietta departed for Ruth's house, it occurred to Hunter that his spiteful remarks the previous day probably contributed to Faith's malaise. Overcome with regret, he agonized, *I acted like such a* dummkopf. *How can I ever repair our relationship now?*

That night Hunter counted the minutes ticking by—not because he was waiting for his pain to subside, but because he was afraid when he closed his eyes he'd envision the glacial water closing over Faith again. Although he'd responded swiftly and skillfully during the emergency as it occurred, now that he lay in the secluded dark of his room, he reflected on how horrified he'd been at the possibility she'd slip beyond his reach.

To comfort himself, he said aloud, "But she's alright now. She's alright." With the help of God, he'd found the strength to draw Faith to safety, despite his physical challenges. In fact, he had no idea when or where he discarded his walking stick in the process of rescuing Faith. All he knew was that when he recognized she was in danger, the only thing that mattered was gathering her into his arms.

Hunter suddenly realized there was absolutely no weakness, except his own attitude, stopping him from being a husband one day, and he bolted upright in bed. He'd almost lost Faith once already, and he wasn't about to lose her again. Tomorrow he was going to tell her he no longer wanted to be her friend: if she'd have him, he wanted to be her suitor.

Chapter Twelve

Because the dress Faith wore the previous day was rumpled from her accidental dip in the pond, and her other two workday dresses were dirty, she donned her Sunday dress. Then she inched down the stairs half an hour earlier than usual in order to avoid waking her sister-in-law, who most likely would pressure Faith into staying home to rest. Today was too festive of an occasion to miss going to the bakery.

Dear Henrietta, she wrote on a pad of paper. *Please don't worry about me; tonight Ruth and Wayne will give me a ride, since we'll be delivering pies—including several to our household—and I won't be able to ride my bike home.* Denki, *Faith.*

Since it was the twenty-fourth of December, Faith intended to close the storefront at two o'clock, so she, Pearl and Ivy could dedicate themselves to making pies to give to their neighbors on Main Street, as well to other members in need in their community. The three women would bake enough to take home for their own families, too.

Although Faith looked forward to spreading good cheer, she was filled with nostalgia as she coasted down the hill into town. Because the tenant above the bakery was moving out on the twenty-seventh and Faith was free to move in on the twenty-eighth, this would be one of the last times she'd bike to work. While she wouldn't miss traveling in inclement weather, she always enjoyed the solitude of her early morning ride.

The new year would bring other changes, too; namely, who would lease the cannery space now? Faith's thoughts darted to Hunter. What would he be doing, come January? Two days ago, she couldn't wait for him to leave, but this morning she was surprised by how thoughts of his departure added to her wistfulness. She wished time would stand still a little longer.

"It smells like it's going to snow," Pearl said when she arrived a couple of hours later.

"Jah," Faith agreed loudly as Pearl walked into the hallway to hang her shawl. "My nephews will be thrilled if we have a white *Grischtdaag.* They were disappointed the first snowfall is already nearly gone."

"Faith!" Pearl called from the storefront. "Why did you use so much plastic wrap on these treats?"

"What?" Faith asked, carrying in a fresh tray of sticky bun wreathes. She surveyed the display case for the first time that morning. Then it dawned on her. "Ivy covered those trays last night. I guess she wanted to make sure they stayed fresh."

"Covered them? She *swaddled* them!"

"*Neh*—they're mummified!"

The women were gripped with laughter. After they composed themselves, Faith recounted the story of her unexpected swim in the pond.

"Didn't I say it was a *gut* thing such a fine, strapping man was in town again?" Pearl asked when Faith described how Hunter reeled her ashore.

"That's what you said alright," Faith responded ambiguously, belying the surge of conflicting emotions she felt about Hunter.

Turning the discussion to Pearl's visiting children, Faith tore the plastic from a tray in order to prepare complimentary samples for the customers to nibble on as they sipped free spiced cider, coffee or hot chocolate, a holiday tradition at the bakery.

At midmorning, Faith was surprised to see Hunter emerge from a taxi idling in front of the bakery. Her stomach fluttered, and she would have disappeared into the kitchen to avoid him, but Ivy was in the washroom and Pearl was running a personal errand at the mercantile. Faith's pulse pit-a-patted as Hunter entered the bakery, adroitly maneuvering his cane in rhythm with his footsteps.

"Guder mariye," she said while polishing the countertop.

"Guder mariye," he replied. His eyes were lustrous and a huge grin adorned his face. "How are you feeling?"

"Fine, *denki*. What can I do for you?"

"I need three sticky bun wreathes, please."

"Three?" Faith questioned skeptically.

"Jah," Hunter answered. "I'm accompanying Ruth to the hospital to get her cast off. I was rude to the hospital staff after my injury, so I wanted to bring them a token of apology. I couldn't think of anything better than something you baked."

Hunter seemed to be carrying himself with a new confidence, and his ruddy cheeks created a striking contrast with his dark hair. To be honest, his presence took her breath away, and when he complimented her, she felt her resolve to keep him at a distance melting away, like icing on a warm cake. She couldn't allow that to happen. She'd be cordial, yes, but she wasn't going to let him pretend they hadn't fallen out—even if he *did* save her life. It was fine and good he was apologizing to the hospital staff, but that didn't change things between the two of them.

"I see," she said crisply, and turned boxing the treats.

"Ah, there you are," Faith said when Ivy walked into the room a moment later. "Please assist Hunter if he needs to purchase anything else. I hear the timer going off." Before leaving, she added, "I hope all goes well for Ruth at the hospital. *Mach's gut*, Hunter."

After pulling the bread from the oven, Faith raced into the washroom and splashed water on her face as her heart boomed in her ears. Ruth's cast was coming off, which meant Hunter likely would leave even sooner than expected. *It won't be soon enough*, Faith thought—not because she wanted him gone, but because she was beginning to hope he'd stay.

Hunter sat beside his aunt in the taxi and balanced the boxes on his knees. Faith disappeared before he asked if he could take her home that evening in order to speak with her in private. Although she looked especially lovely and she stated she was fine, there was something about her manner that suggested she was preoccupied. Either that, or she wasn't nearly as pleased to see him as he'd been to see her. Not that she should have been, considering their last full conversation. *Perhaps it's best if I show up unannounced at the end of the day,* he mused. *That way, Faith won't have time to think of an excuse to decline a ride.*

Twisting his head toward Ruth, he cleared his throat. "*Ant* Ruth," he began in *Deitsch* so the driver wouldn't understand him. "I want to apologize for how ungracious I was the other day when you offered my *mamm* and me such a generous gift. I've had a prideful attitude lately, and I'm sorry."

Ruth chortled. "*Jah*, you've been a bit of a bear. But I understand. After my accident, I felt pretty low, too. And the lower I felt, the more puffed up I became, not wanting to admit my weakness. That's why I didn't notify you and your *mamm* about my accident right away. I thought I'd be fine on my own. I didn't want to admit my own limitations."

Hunter nodded. His aunt had hit the nail on the head.

"But it's when we're weak *Gott* is strong," Ruth reminded him. "You're like me. Sometimes you've got to stop trying to do everything by yourself and start relying more on *Gott's* grace and on those who are in the position to help you. And that means accepting the money I set aside for the lease."

"But how can I accept such a big gift, knowing I might not be able to repay it?"

"It's a *gift*, Hunter, not a debt. It's like…like *Gott's* grace to us. We can't repay grace, we can only receive it. And the way we receive it is with humility and a grateful heart."

Hunter nodded again. Then he placed his hand over his aunt's and said, "*Denki*. I appreciate your gift, but with the exception of my recent hospital bills, I've managed to stay on top of our expenses from Indiana. So, if it's alright with you, I'd like to use your gift for the lease after all. That is, I'd like to keep the building space and use it to set up a furniture restoration shop."

"*Wunderbaar!*" Ruth whooped.

Hunter's apologies to the hospital staff were also well received, with several nurses cheering when he announced he brought goodies.

"So where's your 'new best friend'?" Tyler chided with his mouth half-full. "That stick isn't the one we sent you home with."

"*Neh*, this is the Amish version," Hunter joshed, embarrassed about breaking the first one. "I made it. See how I can hold on to it here, or prop it beneath my arm, like so…"

Tyler's eyes widened. "Nice work, but I still

think you'd do better holding hands with a successful, pretty woman who can bake like this." He held up the last of his treat for emphasis before popping it in his mouth.

"Er, actually…" Hunter began. Ordinarily, he wouldn't confide in an *Englisch* acquaintance, but Tyler had been so encouraging that Hunter wanted to share his good news. "Actually, when she gets done with work, I'm asking if I can court her."

"On Christmas Eve? Nice touch, very romantic!" Tyler said, bumping Hunter's shoulder with his fist. Then someone urged him into a patient's room and he was gone.

Ruth was so giddy to have her ankle free of its cast she chatted all the way home, but Hunter could barely concentrate. His most difficult apology lay before him. Would Faith hear him out? Would she accept his offer of courtship? Would she even accept his offer of a ride home?

He spent the afternoon working on the single chair James Palmer left with him as a sample of the furniture set, and then, an hour before hitching the horse, Hunter shaved again and put on a fresh shirt.

"It's so *gut* to see you! How well you appear!" Pearl exclaimed when she unlocked the front door. "How are you feeling?"

Pearl had such a genuine way of inquiring

about his well-being that Hunter's nervousness temporarily vanished. "I'm much better, *denki*," he said. "You must be well, too, now that your *kinner* are home for a visit?"

Their easygoing conversation was interrupted when Faith emerged from the back room with several boxes stacked in her arms. She couldn't see around them, but when she set them down them on the counter, she looked surprised.

"Oh, hello again, Hunter," she said. Over the course of the day, her hair had loosened within its clip, and her skin had a pleasant, arresting glow.

Hunter wiped his palms on his trousers. "Hello again, Faith," he managed to reply.

"There's Wayne's buggy outside," Pearl said as she donned her shawl. "Since I'm eager to get home to my family, Hunter mentioned he'd give you a ride instead, okay? We'll drop the last pies off at Isaac Miller's house, so all you'll have to deliver are the pies going to your own family."

Faith almost imperceptibly cringed, but she politely agreed. They helped Pearl with her pies and then loaded Hunter's backseat with pies for the Yoder family and one for Ruth's household, as well. By the time he was seated side by side with Faith, Hunter's mouth was so dry he didn't know if he could say the words he'd been so desperate to express.

* * *

Hunter directed the horse toward Faith's home, clearing his throat so many times she was about to search her satchel for a lozenge when he announced, "I'm glad you accepted a ride, Faith, because there's something important I want to discuss with you."

Faith interwove her gloved fingers on her lap to steady her hands. Why was she so nervous? "*Jah*, what is it?"

"It's that I'm sorry. Very sorry. For what I said the day you came to Ruth's house with the fry pies." Hunter's voice was guttural and his words came out in spurts. "I said things that were unkind. And misdirected. I said hurtful things. I'm sorry and I hope you'll forgive me."

"There's nothing to forgive," she answered, echoing the words and impervious tone he'd used when she apologized to him for contributing to his injuries. "You were only telling the truth, and you were right. I don't know anything about the extent of your health issues. In some ways, I have made the bakery the center of my life. And my struggles are small compared with yours."

"*Neh!*" Hunter exclaimed. "Those things weren't true expressions of how I felt. I said them because I was in pain. Not just physical pain, either. I was… I was scared, Faith. When you found out about my previous injuries, I felt weak. Exposed. I assumed you thought of me as…as less than a man. And I felt if I hadn't failed you, you wouldn't have had to get a loan. So I lashed out. My behavior was deplorable."

Stirred by Hunter's brave admission and how similar his fears were to her own, Faith had to lick her lips before softly replying, "I understand, Hunter. *Denki* for explaining. I accept your apology."

As her eyes adjusted to the evening light, she could see the grin crinkling his face as he turned toward her, and his voice was filled with relief. "You have no idea how much your forgiveness means to me," he said. "There's something else I want to discuss. How about if we stop here?"

Curious, Faith agreed. Hunter guided the horse until they'd reversed direction on the side of the road and were overlooking Main Street in the valley below. The landscape twinkled with Christmas lights and candles in houses owned by *Englischers* and the Amish, and as if on cue, snowflakes began powdering the landscape. "How pretty!" Faith raved. "I love Willow Creek, don't you?"

"I like it so much I've decided to stay permanently," Hunter replied.

Faith peered at him. "But what will you—"

"*Ant* Ruth has given me the gift of a year's lease on the cannery, which I'm going to convert into a furniture restoration shop. It was your customer, James Palmer, who gave me the idea when he commissioned me to work on another set of antique furniture. I'll probably perform most of the tasks in my *onkel's* old workshop, but I'll need a prominent location in town to attract *Englisch* customers."

"Wow, your own business— I'm so happy for you!"

"*Denki.* If it weren't for accompanying you on that first delivery to the Palmers' house when I offered to fix their chair, I probably never would have had the opportunity."

Faith was every bit as pleased as Hunter was. Adjusting her scarf to better inhale the snappy night air, she silently marveled that the Lord had used her weight—or at least, a fractured chair seat—to help Hunter. *It's not the first time the Lord has used my brokenness as a blessing*, she thought, remembering how her business was born as a result of her surgery. "I'm glad we'll be neighbors on Main Street again," she said.

"Mmm-hmm," Hunter murmured. He was quiet for a pause, and when he spoke again, his voice was raspy. "Actually, I've been reflecting on how well we worked together as business partners—before I started acting like such a *dummkopf,* that is—and I'd like to continue to, er, be paired with you, but not as your business partner or as your neighbor on Main Street. I'd like it to be a more personal partnership. What I'm trying to say, Faith, is that I'd like to court you."

Faith's heart leaped in her chest and just as quickly sank to her feet. This was simultaneously the most wonderful and terrible moment of her past year. She couldn't accept Hunter's offer, nor could she make herself refuse it. Stunned, she sat wordlessly watching as steam puffed from the horse's nostrils in front of them.

When she didn't reply, Hunter said, "I don't take courting lightly, if that's your hesitation. My stance is the same now as when I was sixteen—I wouldn't ask to court you if I didn't think we have a possibility of marrying someday."

"I understand," Faith answered soberly. "Which is why I can't accept your offer of courtship."

"What? Why not?"

The impulse to share her secret was so overwhelming it frightened her. It made her feel, in Hunter's own words, weak and exposed. True, Hunter was very respectful and understanding when she opened up to him about her business concerns and her breakup with Lawrence. Not to mention how compassionately he responded to her breakdown after the incident with the drunken student. There was no doubt he'd witnessed sides of her she wouldn't ordinarily reveal, and she'd grown to trust him to keep her secrets, which was why she had even considered telling him about her health issue the other day. But that was different.

That was before he asked if he could be her suitor. She couldn't risk being that vulnerable now. She couldn't bear to watch his mouth drop open as he struggled to think of a way to rescind his offer. Getting over Lawrence's rejection was difficult enough, but what helped was that Faith rarely saw him after their breakup. She was sure to cross paths with Hunter on a daily basis now that he was opening a shop across the street from her. No, she just couldn't bear the shame. Not again.

"As fond as I am of you and as valuable as your friendship is to me, you and I wouldn't be compatible as a courting couple, Hunter. Our... our shortcomings would end up disappointing each other at some point in the future."

Hunter removed his hat and rubbed his forehead before saying, "I can't promise I'll never disappoint you in the future, Faith. I don't think anyone can promise that to another person because only the Lord is unfailing. But I'll do my best. And if I hurt your feelings or let you down, I pledge to work out our misunderstandings with an attitude of respect and forgiveness."

"We *have* worked out misunderstandings within our friendship with mutual respect. But as you mentioned, courtship leads to marriage and marriage…marriage is an entirely different kind of relationship."

"Which is why we wouldn't rush into it. We'd take our time courting so we could be certain we were ready."

"Time isn't going to make a difference."

"So you're saying you never want to get married at all?"

"I do, but—"

"But not to me." Hunter finished the sentence for her.

"*Neh*, you don't understand." Faith choked out the words as tears streamed down her cheeks. *It's exactly the opposite. If you knew the reason, you'd realize* you *are the one who doesn't want to marry* me.

Faith was right; Hunter didn't understand. Why was she turning him down? What did she mean they wouldn't be compatible as husband and wife? They already proved how well they worked together. Their conversations were easy and genuine, and they enjoyed many good laughs. How could he have been so wrong in thinking Faith shared the same degree of connection to him that he'd felt toward her? Why did she say they'd end up disappointing each other?

"Is it that you don't think I'd make a good provider because of my injuries?" he persisted. "I don't blame you for thinking that. I've thought that myself. But one thing I've learned since coming to Willow Creek is my future is in the Lord's hands, not mine, no matter how hard I work. So, I'll continue to do my best and leave the rest up to Him."

"*Neh*, that's not it." Faith wiped her eyes with the end of her scarf. "Please, Hunter, take me home."

Ignoring her request, he dropped his voice an octave as he asked, "Is it that you don't think I'm strong enough, or manly enough?"

Straightening her posture, Faith snapped, "Of course I think you're manly and strong! Who else could have tugged me ashore so quickly I barely got my stockings wet yesterday? But physical strength is hardly what makes a man a man—it's his character that defines him. I've seen your strength of character, Hunter. I've witnessed how you've been in pain, yet you've fought to overcome obstacles and to help others along the way, especially your family. Especially *me*. The Lord couldn't have blessed me with your friendship at a more crucial time."

Hunter smacked his knees. "That's exactly how I feel about you, too! I believe the Lord intends for us to be each other's helpmate—and not only when we've fallen over a buggy seat or plunged into an icy pond, or even as neighbors on Main Street or *leit* within the same church district. I believe we have a future together as husband and wife."

Faith wouldn't look at him. Shaking her head, she whispered, "I'm sorry but the answer is *neh*."

"You've told me *neh*, but you still haven't told me why."

"I can't."

"You're not being fair," Hunter argued. "You've seen me at my most vulnerable, you've heard me crying like a *bobbel*, yet you refuse to be vulnerable in return. You've accused me of false pride, yet you're being false, too. You're hiding something beneath that *wunderbaar* smile of yours. Please tell me, Faith."

"I want to go home now," she demanded, reaching for the reins, but Hunter held them to the side. This was one conversation that was too important to allow her to disappear before it was finished.

"Talk to me, Faith. Please?" he implored.

Although she shook her head, Hunter sensed she was on the verge of telling him what was troubling her.

"You almost drowned yesterday," he prodded gently. "I risked my life to save you, and I'd do it again in a heartbeat. But now it's your turn to take a risk on my behalf. Don't I deserve that much? Don't I deserve to know why you won't walk out with me?"

"It's me. It's that I'm not... I can't..."

Hunter reached over and squeezed her hand. "Please tell me," he urged.

Faith pulled her arm away and covered her face. "I might not be able to have *kinner* and you want to have lots of them," she wailed. "I had surgery when I was seventeen and I—I—"

Sobs racked her body and she didn't finish her sentence. There was no need; Hunter understood. He slid closer, enveloped her against his chest and rocked back and forth until her shuddering subsided and she'd caught her breath. Then he dabbed the tears from her cheeks and cupped her face in his hands so he could gaze directly into her eyes. "Do you want to have *kinner* when you get married?" he inquired softly.

Faith pulled back, as if stumped by the question. "That's sort of a moot consideration, since I don't really allow myself to think about getting married anymore. But ideally, *jah*, if I were married I'd like to start a family. However, we don't always get what we want. Sometimes the Lord has other plans for us."

"That's true," Hunter agreed. "Although sometimes, the Lord gives us our heart's desires, just not in the manner we had planned." He took a deep breath before asking, "Would you ever consider adoption?"

"*Jah*, absolutely. But it's expensive, time-consuming, and—"

"And worth every penny, every second and every teardrop put into the process," Hunter interjected. "At least, that's what my parents told me."

"You were adopted?"

"*Jah*."

Faith clutched her stomach and bent forward. At first, Hunter thought she had burst into tears again, but then he realized she was laughing, and he laughed along with her until their joy seemed to echo across the valley.

When they quieted, she looked directly at him and said, "Now I'm positive you're *Gott's* gift to me."

Despite the cold, Hunter's insides melted. "I have no doubt you're His gift to me, too."

"And just in time for *Grischtdaag*," she quipped, playfully nudging his arm.

"Does that mean we're walking out now?"

"Are you sure you want to?"

Instead of answering aloud, Hunter leaned closer, placed his hand on the nape of her neck and gently drew her mouth to his. Her lips were plump and velvety, and she smelled faintly of cinnamon.

When they pulled away, Faith opened her eyes halfway and peered at him from beneath her lashes. "I'm sure, too," she said. Then she turned and rested her head against his shoulder.

They sat side by side in silence, admiring the view, until Faith finally suggested, "I suppose we'd better go deliver these pies to my family before they freeze."

"Alright," Hunter reluctantly conceded. This moment had been so long in coming he hated for it to end.

When he reached the Yoders' farm, he said, "I'd like to see you tomorrow. Perhaps I can bring you home from work again?"

"*Neh*, I don't think that's a *gut* idea," Faith replied.

Hunter was confounded. Was she joking? He decided to tease her, too. "You don't need to ride solo on a bicycle built for two anymore, Faith—you have me now."

She covered her mouth with her hand and

giggled. "*Denki*, but I won't be riding my bike anywhere tomorrow—it's *Grischtdaag*!"

"So it is," Hunter sheepishly admitted. Apparently, kissing Faith not only turned his heart inside out, but it turned his brain upside down, and he'd lost all sense of time.

"You're *wilkom* to visit anytime the following day," Faith suggested. The Amish *leit* in their district celebrated Christmas by fasting and worshipping at home with their families and then feasting together in the late afternoon. December 26 was traditionally reserved for visiting friends and extended family, exchanging small gifts and eating treats.

"I'll see you bright and early on the twenty-sixth, then," Hunter promised.

While he enjoyed reading Scripture, singing carols and devouring the meal Ruth was thrilled to be mobile enough to prepare, Hunter was relieved when twilight finally arrived. But once in bed, he tossed and turned. Thoughts of Faith kept him awake. Instead of counting the ticking of the clock, he counted his heartbeats until he'd see her again. It did no good; he still couldn't sleep. He lay awake until almost dawn, and then donned his clothes, grabbed his flashlight and tiptoed outdoors. It had snowed off and on since Christmas Eve, and his footsteps crunched loudly as he made his way toward the stable.

After quietly hitching the horse, he directed it toward the Yoders' house. At the bottom of a big hill, he stopped the buggy, set the brake and cautiously lowered himself onto the ground to trek partway up the incline. His muscles were sore and tight, but after fifteen minutes, he finished his trek and continued in the buggy to Faith's house.

"Hunter!" Faith whispered when she opened the kitchen door. "What are you doing here? The sun isn't even up yet!"

"I said I'd be here bright and early, didn't I? Please, grab your shawl and *kumme* with me. There's something I need to show you."

Faith pursed her lips and shook her head, but she put on her shawl and followed him out the door. Once they were on the road, she asked, "What would you have done if I hadn't been awake?"

"You're a baker. You're always up at this hour," Hunter replied smugly, causing Faith to giggle.

When they reached the bottom of the hill, and he reversed the buggy so they were facing the incline, she asked, "What is it you want to show me? It's too dark to see anything."

"Be patient. You'll find out."

"If I had known we were going to sit out here, I would have brought *kaffi*," she complained good-naturedly. "And a sticky bun."

"*Jah*, I'm hungry enough to eat an entire wreath of them myself."

Faith lifted her hands to her cheeks. "Ach! Speaking of wreaths, I forgot to say *Frehlicher Grischtdaag*!"

"*Frehlicher Grischtdaag*," he echoed as the sun began peeking over the horizon, tinting the snow with a soft orange hue. "There's something else I forgot to say. It might seem premature, but we've been through so much together already and it's something I need to, er, to spell out plainly, so there's no question about it."

Faith tipped her head. *"Jah?"*

Hunter gestured toward the incline on the hill in front of them, where he'd etched the words *I love you, Faith Yoder* in the snow with his boots. When she read it, her face blossomed with pink and she gave him a sideways squeeze.

"I love you, too, Hunter," she declared and nuzzled his cheek.

"Your nose is like an ice cube," he said, chuckling.

"*Jah*, but this cold spell is almost over. It's supposed to get to forty degrees today," Faith replied, sighing. "Which means your message will melt."

"That's alright. I'd rather say the words directly to you than inscribe them in the snow."

"Uh-oh! Did it hurt your legs to tromp about writing that?"

"*Neh*, not really. It's just I prefer whispering 'I love you' because then I'm close enough to do this," Hunter explained softly as he pressed his lips to hers.

She allowed him to kiss her twice before she teased, "*Kumme*, let's go have breakfast. I've been told most people can't do without their morning meal."

"Actually, I was kind of hoping for a treat, maybe a cupcake or...didn't you mention something about sticky buns?" Hunter gibed. As Faith giggled, Hunter picked up the reins with one hand and encircled her waist with the other. The sun had just risen, but it was already one of the happiest days of his life.

Epilogue

When Faith and Hunter were married one week before Christmas the following year, Faith made their wedding cakes: peanut butter sheet cake for the *kinner*, at Andy's request, and pumpkin spice with cream cheese frosting and shaved pecans—in tiers, not rolled—because pumpkin rolls were Hunter's favorite.

"I can't decide between them, so please cut me a sliver of both," Ruth requested after most of the wedding guests had left and the women were in the kitchen, putting away leftovers and doing dishes.

"That sounds *gut*," Iris said. "But I'll serve it—Faith is about to leave."

"That's okay. Hunter is still hitching the buggy," Faith replied. "There's always time for cake!"

"It doesn't appear you've been eating dessert

at all lately," Willa commented. "Is that how you lost so much weight?"

"*Neh*, I still have my share of treats, but this past year I've done more biking than usual."

"Even though you don't have to ride to town anymore?"

"*Jah*. You see, when Hunter first returned to Willow Creek, I nearly ran into him on my bicycle built for two. It was still dark, and he blamed me for not having a headlamp. I blamed him for walking in the middle of the lane. Last *Grischtdaag*, we gave each other funny little gifts. I received batteries for my headlamp from him, and he got a reflective vest from me," Faith explained.

Willa wrinkled her forehead. "But how did that help you lose weight?"

"Well, we decided we couldn't let our presents go to waste, so for the past year, we've been biking together after work as often as the weather allows. With my headlamp and Hunter's vest, drivers can clearly see us from the front or behind. Anyway, Hunter's doctor says cycling has been beneficial for his hips, and I guess it's been beneficial for my hips, too!" Faith said.

"Of course, all of this cycling happened *after* she finally admitted they were courting," Henrietta teased. "She tried to keep it a secret, but I knew right away."

Before Faith could deny it, Iris exclaimed, "So did we, right, Ruth?" Ruth's mouth was too full to reply, but she nodded vehemently.

"*Jah*, anyone could see they were smitten with each other," Willa claimed.

"Hunter Schwartz loves Faith Yoder," Ivy chimed in, and the room filled with peals of laughter.

Standing in the entryway, Hunter cleared his throat and grinned. "You're absolutely right, Ivy," he said. "But now that we're married, Faith's name is Faith Schwartz."

Faith's heart thumped to hear him call her that. "I suppose it's time for me to say good-bye," she said to her friends.

One by one, they embraced her. When it was Henrietta's turn, her sister-in-law held on to her extra long. "I'm going to miss visiting you."

"What do you mean?" Faith asked. "You'll still *kumme* see me, won't you?"

"If I'm still *wilkom*. Things change once a woman becomes a wife."

"Perhaps, but I still very much need—and *want*—close relationships with all my female friends and relatives. Especially you, Henrietta," Faith insisted.

Henrietta beamed and hugged Faith again before ushering her and Hunter out the door. Once they were situated in the buggy, he tucked a wool blanket about Faith's lap.

"Denki," she said. Linking hands with him, she leaned her head against his shoulder as they traveled toward town. Just before they turned onto Main Street, she jerked to an upright position.

"Oh, *neh,*" she fretted aloud. "In my excitement about our wedding, I forgot to replenish the wood box. We'll freeze!"

Hunter threw his head back and laughed. "Hauling wood upstairs will be my chore from now on, Faith. You're not responsible for doing everything anymore. You've got me."

"I've got you," Faith repeated, resting her head again.

Once inside the apartment, she lit an oil lamp while Hunter started a fire. Turning from the stove, he noticed she was shivering. "You're cold," he said. *"Kumme* here."

As he enveloped her in his arms, she suggested, "One *gut* thing about living in such a tiny apartment is it heats up very quickly."

"Is that a *gut* thing? I rather prefer cuddling for warmth."

Faith tittered. "I have to warn you, it can get pretty hot up here in the summer, especially with the ovens going in the bakery below."

"If the Lord keeps blessing our shops with success as He's done this past year, by the summer I'll be able to build a house of our own. Something bigger."

"Bigger?" Faith questioned. "I thought you believed big houses were a waste of resources."

"Only if they're excessive. Besides, our house won't be huge. Its size will be practical for both of us and perhaps someday for our *kinner*," he said, pausing to kiss the tip of her nose. "Maybe we can even build it on a plot of land near the creek."

"Oh, I'd like that!" She kissed him back on the lips.

Then he cautioned, "Of course, we'll have to enroll the *kinner* in swimming lessons, so they'll know what to do if they fall into the water by accident."

It made Faith's heart swell to hear him speaking as if their babies had already been adopted or born. "I'm not worried. With the grace of *Gott*, I trust you to keep them safe," she mumbled dreamily, and nestled deeper into her husband's muscular, loving embrace.

* * * * *

Dear Reader,

My favorite summer job during college was working at a bakery. Unlike Faith, I didn't have a tandem bike, but I did cycle to work in the wee hours of the morning. I loved being the only one on the road that early, and although I frequently sampled the pastries, all my pedaling kept me from gaining weight.

I still enjoy baking, and while I was writing this book I experimented with several new Amish recipes as part of my research. At the same time, I tried to begin a diet. You can probably guess how that went! I'm blessed to have people in my life who support me through my "failures," and who encourage me to lean on Christ instead of depending solely on my own efforts for success.

I'm grateful God can use our so-called weaknesses, no matter how big or small, for His glory and our good, aren't you?

Blessings,
Carrie Lighte

YES! Please send me the **Home on the Ranch Collection** in Larger Print. This collection begins with 3 FREE books and 2 FREE gifts in the first shipment. Along with my 3 free books, I'll also get the next 4 books from the Home on the Ranch Collection, in LARGER PRINT, which I may either return and owe nothing, or keep for the low price of $5.24 U.S./ $5.89 CDN each plus $2.99 for shipping and handling per shipment*. If I decide to continue, about once a month for 8 months I will get 6 or 7 more books, but will only need to pay for 4. That means 2 or 3 books in every shipment will be FREE! If I decide to keep the entire collection, I'll have paid for only 32 books because 19 books are FREE! I understand that accepting the 3 free books and gifts places me under no obligation to buy anything. I can always return a shipment and cancel at any time. My free books and gifts are mine to keep no matter what I decide.

268 HCN 3760 468 HCN 3760

Name	(PLEASE PRINT)	

Address		Apt. #

City	State/Prov.	Zip/Postal Code

Signature (if under 18, a parent or guardian must sign)

Mail to the **Reader Service:**

IN U.S.A.: P.O. Box 1341, Buffalo, New York 14240-8531
IN CANADA: P.O. Box 603, Fort Erie, Ontario L2A 5X3

7127

didn't like being there at the behest of the defense. He didn't like sitting there exposed, missing his sunglasses and hat. More than anything, he didn't like Jordan. Delmore tried to make every question and answer mortal combat.

"When?"

"I told you the date, Deputy. Let me make it clearer for you: Did you visit Kevin Wainwright in Mercy Hospital while Mr. Wainwright was a patient there because of injuries he sustained in a fight with Wayne Orkney?"

"It wasn't a fight, it was a beating."

"Did you see it?"

"I know all about the bea—"

"Did you see it?"

"You don't have to see something to know what—"

"Did—you—see—it?"

"No," the deputy said sullenly.

"Then why don't you confine your answers to the questions I ask you, which I hope will pertain to events you *do* know something about. Do I need to ask the judge to instruct you to do that?"

Delmore just glared. *You won't always be behind a table in a courtroom full of people,* his face said. *You've got to get in your car some time.*

"Did you visit Kevin Wainwright in the hospital?"

"When?"

"Your Honor?" Jordan said helplessly, but the judge was already speaking, leaning over. Delmore leaned away from him as if he could feel the heat of the judge's breath.

"Deputy Delmore, this court has business to conduct, and you are hindering it. You are wasting the *court*'s time. Cease."

"I'm sorry, Your Honor."

Jordan tried to keep smugness out of his voice but not very hard. "Do you remember the question?"

"Yes, I visited Kevin Wainwright in the hospital after his vicious beating by your client."

"Why?" Jordan asked.

"To see if he could make a statement, of course. About his attacker."

"But as you said, everyone knew that."

"Well—I also wanted to ask him about what had happened in Pleasant Grove Park the same day."

"What *had* happened?"

Delmore shifted. "Jenny Fecklewhite was murdered."

"And you were the first officer on the scene of that murder, weren't you, Deputy?"

"Yes."

"Were you assigned to investigate the murder?"

The deputy shifted again uncomfortably. "I was pursuing investigation on my own."

"You mean without the knowledge of your superiors?"

"I was on my own time," Delmore insisted.

Jordan paused. He was leaning back now, apparently relaxed. "Were you one of the people Jenny interviewed for her speech on law enforcement?" he asked knowingly.

Delmore heard the tone. "Yes," he said simply.

"Were you upset about her death?"

Delmore wanted to challenge the question or the word, but it took him too long to think how. When he heard the silence, he said angrily, "Of course."

"And who did you think had killed her?"

"Objection," the district attorney rose to say. It was the first time he had done so during Delmore's testimony. Arriendez seemed to be giving Jordan his head, or enough rope. "Calls for speculation."

"Sustained."

Speculation was exactly what Jordan was hoping for, but not by the witness, by the jury. Delmore had looked suspicious, he hoped. With his next witness, Jordan tried to offer more suspects.

"Evelyn Riegert," he announced.

Laura turned and gave her old friend a quick look as the nurse came up the aisle of the courtroom. Laura's look took in Jordan, too, but when he tried to make eye contact, Laura was already back in her court reporter pose, sitting at attention. Jordan admired her profile, the line of her neck.

"Did you bring the list I asked you to prepare?" Jordan asked after establishing Ms. Riegert's profession and that she had been the head nurse at the time of Kevin Wainwright's short stay in her hospital.

"Yes, sir," Evelyn said quickly. She was a good witness, very serious. She held up a typed list of names.

"Please tell the court what this list is."

"This is the names of people who came to visit Kevin."

"Was it usual for you to keep such a list?"

"Oh, no, I never did before. But a police officer, Officer Wilcox, came when Kevin was admitted and said someone had tried to kill the boy and that Kevin might also be a witness or a suspect in another case, and he asked me to keep a special eye on him. So I made notes of who came to see him in case he came to and said something to one of them."

"So this isn't a list you made from memory, this is a list you kept at the time."

"Yes, sir. Well, a copy of my list."

"I understand. But couldn't Kevin have had other visitors when you weren't there?"

"I was the day nurse. He shouldn't have had visitors after I left for the day. But I asked the other nurses to let me know if he did, and I added the names they told me."

As he approached the witness, Jordan asked, "Do you know if Kevin said anything to any of his visitors?"

"Object to any hearsay," the prosecutor interjected.

Evelyn understood. "I was in the room with two or three of them," she said to Arriendez. "Kevin never came to enough to say anything. Not when I was there, and everyone seemed to go away disappointed."

"May I see the list, please?"

"Certainly."

Jordan skimmed the list of Kevin Wainwright's visitors quickly. There were eight or nine names: cops, family members, friends, even Wayne's parents. Jordan blinked. He stood at his chair and went through the names again carefully.

He looked at Evelyn Riegert. "Is this list complete?"

"Yes, sir."

Jordan stared at the piece of paper, not wanting to lift his eyes from it. He was so obviously shaken by what he saw that Wayne leaned close to him to whisper, "What is it? Which name?"

Jordan didn't answer. He was vaguely aware of the stares on him but was recalled to his duties only by the judge's voice. "Mr. Marshall? Will you continue?"

"I'm sorry, Your Honor." He looked at Evelyn Riegert and couldn't think of anything he dared to ask her. The nurse stared back at him as if concerned for his health. Jordan walked stiffly to Laura's desk. "Mark this, please," he said.

Laura had a sheet of stickers close at hand. As she wrote "Defense Exhibit #1" on one, she scanned the page before her. She affixed the sticker and looked up at Jordan as she handed the list back to him, their fingers brushing.

"I'll offer this list as defense exhibit number one, Your Honor."

Jordan handed the list to Mike Arriendez, who scanned it curiously. Nothing seemed to catch his eye. "Relevance?" he asked.

"Since we've already offered evidence of the possibility that Kevin Wainwright suffered his fatal injury in the hospital," Jordan said slowly, "the list offers other—"

"I understand, Mr. Marshall. The objection is overruled. Defense exhibit one is admitted." Even Judge Waverly was looking at Jordan concernedly.

"I have no more questions," Jordan said.

Arriendez questioned Evelyn briefly as to whether she'd seen any indication that Kevin had died as a result of something that had happened to him in the hospital. The nurse answered in the adamant negative. Then the prosecutor asked, "What was Kevin Wainwright's time of death?"

"I only found out afterward," Evelyn said—Jordan didn't object to the hearsay—"but our records listed the time of death as six-twelve P.M., July twentieth."

The day after his first appearance in this case, Jordan thought, remembering standing in this courtroom in his shorts. So much time seemed to have passed since then.

"Was anyone on this list in the room with Kevin shortly before that time?" Arriendez continued.

"That would have been after my shift ended," the nurse said, sorry not to be helpful. "I wouldn't know."

When she was returned to him, Jordan still had no questions. He managed something like a smile at his witness as she departed.

"Your Honor, may I check the hallway to see if my next witness has arrived?"

Permission was a nod. As he left, Jordan looked back over his shoulder to see his list, his exhibit, being circulated among the jurors. They were looking it over curiously, obviously recognizing the names. "Everybody knew" was the phrase that kept beating in Jordan's head, excluding other thoughts. It was a phrase he'd heard so many times since his arrival in Green Hills. "Everybody knows . . ." "Everybody knew." The common knowledge.

He was in the hallway longer than a minute, prompting one or two people in the courtroom to wonder if he'd fled. But when Jordan returned, it was with his steadiness regained, at least in his voice.

"The defense recalls Dr. Bob Wyntlowski."

The medical examiner came down the aisle only a few steps behind Jordan. Both drew curious stares.

After Wyntlowski took the witness stand, Jordan asked briskly, rising to his feet, "Doctor, do you remember testifying that you thought the person who struck Jenny Fecklewhite was wearing a ring?"

"Yes."

Jordan was at the witness stand. "Is that the ring?" he asked, dropping Wayne's gold ring on the railing. Hideous thing, with its jagged edges.

Wyntlowski didn't take long to look it over. He had already done so in the hallway. "Yes, sir. I'd say that's the one."

Murmurings broke out in the crowd, but fewer of them and quieter than Jordan might have expected. He wondered how many people in the courtroom had already known about the ring before trial had started this morning.

"Can you be positive?"

"No, I can't. It's not like fingerprints. But this is a very unusual ring, and its sharp edges align with the torn skin in the victim's wound. And I believe this is dried blood in the crevices of the ring's crown."

The murmurings crested. Jordan was looking at the judge, leaning toward the witness, and at Laura, whose head was also turned toward the doctor as if to read his lips. Dr. Wyntlowski scraped a fingernail inside the ring's moon-cratered face and sniffed at what he dislodged. He nodded at Jordan.

"Thank you, Doctor. Oh—You remember the autopsy summary of Kevin Wainwright that you examined?"

"Yes."

"Do you still have the file with you?"

"Yes." The doctor displayed it.

"Is there a preautopsy photo of Kevin? That's it. Does it show a wound similar to the one you found on Jenny Fecklewhite?"

Dr. Wyntlowski examined the photo anew. "No," he concluded.

"But there is a cut on the face?"

"Yes, a bruise, but nothing like the deep gouge on the other victim."

"Thank you, Doctor. We'll offer the ring as defense exhibit number two and this photo as defense exhibit three. And pass the witness."

Mike Arriendez had been sitting placidly through the medical examiner's testimony until the last few questions. Now he was frowning, but he still asked no questions. The ring didn't bother Mike Arriendez. Emilio had said everybody knew the ring was Wayne's. Jordan wondered how many people in the courtroom—how many on the jury—were equipped with that piece of information. It didn't matter, the district attorney would certainly call a witness in rebuttal to let them know.

"Call your next witness."

"The defense calls Dale Hines, Your Honor."

The manager of the Pizza Hut had gotten dressed up for

his appearance in a blue suit, white shirt, and red tie. He'd gotten a haircut, too; his pale scalp gleamed through his brush cut. Jordan liked to see witnesses who took their testimony seriously. Unfortunately, with the increased formality of his appearance, Hines had suffered memory problems. Jordan had seen that happen before, too. What people would tell him freely and easily in the great outside world, they suddenly became not so sure of once they were impressed with the importance of the information.

"Mr. Hines, did you see my client, Wayne Orkney, in your restaurant around noon on July fifteenth, the date Jenny Fecklewhite was killed and Kevin Wainwright got beaten up?"

"Yes, sir. I guess it was around noon. I'm not sure of the time."

"Who was with him?"

"Kevin Wainwright."

No stirring among the spectators this time. Dale Hines must have spread his story around already.

"Was that unusual to see the two of them together?"

"No, sir. They were friends, I'd seen them in the restaurant before, lots of times."

"What were they doing on the day I'm asking about?"

"Talking, I guess. I can't remember what they ordered."

Jordan was coming forward briskly. "Do you recognize this?"

Hines examined the ring closely. "It *looks* like a ring that Wayne used to wear."

"Looks exactly like it, doesn't it?"

Hines shook his head determinedly. "I couldn't say *exactly*. I never studied Wayne's ring before."

"All right. But did you see this ring or one very similar to it that day in the Pizza Hut?"

"Yes, sir. Similar."

"Where was it?"

"Well, Wayne had it at first. And it was on the table."

"Then what happened?"

"I'm not sure," Dale Hines said, looking down so he wouldn't have to confront Jordan's disappointment. "I was busy, taking orders and clearing other tables. I wasn't just staring at Wayne and Kevin."

Jordan's exasperation flared quickly. "Mr. Hines," he said, "is it commonplace to see men giving rings to other men in your restaurant?"

Dale Hines's head came up quickly, glaring at the lawyer. "Not only is my place not that kind of place," he said sternly, "but we don't *have* that kind of place in Green Hills."

"Then this *was* an unusual event, you did take notice of it."

"Well—yes."

"And what was the unusual event? What did you see?"

Hines said slowly, "I saw Wayne give Kevin his ring."

"When Kevin left, was he wearing the ring?"

"I didn't notice," Hines said staunchly.

"When you went to the table to give Wayne the check or ask if he wanted anything, did you see whether he still had the ring?"

Hines frowned. "No, I didn't see it there."

Jordan let his breath out silently. That had been an unexpected ordeal. He suddenly became aware again of Wayne beside him. Wayne was sitting as stiffly as a prisoner in the electric chair and in the same position, his arms on the arms of his chair, staring straight ahead. Jordan touched his arm calmingly.

Turning to see his client had also given him a view of the audience. His quick scan caught on Swin Wainwright, who was stiff as Wayne, his mouth a tight lipless line. Mr. Wainwright was staring not at the witness but at Jordan. Jordan felt the stare even after he turned back.

"I have one other thing to ask you about, Mr. Hines. Is your Pizza Hut a popular gathering spot for teenaged couples?"

"Oh, yes. The *most* popular." Hines wasn't embarrassed to give himself a plug.

"You must see all the teenaged couples in town."

"Well, I don't pay much attention. They're just kids, you know. But yes, I guess I see them all."

"Had you ever seen Kevin in there with girls?"

"The last year or so only one girl," Hines said respectfully.

"Yes, but before this year, had you seen him with other girls, a variety of girls?"

"Well, I wouldn't say a variety, but two or three."

"How would they act?"

"Oh, all different ways. Sometimes happy, sometimes quiet. You know: kids."

"I object to this, Your Honor." Mike Arriendez stood looking as if his patience had run out. "Where is this leading?"

"Give me two more questions and I'll show you," Jordan answered.

"Overruled," Judge Waverly said quickly, waving them both to silence, then motioned for Jordan to continue.

"Did you ever see Kevin having an argument with one of his girl friends?"

"I guess you could say that," the Pizza Hut owner said judiciously.

"Did you ever see him hit her?"

Dale Hines was terribly uncomfortable. His discomfort translated into anger. "Not in *my* place," he said, pointing a stern finger. " 'F he'd ever tried something like that inside my place, he would've been through the door and down on his face so fast he wouldn't've known what happened." Hines shifted and the anger died, leaving him uncomfortable again. "But once," he went on more slowly, "Kevin was having an argument with this girl, and it was getting bad enough that I was about to go over, when the girl suddenly jumped up and ran out. And Kevin ran out after her, and like I said, it had been pretty bad, so I kept watching them. I saw Kevin catch up to the girl in the parking lot and grab her arm, and when she yelled at him again, he slapped her."

Silence held the courtroom when Hines's voice died. Hines seemed to feel guilty about the silence; he hastened to cover it.

"It was only one slap. I was heading for the door, but

before I got there, the girl took off in her car, so I just let it go."

Hines shook his head, seeing the scene again in a new light, one that gave his face a regretful frown.

"Thank you, Mr. Hines. I pass the witness."

Mike Arriendez only asked one question. "Was it Jenny Fecklewhite you saw Kevin slap, Mr. Hines?"

"No, not Jenny."

When he was dismissed, Hines shuffled slowly up the courtroom aisle and found a place in the audience. Jordan watched him and saw that Swin Wainwright was still staring at him, the tightness of his face holding back an obvious plea, one Wainwright was too proud to make openly.

"Do you have another witness, Mr. Marshall?"

Jordan turned his attention to the judge. "Yes, sir. The defense calls Wayne Orkney."

Judge Waverly made the oath sound very solemn, like an initiation rite into a secret society. "Do you swear that your testimony will be the truth and nothing but the truth, so help you God?"

"Yes, sir, I do."

Wayne's uplifted arm looked very skinny. When he lowered it, his white cuff dropped three inches out of the sleeve of his black suit. Jordan realized that Wayne, thin to begin with, had lost weight even during the short time Jordan had known him. His neck seemed to have grown longer. His jail haircut looked like it had been administered with the aid of a bowl. Wayne was clean-shaven and nervous and looked very young, the youngest person in the courtroom.

"You know the day I'm going to ask you about, Wayne."

"Yes, sir."

"The last day you saw Kevin. When did you first see him that day, Wayne?"

"That morning. He come by the gas station."

"Did you notice anything unusual about him?"

"He was real agitated." Wayne almost chuckled, but it passed quickly. "And he'd had at least one drink already. I could smell it. He said he was trying to get his courage up."

"Why?"

"I object to hearsay," the prosecutor said.

Jordan started to answer, "It's not offered for the truth, your—" but Judge Waverly quickly overruled the objection. The judge was turned toward Wayne, listening closely.

"Go ahead, Wayne."

"He said he was going to ask Jenny to marry him."

Jordan felt sure he'd been the only other person in the courtroom in possession of this news, but the silence held—a strained, listening silence.

"What did the two of you do?"

"We went to the Pizza Hut for lunch, so we could talk."

"Did you congratulate your friend on his decision?"

"No, I tried to talk him out of it."

In his peripheral vision, Jordan detected a couple of approving nods.

"Why?"

"I thought it was a bad idea."

"Did you talk Kevin out of it?"

"No." Wayne shook his head. "He had his mind made up."

"Were he and Jenny so much in love?" Jordan asked.

"It was more like a test. That's why Kevin wanted to ask her to get married. He was scared. Jenny didn't treat him the way she used to. Kevin had started getting crazy about her."

"Crazy in love?"

"No, sir, just crazy."

"What do you mean? What would he do?"

"Follow her around." Wayne was rubbing his hand, the enlarged knuckles. He sniffed, a raw sound, and cleared his throat. Jordan could feel his client's physical discomfort. "He got me to go with him a few times. We'd sneak around after her, see where she went after school or whether she was really baby-sitting or had cheerleader practice like she'd told Kevin."

"Did you ever see her with someone else, some boy or man besides Kevin?"

"Yes."

Wayne glanced to the side. Jordan also looked at Judge Waverly. The judge looked intently miserable, not like a man ashamed, like a man in pain. But his pain wasn't distracting him; he was studying Wayne as if he would kill him in open court if he found out Wayne was lying.

"How did Kevin react to that?" Jordan asked.

"That's what I mean about going crazy. Seeing her with somebody else just drove him bug-eyed. One time he just spun around in the street like a top. He wanted to do something so bad and couldn't think what to do."

"Now back to that day in July," Jordan said. He sensed relief that he hadn't pursued the topic of the identity of the man Jenny had been seen with, but the relief wasn't the judge's. Judge Waverly was still watching Wayne with utter absorption. "Were you wearing your ring?"

"Yes, sir. I always wore it."

"Did something happen that day with regard to your ring?"

"Yes, sir, Kevin asked me for it."

"Why?"

"Because he didn't have one, and he wanted to give Jenny one when he asked her to marry him."

"But he hadn't bought her one?"

"No, sir."

The implications of that seemed clear: Kevin's impulsiveness or his uncertainty of his beloved's response to his marriage proposal. Jordan let the jury worry it out on their own.

"Did you give him your ring, Wayne?"

"Yes, sir."

"That ring beside you on the bench marked as a defense exhibit?"

Wayne glanced at it apprehensively. "Yes, sir."

"Did Kevin put it on?"

"Yes. He acted a little nervous—ever'body knew about Kevin and rings—but he kept it on and laughed and said it was a good fit. That's when I was sure he'd been drinking."

"What happened next?"

"Kevin left to go meet Jenny."

"What did you do, Wayne?"

"Just sat there for a while." But Wayne had had an uneasy feeling. He described it for the jury and the judge, who seemed to be accepting his story. They had the faces of children listening to a good storyteller—or of adults finally getting the inside story.

"I knew Jenny wouldn't tell him yes. I didn't think Kevin even expected her to. It was just a—a challenge he was giving her. I sat there trying to think what he'd do when she said no. Because the way he'd been—Kevin'd broken up with girls before, it never seemed to mean much to him one way or the other. But he'd never gone followin' one around before. He'd never asked one to marry him. I was afraid."

"Didn't you think there was a chance she'd accept his proposal?"

"Jenny marry Kevin? No, sir, I didn't give that much thought." Even now Wayne looked surprised at the suggestion.

"So what did you do?"

"I left, and I started back to work, but when I got there, I couldn't get out of my truck. I couldn't just work all afternoon and wait to hear what'd happened. So I drove out to the park."

"You knew where Kevin was meeting Jenny?"

Wayne nodded. "On the way, I saw Kevin in his truck coming back. He just flew right by me."

"Do you think he'd seen you?"

"He couldn't have missed me. He sure knew my truck. That made me even more scared, that Kevin wouldn't stop. I kept thinkin'—hopin'—he was just embarrassed, but that's not what I really thought. I drove a lot faster then."

"You knew Kevin and Jenny's spot in the park, the place where they liked to meet?"

"Oh, their spot," Wayne said scornfully. "It wasn't just their spot, it was ever'body's spot. Yeah, I knew it. When I got there, I saw Jenny's car."

"What did that make you think, Wayne?"

"I don't remember." Wayne's voice was quiet, but it didn't lack force. It sounded as if it took great strength to force his voice through his throat. He sat stiffly, hands clenched. His dress clothes made him look even more out of place, as if what he were describing had changed him forever. "I don't remember thinking anything from then on. I just crept up through the bushes and I saw her. Laid out flat with a little line of blood running down from the corner of her mouth. Not moving. I could see from ten feet away she was dead."

"How were her hands, Wayne?"

"Her hands?" Wayne's wet eyes glazed over again as he consulted his memory picture again. "They were folded on her chest."

"Then what did you do?" Jordan's voice was quiet, too. He hardly felt the need to speak at all. From Wayne's look, the story had played out in his head again and again in the last two months to the exclusion of any other life. It would have continued unspooling now with or without Jordan's help.

"I drove back into town."

"Fast?"

"Fast?" Wayne asked, baffled. "I don't know, I just knew I had to get there as fast as I could. I drove down Main, and I saw Kevin. I guess I stopped the truck, because the next thing I remember is hitting him."

"Did you yell something, Wayne?"

"I—I guess I did. I believe those people, but I don't remember anything except needing to get my hands on Kevin."

"Did you intend to kill him?"

"No, sir. I mean, I didn't have any intention except to hurt him."

"Why did you hit him?"

"I was so damn' mad. I knew he'd killed Jenny. I knew when she told him no, Kevin'd get mad and whine and try to talk her into it until she got tired of him, and when she tried to leave, he'd stop her—"

"Objection," said the district attorney. "This is all speculation."

Judge Waverly waved the objection away before Jordan could even rise. Waverly was engrossed in the story, leaning toward Wayne as if the judge, too, could see it happening as Wayne spoke. He motioned for Wayne to continue. Wayne looked at him, embarrassed by the eye contact, and hurried on.

"And I knew he'd hit her, because that's what Kevin always did when he didn't know what else to do, and that would just make Jenny crazy."

Because she was the golden girl, no one dared lift a hand to her. The judge nodded. There were other knowing looks in the courtroom.

"And when she fought back, he'd hit her again. When I got to the park, I could see that's what had happened. And I just snapped. I wanted to hurt Kevin—"

Because Wayne was the same way, when something went wrong, he didn't know what to do except hit.

"It was just so damn' unfair. It shouldn't've been Jenny, it should've ... Not her. And I was mad at myself, too, because I knew what was going to happen, and I didn't get there in time to stop it."

"Wayne, you got arrested. Why didn't you tell the police why you'd beaten Kevin?"

"I didn't want to get him in trouble." Because Kevin had still been alive, and he was still Wayne's friend.

Jordan felt again like an intruder in the town. He felt like the invisible man. His questions were insignificant. Everyone was watching Wayne with sympathetic looks or angry looks or dumbfounded looks. But everyone else in the courtroom appearing even now, removed by time and distance, part of the story. Even Laura had lost her robotic pose and was turned to watch the witness or maybe the judge. Jordan realized again that he would never know her, not completely.

It was the judge who drew most of his attention. Jordan's case wasn't aimed primarily at the jury, it was aimed at Judge Waverly. The judge looked like a man who had taken the brunt of the attack.

"I pass the witness," Jordan said.

"Wayne, do you mean to say you didn't know how hard you were hitting Kevin?" Mike Arriendez asked aggressively, but he seemed to have lost his steam even before he reached the end of the question.

"I meant to hit him hard, sir. I just didn't know how bad it would hurt him."

"And you would have the jury believe you didn't intend to kill him even though that's what you shouted?"

"Like I said, I don't . . ."

Jordan tried hard to pay attention to the questions and Wayne's answers, but he had lost steam, too. When his turn came again, he only had one question to ask: "When you helped lift Kevin into the ambulance and rode with him to the hospital, Wayne, did he look like someone who was dying?"

"No, sir. He spoke to me. He told me it was okay."

The prosecutor followed up with a last question or two demonstrating Wayne's lack of diagnostic training. Jordan was watching the judge, whose gaze had left the witness and crossed the courtroom. When there was silence, the judge's eyes descended to Jordan's expectantly. Jordan had a hard time remembering what he was supposed to do. He looked at his notes, at his client on the stand, and across the front of the courtroom. That was where his gaze lingered longest, until with sudden decision he spoke up.

"The defense rests," he said.

13

Your Honor, the State hasn't proven a case of murder." The defense had, Jordan thought ironically; only he'd proven it against someone other than the defendant. "The defense has certainly carried its burden of showing that the defendant did what he did as a result of sudden passion rising from adequate cause. That's voluntary manslaughter, not murder. The State did nothing to refute the sudden passion *or* the adequate cause. Even the State's witnesses testified that Wayne looked and acted like someone who couldn't control his actions. His very act of attacking the deceased in front of so many witnesses proves that."

It was beautiful to use the strength of the prosecution's case against them. But Mike Arriendez didn't look worried as he and Jordan stood in front of the judge's bench beside Laura in the otherwise empty courtroom, arguing about what instructions should be given to the jury.

"As for adequate cause," Jordan continued, "Wayne testified why he did what he did, and no one has disputed what he saw, and certainly no one has claimed that what he discovered in Pleasant Grove Park wasn't adequate to inspire sudden rage."

As he argued, Jordan felt as if he and the judge were in collusion. If one person in Green Hills felt that Wayne's beating of Kevin was justified by what Wayne had seen in the park, it was the judge.

But Arriendez argued confidently that the State had presented a case of murder that should go to the jury. "Intent can be found in the methodicalness of the beating," he said among other things. And his confidence was demonstrated by how shaken he looked when Judge Waverly hesitated over his ruling.

It was with an apologetic sigh that the judge finally raised his head to say; "I agree with the defense. That's exactly how I would find if I were the trier of fact." His voice gained strength as he continued. "But I am not. The State has arguably presented evidence of murder to the jury, and the decision should be left to that jury."

The judge suddenly regained a measure of his old fierceness as he shot glares at both lawyers, expecting further argument. But Mike Arriendez was satisfied with the decision, though he looked puzzled. And Jordan just stared back at the judge, asking nothing more. His face, in fact, appeared to offer help rather than request it.

Judge Waverly abruptly rose and turned away. "Arguments in ten minutes," his disembodied voice drifted back. The district attorney hurried away to begin preparing. Jordan just stood.

Laura looked up at him. What was in her face? Sadness: The tragedy that had played out in the courtroom hadn't left her unaffected. Her expression was also compounded with something as she looked at Jordan. Not love, he couldn't convince himself of that, but certainly concern. She took his hand. The concern deepened.

"You're shaking," she said.

His heart was beating him, making his whole body tremble, but he hadn't known it until Laura told him. He was thinking of her. He wanted to hold her, but he was afraid. "I'm sorry," he said.

She leaned her head briefly against his arm. "It'll be over soon," she assured him.

"Wayne knew what was going to happen. It didn't take a genius. After what we heard in this courtroom, any of us could have predicted the same thing. But especially Wayne, who knew Kevin better than anyone. Who'd watched him over the course of weeks, turning crazy over a girl, acting ways Kevin had never acted before. Skulking around after her, learning things that made him even crazier. Haven't we all seen people possessed by that kind of emotion? We call it love, but it's something more. Something worse.

"Kevin was afraid of losing Jenny, and he could only think of one more way to hold her. He was going to propose marriage. Not, Wayne thought, because Kevin expected her to say yes or even because he really wanted to marry Jenny Fecklewhite, but only as a way of testing to see whether she loved him. So Wayne sat in that Pizza Hut and thought about what would happen when Jenny said no.

"But he didn't really have to speculate, did he? He knew from experience what Kevin did when he got mad and frustrated. Dale Hines knows; he'd seen it. A few other girls in Green Hills know, too, what happened when Kevin Wainwright got mad at them."

"Objection," Mike Arriendez said. "That's arguing outside the record."

Indeed it was. Outside the record, but not outside the collective memory of his audience, Jordan thought. He stood close in front of the jury, leaning on the railing, talking to them as if he and they were all long-time residents of the town, who had known all its citizens well since childhood. The jurors' expressions as they watched him attentively made him feel they were accepting his pose. One or two nodded slightly at where he was heading. They were all there ahead of him.

The objection was sustained in a quiet, distracted voice. Jordan didn't glance at the judge.

"He'd hit," Jordan said simply. "Wayne knew it. He'd seen it before. When Jenny refused Kevin, when she tried to walk away, when Kevin was so hurt and angry he didn't know what else to do, he'd hit her."

Jordan waited for acknowledging looks. "But he made a bad mistake when he hit Jenny Fecklewhite, didn't he? Because Jenny wasn't like other girls. Maybe it was just a little open-handed slap, but Jenny wouldn't let it pass. She wasn't the meek type, was she? She'd hit back. Or maybe say something that would cut him worse than a blow. Whatever she did to goad him, it made Kevin furious. And Kevin knew what you do when somebody hurts you. You hit back even harder.

"That's what Kevin Wainwright did. That's when he punched Jenny right in the face, wearing the ring he'd borrowed to give to her. Instead he hit her with it. He marked her face so badly that Dr. Wyntlowski could identify the ring by the wound it had left, like a brand."

He must have been painting the picture vividly, or his listeners didn't need much help to see it clearly. When Jordan turned aside, he saw the judge's head bowed in his hands. Laura's head was up, but two long tear tracks brightened her cheeks. Jordan was stricken by the pain he'd inflicted. He tried to soften it.

"And she fell back," he said quietly, "and something terrible happened, something Kevin never intended. They both had a horribly unlucky moment, because Jenny landed exactly wrong, and what should have been only a little spat left her dead.

"Wayne pictured everything that had happened. He told you that. When he found Jenny's body after he'd seen Kevin racing away from the park, Wayne saw exactly what his friend had done. He saw her lying there and he saw her hands folded on her chest. That's not how a person falls, we know that. Someone, after the terrible accident, had tried to do what he could for her. He'd tried to make her look peaceful. It was a crazy act, maybe, but that's how Kevin had been acting, crazy. Those hands told Wayne the story, too: that Jenny had been killed by someone who loved her."

Another reason Jordan had suspected the judge. He glanced again at Laura, thinking she was the only other person who understood what he was saying. Laura didn't look back at him. Her face had hardened slightly. The tear tracks still glistened on her cheeks, but there were no new tears.

"And in turn what he pictured drove Wayne a little crazy. He raced back into town himself, following his friend's track. And he found him right away, before Wayne had had time to cool down. He saw Kevin on the street and Wayne jumped out and screamed the worst threat he could think of, something people say automatically when they're so mad they can't stand it, and he ran up and punched Kevin as hard as he could, right in the face.

"Right in the face," Jordan repeated, touching his own cheek. "Hit him so hard he cracked Kevin's cheekbone and cut his face, but the cut was nothing like the one on Jenny's face. That's what Dr. Wyntlowski testified, and he's the expert. But you don't have to be an expert, you can see for yourself from the autopsy photos."

He held up the pictures, one in each hand. Some of the jurors lowered their eyes, unwilling to study the cut on Kevin Wainwright's cheek, the much worse wound on Jenny's face. Others in the jury stared at the twin photographs with a strange absorption, the autopsy portraits that strangely joined Kevin and Jenny, made them the couple they had been in everyone's minds.

"Another indication," Jordan concluded, "that the person who struck Jenny wasn't the same as the person who hit Kevin.

"For further proof," he continued after a pause, "we have the way Kevin acted afterward. What did all the witnesses say about Kevin as he was walking down the street just before Wayne's truck screeched to a stop in front of him? He was dazed. He didn't even seem to recognize his best friend. And when Wayne came running up and it was perfectly obvious he was going to punch Kevin, Kevin didn't even raise his hands to defend himself. Hiram Lester said he'd never seen anything like it. What he saw was helpless, stunned guilt. Kevin didn't defend himself from Wayne's blows because he knew he had them coming after what he'd done."

His slow pacing had brought Jordan close to the district attorney. Arriendez was watching him thoughtfully, an unconvinced expression on his face. Jordan acknowledged him with a rising hand.

"He's going to tell you, So what?" he told the jury. "Mr. Arriendez is going to tell you, quite correctly, that Wayne isn't charged with murdering Jenny Fecklewhite. So even if I got up here and proved to your absolute satisfaction that someone else killed Jenny, that doesn't matter in this case.

"But it mattered to Wayne. That's why it's relevant in this trial. Jenny's killing sent Wayne over the edge. It was the only reason for what he did. Do you think Wayne would have beaten his best friend as badly as he did without some terrible provocation? Look at him."

Jordan hadn't glanced over his shoulder and he hadn't prepped his client, but he knew what he'd find when he turned, drawing the jury's attention to Wayne. Wayne tried to straighten his shoulders, regain his manliness, but the attempt only emphasized his red eyes, his emaciated frame. Again his shirt and suit cuffs fell down his skinny wrist as he lifted his hand to wipe his nose and kept the hand there covering his mouth and half his face. His temples and forehead crawled with the effort to maintain. Jordan watched him for a long moment, seeing his client's pain over his lost friend. He had only found two people—no, three—in Green Hills to whom Kevin Wainwright's death really mattered, and one of them was Wayne.

"Judge Waverly has instructed you on three crimes," Jordan continued, having to pull his eyes and his thoughts away from Wayne to talk about the abstract Wayne of his argument. "Murder, which you understand. Murder means you intended to kill someone and did it. Then there's voluntary manslaughter. Voluntary manslaughter also means you killed someone, but that you were acting under the influence of what the law calls 'sudden passion.' Sudden passion isn't just anger. It means emotion so strong you can't control yourself. You could scream that you're going to kill someone without even hearing yourself. You could beat your best friend without even noticing that he's not fighting back. Sudden passion has to be an emotion that has such a grip on you that you do something terrible without even realizing it until afterward, when you're so sorry you feel empty, because the rage is gone and that's the only thing that was controlling you. Isn't that exactly what you heard described? Not just by Wayne Orkney but by the prosecution witnesses as well? If Wayne could have stopped himself, would he have hurt his best friend the way he did and would he have done it so stupidly? Wayne acted in front of the State's long parade of witnesses because Wayne didn't even know they were there. All he was seeing was the terrible sight he'd seen in Pleasant Grove Park."

Jordan glanced at the copy of the judge's jury instructions he held in his hand. "The other requirement of voluntary manslaughter is that the sudden passion has to have been prompted by 'adequate cause.' It can't be over something trivial. I'm not even going to discuss that. If Wayne's discovery of Jenny's body and his realization that Kevin had killed her doesn't amount to adequate cause, then there's no such thing as adequate cause. We wouldn't even have a law mentioning it."

Jordan stood in front of the jury feeling suddenly hollow himself, feeling resolve drain out of him. He looked at the recognizable, worn, earnest faces that in turn were looking back at him. He had the familiar feeling they were just wishing he'd get the hell on with it.

"The third crime you could find Wayne guilty of is the last one explained in the instructions, aggravated assault. That's just a beating. We've probably all seen aggravated assault happen. Sometimes it's just a fight that gets out of hand. No one intends to kill anyone, he just hits, and someone else gets hurt badly." He raised his eyebrows, waiting for looks of recognition. "Isn't that what happened here? I'll acknowledge that Wayne hurt Kevin, there's no way to dispute that after all the witnesses you heard, but he didn't intend to kill him. Not his best friend, no matter what Kevin had done."

Jordan stood very still, forcing himself not to glance aside. He wondered if this was where he should stop. But after a moment he continued.

"Wayne didn't *intend* to kill Kevin, and maybe he *didn't* kill him. Remember the testimony you heard from the defense witnesses. Dr. Wyntlowski was puzzled by the autopsy report on Kevin. It didn't go far enough. Kevin should have recovered, he said. Even Dr. Prouty said that could have happened. Dr. Wyntlowski saw the possibility that something could have happened to Kevin in the hospital, something that overworked his heart just enough to cause his death."

Such a tender muscle, the heart. Jordan could feel his own beating in his ears.

"And look at all the visitors Kevin had in the hospital. You have the list. People who could easily have reached the same conclusion that Wayne had, that it was Kevin who had killed Jenny in the park. Police had never arrested a suspect in Jenny's death. One told you that was because Wayne was their best suspect, but they never charged him, did they? It might also be they never made an arrest because their best suspect was dead. That's what Nurse Riegert said, that one of the officers told her Kevin might be a suspect in the other murder.

"So someone could have figured it out, and there were people in the hospital who cared about Jenny Fecklewhite. Officer Briggs, who rushed outside his jurisdiction to see her body. Deputy Delmore, who continued investigating her death even on his own time. Imagine them sitting there looking at the man who had murdered her and in a moment of anger doing something—some little thing, putting a hand over his mouth, twisting a blood line—some thing that wouldn't even take a minute and that normally wouldn't do any damage except to a man already struggling to recover. That's where Kevin Wainwright died, in the hospital, days after Wayne attacked him. Maybe that's where his death was caused, too."

Jordan waved away all he'd just said. "But it doesn't matter. I'm not saying someone else killed Kevin necessarily. That doesn't matter to this trial. What matters is that Wayne didn't *intend* to kill Kevin. That's all you need to decide to bring a verdict of aggravated assault.

"And finally you could reach a verdict of not guilty. You could find that Wayne was justified in what he did, that he had no—"

"Objection, Your Honor," Arriendez said suddenly and strenuously. "There is no instruction in the charge that would allow the jury to find justification."

"That is true," Judge Waverly said slowly. "No matter

what you may have heard, there is no such defense in Texas as justifiable homicide. Not any more. The objection is sustained. Please disregard that argument."

The judge looked from juror to juror as he delivered his instruction but without his usual black glare. His voice left the district attorney staring at the judge. Jordan turned to look up at him as well. It almost sounded as if Judge Waverly had been sending a message to the jury entirely different from what his words had said.

"No, but—" Jordan hesitantly picked up the thread of his argument again. "All these crimes require a certain mental state. All of them mean you must find the defendant acted 'intentionally.' You *would* be justified in finding that Wayne was so overwhelmed by emotion that he had no intention at all when he attacked his old friend. That he was simply lost in pain and rage."

He turned to look at his client again. Wayne's face was the best support for this argument. Even today he looked still dazed by what had happened. Jordan let the jury study him and didn't want to distract their attention.

"Deliberate carefully," he said quietly. "Thank you for your attention."

Before he even sat, Mike Arriendez was on his feet. "Does this look unintentional?" he asked, interrupting the jurors' gazes with his own exhibits, the autopsy photo of Kevin and a chart from the autopsy report, an outline of a human form with Kevin's injuries marked. "Not one punch," Arriendez continued. "Not just one kick. But here and here and here and here. And on and on. Look at the extent of these injuries. If the defendant had thrown only one punch, we might accept that as a man out of control. But at some point don't we require him to regain control? Don't we require him to see what he's doing? And isn't that point some time before he beats a man to death?"

Jordan could have made the district attorney's argument for him. He *had* made such arguments often as a prosecutor himself. He remembered very few occasions when he'd felt he had to expend much effort to refute the defense's arguments. He wondered if this was such an occasion for Mike

Arriendez. The things Jordan had said now sounded jumbled and forceless in his memory. But Arriendez was attacking them with intensity.

"The defense relies on the burden of proof, the favorite weapon in any defense's arsenal. The State has to prove the defendant guilty of murder. The defense doesn't have to prove anything. They just have to raise *possibilities*. They can throw out any number of theories they can think of. They can bring in an entirely different case to try to distract you. And they don't have to prove anything. They don't have to prove that the victim in this case killed someone else. They don't have to prove someone else murdered Kevin Wainwright in the hospital. They can just toss out the possibilities like birdshot."

Jordan sat stiffly. He was looking down at the table in front of him, nowhere else, bowing his head under Arriendez's attack.

"But their possibilities are ridiculous. Did they offer any *evidence* to support their suggestions? No. Their doctor testified that if he had done the autopsy on Kevin he might have done this, this, and this extra, but did he say there was any evidence from the report that someone else *had* caused Kevin's death? No. No evidence, just speculation. Nitpicking another man's work the way anyone's work can be picked to death. But Dr. Prouty, who was more perfectly familiar with the case and the facts, testified that Kevin was never on the road to recovery after he was savagely beaten by the defendant."

The prosecutor took a long moment to stare at Wayne Orkney. Wayne still looked shaken, but under the weight of silence he looked up, puzzled and a little frightened. It was a better expression from the prosecution point of view, the one Mike Arriendez had been waiting for.

"Let me suggest another interpretation of the facts," he said quietly. "One the defense's evidence also suggests. They would have you believe that the defendant was completely overwhelmed by the sight of Jenny Fecklewhite's murdered body. So stricken that he couldn't recover his senses all the way through the long drive back into town. He had no idea what he was doing, he was so gripped by sudden passion. Yet he had the presence of mind to drive precisely into Green Hills, to decide where he'd be most likely to find Kevin Wainwright, to track him down. How likely do you find that? That a man could be overcome by emotion yet thread his way so accurately to his goal?"

Jordan was poised to object but hadn't thought how. What he really wanted was to refute the district attorney's argument, but he wouldn't get the chance to do that. The State always got the last word. Before Jordan could rise to his feet, Arriendez changed course.

"But I want to examine another aspect of Wayne's mental state. Why was he so upset over Jenny's death? I grant you, it would have been terrible to see such a thing. A young girl so full of promise cut down so suddenly. The sight of that would have shaken anyone."

Arriendez's voice was growing harder. "But it didn't just shake Wayne Orkney. It enraged him. It made him so uncontrollably furious, the defense would have you believe, that he beat his best friend to death without even realizing it."

"Objection," Jordan said. "That's a mischaracterization of the defense argument. We suggested that Wayne in fact *didn't* kill the—"

"Beat him so badly he required hospitalization then," Arriendez interrupted. It had been a feeble objection, one Judge Waverly didn't even stir himself to rule on. Jordan had just wanted to break the flow of the DA's argument, but it went relentlessly on.

"Why? Why did Jenny's death affect the defendant so profoundly? I don't have to tell you the answer."

He didn't. Wayne's face helped tell it. Jordan looked at him and saw Wayne blushing. Wayne sat there as stiffly as before, but his face was burning with a new emotion.

"He loved her," Arriendez said anticlimactically. "Wayne loved Jenny Fecklewhite or he wouldn't have reacted the way he did. Now that we've established that, let's back up. Wayne didn't just suddenly discover his love for Jenny when he saw her lying dead. He must have known it earlier."

But it can *happen that abruptly,* Jordan wanted to say, but that wasn't a legal objection.

"Wayne loved Jenny, and his best friend stood in his way. Now let's look at the evidence in that light. We know before the murders Wayne and Kevin were in the Pizza Hut together. They had a discussion, maybe an argument. The ring played a part. Maybe Kevin did ask to borrow it, maybe he told his friend of his plan to propose. Maybe that's what set Wayne off.

"We don't know who left with the ring. We know they left at different times but not where they each went next. We only have the defendant's word that Kevin went to Pleasant Grove Park first. It's just as likely that Wayne Orkney sat there in indecision for a few minutes, then realized he could beat his friend to the punch. It's just as likely that he raced ahead to the park to meet Jenny himself.

"And then?" Arriendez said more softly, trying to withdraw his own influence from the scene he was painting. "Then the story is exactly the same as the defense's, except with two characters switched. It could just as easily have been Wayne who had the fatal confrontation with Jenny. Wayne who declared his love for her and was rejected. Wayne who responded brutally, as we know he was prone to do. Exactly the same logical progression of events, but with this defendant as the one who struck down Jenny Fecklewhite and realized she was dead and panicked. He raced away from the scene but on the way passed Kevin's truck going the other way. He knew what Kevin would find, he knew what he'd done.

"Imagine the defendant staring in horror at the blood-covered ring on his hand and tearing it off. Could anyone have looked at this wound"—Arriendez held up Jenny's autopsy photo again; this time the jurors stared at it with more penetrating interest—"and not seen what he'd done with that ring?

"But then—he came up with a plan. The defendant waited. Waited until his friend, the only witness to the murder Wayne had committed, made his dazed way back into town, probably trying to decide what he should do. And *that's* when Wayne screeched to a stop in front of him and leaped out and struck Kevin down before he could recover himself, before he could say anything to anyone, and hit him again and again. The defendant had to destroy Kevin; he had to stop his tongue. And he was safe to do it in front of witnesses, because he'd already decided what he was going to do: blame Jenny's murder on his best friend and then stop Kevin from ever being able to deny it."

Jordan was sitting stunned at Arriendez's brilliance in turning all Jordan's own evidence and theories against him. As the DA talked, his scenario seemed as plausible as the one Jordan had described, especially with the evidence of Wayne's blush—his face's plain admission of love.

But there was one thing wrong with the prosecutor's theory. Jordan couldn't quite put his finger on it—and it wouldn't matter if he did, because he wouldn't get to present it to the jury. He'd already had his one opportunity to speak. It was gone, leaving the prosecutor free to destroy him unrefuted.

"After Wayne was pulled off his friend, there was one part of the act left to perform. Then he had to look stunned. He had to sob and say he hadn't known what he was doing. He had to act remorseful and hover over his friend as if to do all he could for him and finally climb into the ambulance to accompany him to the hospital. Not out of tender concern for his friend," Arriendez said with sudden harshness, "but for the opportunity to take that fatal ring, the one Wayne knew incriminated him in Jenny's murder and to slip it onto his friend's finger to incriminate *Kevin* instead. It was the defendant's last betrayal of his friend. Doesn't that make more sense to you than that Kevin, who hated rings, who was terrified of them, put one on on that fatal day?"

Well, maybe, Jordan thought, still looking for the flaw in the DA's theory. His eyes were down, flicking back and forth on the table. He didn't know anything that would refute Arriendez's surprise case.

"And now I am going to say to you what he predicted I would say," Mike Arriendez continued with confident authority. "It doesn't matter. In this room, today, it doesn't matter which of them killed Jenny Fecklewhite. Even if you accept the defense's theory, you see what it reveals about the defendant. About his secret love for the poor deceased. If he acted from finding her dead, that love was his motive. Not simple rage. Not so overwhelming that he didn't know what he was doing. He had time to think on his way back into town. He had time to track his friend down, he had time to calm down and back away, but he didn't. He had time to plan what he committed in front of all these witnesses, which was cold-blooded murder."

Jordan knew an exit line when he heard one. He knew a powerful closing argument as well; he felt completely battered by this one. He glanced at his client in a sort of farewell and suddenly saw what was wrong with the district attorney's theory.

"Thank you," Mike Arriendez said to the jury, and walked briskly to his chair. And Jordan did the one thing he could to refute the prosecutor's argument. He pushed back his chair creakingly, scraping the metal-tipped legs loudly across the floor. He pushed back as if he would rise, but that wasn't his intention. He only wanted to draw the jury's attention, as he did; Jordan had pushed himself back so as not to block their vision, so that when he turned to look at his client, Wayne Orkney was the most prominent person in the courtroom, and all the jurors turned their attention on him.

Wayne didn't notice. He sat there with a small frown on his face. Grief had returned to his expression, but it was compounded now not with embarrassment over the revelation of his feeling for Jenny. That emotion had been replaced by puzzlement. Wayne's lips were moving slightly and his hands were touching each other in distraction as he tried to follow what Mike Arriendez had just explained to the jury and the audience in the courtroom. Wayne didn't look guilty, he looked confused. He didn't get it.

Don't you see? Jordan wanted to shout. A smart lawyer could work out that plot with Wayne portrayed as the cunning double murderer, but Wayne couldn't! He wasn't smart enough to have thought that fast. It seemed perfectly obvious to Jordan.

But the jurors were rising. Judge Waverly had instructed them to begin their deliberations. Jordan stood and pulled Wayne to his feet as well. The defense lawyer was hoping the jurors would glance back at his best exhibit, his befuddled client, but the jurors were concentrating on falling into line and not tripping as they made their way out of the box. The door closed behind them.

Jordan and Mike Arriendez turned to each other. Neither spoke for a moment. They just regarded each other as if they hadn't known each other until now.

"That was a hell of a piece of work," Jordan finally said.

Arriendez didn't smile. "I was up all night thinking of it. And I shouldn't have had to do any thinking at all in this case. It was an absolute lay-down until you put on your evidence."

They didn't shake hands. They only nodded and turned away, Jordan to his client. Spontaneously, he put his arm around him. Wayne didn't respond to the touch.

"How could he say I killed them both?" he asked bewilderedly.

"He was only telling the jury what the evidence *might* show. Nobody can ever know what really happened. We don't know enough."

That was everything Jordan had learned about trials, but as distilled wisdom it wasn't much, and it was no comfort at all.

"Why don't we get your parents up here to sit with you for a while? There's no telling how long the jury'll be out, but maybe your guard will be kind enough—"

Jordan almost bumped into the iron-faced deputy in the amber glasses as he turned. Jordan still felt a strange mix of emotions: at once removed from all humanity, yet able to see people more clearly, enough so that he could see there were so many facets to people he had already categorized and dismissed that he could barely hope to understand any of them. The feeling made him restrained in everything he did.

He didn't glare at the deputy or look around for other authority to back him up. "Would that be all right with you, sir?" he asked. "If Wayne has a few minutes alone with his parents?"

The deputy glanced up the aisle, at Mr. and Mrs. Orkney drawing close, threading through the lingering spectator traffic going the other direction. "Hello, Charlotte," the deputy said, and Mrs. Orkney responded casually, "Hi, Jim. How's your mama and them?"

The deputy turned back to Jordan. "Okay with me," he said.

Jordan, taken aback, offered a concession of his own. "You could handcuff him to the chair if you want."

The deputy snorted softly. With amiable contempt he said, "What's he gonna do, grab a car and flee to Mexico?" He walked away casually.

His feeling of inability to understand anything reinforced, Jordan accepted Mr. Orkney's congratulations. *"I* wouldn't convict him of anything after that."

"I would," Charlotte Orkney said. Then she thawed. "But maybe not of much," she said, and shook Jordan's hand.

"I'll leave y'all alone." Jordan looked past them. The front of the courtroom had emptied almost as quickly as the jury box, except for Laura. She sat still poised as if testimony might resume at any moment. Jordan caught her eye. She didn't smile at him. Her expression was abstracted; she might have still been lost in the arguments. Jordan couldn't imagine what his own expression was like. He yearned toward her, but it seemed impossible to disentangle himself from the remains of the case.

Laura suddenly rose and walked out to join the other court staff in their hidden offices.

Jordan went to find a quiet place. He still had work to do. But his path out of the courtroom was not clear. Swin Wainwright stood there looking menacing, not because of his expression, but simply from the curve of his posture, the strength and competence of his sinewy arms. His eyes smoldered beneath their heavy brows. Jordan tried to brush by him with a nod, but Wainwright put out the hand with the missing finger and stopped him.

"You had to have a bad guy, didn't you?" he said. "And it couldn't be poor little Wayne because he was your client, so it had to be my boy. You had to make Kevin look as bad as possible, not just a murderer, but a stupid, dim-witted murderer."

"I'm sorry, Mr. Wainwright, but the facts—"

"There ain't any facts here! Not in this goddamned place. There's only what you lawyers say." His fist was clenched. Swin Wainwright could only find strength in anger. But he couldn't sustain it. His voice threatened to break as he pointed a finger in Jordan's face. "I want you to remember this. The funeral's over a long time ago. What you said here's probably the last public words anybody'll ever say about Kevin. This is how people'll remember him. He doesn't even have a real memory any more."

The threat of violence had passed. Swin Wainwright stalked out like a man leaving a place for the last time. Jordan just stood, holding his briefcase, feeling the few remaining eyes in the courtroom on him.

You couldn't move in this place without stepping on toes. "I didn't know him," Jordan said loudly, then more softly, "I don't know anybody."

And he walked out to look for a phone.

14

It seemed a very short time later that Jordan was startled by Emilio's opening the door. Jordan sat at the table in the cramped conference room/law library across the hall from the courtroom, the old-fashioned heavy black phone close to his hand. His stare into space was interrupted by the door's opening.

"They're back," the bailiff said.

"Back? Who?" Not the jury. Jordan found his watch. They'd barely been out an hour. "How do they look?" he asked.

"Not happy," Emilio said quietly and left.

God, he hadn't even kept them out long. Defense lawyers have to find victories wherever they can, sometimes in nothing more than confusing jurors enough to keep them arguing for a few hours before coming back with their guilty verdict. Jordan hadn't even managed that.

He hadn't taken any time to prepare his client for the verdict and the punishment phase to follow. He hadn't even prepared himself. Jordan hurried up the courtroom aisle shrugging his jacket straight and trying to recollect himself. As usual, the grapevine was working without breakdown; the spectator seats were already half-refilled, and people were still filing in. He saw Mrs. McElroy in her usual seat and also near the front Chris Cavaletti, the teacher. He reflected that Swin Wainwright had been right: This trial was the final public ceremony for both Kevin Wainwright and Jenny and, in a stranger way, for Wayne.

Wayne didn't seem to have moved. His parents were still

with him. Mrs. Orkney's face was both wet and red. "Stay," Jordan said as the Orkneys started to rise and move back. He pulled up a chair on Wayne's other side, put his arm around him, and began instructing him.

"All rise."

Judge Waverly glanced at the civilians at the defense table, but his face didn't even flicker with disapproval. "Be seated, please. Let's have the jury in."

The judge glanced out, back down, then swiveled his chair to stare over the heads of the jurors shuffling into their seats. Jordan looked at Laura poised below her judge. She too was gazing out into space, her customary courtroom blankness of face looking somehow abstracted rather than officious. Or maybe he was just reading too much into everyone.

The jurors were still settling into their seats when Judge Waverly's voice calmed the room. "Do you have a verdict, Mr. Foreman?"

"Yes, sir. Yes, Your Honor," said a thin, deeply tanned man in the front corner of the jury box, a surveyor for the highway department, Jordan remembered.

Mike Arriendez, Jordan, and Wayne stood. Wayne's parents kept their seats, but Mrs. Orkney held onto her son's hand. Mr. Orkney's arm encircled his wife's shoulders as if there were a current running through the three of them.

Judge Waverly only lifted a hand, relinquishing stage center to the surveyor-foreman, who, without consulting the slip of paper held in one of his clasped hands, stood straight and delivered his verdict to the judge: "We find the defendant guilty, Your Honor—of aggravated assault."

The murmuring soon began, the voices behind him rising to the level of ordinary street conversation, but the moment that extended itself for Jordan was the long few seconds of silence that preceded the murmuring. There were no immediate wails of disappointment, no cry of triumph. The verdict was one calculated to induce thought. People still stood in a listening posture as if there would be more from the jury. Mike Arriendez's face was caught between a smile and a frown. The three Orkneys showed a family resemblance in identical open mouths. Even Laura Stefone had given up her usual blankness for thoughtful blinking.

And Judge Waverly, in minute, unconscious acquiescence, nodded.

Jordan suddenly leaned close to his client's ear as the wave of spectator noise finally broke over them. As he whispered, Jordan kept his eye on the judge. Wayne looked in the same direction and finally nodded.

Judge Waverly looked like a broken man. He had barely moved, but his face had suddenly begun a rapid descent into old age. Jordan knew what was killing the judge. It was Judge Waverly's poorly kept secret relationship with Jenny that had gotten her killed. Because Kevin, poor dumb cluck, had found out about the other man in his girl friend's life and had gotten jealous. That was what had led, with the help of misunderstanding and stupidity and terrible bad luck, to Jenny's death. And Judge Waverly had loved the girl. That was perfectly clear to Jordan as if now he could read everyone in Green Hills.

"Your Honor," Jordan said suddenly, his voice cutting through the clamor, "the defense would like to withdraw its request that the jury assess punishment."

Judge Waverly blinked. He didn't regain his old ferocity, but he was back to business. "State?" he asked.

Mike Arriendez, still trying to absorb the verdict, had only moments to mull this new dilemma. His consent was required for the defendant at this point to change his mind about whether the judge or jury would decide his punishment. But it wasn't a decision that required much thought on the part of the prosecutor. Arriendez was in many ways a prisoner of the court. His judge was the only judge the DA faced, almost daily. To deny his consent to this request would be to publicly announce that Arriendez didn't trust Judge Waverly. Arriendez would never make such an announcement—until, perhaps, he was ready to run for judge himself.

"The State agrees," he said.

The judge turned to the jurors. "This jury has done admirable work. The court appreciates both your thoughtfulness and your swiftness. You are dismissed. Go on with your lives."

A little surprised by their dismissal, the jurors made their slow way out of the box and through the front of the courtroom, stopping to whisper to each other, to nod to court personnel. One almost-elderly man, veins knotted from a lifetime of hard work in the fields, stopped to clap the district attorney on the shoulder. "One fine speech, Miguelito. But nobody believed Wayne's as smart as you. He couldn't've come up with that plan. Certainly not that fast."

The man departed. Jordan muttered, loudly enough for the prosecutor to hear, "Hometown juries. They're great." He was chiding himself as well. His last courtroom tactic had been a waste of theatrics. The jurors knew the players in the drama. They hadn't needed a last, riveting glance at the defendant.

Courtroom decorum was breached with civilians inside the bar and the spectators' discussions continuing. Judge Waverly didn't attempt to restore impeccable order, but he didn't dismiss the proceedings either. "Now?" he said unreadably.

Jordan had the familiar feeling of being caught unprepared. This time, though, he sensed he was on an equal footing with the prosecutor. "Now would be fine, Your Honor."

"Fine," Arriendez echoed. The judge motioned them forward, Wayne accompanying. Jordan's hand moved as if quite naturally to rest on Laura's shoulder. He stopped himself but stood close to her.

"You have evidence to present on punishment?" Judge Waverly asked the prosecutor.

"Only the evidence of the offense itself, Your Honor. Other than that, the State rests on punishment."

"Mr. Marshall?"

Jordan turned to his client. "Wayne, have you ever been convicted of a felony?"

"No, sir. One DWI and a public intox—"

"No prior convictions relevant to this sentencing," Jordan interrupted. "And the court has our sworn application for probation, stating the same thing. Just one more question. Did you mean to kill Kevin, Wayne?"

"Never, never. If I could take it back I'da done it a thousand times by now. I swear to God, I never meant to hurt him that bad."

"And the jury so found by their verdict," Jordan said to the judge.

"I understand the meaning of the jury's verdict, Mr. Marshall. Do you have any more evidence to present?"

"Just one other thing. How old are you, Wayne?"

"I turned twenty yesterday."

Jordan almost laughed, a bitter chuckle. Instead he said, "The defense rests, Your Honor."

"Argument?" Judge Waverly asked blandly.

Jordan said immediately, "Your Honor, there's only one living person left from this whole tragic episode, and you have his life in your hands. Prison would set Wayne on a course that would ensure that his life would be wasted, too. That would be the final tragedy. What he needs is supervision, Your Honor, as this boy makes the difficult transition to adulthood."

Jordan thought he should say more, in a normal case he would have, but he also understood the negligible effect his words would have on the man before him. Jordan shrugged and subsided.

"From the State?" Judge Waverly asked quietly.

"The jury has found this was only a case of aggravated assault, but it was the worst possible example of an aggravated assault, resulting in prolonged hospitalization and eventually the victim's death." Arriendez glared at Jordan, defying him to contradict. Jordan didn't respond at all. He was watching the judge.

"The victim was the defendant's best friend," Arriendez continued. "The defendant has a history of alcohol abuse, but there's no evidence alcohol was involved in this offense. His only defense was that he flew into an uncontrollable rage. That doesn't bode well for the citizens of this community if Mr. Orkney is allowed to remain free among us. The offense was the worst possible—"

The DA suddenly looked up at his judge and saw that his words were having no effect. Like Jordan, the prosecutor wound down abruptly, with much of his thoughts left unsaid. "It calls for the maximum sentence of ten years," he concluded simply.

Judge Waverly hadn't let either lawyer catch his eye. It didn't appear to be deliberate evasion, he simply wasn't paying attention to them; he was listening to an argument inside his head. That argument seemed to have concluded. The judge tapped the gavel lightly and with no more deliberation said, "Wayne Orkney, the jury having found you guilty of aggravated assault, I sentence you to serve a term of ten years' imprisonment."

Jordan was shocked. He felt himself suddenly surrounded by an aura of cold electricity. His hair felt as if it were standing on end.

"Now let us consider the application for probation," Judge Waverly continued, his voice a strange mix of sternness and detachment. "Wayne, if I send you to prison, you'll be out in a year or two, but your life will never be the same. You will forever be an ex-convict. Besides certain loss of rights and difficulties in finding employment, you'll find that prison is a stigma you can never shake. And as your attorney said, it will alter the whole course of your life.

"On the other hand, granting you probation might put this whole community at risk, as the district attorney has said. I would be a fool to take that risk, wouldn't I?"

Under the judge's words and gaze, Wayne had emerged both from the weight of the trial and from his endless self-study. He spoke up earnestly. "I know I'll never hurt anybody again, Judge. I don't think I could touch anybody. I—" He held up a hand and it was trembling. "Sometimes I think about cutting them off," he said softly.

"Probation doesn't mean walking free," Judge Waverly continued. "It means community service, it means reporting to a probation officer very regularly, it means reforming your habits, it means never getting arrested again for *any*-thing. It would last ten long years. When it's over, you won't be a boy of twenty any more, you'll be a man—or you will have broken your covenant with me and then you *will* go to prison, even if you don't make a mistake until the last day of your probationary term. Can you live up to those conditions, Wayne?"

Wayne looked shaken, but not as he usually had since Jordan had known him, when Wayne had been driven inward by his pain. Judge Waverly's lecture had had the effect of shaking Wayne back out into the world again.

And the idea of aging to thirty was probably more of a threat in the boy's mind than prison was.

"Yes, sir, Your Honor. I won't ever be no trouble to nobody again."

"That's exactly right, Wayne. Or you'll answer to me. I grant the application for probation. The sentence of ten years' confinement is suspended."

Jordan routinely clapped his client on the back in congratulations, but his attention was still centered on the judge. Judge Waverly finally returned his stare. His expression was one of unpleading interrogation; Jordan took it to mean the judge was asking if he and Jordan had formed a covenant as well.

"Thank you, Your Honor. May we be dismissed?"

"You all are." As was his habit, the judge disappeared quickly, seeming to vanish into the blackness of his robe.

"I *told* you it was a probation case," Jordan said to Mike Arriendez as they turned. "Why'd you put us through all this grief?"

The DA made a gun of his thumb and forefinger and pointed it at Jordan. "Next time," he said.

Jordan snorted. "Be a cold day on the highway before you see me in *this* building again."

The Orkneys were upon him. Mrs. Orkney detached herself from her son long enough to give Jordan a quick, wet hug, then they were huddled into themselves again and he let them go.

There were milling crowds in the courtroom, people standing but not moving to leave, like people discussing an interesting play. Jordan had no inclination to pass among them. Instead he finally gave in to the tug in the opposite direction. He turned to Laura.

Her chair was empty. She was gone as suddenly as her judge.

Jordan followed what must have been her path back into the court offices. But when he passed through the short hall and opened the office door, it was into nightmare. Deputy Delmore stood there, inches from Jordan's face, hat and sunglasses restored to their proper places, and gunbelt heavy on his hip. Delmore thrust a finger into Jordan's chest.

"You called me a murderer, you son of a bitch."

Jordan didn't answer. The door into the courtroom was behind him, closed. He didn't dare turn his back on Delmore.

"I live in this town," the deputy continued, advancing on him. "I'm not just some arrogant son of a bitch out-of-town bastard passing through, dropping insinuations like birdshit. I've got a name in this town. People respect me. I won't have 'em lookin' sly at me, wondering what I did, just because some smartass lawyer—"

"What do you want me to do, issue a retraction?"

Delmore had him pinned against the door. He grabbed Jordan's arm, squeezing so hard Jordan could feel his arm bruising even beneath the protection of his suit coat and shirt. "I want to take your head off," Delmore almost shouted.

Jordan could taste the deputy's breath, sour with undigested hamburger and beer and hatred.

"You take your hand off me or you're gonna need some new sunglasses," Jordan said.

Delmore grinned evilly. He did remove his hand, but only to draw it back into a fist. Jordan shoved him away and Delmore's hand fell to his gun belt instead.

"Tommy!"

Laura had appeared in the far doorway. Delmore didn't turn to her, but it was clear he recognized her voice, maybe aided by her use of an old nickname.

"Back off, T. J. Nobody thinks you killed that boy. Unless you start acting like a crazy person now."

Still staring at Jordan, Delmore said relentlessly, "He's gonna apologize, or he's gonna—"

"He doesn't have anything to apologize for, T. J. He was just doing his job. Why don't you go do yours? Before you get fired from it for conduct unbecoming an officer—or excessive nitwittery on duty."

"Shut up, Laura."

"Say that to my face, Tommy."

Delmore hesitated. He managed to make the turn toward her, but his eyes barely raked her. He slammed his fist against the nearby wall. There were two doors out of the passageway: Laura stood in one doorway and Jordan was blocking the other. The deputy chose Jordan. He stalked past him. "Watch it!" he said loudly to someone and slammed the door behind him.

Laura was looking at Jordan appraisingly as if nothing had just happened, but when she spoke, it was about Delmore.

"How many of our local law enforcement officers am I going to have to rescue you from?"

"I don't know. How many ex-boy friends have you got?"

"*Don't* be insulting." There was a lightness to her words but not in her tone or her face. Her next sentence revealed why. "I guess you're on your way out of town now."

"Laura," he said reproachfully, coming close to her.

"Well, I *was* hoping you'd stop by on your way out." But she was looking at him so strangely, as if Jordan had again become the stranger he'd been when she'd first seen him, but a stranger who stirred dreamlike memories of intimacy.

Jordan wasn't smiling either. "Let's go now," he said.

She didn't ask where he wanted to go. On the way to her house he told her about his encounter with Swin Wainwright. "Hell of a thing when you can't even win a trial and feel completely good about it afterward."

"This was a win?" Laura teased. "I thought I heard the jury say guilty."

"Darling, in a defense lawyer's book, this was a major, major victory."

They both grew quiet and somber as they crossed her

front porch. The house felt different, more formal. Jordan wondered if Laura felt the change, too, if she was responsible for it.

He brought up the case again. It gave the illusion of safe ground. "In a way Wayne got the harshest sentence he could have. The judge was right, the way parole is now he wouldn't have spent much time in prison. But he'll be under Judge Waverly's thumb for ten years."

Laura was pensive. She stood by the sofa in her living room, one hand touching the sofa's back, her head bowed. Jordan, still close to her front door, thought maybe she was expending a little thought on him, on the fact that there was nothing to keep Jordan in Green Hills now that the trial was ended. But he knew he wasn't the only thing on her mind. There was no reason for Laura to stay here either. Not any more.

"The judge won't ever revoke Wayne, though."

"Why not?" Laura asked, looking up.

"I don't think the judge will want to reopen the case."

Waverly would brood over it, though, many a long night. What had been touched on but not revealed in court threw a wholly new light over the judge's whole life.

"But you don't have to be here to see it," Jordan told Laura. "There's nothing to hold you in Green Hills now that Jenny's not here."

Laura began crying, one welling tear diving down her cheek. She didn't turn away from him.

"I called Midland and I called Chicago," Jordan said. "I talked to a lot of people, a lot of clerks and recordkeepers. Jenny wasn't Joan Fecklewhite's wild sister's daughter. She was yours. You left town to have her and you stayed away too long, until her father had to insist you come back. And you couldn't keep the baby, not in this little town, so the judge found a family to raise her. He already knew the Fecklewhites because he'd represented Ed and investigated them, I guess, and thought they'd do."

Laura didn't speak, so he went on, studying her face. "After I realized it, God, I could see her face in yours. I'm surprised nobody else's seen it over the years. But gossip had already solved that little mystery to everyone's satisfaction. Did you start that rumor yourself about Joan Fecklewhite's sister? It wouldn't have taken much of a hint to the right person."

"What gave you this idea?" Laura asked. Her voice didn't go with her wet cheek. Her voice was strong. Just hearing it, a listener wouldn't have guessed how she was holding herself as if she were freezing to death.

"I kept working on the assumption you were lying to me, but after a while I thought what if you were telling the truth about Jenny not being the judge's girl friend? 'People are so stupid,' you said. That sentence was just ripped out of you, you couldn't put up with the nastiness the idea implied about Jenny. But you couldn't deny how the judge took an extraordinary interest in her. How he practically took over her life, displacing her own father. Her adopted father. Judge Waverly couldn't keep out of her life, could he? She was his only child."

Jordan's realization had explained everything else. That Laura had left town right after working for Judge Waverly during high school, and he had paid for her further education. And at about the same time she came back, a baby girl was adopted by the Fecklewhites, a girl who transcended her origins and in whom both Laura and the judge took an abiding interest. And it explained why Laura could never bring herself to leave Green Hills. She couldn't go away and not see her daughter grow up. It explained Judge Waverly's confession about finding a quick, bright girl and reaching out for her: not Jenny—Laura, who became Jenny's mother.

"Did you ever tell her? Did she know you were her mother?"

Laura's arms were still wrapped around herself. "She just knew I cared about her. I wanted to hear what was happening to her. I'd track her down to hear about her life, and sometimes *she*'d come to find me." Proudly. "Because we were friends. It was better than being mother and daughter—I guess. She'd tell me things she wouldn't tell her mother. She knew I loved her because of who she was, not what she was."

Another tear washed her cheek, but Laura still looked rigid. The discipline of a lifetime of keeping her strongest feelings hidden had become part of her. But now the discipline was making her immobile.

"It's amazing you could have kept a secret like that in this town," Jordan said.

And horrible. He couldn't imagine Laura's life. To have spent years close to her only daughter but unable to touch her, to tuck her in bed at night. To be unable to take open pride in her and have her mother's love acknowledged.

"You don't even have a picture of her," Jordan said wonderingly.

"Picture?" A sob broke from Laura. It was a sound so alien to her it could have come from outside. But that one cry utterly remade Laura. She lost any trace of composure and rigidity. She flew across the room.

"I have pictures!" she shouted, openly crying now, wracked by crying, shoulders shaking, but somehow energized by it, too. Across the room, she tore open the doors of one of the cabinets beneath her bookcases. The cabinet was deeper than Jordan had suspected. Laura pushed aside some junk—frames, vases, fake ferns—that acted as concealment for a good-sized cardboard box, probably two feet long on each side. Laura pulled the box into the light. It was sealed with tape, but the tape was curling up at the ends, obviously pulled up and pressed down again several times. Now Laura broke the tapes, tore open the top of the box, and spilled out its contents.

"My God," Jordan said.

They were all photos of Jenny. Eight-by-tens, wallet-size school pictures, Polaroid snapshots. The photos weren't laid down in chronological layers within the box. Some baby pictures were near the top. Jordan knelt and touched one of the pictures, separating it from the others. The photo, not very clear, apparently taken by someone operating a cheap camera with which he was not familiar, showed a very young Laura wearing a blouse not even stylish more than fifteen years ago when the picture was taken. She was holding a tiny baby, no more than two months old. And beaming.

Looking at the picture, Jordan realized he had never seen Laura smile. What he had taken for smiles weren't even bitter shadows of the grin this eighteen-year-old girl was showing the world, this dazzlement of delight and pride and love.

Laura was holding another picture, one she hadn't had to sort through the pile to find. It had been on top. Jordan looked over her shoulder and saw a Jenny fifteen or sixteen years old, almost as old as she'd ever gotten, smiling at the camera, wearing almost that same smile, the one Laura had displayed in Chicago years earlier. The later picture had been taken outdoors. In the background were trees, a banner of some kind, people strolling. Standing close beside Jenny was Laura almost as Jordan knew her. Jenny had her arm around Laura. It looked spontaneous, as if Jenny had hugged Laura just as the picture was being taken. Laura's arms were just beginning to unfold and so was her face, being startled into another smile. But still wearing that awareness of other people around.

"I'd say to people, 'Take our picture,' Casually, like I'd just thought of it. I always had my camera with me. In my desk at the courthouse, in my purse at county fairs or livestock shows or picnics. I had to take a dozen pictures of other people to get one of Jenny. People thought it was my hobby." Laura was crying steadily. Only her hand holding the picture didn't shake. She couldn't risk crumpling the picture. It had been obtained at too great a risk. It was irreplaceable.

"But some of these others," Jordan said. "School pictures and studio photographs—"

"I paid Joan to make copies for me. Joan knew, of course. I was the one who handed Jenny over to her. The judge wanted to do it, so they wouldn't know about me, but I said no, I want her to know. I put that baby into her arms and I said, 'If you—If she ever—' and Joan just hugged me and said, 'Honey, I know.'

"I was always there for her," Laura said loudly. "Whenever Jenny needed me. Even when she didn't know she did. One day Joan called me at the courthouse and said Jenny's about to talk. I ran out of that courthouse, I don't know if they got another court reporter or had to stop the hearing, I didn't care, if anybody'd tried to stop me, I would have run them down. I was at their house almost before Joan hung up the phone. The baby came right to me. Back then she still remembered me. I held her and Joan said, 'Say it, baby. Say it, Jenny.' "

Laura wiped her hand across her eyes. She sorted through the pictures and found one of Jenny close to the age she was talking about, a little more than a year old. Joan Fecklewhite was holding the little girl in that photo.

"But they won't do it on cue at that age, you know," Laura said. "I had to stay there all afternoon. After her nap, as soon as she opened her eyes, Jenny saw me and said, 'Ma-ma.' "

Laura had to stop talking. She even put the picture down on the floor, so she could clench her fists. She lowered her head onto them.

Jordan wanted to hold her, but he felt excluded by Laura's past and by what he knew about her. He didn't think she would have recognized him if she had turned.

After a minute, her muffled voice came. "Joan told me it was her first words. I knew she was lying—How could she have known she was going to say it if she hadn't said it already?—but I pretended."

Jenny's learning to talk must not have been entirely happy for Laura. As Jenny had become more aware, Laura had had to withdraw to preserve the secret. Jordan could see it in the progression of the pictures. From baby pictures of Laura holding Jenny, they passed to pictures of them standing side by side or of Laura only in the background or not in the picture at all.

"But I was always there," Laura said. She was kneeling amid the pictures but no longer looking at any of them. She was still crying, but the racking sobs had passed. She was staring across the room. Laura drew a deep ragged breath that was rich with release. This might have been the first time she had ever talked to anyone about Jenny. "When she graduated from kindergarten, from elementary school, from middle school. I would've been there—"

Another sob stopped her, not as strong as the first but just as wrenching, because Laura was weaker now. She crawled away, careful not to touch any of the pictures, and pulled herself up onto the couch. Jordan looked down at the array of pictures of the pretty girl turning beautiful. There, he noticed for the first time, was a copy of the one Evelyn Riegert had given him, the picture of laughing Jenny from her hospital file. Maybe he hadn't been the first to guess Laura's secret.

"I thought it wouldn't be so bad," Laura said. She might have thought she was speaking in a normal tone, but her voice had lost its rich confidence. It squeaked. "When Richard told me it was what we had to do, I told him no"—it was the first time Jordan had heard her call Judge Waverly by his first name—"I told him I'd run with her, I told him if he dragged me back, I'd tell everyone. And all he said was he'd fight me for custody and he'd win. And he would have. He had so much more to give her than I did."

And it wouldn't have been a fair fight, Jordan thought. Richard Waverly would have pulled every legal string he had, and he had them all, even that long ago. Laura would have known that, too.

"He told me this was the only way we could both have her, we could both stay close to her. And I agreed, and I came back, and I let them—take her.

"I should have run!" Laura suddenly screamed, driven to her feet. "I should have taken her to France. To Australia. Somewhere where she'd still be alive, where I'd still have her! I should have—"

"You can't know," Jordan said quietly. "You might have lost her anyway, another way. She would have wanted to know where she came from. She might have ended up hating you for taking her away from the life she could have had here."

Laura's face twisted. She was trying to make the comparison—Jenny's hating her versus Jenny's being dead—and the choices were so horrible she was lost again.

Jordan was across the room in two steps, holding her. He shouldn't have, he'd been consciously resisting comforting Laura, but when her face turned tormented again, it was no longer a matter of volition for him. He was just there, holding her.

Laura wasn't used to comfort. She just stood with her arms at her sides for a long minute. Then she put her arms around Jordan and held him so tight he lost his breath. She sobbed harder for a minute, but she didn't have the strength for that any more. Her arms loosened as her cries diminished. Jordan let her go. She slipped down to the couch again. Jordan took a few steps away, toward the door.

"The worst part is you start to forget," Laura said quietly. "I actually had a life sometimes. After a while I'd go for a day or two without even thinking about her. Well, after they get to be teenagers, you start losing them anyway. Don't you?" she asked with the anxiety again cutting through her voice.

"Yes," Jordan said as if he knew.

Laura looked at him, maybe for the first time since she'd pulled out the box of pictures. She was coming slowly forward out of the past.

"When I realized your secret," Jordan said, "I realized that's why you'd gotten close to me. So you could keep up with what I was finding out, and guide me, too, if I got too close to the truth."

"That's why," Laura said. She was past lying.

And maybe once she'd learned a little about him, the losses Jordan had suffered had appealed to the emptiness in Laura. Maybe she'd been surprised by growing fond of him. Remembering their times together, Jordan couldn't help but believe that. Couldn't believe it had all been artifice and deception.

"Because you had another secret to protect, didn't you?" Jordan said, watching her face. Laura didn't look startled. She winced slightly as if with a twinge of physical pain, but she didn't look away from him. "So you can tell the judge I know," Jordan continued slowly, "if you think he should know. Or does he already know all of it? Did he send you to see Kevin in the hospital?"

Laura took a deep breath, but she didn't say anything.

"That's what I suddenly knew during trial when Evelyn Riegert handed me her list. Your old friend Evelyn who had learned Kevin's time of death and realized it was the same time when you had come to see him. Because the first time I talked to Evelyn she *didn't* know the time of death yet— she hadn't been on duty—and she made a mistake and told me someone from the court had come to get a statement from Kevin. That always bothered me, because it was way too early in the process for anyone from the court to get involved. A police officer would have tried to get a statement, but no one else. But if someone from the court did come, it would be someone who could take a statement. It would be the court reporter. At least that's what you would have told Evelyn when she asked why you'd been there. And she believed you until later when the autopsy had established Kevin's time of death and Evelyn realized it was during your visit. So she covered up for you because you were her old friend. That's what I realized when she handed me her list in court and your name wasn't on it and neither was the name of anyone else from the court.

"You were Kevin's last visitor, weren't you?"

Laura stayed quiet for a moment, as if she would let silence deny his accusation. Jordan became aware again of the photographs arrayed on the living room rug. Laura didn't glance in their direction, but her thoughts did.

"He killed my baby," she said. Her voice shook. "I knew he did as soon as I heard that Jenny was ..." When she hesitated, her voice turned questioning, as if she still couldn't believe it. "... was dead? Dead? Murdered? And Kevin was in the hospital and Wayne in jail for beating him up. Like you said, it didn't take a genius to figure it out. I knew what Kevin was like, and I knew the confrontation he and Jenny'd been headed for. Some people were saying Wayne, but Wayne didn't have any reason for killing Jenny."

The last phrase made her lips clamp down. Jordan's hand

twitched. But he felt immobilized by the contradictions of his obligations.

"And I was hearing in the courthouse how hard the case against him would be," Laura continued. Her hands moved slightly. She held herself back, then made the gesture after all, reaching with empty hands for options that weren't there. "And the judge just seemed paralyzed, I could see he wasn't going to do anything but let the law take its course."

"And I helped, didn't I?" Jordan said. That first day in court, in his short pants, when he hadn't known anything, when he was just tossing out possibilities, he'd hit on a real one, that after Kevin recovered, he and Wayne might refuse to testify against each other, so that a case couldn't be made against either of them. Laura had sat there in the courtroom copying down his words, understanding them completely: that her daughter was dead and the "justice system" wasn't going to do anything about it.

It was the next day that Kevin had died.

"Maybe it was more an accident than anything," Jordan said slowly, spinning out possibilities the way he had that day in court. "You didn't realize how weak Kevin was, how even a little touch might be enough to—"

Laura interrupted him. "It wasn't an accident. It didn't take anywhere near the effort or time I'd been afraid it would. Maybe if it had, I would have lost my nerve. But I did what I intended to do. And I'm not sorry."

Jordan couldn't blame her. If someone hurt his daughter, he thought he would do the same thing Laura had done. But Laura was looking at him as if she didn't understand that. She looked ready to be taken away. Laura was reassembling herself. She crossed her arms and stood in a posture that showed her strength, the strength that had carried her through her daughter's life and death and the mother's revenge Laura had taken for her.

"What are you going to do about it?" Laura asked, watching Jordan as if that weren't her real question.

He spoke with assurance, which was strange, because he hadn't known what he was going to say until the words were out of his mouth. "I'm not a law enforcement officer and it's not my case. I'm not going to do anything. I don't even live here."

He turned away.

"Jordan?"

He was standing inside her screen door, looking out at the dazzle of day. Laura's voice came more softly.

"You know what happened between the judge and me was a long time ago, and it was *over* a long time ago."

He nodded.

"You guessed right," she said. "I got close to you so I could find out what you were learning. That's why I started. I didn't know what would come of it. Did you? I didn't know how I'd start to feel about you. As if when everything had crashed and burned and there was nothing left and I saw that my life was over, suddenly here *came* my life, speeding by on the interstate and getting dragged right into my courtroom, like I'd ordered you up."

It would be nice to believe that. He *did* believe her, because when Laura spoke, Jordan couldn't disbelieve. It was like part of himself talking. He yearned toward her even as he stood rooted to the spot.

"I love you, Jordan."

He believed her. She had no reason to lie to him now that he had already said he wasn't going to betray her. But how could he stay with her? How could they get over their origins? That she had come to him only to lie to him, to cover up the murder she'd committed. Would she ever be able to forget that he knew that? How could they discard their separate pasts: his daughter, her dead daughter, the judge? Jordan had had time to think it all out and decide what he had to do, which was to walk away, to try to let both their lives heal. He was determined to leave, but he couldn't make himself move. He was looking out at the street, picturing where it led: down to the corner, turn at Mrs. Johnson's house, onto Main Street, past the Texaco where Wayne pumped gas, past the courthouse. Away from Laura.

And in a few short blocks the street would take him to the interstate.

A long, boring highway with nothing much at either end.

The decision to leave had been a theory, and Laura was real. He pictured her perfectly behind him as if he hadn't turned away. He saw her lifting her hand, and he knew which fingernail she was biting.

"I don't even belong here," he said. "What a fluke." His voice became firm with sudden resolution. "I was on my way to the beach when I hit this town. I *am* going to the beach." He nodded, approving his decision.

He turned around. Laura was standing just as he'd pictured her. Another tear hung on the rim of her eye, but she wasn't trembling. She was looking at him steadily, regretfully, but with determination in her posture. Looking at her full on, he saw again the slight unevenness of her face, so slight that Jordan was probably the only person who had ever noticed it.

"How long will it take you to pack?" he said.

**POCKET BOOKS
PROUDLY PRESENTS**

DEFIANCE COUNTY

JAY BRANDON

**Coming mid-May
in Hardcover from
Pocket Books**

The following is a preview of
Defiance County. . . .

It was Thanksgiving week. No prospective jurors had been called, the courthouse was quiet. In Judge Saunders's courtroom a few lawyers halfheartedly argued motions that wouldn't take long to dispose of. When Kelsey's turn came the court's business was done, at ten-forty-five in the morning, but a couple of the lawyers lingered. Kelsey could feel their eyes on her back.

Judge Saunders sat back in her tall chair. The zipper of her black robe was pulled down several inches below her neck, displaying the cream-colored scalloped collar of her blouse. The judge raised one eyebrow at Kelsey. "Should I have Clyde Wolverton come over for this?" she asked.

"It isn't an adversarial proceeding, Your Honor. But I'm ready to make it one. I'd like you to convene the grand jury you told me I could have when I was ready."

In the pause that followed, Judge Saunders seemed to be studying Kelsey rather than what the prosecutor had said. Kelsey watched the judge as well. Linda Saunders and Morgan Fletcher had dated when they were young. That past could cover wide ground: forgotten minor incidents, lifelong lingering love, everything in between. Kelsey had seen that some affection remained between Morgan and the judge.

"Actually, there's a grand jury finishing up its term today," Judge Saunders said. "But maybe you'd like to wait to convene a new one, even a special—"

"No, thank you, Your Honor. I wouldn't want to put

the court to any special trouble." *Of hand-picking a grand jury for me to try to sell on indicting Billy Fletcher.* Better to try her luck with leftovers. As it was, it probably wasn't possible to convene a grand jury in Galilee that wouldn't include friends of Billy's.

"I was going to dismiss them this afternoon," Judge Saunders said. "I could give them to you instead. Tomorrow morning."

"I'm ready now, Your Honor." Time was not Kelsey's friend. She knew in a matter of moments word of what she was about to do would start spreading, and the grand jurors would start getting phone calls.

"After lunch, then," the judge said. "Two o'clock. Does anyone else have business with the court? We're adjourned, then."

When Kelsey returned from a solitary, distracted lunch, the story had spread quickly. A glaring Clyde Wolverton, accompanied by his client, met her on the first floor of the courthouse. "I understand you think you have something worth taking to a grand jury," he said. He sounded restrained, but his face was red.

"Yes," Kelsey said shortly, and started past him, but Wolverton grabbed the prosecutor's arm to stop her. "Doesn't it offend you to prostitute yourself like this? Everybody in Galilee knows who is behind this prosecution! Before I'm done, everyone in the state will know you are just the puppet of a vindictive woman. The attorney general will have no choice but to fire you in disgrace. Such blatant disregard for truth—"

Kelsey had resolved to let him talk himself out, but as he did she got mad, until she leaned forward and blasted him back. "If she's vindictive, it's because Billy Fletcher murdered her child! *I* don't have any personal stake in this case. The truth is all I care about. Personal motives don't matter as long as I have the evidence. And I do, Mr. Wolverton. You ask your client whose blood is in his car!"

Billy started to shout something, but his attorney, finally controlled, put a hand on Billy's chest and quieted him. Wolverton looked stonily at Kelsey. "I hope some other profession interests you, Ms. Thatch. After this proceeding you will be such damaged goods that no one will hire you to practice law anywhere in this state."

Well pleased with this exit line, the defense lawyer turned smartly and took his client in tow. Billy Fletcher was furious, but expostulations so crowded his throat he couldn't say anything until he was almost out of sight down the corridor, when he screamed, "Don't you have a conscience?"

Kelsey didn't reply. As she stood watching Billy and his lawyer disappear out the doors of the courthouse, she realized someone was standing just behind her. She felt his presence as a blocky warmth, and knew who it was even before Morgan Fletcher put his hands on her shoulders. "Of course you do," he said of Kelsey's conscience. "Don't mind—"

"I don't," Kelsey said. There was something frighteningly alluring about Morgan standing close behind her, so that she was immobilized. She knew she should step away from him, but she wanted more to put her hand over his. Obviously sensing her feeling, Morgan kept his hands on her shoulders, holding her for a long minute in the empty hallway.

There was another surprise visitor to the courthouse, sitting on a hard bench outside the grand jury room.

"Mrs. Beaumont," Kelsey said. "Can I help you?"

"No, thank you. Move aside, please, dear."

Kelsey did so, puzzled, and saw that Mrs. Beaumont was craning her neck to watch the grand jurors approach. They did so in straggling order, in no hurry, men in suits, women in dresses nice enough for church. Some of them were chatting as they came down the courthouse hallway. Each stopped or glanced nervously upon sight of Alice Beaumont.

"Ed. Gordon. Hello, Mrs. Davies." Mrs. Beaumont spoke to some of the grand jurors. Each she fixed with a steely eye. The reason for her presence was clear. She was watching them: they had better do what was expected of them.

But Kelsey walked away a few steps and saw what Alice Beaumont couldn't see. As they saw her, each man or woman on the grand jury acknowledged the matriarch. But as they passed out of her sight, their faces changed. It was those faces they presented to Kelsey when she followed them into the narrow grand jury room and shut the door behind her: skeptical faces. A few, particularly among the seven men, actively frowned at her. Mrs. Beaumont had had the opposite effect from what she'd wanted. She had stiffened the grand jurors' resolve not to be sheep. Not to do as they were implicitly ordered by the woman who controlled the fate of their town.

These were Billy Fletcher's people. Not Alice Beaumont's, and certainly not Kelsey's.

"You are the grand jury. I'm coming in late, I didn't hear your instructions. Did they tell you about how historically you're the body of citizens who stand between someone accused of a crime and the power of the state?"

One woman nodded. The grand jurors were casually arrayed around the room, only about half of them sitting at the long conference table. Two of the women and one of the men looked familiar to Kelsey; she hadn't met them but she had seen them, in the town or during her evening at the country club. Solid citizens, they all looked like. The average age was about fifty, and she couldn't tell from their hands or their faces which worked in offices and which had spent years in the farm fields. They all looked like hard workers. They looked like Billy Fletcher's peers.

"Well, I'm the power of the state," Kelsey continued. She hoped to draw a chuckle, at least a few wry smiles. Make the grand jurors acknowledge that in this case the array of power was behind the suspect, not the prosecutor.

But no one acknowledged her little joke. They stared at her grimly. The best she got was a look of quiet neutrality, from a lady wearing a cotton print dress and a small hat. Her green sweater was draped over her shoulders, as if she were cold or as if she didn't expect Kelsey's presentation to detain her long.

"My job as the prosecutor is to present to you the evidence I've been given in this case, to convince you that enough evidence exists to put my suspect to trial. *Not* to convince you of his guilt. Guilt isn't an issue here. Your job is only to say whether I have probable cause—just enough evidence that you think I should have to go to trial and let a jury decide whether the defendant is guilty or not guilty. You're not calling him a criminal just by issuing the indictment. You're just saying the case should go to trial."

Kelsey spoke firmly and professionally. She wasn't going to rely on emotion.

"The cases I'm presenting to you are the murders of Ronald Blystone and Lorrie Blystone, and the kidnapping of their daughter Taylor. I'm going to ask you to indict Billy Fletcher for those crimes."

There was only a gentle stir. They all knew why they were there. Kelsey outlined the facts of the cases, facts with which the grand jurors must be as familiar as she was. Kelsey passed around pictures of the crime scene, of the bodies, the pool of blood. Some grand jurors studied the pictures briefly, others only glanced at them, wincing. The lady in the green sweater didn't do that much, just took each photo in turn and passed it on, without looking at any.

"Shortly before the murders, Andrew Sims witnessed a very angry argument between Billy Fletcher and Ronald Blystone," Kelsey continued, but was interrupted by a standing man who spoke to the room at large, not bothering to whisper:

"Not safe to have an argument with anybody anymore. You'd better not say what you think in this town. Next thing you know somebody'll be dead and you'll be blamed for it."

"Would you rather I not tell you the evidence I have?" Kelsey asked, walking around the table toward the man, who stiffened and glared at her.

"Hush, Norman," one of the women at the table said softly. "Let her talk."

The admonition did not reassure Kelsey. It sounded to her as if the woman meant they should let the special prosecutor finish as quickly as possible so they could all do what they'd come to do.

Kelsey told them about Billy Fletcher's fingerprint on the murder weapon. In a grand jury proceeding she didn't have to present live witnesses, she could simply describe the evidence she had. Kelsey was the only witness the grand jury would hear. She tried to keep her voice level and detached, as if she had already made the judgment for them. But some of the things she chose to tell them were very brutal.

"The baby crawled in her mother's blood. Then someone put the baby back in her crib. We know that from the bloodstains on the baby's sheets. Then someone took the baby. I expect her little hands and gown were still bloody."

The room was dead still. The air was very close. The heat was on that morning in the courthouse, and in the little grand jury room the heat breathed in through the vent and had nowhere to escape.

Some of the grand jurors frowned down at the table. A few frowned at Kelsey. She knew they didn't like to hear about the baby. Hadn't someone warned her that the kidnapping of the baby actually weakened her case against Billy Fletcher? Because while people might be convinced that he had killed Ronald and even Lorrie Blystone in the heat of passion, taking the baby was the act of a madman, and no one in Galilee could believe good old bluff Billy Fletcher capable of such an act.

Kelsey might have been well-advised to lay off the baby. But today that was her trump card.

"Yesterday morning I seized Billy Fletcher's car and had it searched. An assistant medical examiner in Houston examined the car and confirmed that what she found in the front passenger seat was traces of dried blood."

Now she did get gasps. Some of them looked shocked. All stared at Kelsey.

"The baby's blood?" one woman asked quietly.

Kelsey shook her head. "I assume it's Lorrie Blystone's blood that the baby had on her hands and clothes." A couple of people nodded, having followed her reasoning. "I don't know yet, it will take a while for tests to determine whose blood it is. What I'm telling you this morning is that the man who argued with Ronald Blystone, whose job was threatened by Ronald and his wife, whose fingerprint is on the gun that killed both of them, who was the only one we know of in a position to take the baby—that that man has traces of blood in his car. Traces such as the baby would have left when he took her with him when he drove away."

Kelsey saw her words take effect. The man who had interrupted her looked down at the table, lips moving as he mumbled something inaudible. He had the look of a man trying to explain a puzzle. Others wore the same expression. A few simply looked horrified. "That's my evidence," Kelsey said. She closed her file and picked it up, ready to walk out. The law required her to leave while the grand jury voted. They could do what they wanted behind her back.

Kelsey was proud of herself for the professional way she'd presented the case. She hadn't raised her voice and she hadn't argued. She hoped her quiet authority had convinced them.

But she didn't think so.

It was a relief, though, to be finished. As she turned to go, Kelsey had the ugly thought that it would be okay if it did end here, if the grand jury did refuse to indict and she could go home, to tell people it had just been too tough a case, too much of a hometown boy for a suspect.

Then she turned back to the grand jurors.

"You may think you'll be doing Billy Fletcher a favor if you refuse to indict him," she said harshly. "But you took an oath not to do any favors for anybody. And I'm not sure you'd be doing Mr. Fletcher any good by not indicting him. Everyone's going to know what I've discovered. And even if you no-bill Billy Fletcher, after his friends congratulate him and he goes back about his normal business, everyone will remember for the rest of his life. Everyone will wonder. Won't they? Imagine him in church someday ten years from now, passing around the collection plate, and someone nudges a new member and whispers. Someday somebody will even say it to his face: murderer. And the only thing Billy will be able to say in return is, I never got indicted. But everybody will know that had nothing to do with whether he did it or not."

"You'd better watch your—" the gruff standing man began, but Kelsey looked at him and he subsided. She swept her gaze around the table. Anybody else?

"If you want to give Billy Fletcher his only chance to clear his name, if you want this thing thoroughly thrashed out to a conclusion that will satisfy everyone, issue the indictment."

Only a couple of them looked as if they found that convincing. Kelsey said the last thing she had to say.

"If you give a damn about the truth— If you want to know about that blood— If you want to know where the baby is, issue the indictment."

She stood and looked at them all, but no more than five or six of the grand jurors met her eyes.

Alice Beaumont was waiting for her when Kelsey came out of the grand jury room. "What did they decide?" she asked quickly.

"They're deciding now." Kelsey felt tired. She needed to run again.

"They'd better do the right thing," Mrs. Beaumont said.

Mrs. Beaumont was wearing a green dress, dark but with white highlights at the collar and wrists that saved the dress, and her, from drabness. She carried a black shawl, a mourning cloak she could put on or off. Mrs. Beaumont stood so erect that in her heels she was taller than Kelsey.

Kelsey had the drained feeling that her time in Galilee was over. But there was still much she wanted to do here, and even more she wanted to understand, starting with Alice Beaumont herself. She was a woman who insisted on being in charge. Her life had been devoted to gaining dominance over her whole world. If people got hurt along the way, if bystanders like Kelsey had their lives changed, that hadn't mattered to Alice Beaumont. Why? What had she been after?

Kelsey felt free enough, almost on the highway out of town, to ask her. "Mrs. Beaumont, did you ever have a plan?"

The old lady looked at her, startled.

"Everybody says what a great thing you did for the town, getting your husband to build the Smoothskins factory. And the way you've used the factory ever since to keep everybody in line— What did you want from it all? Was there some goal, or was it just beating down resistance just for exercise? What did you want?"

Alice Beaumont peered at her as if trying to discern what Kelsey was asking. The woman's eyes didn't look as piercing as Kelsey remembered, they were the faded shade of bluebonnets in May, but Mrs. Beaumont squinted them as if trying to make her eyes see as sharply as ever. Then her voice came out angrily.

"I wanted what anybody wants. Everybody. I just worked harder for it than most people are willing to. I wanted my children around me. I wanted family, babies crawling under the table. Playing in the yard, not having to worry. I wanted to sit on my porch and watch them . . ."

Her voice softened and her lower lip began to tremble. "One baby, that's all I had," she sobbed. "One baby to watch grow up. To remember me. And he—"

Kelsey put her arms out and Mrs. Beaumont lowered her head to Kelsey's shoulder, but as soon as they touched, the older woman stiffened again. She drew back and her eyes went fierce. "What do I want?" She clenched her fist and said, "I want the respect I've earned. But they wouldn't let me have any of that." She glared at Kelsey. "Now I want what the law owes me: revenge. Or I'll kill this town."

It was a death threat cold with sincerity and stony with the power to carry out the threat. If Alice Beaumont's target had been a person instead of an entire town, she would have been arrested.

Kelsey stared at her, somehow looking for a resemblance to herself. In a way Mrs. Beaumont was an admirable woman, a role model. Young during an age when a woman could never seize her full potential, Alice Beaumont had learned through romance and ingenuity and finally brute force to control her life and every life around her. But in the end her power hadn't even protected her family. And she was counting on Kelsey to right that wrong.

They heard the sound of rising voices from the grand jury room, but not what they were saying. The vote on Billy Fletcher's indictment was not going smoothly. "At least I got to some of them," Kelsey said.

"I did," Alice Beaumont corrected her.

But Kelsey knew she herself was the one who'd won over some of the grand jurors. She'd seen it in the anguish in their faces during her final short speech about the baby. She wanted to burst back into the room and say more.

There was silence. It went on, the silence of justice fled. Kelsey was suddenly angry. She was walking toward the grand jury room door when it opened. The woman in the green sweater said, "Ms. Thatch, we're ready for you."

And Kelsey was ready for them. *You've disgraced this*

town, she was going to say. She wasn't going to let any of them off. She had changed her mind. She wouldn't let it die here. She would ask for another grand jury. She would find more evidence. She—

"There," said the tall man she'd clashed with before. He threw her papers down on the table, scowling, "There's your damned indictment," he said angrily.

"All right," Kelsey snapped. "If you won't do your job—" But then she looked at the document before her and saw that it was signed. She also saw that the angry man throwing down the indictment was the foreman of the grand jury. He was the one who had signed the indictment: Norman Gray.

"Thank you, Mr. Gray," she said levelly. She looked around at all the faces. None of them looked happy. The lady in the green sweater, though, who had taken her seat at the table, had a certain look of satisfaction, and she gave Kelsey a nod of approval.

"I'd like one more thing. I'd like you all to sign. Everyone who voted to issue this indictment. I'd like you all to put your names to it."

They didn't like that suggestion, but none of them balked. It turned out to have been unanimous. Maybe some of them had voted out of fear of Alice Beaumont, rather than Kelsey's persuasiveness, but it didn't matter. She had her indictment. Billy Fletcher was going to trial.

Coming out of the courthouse, Kelsey turned in a slow half-circle. It was a habit she'd developed in Defiance County, perhaps the habit of a woman who had no one to watch her back. Today, though, she felt a proprietary interest in the town she saw arrayed before her. She was going to be here a while longer.

She lifted her eyes to the horizon, the pine trees as always drawing her gaze. She hadn't thought she was looking for anything in particular, until she saw it:

Smoke rising.

It had been days since she'd seen one of the thin columns of smoke. This one was just starting: a crinkle in the sky, a shimmering of the air, then the smoke. Thicker this time than she'd seen it before.

Kelsey ran toward her car.

Look for
Defiance County
Wherever Hardcover Books
Are Sold
June 1996